"Excuse me, is it Mrs. Rennie?"

She looked at the man standing there on her front doorstep, hands in his coat pockets, an open smile on his face, dark hair nicely parted.

"Yes, that's right."

Very quietly he said, "Put your hands behind your head, keep them there and don't shout. Don't make any move. I know the kids are here."

She watched helplessly as through his coat, unbuttoned and opened, he drew out the ugly squat black shape of the Armalite. Holding it in one hand, with the stock still folded, he prodded her with the barrel back into the hallway.

"Just remember this. If you try anything, I'll kill you. You, and the children. Don't forget it when you want to play the bloody heroine. We're going to sit in there and wait for that bastard husband of yours."

"I'll warn you, missus," the Man continued, "any moves, anything clever, and you'll be dead, the lot of you. Just remember I'm watching you. Watching you all the time. So be very careful. Right, missus?"

The Man paused and let the effect of his words sink in on the small room.

"We're just going to wait," he said.

HARRY'S GAME

Gerald Seymour

A FAWCETT CREST BOOK

Fawcett Publications, Inc., Greenwich, Connecticut

HARRY'S GAME

THIS BOOK CONTAINS THE COMPLETE TEXT OF
THE ORIGINAL HARDCOVER EDITION.

A Fawcett Crest Book reprinted by arrangement with
Random House, Inc.

ISBN 0-449-23019-8

Selection of the Book-of-the-Month Club, Fall 1975
Selection of the Reader's Digest Condensed Book Club,
August 1975

Printed in the United States of America

10   9   8   7   6   5   4   3   2   1

To
William Kean Seymour

■ 1 ■

The Man was panting slightly, not from the exertion of pushing his way through the shapeless, ungiving mass of the crowd but from the frustration of the delay.

He drove himself at the knot of people that had formed a defensive wall around the Underground ticket machine, reaching out through their bodies with his money for the slot, only to be swept back as the crowd formed its own line. It took him fifteen seconds more than two minutes to get his ticket, but that was still quick, set against the endless shuffling line approaching the ticket kiosk.

He moved on to the automatic barrier, inserted his ticket into the machine and watched it bend upward to admit him. There was space around him now. His stride lengthened. Bottled up among the mass on the far side of the barrier, with the clock moving, he'd felt the constriction, his inability to get away.

Now, in the open at last, he cannoned off an elderly man, deep in his paper, making him stumble. As he tried to sidestep his way out of the collision, he knocked into a girl loaded for the launderette, hitting her hard with his left elbow. She looked startled, half focusing on him, half concentrating on holding her balance, her arms out of action clinging to the plastic bag pressed into her breasts. He saw the look of surprise fill her face, watched her as she waited for the explanation, the mumbled apology and helping hand—the usual etiquette of Oxford Circus Station at 8:45 in the morning.

He froze the words in his mouth, the discipline of his briefing winning through. They'd told him not to speak en route to the target. Act dumb, rude, anything, but don't open your big mouth, they'd said. It had been drilled into him—not to let anyone hear the hard, nasal accent of West Belfast.

As the Man sped from the fracas, leaving the elderly man to grope among a mass of shoes for his paper, the girl to regain her feet with the help of a clutch of hands, he could sense the eyes of the witnesses boring into him; it was enough of an incident to be remembered.

He ran away toward the tunnel and the escalator leading to the Victoria Line. Reaching it, he was aware of his stupidity in the hall area, conscious that he'd antagonized people who would recognize him, and he felt the slight trembling again in his hands and feet that he'd noticed several times since he'd come across the water. With his right hand, awkwardly and across his body, he gripped the escalator rail to steady himself. His fingers tightened on the hard rubber, holding on till he reached the bottom and skipped clear of the sieve where the stair drove its way under the floor. The movement and the push of a young man behind him made the Man stumble a little, and with his right hand he reached out for the shoulder of a woman in front of him. She smiled warmly and openly at him as he found his feet again, and a little hesitantly he smiled back, and was away. Better that time, he thought, no tension, no incident, no recognition. Cool it, sunshine. Take it easy. He walked through, carried forward by the crowd onto the platform. They'd timed the frequency of the trains; at worst he'd wait less than a minute.

His left arm, pressed against his chest, disappeared into the gap between the buttons of his raincoat. His left hand held tightly onto the barrel of the Kalashnikov automatic rifle he'd strapped to his body before leaving the North

London boarding house two hours and twenty minutes earlier. In that time the hand had never left the cold metal, and the skin under his thumb was numb from the indentation of the master sight. The barrel and weapon mechanism were little more than twenty inches long, with the shoulder stock of tubular steel folded back alongside it. The magazine was in his hip pocket. The train blurted its way out of the darkened tunnel, braked, and the doors slid back. As he wormed his way into a seat and the doors closed, he edged his weight off the magazine, and the thirty live rounds inside it.

It was 8:51 on the cheap watch on his wrist, just visible if he moved the gun toward the coat buttonholes. Five minutes maximum to Victoria, three minutes from the Underground platform to the street, and taking it gently, seven minutes from there to his target. 9:06 on location. The train pulled abruptly into Green Park Station, waited little more than forty-five seconds as a trickle of passengers got off, a few moments more to let others on, and the doors, to the shout of the big West Indian guard, were closing.

9:06 on location meant that he had two minutes in hand, perhaps three at the most, primarily to assemble the gun and pick his firing position. It was a close schedule now, and he began again to feel the trembling that had dogged him since Rosslare and the ferry, and that he had first felt acutely at Fishguard as he walked with the Kalashnikov past the cold eyes of the Special Branch section watching the ferry passengers coming over from Ireland. He'd gone right by them then, waving furiously to a nonexistent relative in the middle distance beyond the checkpoint and suddenly realizing that he was through and on his way. At his briefing they'd told him the worst part before the shooting would be at Fishguard. He'd seen when he was at the back of the queue how they watched the men coming through, watched hard and expressionless, taking them apart. But no one from his ferry had been stopped. At the briefing they had explained that in his favor was his lack of form, never fingerprinted, never photographed, that he was an unknown face, that if he kept his nerve, he'd get away with it and make it out as well. No sympathizers' homes in London were being used, no contact with anyone, keep it tight as an Orangeman's drum, one said. They'd all laughed. The train jolted to a halt, the carriage emptied. Victoria. The Man pulled himself up with his right hand on the pole support by the door, and stepped out onto the platform. Instinctively he began to hurry, then checked himself, slowed and headed for the neon *Way Out* sign.

By the start of the nine o'clock news something approaching order was returning to the Minister's home. Three children already on their way to school, two more still wrestling with overcoats, scarfs, hockey sticks and satchels. The au pair girl in the hall with them and the Ministers' Afghan hound tangled around their legs.

The Minister was alone at the long refectory table in the breakfast room, newspapers spread out where the children's cereal bowls had been, attacking first the editorial columns, then on through the parliamentary reports, and finally to the front-page news. He read quickly, with little outward sign of annoyance or pleasure; both were reflected only by a slight snort. It was said that only his closest parliamentary colleagues, and that meant about four in the Cabinet, could spot his moods at a time like this. But the selection of papers offered him little more than the trivial interest in the fortunes of his colleagues. Since his eighteen months as second man in Belfast, and the attendant publicity, his promotion to Social Services overlord and a place in the Cabinet had taken him back out of the public eye and reduced his exposure. His major speeches in the House were fully reported, but his monolithic department ticked along, barely feeling his touch at the helm. This morning he wasn't mentioned, and his department figured only in the continuing story of a grandmother in the North East who had been taken to the hospital penniless and suffering from malnutrition and then told local officials that she'd never drawn her pension, and believed people should look after themselves anyway. Lunatic, stupid woman, he muttered.

The news was mostly foreign, South Africa and the mine strike, Middle East cease-fire violations, Kremlin reshuffle. "In Belfast"—suddenly he was concentrating— "a city centre pub was destroyed by a car bomb. Two masked men had warned the customers to leave, but the bomb went off before the area could be fully evacuated. Three men were taken to a hospital suffering from shock, but a spokesman said no one was seriously hurt." Belfast was pretty far down these days, he reflected. Just time left to see what football manager was leaving where, and then the weather, and it would be five-past. He shuffled his papers together and reached for his briefcase under the table; the car would be at the door in three minutes. "Moving off, sweetheart," he called, and made for the hall.

The Afghan was now sitting quietly on the doormat, the children ready, as the Minister put on his heavy darkblue overcoat, paused and contemplated the scarf on the hook, decided against it, gave his wife's offered cheek a kiss, and opened the door into Belgrave Square. The Afghan and au pair led the way down the steps to the pavement, then the children, and after a moment, the Minister and his wife. To his right he saw the black Austin Princess turning out of Halkin Street, seventy-five yards away, to pick him up. The children, holding their hockey gear, straggled after the dog and au pair as they walked left toward Chapel Street, and across the road a short, dark-haired Man slouched against the square's fence, then stiffened and moved forward.

The Minister's huge voice bellowed after his children: "Have a nice day, darlings, and don't do any damage with those sticks." He was still smiling at the over-the-shoulder grimace from the elder girl down the street, when he saw the rifle come from under the coat of the Man across the street and move to his shoulder. The Minister was standing on the pavement now, some yards away from the house, as he turned and looked for the sanctuary of the door in front of which his wife was standing, intent on her children.

He had started to shout a warning to her when the Man fired his first shot. For the Minister the street exploded in noise as he felt the sledge-hammer blow of the 7.62-mm shell crashing into his chest, searing into the soft flesh on its way through a splintered rib cage, puncturing the tissue of his lungs, gouging muscle and bone from his backbone and bursting out through his clothes before, a shapeless mass of lead, it buried itself in the white façade of the house. The force of that first shot spun and felled the Minister, causing the second shot to miss and fly into the hallway, fracturing a mirror beside the lounge door. As the Man aimed for his third shot—"Keep steady, aim," they'd told him, "don't blaze, and for Christ's sake, be quick"—he heard the screaming. The Minister's wife was crawling down the steps to where her husband writhed in his attempt to get away from the pain. The Man fired two more shots. This time there were no misses, and he watched with detached fascination as the back of the sleek groomed head disintegrated. It was his last sight of the target before the woman who had been screaming flung herself over it, swamping it from his view. He looked to his left and saw the big car stranded, its engine racing in the middle of the road. To the right on the pavement he saw children, immobile, like statues, with the dog straining at its leash to escape the noise.

Automatically the Man flicked the safety catch to On, deflated the catch at the top of the stock, bent the shoulder rest back alongside the barrel and dropped the weapon into the sheath they'd built to be strapped under his coat. Then he ran, jumping out of the way of a woman as he went. He turned into Chapel Street, sprinting now. Right next into Grosvenor Place. Must get across the road, get a line of traffic between you and them, he told himself. Alongside him now was the high spiked wall of Buckingham Palace. People saw him coming and moved out of his path. He clutched his unbuttoned coat tight to his body. The rifle was awkward now, the curved magazine digging into his ribs. While he was running he was vulnerable, he knew that. His mind didn't tell him that no one had cause to stop him, but focused almost exclusively on the road, the traffic, and at what moment he would see a hole in the river of buses and cabs and lorries. Get across Buckingham Palace Road and then into the safety and anonymity of the tube station at Victoria. Hard out of breath, he stumbled into the station. He took two ten-pence pieces from his pocket and pushed them into the automatic machine. Remember, they'd said, the law will expect a car; you're better on the tube. They'd given him a route, Victoria to Oxford Circus on the Victoria Line, the Circus to Notting Hill Gate on the Central Line, then the District Line to Edgware Road, then Bakerloo to Watford. He was on a train and moving and his watch showed 9:12.

The sirens of the patrol cars blotted out the screaming of the Minister's wife as she lay over the body. They'd been diverted there just ninety seconds before with the brief message: "Man shot in Belgrave Square." The two constables were still mentally tuned to the traffic blockages at the Knightsbridge underpass as they spilled out into the street. George Davies, twenty-two years old and only three years in the Metropolitan Police, was first out.

He saw the woman, the body of the man under her and the brain tissue on the steps. The sight stopped him in midstride as he felt nausea rising into his mouth. Frank Smith, twice his age, screamed. "Don't stop, you little bugger, move," ran past him to the huddle on the steps and pulled the Minister's wife from her husband's body. "Give him air," he yelled before he took in the wrecked skull, the human debris on the flagstones and the woman's housecoat. Smith sucked in the air, mumbled inaudibly and turned on his knees to the pale-faced Davies ten paces behind him. "Ambulance, reinforcements, tell 'em it's big, and move it fast." When Smith looked again at the Minister's wife, he recognized her. "It's Mrs. Danby?" he whispered. It was a statement, but he put the question into it. She nodded. "Your husband?" She nodded again. She was silent now and the children had edged close to her.

Smith took the scene in. "Get them inside, ma'am." It was an instruction, and they obeyed, slowly and numbly going through the door and off the street.

Smith got up off his knees and lumbered back to the squad car. "Davies, don't let anyone near him. Get a description."

On the radio he put out a staccato message: "Tango George, in Belgrave Square. Henry Danby has been shot. He's dead, from all I can see. Ambulance and reinforcements already requested."

The street was beginning to fill. The Ministry driver of the Austin Princess had recovered from the initial shock and was able to move the car into a parking meter bay. Two more police cars pulled up, lights flashing, uniformed and CID men jumping clear before they'd stopped. The ambulance was sounding the warning of its approach on the half-mile journey from St. George's Hospital at Hyde Park Corner. The Special Patrol Group Land-Rover, on stand-by at Scotland Yard, blocked the south side of the square. One of its constables stood beside it, his black short-barreled Smith and Wesson .38-caliber in his hand.

"Put the thing away," said his colleague, "we're light-years too bloody late."

At Oxford Circus the Man debated quickly whether to break his journey, head for the Gents and take the magazine off his Kalashnikov. He decided against it, and ran for the escalator to bring him up from the Victoria Line to the level of the Central Line. He thought there would be time to worry about the gun later. Now distance concerned him. His mind was still racing, unable to take in the speed and violence of the scene behind him. His only reaction was that there had been something terribly simple about it all, that for all the work and preparation that had gone into it, the killing should have been harder. He remembered the woman over the body, the children and the dog on the pavement, the old woman he had avoided on the pavement outside the house. But none of them registered: his only compulsion now was to get clear of the city.

The first reports of the shooting reached the Commissioner's desk a mile away at Scotland Yard at 9:25. He was slipping out of his coat after the drive from Epsom when his aide came in with the first flashes. The Commissioner looked up sharply, noting there had been no knock on his door before the young officer was in front of him, thrusting a piece of paper at him. As he read the message he saw it was torn at the bottom, ripped off a teleprinter. He said, "Get me C1, Special Branch and SPG here in five minutes." He went over to his desk, pressed the intercom button, announced sharply "Prime Minister, please" and flicked the switch back.

When the orange light flashed in the center of the console, the Commissioner straightened a little in his seat, subconsciously adjusted his tie, then picked up his phone. A voice remote, Etonian and clipped said on the line, "Hello, Commissioner, we're just raking him up, won't be a second." Then another click. "Yes, right, you've found me, good morning, Commissioner, what can I do for you?"

The Commissioner took it slowly. First reports, much regret, your colleague Henry Danby, dead on arrival in the hospital. Seems on first impression the work of an assassin, very major police activity, but few other details available. He spoke quietly into the phone and was heard out in silence. When he finished, the voice at the end of the line, in the first-floor office overlooking Downing Street and the Foreign Office arch, said, "Nothing else?" "No, sir. It's early, though." "You'll shout if you want help—army, air force, intelligence, anything you need?"

There was no reply from the Commissioner. The Prime Minister went on: "I'll get out of your hair—call me in half an hour. I'll get one of our people to put it out to the Press Association."

The Commissioner smiled to himself bleakly. A press release straightaway—the political mind taking stock. He grimaced, putting his phone down as the door opened and the three men he'd summoned came in. They headed critical departments: C1—the elite crime investigation unit; the Special Branch—Scotland Yard's counterterrorist and surveillance force; and the Special Patrol Group—the specialist unit trained to deal with major incidents. All were commanders, but only the head of the SPG was in uniform.

The Commissioner kept his office Spartan and without frills, and the commanders collected the armless chairs from the sides of the room and brought them toward the desk.

He spoke first to the Special Patrol Group commander and asked him abruptly what was known.

"Not much, sir. Happened at 9:07. Danby comes down his front steps regular time, regular everything—he's waiting for the Ministry car. A man steps out into the street on the other side and lets fly, fires several shots, multiple wounds, and runs for it in the direction of Victoria. Not much good for eyewitnesses at this stage, not much about. There's a woman on the pavement had a good look at him, but she's a bit shocked at the moment. We've got he's about five-eight, younger than middle-aged, say thirtyish, and what she calls so far a pinched sort of face, dark hair. Clothes aren't much good—dark trousers under a biscuit-colored mac. That's it."

"And the gun?"

"Can't be definite." It was the Special Branch man. "Seems from what the woman said, it's an AK 47, usually called a Kalashnikov. Russians use it. VC in Vietnam, the Aden people, the Black September crowd. It's Czech-designed, quite old now, but it's never showed up here before. The IRA have tried to get them into Ulster, but always failed. The *Claudia*—that fishing boat up to the gills in arms—was running them when intercepted. It's a classic weapon, semiautomatic or virtually automatic—four hundred rounds a minute, if you could get that many up the spout. Muzzle velocity around two thousand feet a second. Effective killing range comfortable at half a mile. The latest version has a folding stock—you could get it into a big briefcase. It's accurate and doesn't jam. It's a hell of a weapon for this sort of thing. Its caliber is fractionally bigger than ours, so it fires Iron Curtain ammo, or ours at a pinch. We've found four shell cases, but no detail on them yet. It's got a noise all its own, a crack that people who've heard it say is distinctive. From what the woman said to the people down there, it fits with the Kalashnikov."

"And the conclusion?"

"It's not an amateur's weapon. We haven't traced them

coming in here yet. If it is a Kalashnikov, we're not up against second division. If they can get one of these things, then they're big and know what they're about."

That struck the chord. All four stayed quiet for a moment; it was a depressing thought. The professional political assassin on their hands. It went through the Commissioner's mind before he spoke that a man who troubled to get the ideal gun for the killing, the favorite terrorist weapon in the world, would spend time on the other details of the operation.

He lit his first cigarette of the day, two hours ahead of the schedule he'd disciplined himself to after his last medical check, and broke the silence. "He'll have thought out his escape route. It'll be good. Where are we, how do we block him?"

The Murder Squad chief took it up. "Usual, sir, at this stage. Ports, ferries, airports, private strips as soon as we can get men to them. Phone calls ahead to the control towers. I've got as many men as possible concentrated on the tube stations, and particularly exit points on the outskirts. He went towards Victoria, could be the tube, could be the train. We're trying to seal it, but that takes a bit . . ."

He tailed away. He'd said enough. The Commissioner drummed his desk top with the filter of his cigarette. The others waited, anxious to get the meeting over and get back to their desks, their teams and the reports that were beginning to build.

The Commissioner reacted, sensing the mood. "Right, I take it we all accept Danby was the target because of his work in Northern Ireland, though God knows, a less controversial Minister I never met. Like a bloody willow tree. It's not a nut, because nutters don't get modern Commie assault rifles to run round Belgrave Square. So look for a top man, in the IRA. Right? I'm putting Charlie in overall control. He'll coordinate. By this afternoon I want the whole thing flooded, get the manpower out. Bank on Belfast, we'll get something out of there. Good luck."

The last was a touch subdued. You couldn't give a pep talk to the three men he had in the room, yet for the first time since he'd eased himself into Commissioner's chair he'd felt something was required of him. Bloody stupid, he thought as the door closed on the Special Patrol Group commander.

His yellow light was flashing again on the telephone console. When he picked up his phone his secretary told him the Prime Minister had called an emergency Cabinet meeting for 2:30, and would require him to deliver a situation report to Ministers at the start of their meeting.

"Get me Assistant Commissioner Crime Charlie Henderson," he said after he'd scribbled down the message from Downing Street on his memory pad.

At a quarter to eleven the BBC broke into its television transmissions to schools, and after two seconds of blank screen went to a "Newsflash" caption. It then dissolved to an announcer, who paused, hesitated for a moment, and then, head down on his script, read:

"Here is a newsflash. Just after nine this morning a gunman shot and killed the Secretary of State for the Social Services, Mr. Henry Danby. Mr. Danby was about to leave his Belgrave Square home when he was fired on by a man apparently on the other side of the street. He was dead on arrival in the hospital. Our outside broadcast unit is now outside Mr. Danby's home, and we go over there now to our reporter, James Lyons."

"It's difficult from Belgrave Square to piece together exactly what happened this morning as Mr. Henry Danby, the Social Services Minister, left his home and was ambushed on his front doorstep. The police are at the moment keeping us a hundred yards back from the doorway as they comb the street for clues, particularly the cartridge cases of the murder weapon. But with me here is a lady who was walking her dog just round the corner of the square when the first shot was fired."

Q. What did you see?

A. Well, I was walking the dog, and I heard the bang, the first bang, and I thought that doesn't sound like a car. And I came round the corner and I saw this man holding this little rifle or gun up to his—

Q. Could you see the Minister—Mr. Danby?

A. I saw him, he was sort of crouched, this man in his doorway, he was trying to crawl, then came the second shot. I just stood there, and he fired again and again, and the woman—

Q. Mrs. Danby?

A. The woman in the doorway was screaming. I've never heard such a noise, it was dreadful, dreadful . . . I can't say any more . . . he just ran. The poor man was lying there, bleeding. And the woman just went on screaming . . . it was awful.

Q. Did you see the man, the gunman?

A. Well, yes and no, he came past me, but he came fast, he was running.

Q. What did he look like?

A. Nothing special, he wasn't very tall, he was dark.

Q. How old—could you guess?

A. Not old, late twenties, but it was very fast.

Q. And what was he wearing? Could you see?

A. He had a brown mac on, a sort of fawn color. I saw it had a tartan lining. I could see that he put the gun inside, in a sort of pouch. He just ran straight past me. I couldn't move. There's nothing more.

They'd told the Man that simplicity would see him through. That if they kept it easy, with no frills, they'd get him back. He got off the train at Warford Junction and began to walk toward the barrier, eyes going 180 degrees in front of him. The detectives he spotted were close to the ticket barrier, not looking down the platform but intent on the passengers. He walked away from the barrier toward the Gents, went into the graffiti-scrawled cubicle and took off his coat. He hung it carefully behind a door. He unfastened the shoulder strap, unclipped the magazine from the gun, took off his jacket and put the improvised holster back on. With his jacket over the top, the rifle fitted unseen close to his armpit. It gave him a stockiness that wasn't his and showed his jacket as a poor fit, but that was all. Trembling again in his fingers, he walked toward the barrier. The CID men, both local, had been told the Minister had been shot at home in Belgrave Square, they'd been told the man might have got away by Underground, they'd been told he was in a fawn-brown macintosh and was carrying an automatic rifle.

They hadn't been told that if the killer was on the tube, he had traveled from Victoria, and for the half-second that the ticket was between the Man and the collector, neither noticed it. In effect, they'd ruled him out in the five yards before he handed it over—no mac and no place to hide a gun. Nor had they been told the Kalashnikov could be folded.

He walked away from them, panting quietly to himself, his forehead cold with sweat, waiting for the shout behind him or the heavy hand falling on his shoulder, and felt nothing. He walked out of the station to the car park, where the Avis Cortina waited. He stowed the gun under the driver's seat and set off for Heathrow. There's no way they'll get you if you stay cool. That was the advice.

In the late morning traffic the journey took him an hour. He'd anticipated it would, and he found he'd left himself ninety minutes for his flight when he'd left the car in the No. 1 terminal car park. He locked the car, leaving the rifle under the seat with its magazine along with it.

The police were staked out at all corners of the terminal. The Man saw the different groups, reflected in their shoulder markings. Airport Police, Metropolitan Police, Special Patrol Group. He knew the last were armed, which gave him a chilled feeling in his belly. If they shouted and he ran, would they shoot him . . . ? He clenched his fist and walked up to the British Airways ticket desk. "The name is Jones . . . you've a ticket waiting for me. The one o'clock to Amsterdam, BE 467."

The girl behind the counter smiled, nodded, and began to beat out the instruction of the flight into her personal reservations computer. The flight was confirmed, and as she made the ticket out, the terminal loudspeakers warned passengers of delays on all flights to Dublin, Cork and Shannon and Belfast. No reason was given. But that's where all the effort will be, they'd told him. They haven't the manpower for the lot.

The Man brought out the new British passport supplied for him by his unit quartermaster and walked through immigration control.

■ 2 ■

Normally the Commissioner traveled alone, with only the elderly driver for company. That afternoon, sitting in the front with the driver was an armed detective. The car turned into Downing Street through the crash barriers that had been put into position half an hour after the shooting was reported. The dark, shaded street was empty of ministerial cars, and sightseers were banned for the day. By the door two constables had established their will on the group of photographers gathered to record all comings and goings, and shepherded them into a line stretching from the railings, over the pavement and out into the parking area.

The Commissioner was met in the hall, warm with its red carpets and chandeliers, and escorted to the lift. As he passed the small room to the right of the door he noted the four plainclothesmen sitting there. His order that the Prime Minister's guard should be doubled had been carried out. Two floors later he was led into the Prime Minister's study.

"I just wanted to see if there was anything you wanted to say before we get involved in the main scene downstairs."

"All I can do now, sir, is say what we know, what we're doing. Not much of the first, a lot of the second."

"There'll be a fair amount of questioning about the security round the Minister . . ."

The Commissioner said nothing. It was an atmosphere he was not happy in; he reflected that in his three years as Commissioner and the country's top policeman, he'd never got into this marble tower before, never got beyond the first-floor reception salons. On the way to Whitehall he had primed himself not to allow the police to become the scapegoat, and after thirty-six years on the Force his greater inclination was to be back at Scotland Yard hovering on the fifth floor by the control room, irregular as it was, but at least doing something.

There was little contact, and both acknowledged it. The Prime Minister rose and motioned with his hand to the door. "Come on," he murmured, "let's go and meet them. Frank Scott of the RUC and General Fairbairn are coming in from Belfast in an hour or so. We'll hear them after you."

The Man was striding his way along the vast pier of Schiphol Airport, Amsterdam, toward the central transit area. If his connections were working, he had fifty-eight minutes till the Aer Lingus 727 took off for Dublin airport. He saw the special airport police with their short-barreled, lightweight carbines patroling the entrance to the pier where the El Al jumbo was loading, and had noticed the armored personnel carriers on the aprons. All the precautions of the antihijack program, but nothing to concern him. He went to the Aer Lingus desk, collected the ticket waiting for him and drifted away to the duty-free lounge. They'd told him not to miss the duty-free lounge: the best in Europe, they'd said. Belgrave Square and the noise and the screaming were far away; for the first time in the day he felt a degree of calm.

In the first-floor Cabinet Room, the Commissioner stood to deliver his briefing. He spoke slowly, picking his words with care, and aware that the Ministers were shocked, suspicious and even hostile to what he had to say. There was little comfort for them. On top of what they had seen on the television lunchtime news they were told that a new and better description was being circulated; for the first time the policeman had the full attention of his audience.

"There was a slight jostling incident at Oxford Circus this morning. A man barged his way through; nearly knocking people over, and noticeably didn't stop to apologize. Not the sort of thing that you expect people to remember, but two women independently saw the television interview from Belgrave Square this morning and phoned the Yard—put the two together. It's the same sort of man they're talking about as we'd already heard of, but a better description. We'll have a photokit by four o'clock—"

He was interrupted by the slight knock on the door, and

the arrival of the Royal Ulster Constabulary Chief Constable Frank Scott and General Sir Jocelyn Fairbairn, GOC Northern Ireland. When they'd sat down, crowded in at the far end of the table, the Prime Minister began.

"We all take it this is an IRA assassination. We don't know for what motive, whether it is the first of several attempts or a one-off. I want the maximum effort to get the killer—and fast. I don't want an investigation that runs a month, two months, six months. Every day that these thugs get away with it is a massive plus to them. How it happened that Danby's detective was withdrawn from him so soon after he'd left the Ulster job is a mystery to me. The Home Secretary will report to us tomorrow on that, and also on what else is being done to prevent a recurrence of such attacks."

He stopped. The room was silent, disliking the schoolroom lecture. The Commissioner wondered for a moment whether to explain that Danby himself had decided to do without the armed guard, ridiculing the detective sergeant's efforts to watch him. He thought better of it and decided to let the Prime Minister hear it from his Home Secretary.

The Prime Minister gestured to the RUC man.

"Well, sir . . . gentlemen," he started in the soft Scots burr of so many of the Ulstermen. He tugged at the jacket of his bottle-green uniform and moved his blackthorn cane fractionally across the table. "If he's in Belfast, we'll get him. It would be very difficult for them to organize an operation of this scale and not involve so many people that we'll grab one and he'll bend. It's a lot easier to get them to talk these days. The hard men are locked up; the new generation talks. If he's in Belfast, we'll get him."

It was past five and dark outside when the Ministers, and the General and the Prime Minister again, had had their say. The Prime Minister had called a full meeting of all present for the day after tomorrow, and reiterated his demand for action and speed, when a private secretary slipped into the room, whispered in the Commissioner's ear and ushered him out. Those next to him had heard the word "urgent" used.

When the Commissioner came back into the room two minutes later the Prime Minister saw his face and stopped in midsentence. The eyes of the eighteen politicians and the Ulster policeman and the General were on the Commissioner as he said:

"We have some rather bad news. Police officers at Heathrow have discovered a hired car in the terminal car park near No. 1 building. Under the driver's seat was a Kalashnikov rifle. The car-park ticket would have given a passenger time to take flights to Vienna, Stockholm, Madrid, Rome and Amsterdam. The crew of the British Airways flight to Amsterdam are already back at Heathrow, and we are sending a photokit down to the airport, it's on its way, but one of the stewardesses thinks a man who fits our primary description, the rough one we had at first, was in the fifteenth row in a window seat. We are also in touch with Schiphol police, and are wiring the picture, but from that flight there was ample time to make a Dublin connection. The Aer Lingus Amsterdam/Dublin flight landed in Dublin twenty-five minutes ago, and they are holding all passengers in the baggage reclaim hall."

There was a common gasp of relief around the Cabinet Room, then the Commissioner went on: "But the Dublin airport police report that those passengers without baggage went through immigration control before we notified them."

"Would he have had baggage?" It was the Prime Minister, speaking very quietly.

"I doubt it, sir, but we're trying to establish that with the ticket desk and check-in counter."

"What a cock-up." The Prime Minister was virtually inaudible. "We'll need some results, and soon."

From Heathrow the Kalashnikov, swaddled in a cellophane wrapping, was rushed by squad car to Woolwich, on the far side of the city, to the police test-firing range. It was still white from the chalklike fingerprint powder brushed on at the airport police station, but the airport's resident fingerprint man had declared it clean. "Doesn't look like a gloves job," he said. "He must have wiped it— a cloth, or something. But it's thorough; he's missed nothing."

In the suburbs of Dublin in the big open-plan newsroom of RTE, the Republic of Ireland's television service, the central phone in the bank used by the news editor rang at exactly six o'clock.

"Listen carefully, I'm only going to say this once. This is a spokesman for the military wing of the Provisional IRA. An active-service unit of the Provisional IRA today carried out a court-martial execution order on Henry DeLacey Danby, an enemy of the people of Ireland and servant of the British occupation forces in Ireland. During the eighteen months spent in Ireland, one of his duties was responsibility for the concentration camp at Long Kesh. He was repeatedly warned that if the regime of the camp did not change, action would be taken against him. That's it."

The phone clicked off, and the news editor began to read back his shorthand.

Ten hours later the Saracens and Pigs, on dimmed headlights, were moving off from the Belfast police stations, heading out of the sandbagged tin- and chicken-wire fortresses of Andersonstown, Hasting Street, Flax Street, Glenravel Street and Mountpottinger. Sentries in steel helmets and shrapnel-proof jerkins, their automatic rifles strapped to their wrists, pulled aside the heavy wood and barb-wire barricades at the entrances of the battalion and company headquarters, and the convoys inched their way into the darkness. Inside the armored cars the troops huddled together, their faces blackened with boot polish, their bodies laden with gas masks, emergency wound dressings, rubber-bullet guns, truncheons and the medieval Macron see-through shields. In addition, they carried their high-velocity NATO rifles. Few of the men had slept more than a few hours, and that catnapping had been in their uniforms, their only luxury that of being able to take off their boots. Their officers and senior NCOs, who had attended the operational briefings for the raids, had slept even less. There was no talk, no conversation, only the knowledge that the day would be long, tiring, cold and probably wet. There was nothing for the men to look at.

Each car was battened down against possible sniper attacks; only the driver, the rifleman beside him and the rifleman at the back, with his barrel poked through the fine visibility slit, had any sight of the darkened, rain-swept streets. No house lights were on, no shop windows were illuminated, and only occasionally was there a high street lamp that had survived the attempts of both sides over the last four years to destroy its brightness.

Within a few minutes the convoys had swung off the main roads and were splitting up in the housing estates, all but one on the west side of the city. Two thousand troops, drawn from six battalions, were sealing off the streets that have the Falls Road as their spinal cord—the Catholic artery out of the west side of the city, and the route to Dublin. As the armored cars pulled across the streets, paratroopers, marines and men from the old county infantry units flung open the reinforced doors and ran for the security of their fire positions. In the extreme west, on the Andersonstown and Suffolk border, where the houses are newer and the sight therefore more incongruous, the troops were from a heavy-artillery unit—men more used to maneuvering with the long-range Abbot gun than looking for cover in front gardens and behind dust-bins. Away across the city from the Falls, more troops were spreading into the Ardoyne, and on the east side of the Lagan, the Short Strand area was sealed.

When their men were in position the officers waited for first light. Cars that tried to enter or leave the cordoned streets were sent back. In a gradual drizzle the troops lay and crouched in the cover that they had found, thumb on the safety catch. The selected marksmen cradled their rifles, made heavier by the attachment of the Starscope, the night vision aid.

The noise started as the soldiers began the house-to-house searches. Women, mighty in dressing gowns, with hair piled high by their bright plastic-coated curlers, surged from the houses to blow whistles, howl abuse and crash the dustbin lids. Amid the cacophony came the beating of rifle butts on doors, and the thud of the axes and sledge hammers when there was no ready answer. Within minutes there were as many civilians on the street as soldiers, bouncing their epithets and insults off the unmoving faces of the military. Protected by small knots of soldiers were the unhappy-looking civilian police, usually with their panting gelignite-sniffer Labradors close by. Occasionally there would come a shout of excitement from one of the small terraced houses, the accent North Country or Welsh or Cockney, and a small shining rifle or pistol would be carried into the street, wrapped to prevent the loss of the clues that would convict the still half-asleep man bundled down the pavement and into the back of an armored truck. But this was not often. Four years of searches and swoops and cordons and arrests had left little to find.

By dawn—and it comes late as far north as Belfast, and then takes a long time coming—there was little to show for the night's work. Some Japanese-made Armalite rifles, some pistols, a sackful of ammunition, and crocodile lines of men for questioning by the Special Branch, along with the paraphernalia of terrorism—batteries, lengths of flex, alarm clocks and sacks of potent weed-killer. All were itemized and shipped back to the police stations.

With the light came the stones, and the semiorderliness of the searches gave way to the crack of rubber bullets being fired; the streets swirled with CS gas, and always at the end of the narrow line of houses were the kids heaving their fractured paving stones at the military.

Unaware of the searches, bus drivers down the Falls Road, stopping at the lights, found youths climbing into their cabs, a variety of pistols threatening them, and handed over their double-deckers. By nine o'clock the Falls was blocked in four places, and local radio bulletins were warning motorists once again to stick to alternative routes.

As the soldiers withdrew from the streets there were infrequent bursts of automatic fire, not pressed home and causing no casualties. Only on one occasion did troops have enough of a target to fire back, and then they claimed no hit.

For both sides the raid had its achievements. The army and police had to stir up the pool and muddy the water, get the top men on the other side on the move, perhaps panic one of them into a false step or a vital admission. The street leaders could also claim some benefit from the morning. After the lull of several weeks the army had arrived to kick in the doors, take away the men, break up the rooms, prise out the floorboards. At street level that was valuable currency.

The Man had seen the police convoy racing into the airport as he'd left carrying, as his sole possessions, the Schiphol duty-free bag with two hundred cigarettes and a bottle of Scotch. As he'd come through, a young man had stepped forward and asked him if he was Mr. Jones. He'd nodded, nothing more was required of him, and followed the young man out of the new terminal and into the car park.

As they had driven past the airport hotel, they'd seen the Garda cars and a van go by. Neither driver nor passenger spoke. The Man had been told he would be met, and reminded that he must not speak at all on the journey, not even on the home trip. The car took the Dundalk road, and then on the stretch between Drogheda and Dundalk, turned left and inland toward the hills.

"We'll be away over near Forkhill," muttered the driver.

The Man said nothing as the car bumped its way down the side road. After fifteen minutes at a crossroads, where the only building was a corrugated iron-roofed store, the driver stopped, got out and went inside, saying he'd be a minute and had to telephone. The Man sat in the car, the light-headedness he'd felt at Schiphol that afternoon suddenly gone; it was not that he was alone that worried him, but that his movements and immediate future were not in his own hands. He had started to conjure up images of betrayal and capture, of himself left abandoned near the border and unarmed, when the driver walked back to the car and got in.

"Forkhill's tight, we're going further down towards the Cullyhanna road. Don't worry, you're home and dry."

The Man felt ashamed that the stranger could sense his suspicion and nervousness. As a gesture, he tried to sleep, leaning his head against his safety belt. He stayed in this position till the car suddenly jerked and flung his head hard against the window of the door. He shot forward.

"Don't worry"—again the self-assured, almost patronizing approach of the driver. "That was the crater we filled in two years ago. You're in the North now. Home in two hours."

The driver cut back to the east, through Bessbrook and on to the north of Newry and the main road to Belfast. The Man allowed himself a smile. There was a wide road now, and a good fast one. After a while the driver pulled up outside Hillsborough and motioned to the duty-free bag on the back seat under the Man's coat. "Sorry, boy. I don't want that as we come into town. Ditch it."

The Man wound down his window and flung the plastic bag across the lay-by and into a hedge. The car was moving again. The next sign showed Belfast to be five miles away.

On his return from London the previous evening, the Chief Constable had put a picked team of detectives on stand-by to wait for information over the confidential phone, the heavily publicized Belfast phone numbers over which information is passed anonymously to the police. They waited through the day in their ready room, but the call they hoped for never came. There was the usual collection of breathy messages naming people in connection with bombs, shootings, locating the dumping of fire-arms—but not even a word of rumor about the Danby killing. In three pubs in the center of Belfast, British army intelligence officers met their contacts and talked, huddled forward in the little cubicles they favored. All were to report later that night to their controller that nothing was known. While they talked, threatening, cajoling, bribing their sources, military police Land-Rovers cruised close by. The Red Caps had not been told who they were guarding, just detailed to watch and prevent the sudden entry of a number of men into those pubs.

The blowing of the laundry-van intelligence surveillance unit, when soldiers kept watch on an IRA base area from the false ceiling of a laundry van while their colleagues plied for trade below, had awakened the operation directors to the needs for safeguards when their men were in the field. That was thirty months back. The tortured and mutilated body of a Royal Tank Regiment captain found just three months ago had demonstrated the probability of a security leak close to the heart of the unit, and the public outcry at home at the exposing of soldiers to these out-of-uniform dangers had led to a Ministry directive that military personnel were no longer to infiltrate the Catholic community, but instead stay out and cultivate their informers. Funds and the availability of one-way air tickets to Canada were stepped up.

Quite separate from the military intelligence team, the RUC's Special Branch was also out that night—men who for three years had slept with their snub-nosed PPK Walthers on the bedside table, who kept a stock of spare plates at the back of the garage, who stood to the side at the well-photographed police funerals. They, too, were to report that there was no talk about the Danby killing.

Just before midnight came the first positive information that the killer was back in the city. The duty major in the intelligence section at Lisburn military headquarters, leafing through the situation reports of the evening, read that a patrol of the Lifeguards had for fifteen minutes closed the Hillsborough to Banbridge road while they investigated a package at the side of the road. It was cleared after the bomb-disposal expert arrived and found the bag contained a carton of cigarettes and a bottle of Scotch, duty-free and bought at Schiphol Airport. He hurriedly phoned his chief at home and the RUC control center. But nagging at him was the question of how such an operation as the Danby killing could have been mounted, with no word coming out.

The Man was asleep now, in the spare back bedroom of a small terraced house off the Ballymurphy Bull Ring. At 11:25 he'd come up from Whiterock, where he had stayed since arriving in Belfast. Around him a safety system was building, with the arrangement that he'd sleep till 5:30, then move again up into New Barnsley. The Brigade staff in Belfast was anxious not to keep him long in one place, to hustle him around. Only the Brigade commander knew the value of the man the precautions were made for—no one else was told, and in the house he was greeted with silence. He came in fast over the back fence, avoiding kids' bikes, ducked under the washing lines and made his way through the damp, filthy scullery into the back room. The family was gathered in semidarkness with the television on loud—Channel 9. His escort whispered into the ear of the man of the house, and was gone, leaving him. The Man was not from this part of the city, and was not known anyway.

His arrival and needs, after four years of warfare, were unremarkable. In the "Murph" his name could be kept secret, not his reason for running—not after the Scotland Yard photokit had been flashed up onto the screen during the late-night news. On orders from London, the photo had been withheld until after the intelligence and Special Branch officers had attempted to identify the killer. With their failure, the picture had been released.

The family gathered around the set to hear the announcer:

"Scotland Yard had just issued a photokit picture of the man they wish to interview in connection with the murder of Mr. Henry Danby, the Minister of Social Security, at his home in central London yesterday morning. The picture has been compiled from the descriptions of several eyewitnesses. Scotland Yard says the man is aged about thirty, has short hair, with a parting on the left side, a narrow face, with what a witness calls 'pinched cheeks.' The man is of light build, and about five feet nine inches tall. When last seen he was wearing grey trousers and a dark-brown jacket. He may also have a fawn-colored macintosh with him. Anyone who can identify this man is asked to get in touch immediately with the police on the confidential line of Belfast 227756 or 226837."

High on the fireplace over the small fire grate was a carved and painted model of a Thompson machine gun, the present to the family from their eldest son Eamon, held for two years in Long Kesh. It was dated Christmas 1973. Below the gun the family registered no reaction to the picture shown on their screen.

In the small hours Theresa, Eamon's sister, tiptoed her way around the scarred door of the back room. She eased her path over the floorboards, still loosened and noisy since the army came to look for her brother. In the darkness she saw the face of the Man, out from under his blankets; his arms were wrapped around his pillow like a child holding a favorite doll. She was shivering in the thin nightdress, transparent and reaching barely below her hips. She had selected it two hours before and then waited to be sure her people were asleep. Very gently at first, she shook the shoulder of the Man, till he started half out of bed, gripped her wrist, and then in one movement pulled her down, but as a prisoner.

"Who's that?" He said it hard, with fear in his voice.

"It's Theresa." There was a silence, just the Man's breathing, and still he held her wrist, vicelike. With her free hand she pushed back the bedclothes and moved her body alongside his. He was naked and cold; across the room she saw his clothes strewn over the chair by the window.

"You can let go," she said and tried to move closer to him, only to find him backing away till the edge of the single bed stopped his movement.

"Why did you come?"

"To see you."

"Why did you come?" Again, harsher, louder.

"They showed your picture . . . on the telly . . . just now . . . on the late news."

The hand released her wrist. The Man flopped back on

the pillow, tension draining out of him. Theresa pressed against his body, but found no response, no acknowledgment of her presence.

"You had to know, for when they move you on. I had to tell you . . . we aren't your enemies. You're safe with us . . . there's no danger."

"There are six men in the city who know I'm here—and you . . ."

A little more nervously she whispered back, "Don't worry yourself, there's no narks here, not in this street, not since the McCoy girl . . . they shot her." It was an afterthought—Roisin McCoy, soldier's girl friend, part-time informer, found shot dead under Divis mountain. Big outcry, no arrests.

"I'm not saying anything."

"I didn't come to talk, and it's freezing, half out of the bloody clothes."

He pulled her down, close now against him, the nylon of her nightdress riding up over her hips and her breasts. She pushed against him, screwing her nipples against the black hair of his chest.

"Not much, are they?" she murmured. "Couple of bloody bee stings."

The Man smiled, and the hand that had grasped her wrist to the point of half stopping the blood flow now stroked and rubbed urgently at the soft white inside of her thighs. She reached down and felt his stomach back away as she took hold of him, limp and lifeless, pliable in her hand. Slowly, then frantically to match her own sensations, she stroked and kneaded him, but without success.

Abruptly the Man stopped his movements, pulled his hand away from the moist warmth.

"Get out. Bugger off. Get out."

Theresa, nineteen years old, four of them spent on the mill weaving line, had heard and seen enough in her life to say, "Was it that bad . . . London . . . was it . . . ?"

The interruption was a stinging blow across the right side of her face. His cheap onyx wedding ring gouged skin below the eye. She was gone, out through the door across the passage to her bed; there she lay, legs clenched together, fascinated and horrified at the knowledge she had.

In her half-sleep she heard the whisper of voices and the footsteps on the stairs as the Man was taken to his next place of hiding.

In the Cabinet Room, the Prime Minister was showing little patience for the lack of a quick arrest. He had heard the Commissioner say that the case was static in London now, and that the main police effort was to establish how and where the man had entered the country. The boarding house in Euston where he had slept the night before the shooting had been searched, but nothing found. As expected, the gun had yielded no fingerprints, and the same process of elimination was being used on the car. Here it was pointed out that the police had to identify the fingerprints of everyone who had handled the car over the previous six weeks or so before they could begin to come up with a worthwhile print and say this was the killer's. It would take a long time, said the Commissioner, and involved drivers, Avis staff, garage personnel. Nothing had been found on the basics—steering wheel, door handle, gear lever. He reported on the new security measures surrounding Ministers, pointed out that they were nearly if not totally a waste of time if politicians did not cooperate, and urged no repetitions of the situation by which the murdered Minister had been able to decide for himself that he no longer wanted protection. He finished by putting the proposition that the killer had no contact in Britain, and had operated completely on his own. Reservations for tickets, in Dublin, Heathrow and Amsterdam, had all been made over the phone and were untraceable. He fell back on the theme that the solving of the crime would happen in Belfast, and that yesterday a chief superintendent from the Murder Squad had gone to Belfast to liaise with the RUC.

Frank Scott, the Chief Constable, reported nothing had come in on the confidential phones, and as yet there had been no whisper on the Special Branch net. "Now we know he's in the city, we'll get him, but it may not be fast —that's the situation." It had been left to him to report the finding of the Amsterdam duty-free bag.

"That's what you said two days ago," snapped the Prime Minister.

"And it's still the situation." The Chief Constable was not prepared to give ground. The Northern Ireland Secretary chipped in, "I think we all accept, Frank, that it's near impossible to stampede this sort of operation."

"But I have to have results." The Prime Minister drummed his knuckles on the table. "We cannot let this one hang about."

"I'm not hanging about, sir, and you well know that no one in my force is."

The Ulster policeman's retort caused a certain fidgeting down the sides of the table from Ministers who had begun to feel their presence was irrelevant to the matter in hand —other than that by their arrivals and departures the cameras could witness the activity and firm hand of government. The Commissioner wished he'd come in faster. One up to the RUC.

The Prime Minister, too, sensed the chilliness of the situation, and invited the opinion of General Fairbairn. As the GOC Northern Ireland, commanding more than fifteen thousand men there, he expected to be listened to.

"The problem, sir, is getting inside the areas the IRA dominate. Getting good information that we can trust and can then act on fast enough while the tips are still hot. Now, we can thrash around as we did yesterday morning, and as we have done to a more limited degree this morning, and though we pick up a bit—a few bodies, a few guns, some bomb-making equipment—we're unlikely to get at the real thing. I would hazard the motive behind the killing was to get us to launch massive reprisal raids, cordon streets off, taking house after house to pieces, lock hundreds up. They want us to hammer them and build a new generation of mini-martyrs. It's been quiet there these last few weeks. They needed a major publicity-attracting operation, and then a big kickback from us to involve people at street level who are beginning to want to disengage. The raids we have been mounting these last thirty-six hours are fair enough as an initial reaction, but if we keep them up, we'll be in danger of reactivating the people who had begun to lose interest in the IRA."

"What about your intelligence men, your men on the inside?"

"We don't go in for that sort of thing so much now, we tend to meet on the outside . . . After the young captain was murdered three months ago, horrible business . . . the Ministry wasn't happy, we suspended that sort of work."

"Suspended it?" The Prime Minister deliberately accentuated the touch of horror in his voice.

"We haven't had an operation of anything like this size to handle for around a year; things have been running down. There hasn't been the need for intelligence operatives. Now we would have to set up a new unit completely —the men we have there at the moment are too compromised. I don't think in your time scale, Prime Minister, we have the time to do it."

He said the last dryly, and with only the faintest hint of sarcasm, sufficiently guarded to be just permissable for a lieutenant general in the Cabinet Room at No. 10 Downing Street.

"I want a man in there . . . nothing else to think about."

The Prime Minister was speaking deliberately, the Agriculture man thought—nice and slowly, just right for the transcript being scribbled in the corner. "I want an experienced agent in there as fast as you can make it. A good man. If we've picked the killer up by then, nothing lost; if not . . . I know what you're going to say, General —if the man is discovered, I will take the rap. That's understood. Well?"

The General had heard enough to realize that the interchange of ideas had been over several minutes earlier. This was an instruction by the Head of Government.

"For a start, sir, you can get the gentleman taking the notes over there by the door to take his last page out of the book, take it over to the fire and burn it. You can also remind everyone in the room of the small print of the Official Secrets Act. Thank you."

The General got up, flushed high in his cheeks, and followed hurriedly by the Chief Constable, who was sharing his RAF plane back to Belfast, left the room.

That afternoon in an upper room above a newsagent's shop near the main square in Clones, just over the border in County Monaghan, half of the twelve-man Army Council of the Provisional IRA met to consider the operation mounted two days earlier in London. Initially, there was some anger that the killing had not been discussed by all members in committee, as was normal. But the chief of staff, a distant, intense man with deep eyes and a reputation for success in pulling the movement together, glossed over the troubles. He emphasized that now the shooting had taken place, the priority in the movement was to keep the Man safe. Unknowingly, he echoed the British Prime Minister five hundred miles away in Whitehall when he said, "Every day we keep the Man free is a victory. Right? They wanted to pull two battalions out next month; how can they when they can't find one man? We have to keep him moving and keep him close. He's a good man, he won't give himself away. But at all costs we have to keep their hands off him. He's better dead than in Long Kesh."

It was getting dark when the RAF Comet took off from Tempelhof Airport, Berlin, with its three passengers. Half-way back and sitting in an aisle seat, Harry still felt bewildered. Two hours earlier he had been called to the Brigade commander's office at HQ under the shadow of the old Nazi Olympic stadium, and been instructed he was going to London on urgent military business. He was told he wouldn't need to go home to get his bag, that was being done, and no, it would not be suitable for him to phone home at this moment, but it would be explained to his wife that he had been called away in a hurry.

Three hours later the plane landed at Northolt and then taxied two hundred yards beyond the main reception area to an unmarked square of tarmac where a solitary set of steps and a civilian Morris 1800 were waiting.

For a captain in transport it was a very remarkable set of circumstances.

■ 3 ■

Harry was awake at first light.

He was in a large room, painted soft pastel-yellow, with fine hard molding around the ceiling. A study of a Victorian matron with a basket of apples and pears faced him from across the room. An empty bookcase against the same wall, a basin, small Ministry-issue thin towel hanging underneath it. There was a chair and table, both with his uniform draped over them. At the foot of the bed he could see the suitcase they said they'd packed for him, with no baggage labels attached to it.

They'd avoided all checks at Northolt, and Harry hadn't been asked to produce his passport or any travel documents. As soon as he was inside the car the two military policemen had peeled away from his side and moved back into the shadows. He'd heard the trunk bang shut to notify that his suitcase was aboard. Then the car had moved off.

"My name's Davidson." The man in the front passenger seat was talking. "Hope you had a good flight. We've got a bit of a drive now. Perhaps you'd like to sleep for a while."

Harry had nodded, accepted the situation with what grace his position allowed, and dozed off.

The car had gone fast out of London, the driver taking them onto the A3, then turning off down to Leatherhead, south to Dorking and then into the narrow winding side roads under Leith Hill. Davidson was beside the driver and Harry had the back seat to himself, and it was only when the night sky was blotted out by the arch of trees over the sunken road that he awoke. The car had driven on some miles, with intent care, before it swept through the wrought-iron gates of one of those great houses, buried deep among their own woods, that lie hidden in the slopes. The drive was rough and in need of repair. Abruptly the rhododendrons gave way to lawns and the car pulled up at a huge porticoed front door.

"Bit formidable, isn't it? The Ministry maintains it's all they could get. Delusions of grandeur. A convent school went broke. Kids all died of exposure, more likely. Come on in."

Davidson, who had opened the door for him, was

speaking. Harry was aware of several other men hovering in the background. The bag was collected, and Davidson went in, followed by Harry.

"We've a long day tomorrow. Lot of talking to do. Let's call it quits, have a good night, and breakfast at seven. Okay?"

Sandwiches and a vacuum flask of coffee were waiting in Harry's room.

The plate and dirtied cup were on the rug by his bed. He put his feet down gingerly and moved to his case. His shaving bag was on top of his neatly folded clothes. He wondered what on earth Mary was making of all this. If they'd sent that dreadful adjutant down to tell her he was called away on urgent business, it would be enough to get him a divorce—better be someone with a little experience in the world of untruths.

No one he'd seen last night had been in uniform. After shaving, he put on a checked shirt, tie and his grey suit. He folded his uniform away in the wardrobe and dispersed his other clothes to the various drawers and cupboards. He sat by the window waiting for someone to come and tell him breakfast was served. From his room on the second floor, he could see he was at the back of the house. Overgrown tennis courts. A vegetable garden. A great line of trees before the ridge of Surrey hills.

Harry was not naïve and had realized he was to be briefed for an intelligence mission. That didn't bother him, he'd decided. It was a little flattering, and was welcome after brigade transport. Perhaps the remarks about nervous collapse had been rather overstressed on his post-Aden reports. Anyway, little had come his way that had stretched him to the degree he thought he was capable of. If they'd brought him from Germany, then the hard assumption would be they were going to use him for something in Berlin. This pleased him, as he prided himself that he had taken the trouble to learn passable German, have a near-taxi-driver knowledge of the city and keep himself discreetly abreast of the trade techniques. His thoughts were full of the Reichstag, watchtowers, walls and clumps of flowers by the little crosses, when the sharp knock came and the door opened.

It began in earnest in what must once have been the drawing room, now furnished in the fashion of the Defence Ministry. Heavy tables, sofas with big pink flowers all over them and deep army chairs with cloth squares at the back to prevent greased hair marking the covers.

Davidson was there, and three others.

Harry was given the armchair to the right of the fireplace, dominated by the oil painting of the Retreat from Kabul in the snows of the Afghanistan passes. One man sat behind him by the window; another, not ostentatiously, close to the door. The third sat at a central table, his files spread out on the drapes that covered the polished oak surface. One was of stiff blue cardboard, its top crossed with red tape. *SECRET* had been written across the front in large letters, and underneath were the words: BROWN, HARRY JAMES, CAPT. Four sheets of closely typed paper were inside—Harry's life history and the assessments of his performance by each of his commanding officers. The first page carried the information they had sought when they had begun the search for the officer they wanted:

Name: Brown, Harry James
Current rank: Captain
Age: 34 years
Born: Portadown, NI, November 1940
Distinguishing marks and description: 5′11″ height, medium build, brown hair, blue eyes, no distinguishing marks, no operation scars
Service UK: Catterick, Plymouth, Tideworth, Ministry of Defence

Service Overseas: Cyprus (2nd Lt), Borneo (2nd Lt), Aden (1st Lt), Berlin (Capt)
Decorations: Cyprus—Mentioned in Despatches. Aden—Military Cross

In the last quarter of the page was the passage that ensured that Harry came into the operation:

Aden citation: For three months this officer lived as a native in the Arab quarter of Sheik Othman, moving inside the community there and supplying most valuable intelligence concerning terrorist operations. As a result of his work, many important arrests were made. It should be stressed that this work was extremely dangerous to the officer, and there was a constant risk that if discovered he would face certain torture and death.

Too bloody right, Harry would have thought if anyone had let him see the file. Day after day, living with those filthy bastards, eating with them, talking with them, crapping with them. Watching for new cars, watching for movement after curfew, observing the huddles in the coffee shops. And always the fear, and the horror if they came too close to him, seemed too interested, talked too much. The terrible fear of discovery, and the pain that would follow. And the know-alls in intelligence back at headquarters who only met an NLF man when he was neatly parceled up in their basement cells, and who pass discreet little messages—about hanging on a few more days, just a little bit longer. They'd seemed surprised when he just walked up to an army patrol one hot, stinking morning, and introduced himself, and walked out of thirteen weeks of naked terror. And no mention in the files on him of the nervous breakdown, and the days of sick leave. Just a metal cross, and an inch square of purple and white cloth to dangle it from, all there was to show for it.

Davidson was moving about the room in sharp darts around the obstacles of furniture.

"I don't have to tell you, from your past experience, that everything that is said in this room this morning goes under the Official Secrets Act. But I'll remind you of that anyway. What we say in here, the people you've seen here, and the building and its location are all secret.

"Your name was put forward when we came into the the market for a new man for an infiltration job. We've seen the files on the Aden experience, and the need has now come up for a man unconnected with any of the normal channels to go in and work in a most sensitive area. The work has been demanded by the Prime Minister. Yesterday afternoon he authorized the mission, and I must say frankly it was against, as I understand it, the advice of his closest military advisors. Perhaps that's putting it a bit strong, but there's some skepticism . . . the PM had a brother in SOE thirty years ago, he has heard over Sunday lunch how the infiltration of agents into enemy country won the war, and they say he's had a bee about it ever since.

"He wants to put a man into the heart of Provo-land, into the Falls in Belfast—a man who is quite clean and has no form in that world at all. The man should not be handled by any of the existing intelligence and undercover groups. He'd be quite new, and to all intents he'd be on his own as far as looking after himself is concerned. I think anyone who has thought even a little about what the PM is asking for knows that the job he has asked us to do is bloody dangerous. I haven't gilded it, Harry. It's a job we've been asked to do, and we all think from what we've read of you that you are the ideal man for it. Putting it formally, this is the bit where you either stand up and say, 'Not effing likely' and walk out through the door and we'll have you on a flight to Berlin in three hours. Or it's the time when you come in and then stay in."

The man at the table with the files shuffled his papers. Harry was a long way from a rational evaluation of the job, whatever it was they were offering. He was just thinking how large a file they'd got on him when he became aware of the silence in the room.

Harry said, "I'll try it."

"You appreciate, Harry, once you say yes, that's it. That has to be the definitive decision."

"Yes, I said yes. I'll try it." Harry was almost impatient with Davidson's caution.

The atmosphere in the room seemed to change. The man behind Harry coughed. Davidson was on the move again, the file now open in his hand.

"We're going to put you into the Falls with the express and only job of listening for any word of the man who shot the Minister, Danby, three days ago. Why aren't they doing it from Belfast? Basic reason is they haven't got an infiltration setup any longer that we're happy with. They used to do it, lost out, and have pretty much withdrawn their men to let them stooge on the outside and collect the stuff they want from informers. The activity has been down over the last few months, and with the risk that exists—I'm being straight with you, Harry—of an undercover man being picked off, and the hullabaloo when it hits the fan, those sorts of operations have been scaled down. There is a thought that the intelligence division over there is not as tight as it ought to be. We've been asked to set up a new operation. Intelligence in Belfast won't handle you, we will. The Special Branch over there won't have heard of you. Whatever else your problems would be, they won't be that someone is going to drop you in it over there, because no one will know of your existence. If you have a message, you pass it to us. A phone

call to us, on the numbers we give you, will be as fast—
if you want to alert the military—as anything you could
do if you were plugged into the regular Lisburn net, working under their control.

"I stress again, this is the PM's idea. He raised it at
the security meeting yesterday and insisted we push it
forward. The RUC don't want you, and the military
regard it as something of a joke. We reckon we'll need you
here for two weeks before we fly you in, and in that time
they may have the man, or at least have a name on him.
If that happens, then we call the whole thing off, and you
can relax and go back to Germany. It's not a bad thing that
they don't want to know—we won't have to tell them
anything till it's ripe, and that way we keep it tight.

"So far, the police and military have put out pictures,
appeals, rewards, launched raids, checked all the usual
angles, and they haven't come up with anything. I don't
know whether you will. The PM decided we try, and
that's what's going to happen.

"I'm sorry, but on this there cannot be a phone call to
your wife. We've told her you've been called away on
urgent posting. This morning she's been told you're on
your way to Muscat, because of your special Aden
knowledge. We have some postcards you can write to
her later and we'll get them posted by the RAF for you.

"I said in the beginning this would be dangerous. I don't
want to minimize that. The IRA shoot intelligence men
they get their hands on. They don't rough them up and
leave them for a patrol to find, they kill them. The last
man of ours that they took was tortured. Catholics who
work for us have been beaten up, burned, lacerated,
hooded and then killed. They're hard bastards . . . but we
want this man badly."

Davidson paused in his stride, jolting Harry's attention.
Harry fidgeted and shifted in the chair. He hated the pep
talks. This one was damn near a carbon copy of the one

he'd had in Aden, though then the PM's name had been left out, and they were quoting top-secret instructions from GOC Land Forces Mideast.

Davidson suggested coffee. The work would start after the break.

The Prime Minister had been hearing a report on the latest speech to a Bulawayo farming conference of the rebel prime minister—his "illegal counterpart," as he liked to call him. He scanned the pages quickly and deftly, assimilating the nuances the Rhodesian's speech writers had written in for the reader on the other side of the world. It was a static situation, he decided, not one for a further initiative at this stage. When his secretary had left him he turned back to his desk from the window and dialed an unlisted number at the Ministry of Defence.

The conversation lasted about twenty-five seconds. The Prime Minister put his opening question, listened, and rang off after saying, "No . . . no . . . I don't want to know any more . . . only that it's happening. Thank you, you'll keep me informed, thank you."

Off the Broadway, halfway up the Falls, the Man and his minder locked the doors of the stolen and resprayed Cortina and moved through the protective cordon of white-painted petrol drums to the door of the pub. The minder had been there from the morning, not knowing and not asking who the man was he had been sent to protect. With the job went the PPK Walther that pulled down his coat pocket. The gun was a prize symbol of the old success days of the local IRA company—taken from the body of a Special Branch constable ambushed as he cruised late at night in the Springfield Road. It was now prized partly for its fire power, partly for its value as a trophy.

The Man led the way into the pub. It was the first time

he had walked the streets of the city since his return, and after two days on the move from house to house and not a straight night's sleep at any of them, he showed the signs of a life on the run. The Army Council had anticipated this and had decided that for his own safety the Man should as soon as possible be reintroduced to his old haunts, as the longer he was away the more likely it was that his name could become associated with the shooting in London.

The pub boasted a single bar, dark, shabby and with a pall of smoke hanging between shoulder height and the low ceiling. A sparse covering of worn lino was on the floor, pocked with cigarette burns. As always, most eyes were facing the door, and conversation died as the Man walked in and went toward the snug, away to the left of the serving area. The minder gripped him by the arm and mouthed quickly in his ear. "They said in the middle of the bar. Show yourself. That's what they told me."

The Man nodded his head, turned to the bar and ordered his drinks. He was known only slightly here, but the man with him was local, and that was the passport of acceptance. The Man felt the tension easing out of him as the conversation again spread through the bar.

Later he was asked by one old man how come he'd not been in. He replied loudly, and with the warm beer moving through him, that his Mam in Cork had been unwell. He'd been to see her, she was better now and he was back. His Mam was better known in these streets than he was, and it was remembered by a few that she'd married a railwayman in Cork three years after her first husband died, and moved away to the South from Belfast. Bloody lucky I was too, she'd say. The railman himself had died now, but she had stayed South. The Man's explanation was more than adequate. There were mutterings of sympathy, and the subject was closed.

His main worry had been the photokit picture. He had

seen it reproduced on the front page of the Belfast *News-letter* on his second day back and read of the efforts to track him down. He'd seen pictures of the troops sealing streets off, looking for him, and looked at quarter-page advertisements taken by the Northern Ireland office urging people to tell all they knew about the killing to the police via the confidential phone. There were reports that a huge reward was to be offered for his capture, but if any of the men in the bar linked him with the picture, there was no sign of it. The Man had decided himself that the picture was not that similar to his features, too pinched in the face, the word the woman had used, with the hair parting too accentuated.

He was on his third pint when the patrol came into the pub.

Eight soldiers, crowding into the small area, ordered everyone to stay still and keep their hands out of their pockets. With the shouting from the troops and the general noise of their entry, no one noticed the minder, leaning against the bar, slide his gun down toward the washing-up bowl. Nor did they see the publican, ostensibly drying his hands before displaying them to the troops, put his cloth over the dark gun metal. With his final action, he flicked cloth and gun onto the floor and kicked them hard toward the kitchen door. The design of the building prevented any of the soldiers seeing the young girl's hand reach around the door in answer to her father's short whistle, gather up the gun and run with it to the coal shed. The men in the bar were lined against the side wall by the empty fireplace and searched. The Man's search was no more, no less thorough than that of the other men. They searched the minder very thoroughly, perhaps because he was sweating, a veil of moisture across his forehead, as he waited their decision on him, not knowing what had happened to the gun that bore his palm prints and could earn him five years plus in the Crumlin Road.

Then, as suddenly as the soldiers had come, they were out, barging their way past the tables, running into the street, and back to their regular routine of patrolling. There was noise again in the bar. The publican pushed the washing-up cloth, now filthy with coal smut, across the wooden bar to the minder. The Man felt noisy. He'd come through the first big test.

At the big house in Surrey, the team around Harry had worked him hard the first day. They'd started by discussing what cover he would want, and rejected the alternatives in favor of a merchant seaman home after five years, but with his parents dead some years back.

"It's too small a place for us to give you a completely safe identity you could rely on. It would mean we'd have to bring other people in who would swear by you. It gets too big that way. We start taking a risk, unnecessary."

Davidson was adamant that the only identity Harry would have would be the one he carried around on his back. If anyone started looking into his story really deeply, then there was no way in which he could survive, strong background story or not.

Harry himself supplied most of what they needed. He'd been born a Catholic in one of the little terraces off Obin Street in Portadown. The houses had been pulled down some years ago and replaced by anonymous blocks of flats and small houses, now daubed with slogans of revolution. With the destruction of the old buildings, inevitably the people had become dispersed.

Portadown, the Orangemen's town with the ghetto around the long sloping passage of Obin Street, still had its vivid teenage memories for Harry. He'd spent his childhood there from the age of five, after his perents had been killed in a car crash. They'd been driving back to Portadown when a local businessman late home on his way back from Armagh had cut across them and sent his father into a ditch and telegraph pole. Harry had stayed with an aunt for twelve years in the Catholic street before joining the army. But his childhood in the town gave him adequate knowledge—enough, Davidson decided, for his cover.

For four hours after lunch they quizzed him on his knowledge of the intricacies of Irish affairs, sharpened him on the names of the new political figures. The major terrorist acts since the summer of 1969 were neatly catalogued on three closely typed sheets. They briefed him particularly on the grievances of the minority.

"You'll want to know what they're beefing about. You know this, they're walking encyclopedias on every shot we fired at them. There's going to be a lot more, but this is the refresher."

Davidson was warming to it now, enjoying these initial stages of the preparation, knowing its thoroughness would be the deciding factor as to whether their agent survived. Davidson had been through this before. Never with Ulster as the target, but in Aden before Harry's duty there, and Cyprus, and once when a Czech refugee was sent into his former homeland. That last time they heard nothing till the man's execution was reported by the Czech news agency half an hour after a stony protest note was delivered to the British ambassador in Prague. Postwar Albania had involved him too. Now it was a new operation, breeding the same compulsion as the first cigarette of the day to an inveterate smoker.

Harry had come up to the table. The papers were spread out in front of him, fingers reaching and pointing at the different essentials for him to take in.

Later he took many of them to his room, asked for some sandwiches and coffee, then sprawled in front of the gas fire, reading them into the small hours till they were second nature. On his own for the first time in the day, he, too, was able to assess the importance of the preparation he was undergoing, and alone in the room, he allowed himself to think of the hazards of the operation in which he was now involved.

It was past two in the morning when he undressed and climbed into bed, the papers still strewn on the rug in front of the fire.

4

Over the next fortnight the street scene in Belfast returned to its pre-Danby level of violence. It was widely recognized that in the wake of the killing, the level of army activity had risen sharply, initially in the use of major cordon and search operations, merging into an increase in the number of spot raids on the homes of known republicans on the run. The army activity meant more men were charged with offenses, but alongside their appearances in court was an upsurge in street rioting, something that had previously been almost eradicated. The army's posture was sharply criticized by the minority politicians, who accused the troops of venting their frustrations at not being able to find Danby's murderer on innocent Catholic householders.

The Secretary of State for Northern Ireland agreed to appear on the local independent TV station and the regional BBC news program to answer the allegations of Protestant papers that not enough was being done—that a British Cabinet Minister had been shot down in cold blood in front of his wife and children, yet his killers were allowed to go free for fear of offending Catholic opinion.

Before appearing on television the Secretary of State called a meeting of his security chiefs, and heard both Frank Scott and General Fairbairn urge caution and patience. The General in particular was concerned lest a show of strength spread over several weeks undo the gradual return to something like normalcy. The three men were soon to leave for their various destinations—the politician for the studio, the General for Lisburn, the Chief Constable for his modern police headquarters—but first they walked on the lawn outside the Stormont residence of the Secretary of State. Away from the listening ears of secretaries, aides and bodyguards, the General reported that his intelligence section had heard nothing of the killer in Belfast and there was some concern about whether the man they sought was even in the city. The Chief Constable added to the politician's cross in reporting that his men, too, had been unable to uncover any hard information on the man. But the head of his Special Branch favored the belief that the killer was in the city, and probably back in circulation. The chief superintendent in charge of picked detectives had a fair insight into the workings of his enemy's minds, and had correctly read the desire of the Provisional IRA Army Council to get their man back into the mainstream.

For three minutes they talked in the center of the lawn. The conversation ended when the Secretary of State quietly, and more than a little hesitantly, asked the General, "Jocelyn, no news I suppose on what the PM was talking about?"

"None, nor will there be."

The General made his way back to his car, turned and shouted a brusque farewell.

As the military convoy pulled away, the politician turned to the policeman. "We have to have this bastard soon. The political scene won't hold up long otherwise. And there's a lot of restiveness among the loyalists. We need him quick, Frank, if the sectarianism isn't to start up again. There's not much time . . ."

He walked quickly now to his big maroon Rover with its reinforced sides and extra-thick windows. He nodded to his driver, and then winced as the detective sitting in front of him loaded the clip of bullets into the butt of the 9-mm Browning.

The car swung out into the open road for the drive into the city, with his escort close behind to prevent any other car clipping between them. "What a bloody carry-on," the politician observed as they swept through the traffic toward the television studio.

The interview of the Secretary of State was embargoed until 1801 hours; its full text was issued by the Northern Ireland press office to Belfast newspapers. In essence the BBC and ITV transmissions were the same, and the public relations men put out only the BBC interview.

Q. Secretary of State, can you report any progress in the hunt for Mr. Danby's killer?

A. Well, I want to emphasize that the security forces are working flat out on this one. I myself have had a meeting just before this broadcast with the army commander and Chief Constable, and I am perfectly satisfied with the investigation and follow-up operations they are mounting. I'm confident we'll round up this gang of thugs quickly.

Q. But have you any leads yet to who the killers are?

A. I think we know who the killers are, they're the Provisional IRA, but I'm sure you wouldn't expect me to talk on television about the details of a police investigation.

Q. It's been pretty quiet for some time in Belfast, and

we were led to believe that most of the IRA commanders were imprisoned . . . Isn't it justifiable to expect rather quicker action, even results at this stage?

A. If you mean to imply we have claimed the IRA weren't capable of mounting this sort of operation, I don't think we have ever made that sort of assumption. We think this is the work of a small group, a very small group. We'll get them soon . . . there's nothing to panic about . . . (It was a bad word, panic, he saw it as soon as he said it. The interviewer nudged him forward.)

Q. I haven't heard the word "panic" used before. Are you implying the public has overreacted towards the killing of a Cabinet Minister in broad daylight in front of his children?

A. Of course this was a dreadful crime. This was a colleague of mine. Of course people should feel strongly; what I'm saying is that this is a last fling of the IRA . . .

Q. A pretty successful last fling.

A. Mr. Danby was unarmed.

Q. In loyalist areas of the city, the government is accused of not going in hard to find the killer because the results could antagonize Catholic opinion.

A. That's untrue, quite untrue. When we have identified the man, we intend to get him. There'll be no holding off.

Q. Secretary of State, thank you very much.

A. Thank you.

Most of the young Protestants who gathered in the side streets off the Albert Bridge Road, pelting the armored vehicles as they went by, hadn't seen the interview. But word had quickly spread through the loyalist heartlands in the east and west of the city that the British had in some way glossed over the killing, not shown the determination to rout out those Provie rats who could murder a man in front of his bairns. The battalion on duty in Mountpottinger police station was put on fifteen-minute readiness, and those making their way to the prosperous suburbs far out to the east of Belfast took long diversions, lest their cars become part of the sprouting barricades that the army crash-charged with their Saracens. Three soldiers were hurt by flying debris, and the Minister's broadcast was put down as the kindling point or the brushfire that was to smolder for more than a week in the Protestant community.

Meanwhile Harry was being prepared for the awesome moment when he would leave the woods of Surrey and fly to Belfast, on his own, leaving the back-up team that now worked with him as assiduously as any heavyweight champion's.

Early on, Davidson had brought him a cassette recorder, complete with four ninety-minute tapes of Belfast accents. They'd been gathered by students from Queens University who believed they were taking part in a national phonetics study, and had taken their microphones into pubs, launderettes, workingmen's clubs and supermarkets. Wherever there were groups gathered and talking in the harsh, cutting accent of Belfast, so different from the slower, more gentle Southern speech, tapes had attempted to pick up the voices and record them. The tapes had been passed to the army press officer via a lecturer at the university, whose brother was on duty on the Brigade commander's staff, and then, addressed to a fictitious major, flown to the Ministry of Defence. The sergeant on Davidson's staff traveled to London to collect them from the dead-letter box in the postal section of the Ministry.

Night after night Harry listened to the tapes, mouthing over the phrases and trying to lock his speech into the accents he heard. After sixteen years in the army, little of it seemed real. He learned again of the abbreviation, the slang, the swearing. He heard the way that years of conflict and alertness had stunted normal conversation; talk was kept to a minimum as people hurried away from shops once their business was done, and barely waited around for a quiet gossip. In the pubs he noticed that men lectured each other, seldom listening to replies or interested in opinions different from their own. His accent would be critical to him, the sort of thing that could awake the first inkling of suspicion that might lead to the further check he knew his cover could not sustain.

His walls, almost bare when he had arrived at the big house, were soon covered with aerial photographs of Belfast. For perhaps an hour a day he was left to memorize the photographs, learn the street patterns of the geometric divisions of the artisan cottages that had been allowed to sprawl out from the center of the city. The developers of the nineteenth century had flung together the narrow streets and their back-to-back terraces along the main roads out of the city. Most relevant to Harry were those on either side of the city's two great ribbons of Falls and Shankill. Pictures of astonishing clarity taken from RAF cameras showed the continuous peace line, or the "interface," as the army called it, the sheets of silvery corrugated iron that separated Protestants from Catholics in the no man's land between the roads.

The photographs gave an idea of total calm, and left no impression of the hatred, terror and bestiality that existed on the ground. The open spaces of bombed devastation in any other British city would have been marked down as clearance areas for urban improvement.

From the distance of Germany—where theorists worked out war games in terms of divisions, tank skirmishes, limited nuclear warheads and the possibility of chemical agents being thrown into a critical battle—it had become difficult for Harry to realize why the twenty or so thousand British soldiers deployed in the province were not able to wind up the Provisional campaign in a matter of months. When he took in the rabbit warren revealed by the reconnaissance photographs, he began to comprehend the complexity of the problem. Displayed on his walls was the perfect guerilla fighting base. A maze of escape routes, ambush positions, back entries, cul-de-sacs and, at strategic crossroads, great towering blocks of flats commanding the approaches to terrorist strongholds.

It was the adventure playground *par excellence* for the urban terrorist, Davidson would say as he fired questions at Harry. He kept at it till he could wheel out at will all the street names they wanted from him—so many of them commemorating the former greatness of British arms: Balkan, Raglan, Alma, Balaclava—their locations and the quickest way to get there. By the second week the knowledge was there and the consolidation toward perfection was under way. Davidson and his colleagues felt now that the filing system had worked well, that this man, given the impossible brief he was working under, would do as well as any.

Also in the bedroom, and facing him as he lay in bed, was the "tribal map" of the city. That was the army phrase, and another beloved by Davidson. It took up sixteen feet of space, with Catholic streets marked in a gentle grass-green, the fierce loyalist strongholds in the hard orange that symbolized their heritage, and the rest in a mustard compromise. Forget that lot, Davidson had said. That had meant something in the early days when the maps were drawn up.

"Nowadays you're in one camp or the other. There are no uncommitted. Mixed areas are three years out of date. In some it's the Prods who've run, in others the other crowd."

It had been so simple in Sheik Othman, when Harry had lived among the Adeni Arabs. The business of survival had occupied him so fully that the sophistications they were teaching him now were unnecessary. And there he had been so far from the help of British troops that he had become totally self-reliant. In Belfast he knew he must guard against the feeling that salvation was always a street corner away. He must reject that and burrow his way into the community if he was to achieve anything.

At one stage it was suggested that Harry should personally meet the eyewitnesses who had been in Belgrave Square, or who had reported the jostling incident with the hurrying man in the Underground ticket area at Oxford Circus. Harry could have gone in the guise of a detective, but Davidson, after mulling it over for thirty-six hours, decided it was an unnecessary risk and sent a video camera from the Ministry to their homes with one of the young officers, in order that they could relive the moments they had been face to face with the gunman. For about fifteen minutes the elderly man who had seen a flash of the face while reading his paper, the girl with the bag of laundry, the woman exercising her dog, the driver of the Ministry car and the woman who had stood immobile as the man weaved away past her had spelled out their recollections. They were taken again and again through the short experience, milked till their impatience with their questioner grew pointed, and then left wondering why so much equipment and time was spent in merely reiterating the statement they had made to the police the previous week.

Endlessly the tapes were rerun, so that the strength of each witness's description could be tested. Hesitations about hair style, eye color, cheekbone make-up, nose size, all the details that make each face unique as a fingerprint were analyzed. Davidson made up a chart where all the strong points were listed in green ink, the next category in red, the doubtful points in blue. These were placed against the photokit picture already issued by the Royal Ulster Constabulary and Scotland Yard.

There were differences, they found. Differences that would have been sufficient to prevent the young soldiers in the pub off the Broadway eight days earlier from connecting the picture they had memorized with the man they had studied, arms up and legs apart, against the wall.

"You have to know him," said Davidson—so often, it became like a broken record. "You have to know about him, have a sense that when he's on the pavement and you're at the other side you'll have him straightaway. It's chemistry, my boy."

Harry thought of it a different way. He thought in a job as daft as this you need everything on your side. He reckoned his chances of seeing the man were about minus nil, though he maintained a more public optimism with Davidson.

The Ministry had designed their own photokit of the man, using the Scotland Yard one as a basis, but from the eyewitness tapes they altered various features slightly, particularly the profile of the face. Their own picture was displayed about treble life-size in the rooms where the team worked—the big living room and the dining area at the back—and more space on Harry's wall was taken up with it, alongside the maps and aerial photographs.

By the fifteenth day they were ready to cut the cord and push Harry out into the field. Other than his sleeping time, and those hours he'd worked in his room on the voice tapes and the maps, he'd been allowed to spend little time on his own. That was Davidson's idea—"For Christ's sake, don't let the poor bugger brood on it," he told the others.

Davidson had wondered whether there ought to be some celebration on Harry's last night, and then decided against it in favor of a few glasses of beer after their final session, and another early night.

"Don't believe all that *Daily Telegraph* stuff about their being beaten, smashed, in their final death throes. It's nonsense. They need time to regroup, and they needed a big morale booster. They've got that, not in the killing itself, but in our failure to nab their man and lock him up. The Prods are restless now, not critical yet, but stirring the pot—just as the Provos want it.

"To be frank, Harry, we all thought they'd have had the sod by now, and for the first week, at least, we may have handled your preparation on that basis. The word I had last night is that they haven't identified any positive clue yet. No one's losing anything by your going in. But in a strange, idiotic way, you have a better chance than the military clumping round and the police. It's not a great chance, but about worth taking."

They wished him luck. A little formal. Harry said nothing, nodded and walked into the hall and up the stairs to his room. They let him go alone.

The fire position was in the roof of a derelict house just to the north of the Falls Road, beyond its junction with Springfield. Four of the houses had been demolished when a nineteen-year-old volunteer in the First Battalion had stumbled, knocking the arm of the battalion's explosive officer as he was putting the final touches to a battery-controlled time fuse on a seventy-five-pound gelignite bomb. The officer's fingers had moved some three-eighths of an inch.

The explosives had left a gouged hole in the street. The first house to the right after the gap was left naked and exposed to the open air. The next house down was in better shape. There was a door still in place and the roof was largely intact. The house was empty because local housing officials had condemned it as unsafe, and gas and electricity had been switched off. The five houses beyond were occupied.

The Man had wedged himself in the angle between the beams and the horizontal struts of the roof. Part of the time his legs were astride the struts, which cut deep into his thighs in spite of the cushions he had brought with him. Otherwise, he knelt, spreading his weight over two of the struts. In that position his balance was more stable, but it hurt more.

Looking down, he could see through a gap in the roof where a tile had slid down into the street, shaken loose by the explosion. The tile had been only slightly above the level of the guttering, and from his position, his eyes were little more than four feet from it. From the hole, his line of visibility took him left to the street, and across and to the right he could see the length of the frontage of three houses. On the same side of the street as the Man's hiding place was the home of a Mrs. Mulvenna, whose husband was currently held in Long Kesh. She always kept her front-room light on, with the curtain drawn back, so that the light illuminated the pavement just beyond the extremity of the Man's field of fire and threw shadows into the area covered by his line of vision. It was his hope that a night patrol, their faces blackened, rubber soles on their boots, would edge away from the brightness in favor of the side of the road where they could find some false refuge in the greyness, but where they would be covered by the Man's sights. He knew enough of the habits of the soldiers to be able to bank on one of the troops in the middle of the patrol lingering uncertainly on the corner. The soldier would need to pause for only two or three seconds to make the Man's vigil worthwhile.

The army was never consistent with their patrol patterns, and in the three days that he had been in the roof, the Man had seen only one group of soldiers. That had been in midmorning, and then, without Mrs. Mulvenna's light to drive them across the street, they had come by, right underneath the hideout and virtually out of sight. He had seen one of them momentarily then, heard their fresh, young English county voices as they passed by, unaware of his presence above.

Across the Man's knee was an Armalite rifle. Small, lightweight, with shocking high-velocity hitting power. The bodywork of the rifle was of black plastic, made in Japan, built under license as a copy of the American infantry's M16 weapon. The Kalashnikov in London had been a luxury, an eccentricity . . . for the more routine job in which he was now engaged the Armalite was totally suitable.

And so he waited in the dark and freezing drafts of the roof for the twenty seconds or so it would take an eight-man patrol to move past the shadows of the three houses opposite. His eyes strained at the darkness, his ears keen to the noise of feet and the different types of shoes the civilians wore. He had catnapped through the day to reserve his concentration for the time, fast and silent, that the soldiers would come.

The lady who had been walking her dog in Belgrave Square now left it at home when she went to the doctor's office. The elderly GP allowed her to talk for at least ten minutes each morning before gently shooing her back to her flat and to the hysteria and depression that had engulfed her since the shooting. The doctor appreciated the need of the widow, who had been his casual and infrequent patient for twenty-three years, to talk to some friend who could comprehend her meticulous description of the screaming woman, the man with that awful banging gun at his shoulder, the petrified children, the sirens, the shouting, helpless policemen.

He gave her mild sedatives but had been unwilling to prescribe habit-forming doses, in the hope that time would eventually erode the images of the killing. He had been surprised and annoyed when she had told him that the detectives had been to see her again, a clear week after they had received her signature on what was described as the final and definitive statement she would need to make. She had told the doctor of the queer equipment they had brought, and how, over and over, she had been made to describe the man with the gun.

It had been enough of an ordeal for her, this last visit, to set back her recovery, and accordingly, the doctor had phoned the Scotland Yard officer who was named in the papers as heading the inquiry. But such was the pressure on his time, and the size of his register, that he had not taken the matter further when told that no policeman had been to visit his patient in the last ten days. He had blustered a bit when he was told that, protested about the obvious inconsistency between the police story and his patient's, and then rung off. But it still puzzled him.

The Secretary of State of Defence was in his office early, clearing his desk for the start of a short holiday and arming himself with the persuasive and informed arguments that he would need for his nine holes with the Prime Minister. The civil servant who was briefing him on the missile gap and the sagging morale of denuded units in Germany continued his lecture in his usual professional manner. This way of speech had infuriated a series of Ministers as the civil servant had progressed upward to his position as a Man Who Ran Things. His role in the vast department was now all-commanding, his power and influence huge. One of the smaller cogs in his well-oiled machine was Davidson, and one of the less frequently mentioned properties on his books was the house near Dorking.

Tentatively, the Minister spoke to him. "That suggestion of the PM about the Danby killing—you remember, putting a chap in there. He'll want to know . . . what's happening?"

"Yes. He phoned last week. I wouldn't worry about it,

Minister. We're still going over feasibility et cetera at the moment. It's not a fast business, you know; not a thing we can successfully knock off overnight."

"Nothing definite yet, then? You've already spoken to him? That's a bit odd, isn't it? On to you direct, and by-passing me? He may be in charge of security and all that, but it's a bit off. What did you tell him?"

"That things were in hand. That he'd get a briefing the moment there was something to report, when there were developments."

"I think you see me as some sort of security risk or something."

The Minister grimaced. The civil servant smiled generously. The subject was terminated. It was back to rocketry and more conventional theaters of war.

■ 5 ■

Twenty-five thousand feet up, between Liverpool and the Isle of Man, Harry was working things out. The reality of it all had been brutally clear as he had stood in the queue waiting to be searched by the Securicor team at the departure gate. Whoever heard of an agent getting his own bags taken apart by his own bloody side? It was painfully clear why his promised Smith and Wesson would have to be picked up at the Belfast main post office, where Davidson was sending it to await collection. He tried to concentrate on his cover story. Merchant seaman going home after years away, land in turmoil, oppression over the minority. Time for all true Irishmen to get back to back, together to withstand the English bastards. Three hundred years post-Cromwell, and nothing changed. Blood of martyrs on the streets again. Would anyone be daft enough to come back to that stinking hole, just because things were getting worse? Be out of their minds. Irish might be daft enough, have to be daft. One thing—bloody English wouldn't come home, they'd all go off to Australia or South Africa. Wouldn't catch them risking their precious lily-white backsides.

He lay, half awake, half asleep, in no man's land. What of the commitment he had taken on? Motivation was vague and unthought-out. It wouldn't be as strong as the other side's. No chance. Motivation was against the code with which he had been instilled. Officers didn't need motivating. It wasn't all clear.

Rights and wrongs, pluses and minuses, blacks and whites were all vague. In Northern Ireland things don't divide and coalesce neatly. That's too easy. What was it the politician had said? "Anyone who thinks he knows the answer to Northern Ireland is ill-informed." Good, that. Lot of ill-informed types in the mess in Germany, then. They all came back with the solution worked out: "saturate them," "pull the plug and leave them." All the answers, none the same, but all spoken with such authority. Amazing how you can learn three hundred years' bigotry in four months' looking after five blocks in a scruffy council estate.

Harry, heavy with sarcasm, had once congratulated a brother in uniform on the good fortune the other had in being able to see things so clearly. To be able with such confidence to apportion his blame and praise, culpability and credit—that made him a lucky man. In Mansoura, just out of Sheik Othman, where the gunmen were running around while the boyos in Ulster were still on their iced lollies and singsongs, it had been so much easier. The Red Cross man from Switzerland, in his little white suit, even with a big bright cross on his hat so they wouldn't throw a grenade at him from a rooftop, had come to visit the unit once. He'd said to the colonel something like, "One man's terrorist is another man's freedom fighter." The colonel hadn't liked that. Pretty heady stuff, they all thought in the mess. Such rubbish. Terrorists they were then, wog terrorists at that.

But in Aden, Harry had thought it was obvious to even the most stupid that British society was in no way being protected by their efforts—business perhaps, but nothing else.

Whatever else men died for in the sharp staccato engagements of small-arms fire, the green fields of home were a touch removed from the Mansoura roundabout picket. Checkpoint Golf or the Chartered Bank in Crater. As an Ulsterman, and so never allowed a posting home to fight, Harry had often wondered whether soldiering there was any different than in Aden. Did all the stuff about duty, purpose and reason mean that much more just because the fighting was down by the local supermarket and not six hours on a VC-10 away? He reckoned he was as disinterested now in the welfare of the great body of society as he had been then. He had been given a job to do, and he was doing it because someone had to, and by a series of accidents he was better equipped than most.

But by the time the Trident was arching over the landfall to the south of Strangford Lough, Harry had decided he was not a little flattered he'd been asked. He had been chosen for a mission, after all, called for by the Prime Minister. In the close heat of the plane he thought of his wife, warmth and closeness flooding through him. It was a pity she couldn't share in his pride. The passenger across the aisle noticed the slow smile spreading across the cheeks of the man slumped by the window.

For a few more seconds Harry indulged himself, conscious of the softness of the moment. He knew from other times of danger that he could cocoon himself in sentimentality for his family, for Mary and the boys. It was part of the mechanism of protection which Harry understood and cherished.

As the airliner began its approach across the small fields toward Aldergrove, Harry fastened his seat belt and let his thoughts turn to the man whose image was imprinted on his mind. He could see the man, could put flesh and color and dimension onto the dark lines of the photokit. The target. Was he an enemy? Not really. What, then, if not an enemy? Just a target. Still to be killed, no question of that. *Eliminate him*—it rolled off Harry's silent tongue. It was the word he liked.

He was jolted awake as the wheels, suspended below the wings, banged down onto the scarred tarmac. The plane surged forward in the air at a little more than ninety miles an hour, bounced again, and began to slow with the application of the engines' reverse thrust.

Terminal 1, Heathrow, the first-floor cafeteria. Davidson was breakfasting with the team who had come up to see Harry off. It was a subdued meal, without the frills of conversation. Not much had been said after Harry had disappeared toward the security checks. Davidson had muttered, almost audibly, "Gutsy little sod . . . I'll take the bill," he had added as they rose from the table, and then, as an afterthought, "I think we've told him all we could in three weeks, but it's bloody little time. To do that job properly, you'd need six months. And then you couldn't be sure. Always the same when the politicians dip their toes in—shortcuts. That's the order of the day. To come through with three weeks behind him he'll need to be lucky, bloody lucky."

The anomaly of going to war in your own country was

not lost on Harry. He came down the steep steps from the plane and hurried past the RAF regiment corporal, who held his rifle diagonally across his thighs, right-hand forefinger extended along the trigger guard. There were coils of barbed wire at the flanks of the terminal building, sprawled across the flower beds that had once been sufficient in themselves to mark the perimeters of the taxiing area. The viewing gallery where people used to wave to their friends and relatives was now fenced with high chicken wire to prevent a bomb being thrown onto the apron; it was out of bounds to civilians, anyway. After getting his bag in the concourse, Harry walked out toward the bus pickup point. Around him was an avenue of white oil drums with heavy planks slung between them—a defense against car bombers moving their lethal loads against the walls of the buildings. He moved by a line of passengers waiting to take the Trident back to London. They stood outside, occasionally shuffling forward with their baggage. Up at the front the searches went on in two green prefab huts. Only rarely did the faces of the travelers match the brightness of their going-away clothes. Children silent, women with their eyes darting around, the men concerned with getting suitcases to the search and then eventually to the plane. Greyness, anxiety, exhaustion.

Harry climbed onto the bus, and was quick enough to ensure himself a window seat near the back.

By the time the bus had left the fields behind and was into the top of the Crumlin Road, the man right behind Harry was in full voice. Taking upon himself the role of guide and raconteur, outmatching those who lead lines of tourists around the Tower of London and Hampton Court, he capitalized on the quiet of the bus to demonstrate his intimate knowledge of the campaign as fought so far.

"Down there on the right—you see the small lane— just round the corner where you can't see—that's where the three Scottish soldiers were murdered . . . the pub

. . . the one that's blown up—the one we're passing—they took 'em from there and killed them down the road when they were having a slash. There's nothing to see there now . . . people used to put flowers . . . but not now . . . nothing to see except there's no grass in the ditch where they got it. . . army dug it all up looking for bullets, and it never grew since. Now on the left, where the road climbs up, towards the quarry, that's where the senator was killed— the Catholic senator with the girl, they were killed up there, stabbed. Last year it was, just before the elections. Look now in front, there she is, the greatest city on earth. Down below, left, not hard left, that's Ardoyne. Over to the right, that's Ballymurphy . . . we're coming into Ligoniel now."

It'll be bloody bus trips for the Japanese next, thought Harry. Once they've stopped looking around Vietnam, you'll be able to flog them Belfast. By special remand after the world's greatest jungle conflict, we offer you reduced rates to the longest-ever urban guerilla war. Roll up! Roll up! Get your tickets now.

"Now wait for the bumps . . ." The man behind was away again as the bus had slowed to a crawl. "Here we go now. See, we're outside a barracks . . . there on the left. They all have bumps outside now . . . stops the Provos belting past and giving the sentry a burst with a Thompson. They used to have luminous paint on them, the bumps, that's gone now. If you don't know where they are, you give the car a hell of a bang . . . hit one of those at fifty and you know about it. That's Ardoyne, now, over on the left, where the policeman is. That's a sight for the English, policemen with bulletproof coats and machine guns . . . won't use the army flak jackets, have their own. We cut across now, they don't rate going down the Crumlin in Ulster bus. We'll use the Shankill. Looks all right, doesn't it, quiet enough? See that hole in the right . . . that's the Four Steps bar . . . killed a fair few when that went up . . . not a breath of warning . . . look there on the same side, see it . . . that hole . . . that was a furniture shop . . . two kiddies died there . . . not old enough to walk . . ."

"Shut up, Joe, nobody gives a fuck now. Just wrap it."

Perhaps Joe felt he had given his virtuoso. He fell silent. Harry watched out the window, horribly fascinated by the sights. At the traffic lights, the driver nudged up to the white line alongside a Saracen armored car. Soldiers were crouched inside the half-open steel back doors, rifles in hand. On the other side of the crossroads, he watched a patrol inching its way through the shopping crowds. On all sides were the yards of pale-brown hardboard that had taken over from glass in the display windows of the stores. The policemen here had discarded their submachine guns, but let their right hands rest securely inside their heavy dark coats. It surprised Harry how much there was to see that could have been part of any other British industrial city—buses, cars, people, clothes, paper stands—all merging in with the great military umbrella that had settled itself on Belfast.

At the bus station, Harry switched to another single-decker that went high up on the Antrim Road to the north, speeding past the troubled New Lodge junction before cutting into residential suburbs. The houses were big, old, tall, red-brick and fading. Davidson had given him the name of a boarding house where he'd said Harry could get a room, three stops up past the New Lodge.

Harry got off the bus at the stop, and looked around to find his bearings. He spotted the house they had chosen for him and moved away from it further down the long hill till he was one hundred and fifty yards from the seedy board with its *Vacancies* sign. Then he waited. He watched the front door for twenty-five minutes before he saw what he'd half expected. A young man came out down the steps that led to the short front path. Clothes not quite right, walk too long, hair a fair bit too short.

Harry boiled. Stupid bastards. Davidson, you prime bastard. Send me to one of your own bloody places. Nice safe little billet for soldiers in a nice Proddy area. Somewhere where you won't find any bloody thing out, but you won't get shot. No, not Davidson, some bugger in intelligence in Belfast, having his own back because it isn't his bloody caper. Sod 'em. Sod 'em all. Not going through all this crap to sit on my arse in Proddyland and come out in a month with sweet bugger all. No way.

He took the next bus into central Belfast from the other side of the road, walked across to the taxi rank in Castle Street and asked for a lift up to mid-Falls. Not Davidson's game, that. He wouldn't know addresses in Belfast, it would have to be one of the minions, flicking through his bloody card index, this looks right to keep him out of mischief. Couldn't infiltrate Mansoura from bloody Steamer Point, not Falls from Prod country.

To the cabdriver he said, "I'm working about halfway up, and looking for someone who takes in lodgers. Not too pricey. Yer know anyone? About halfway, near the Broadway. Is there anyone?"

He waited in the cab for several minutes for the other seats to be taken up in the shuttle service that had now largely replaced the inconsistencies of the bus timetable. The journey he'd made in from the airport out onto the Antrim Road, his wait there, the trip back, the walk to the taxi rank, that delay sitting in the back waiting to go—all had taken their toll in time. Deep greyness was settling over the city, rubbing out its sharp lines, when the taxi, at last full, pulled away.

The first soldier in the patrol was up to the corner and around it before the Man had reacted to the movement. The second gave him a chance to identify it as an army patrol. On the third and fourth he had begun to get an aim, and for the next man he was ready. Rifle at the shoulder—the upper part of the shadow cut out by the V of the leaf mechanism of his rear sight and sliced by the upward thrust of the front sight at the far tip of the barrel. The fifth soldier had come fast around the corner, too close to his colleague in front, and paused for the other to move further away before starting off again himself. He was stationary for one and a half seconds before the Man fired. The shadow fell out from the darkness of the wall toward the corridor of light from Mrs. Mulvenna's front room.

The Man had time to see the stillness of the form, half on the pavement and half on the street, before he wormed and scrambled his way to the center of the roof space— and ran. His escape route took him along a catwalk of planks set across the gaps between the roof beams, in all, traversing the roof space of four homes. In the last house the light shone up among the eaves where the ceiling door had been left open for him. He swung down onto the landing, and then moved to the stairs leading to the back of the house and the kitchen. The Armalite was grabbed from him by a teenager who had been listening for the clatter of the escape across the ceiling. Within three minutes it would be in a plastic bag, sealed and dropped under the grating in the backyard, with a thin line of dark cord tied to the bars to retrieve it later.

The Man went out into the backyard, scrambled over the five-foot-high fence, ducked across the back entry and felt for the rear doors on the far side till he came to the one off the hook. He had only to cut through that house and he was out in the next street. Here he didn't run, but ambled three hundred yards further away from the killing, where he rang a front-door bell. A youth came out immediately, motioned him to a waiting car and drove him away.

There had been no pursuit. No soldier had seen the

flash of the barrel as the Man fired. Five of them, shouting and waving, fear in their eyes, had sunk to firing positions in the doorways of the street. Two more gathered beside their dead colleague. Before the ambulance came it was plain that their efforts were pointless, but they fumbled the medical dressing clear from his webbing belt and placed it over the bleeding chest wound.

The taxi was caught in stationary traffic when Harry heard the single shot from far up the road. As the taxi stayed unmoving, log-jammed in the sea of vehicles, a convoy of armored cars swept by up the wrong side of the road, horns blaring and headlights on. Soldiers jumped from the moving column to take up their shooting positions on the main road, while others poured into the side streets. Harry saw the blue flashing light of an ambulance swing sharply out of a side street, one hundred and fifty yards up on the right, and turn down toward them. The ambulance was a Saracen with huge red crosses on white background painted on the sides. Turning his head, Harry saw, through the flapping open doors at the back, two dark shapes bent over the top end of the stretcher. The handles of the stretcher. Between them a pair of boots stuck out beyond the tailboard of the armored car.

It was some minutes before the traffic moved again. None of the other passengers in the cab—the old lady with her month's best shopping, the two office girls from Andersonstown—spoke a word. When the cab reached the street corner where the ambulance had emerged, the soldier in the middle of the road waved them out and to the wall. He ran his hands fast and effectively over the shoulders, torsos and legs of Harry and the driver, contenting himself with examining the woman's shopping bag and the girls' handbags. He looked very young to Harry.

"What happened?" Harry asked.

"Shut your face, you pig-arsed Mick."

The taxi dropped him off seventy-five yards further on. He was to try Mrs. Duncan's. First left, twelfth door on the right. *Delrosa.*

It didn't take Harry long to settle into the small room that Mrs. Duncan showed him at the back of her two-story house—about as long as it takes to unpack the contents of a small suitcase and put them into a medium-sized chest of drawers and a wardrobe. She suggested he wash his hands and then come down to the big room where the other guests would gather, first for tea, then to watch television. She asked no questions about him, obviously prepared to give the stranger time to make his own explanations and fill in his background at his own pace.

Looking across from his window, Harry could see the Falls Road where the army Land-Rover and Saracens still crisscrossed back and forth.

There were six at tea, all eating urgently and with concentration. The way to avoid talking, thought Harry. Stuff your face, with just a mutter for the milk or the sugar, or the fresh-cut bread, and you don't have to say anything. No one mentioned the shooting, but it came into the room with the BBC local television news. Mrs. Duncan came from the kitchen to the doorway, leaning there, arms folded, in her apron. A single shot had killed the first soldier to die in Northern Ireland in three weeks. The pictures showed troops illuminated in doorways and manning roadblocks. Over the sound track but half drowned by the report came the words "Put that bloody light off," then there was only the meaningless picture of the road with the dark stain on it, something for the color TV people but just a shapeless island on Mrs. Duncan's set. Then out of the blackness, the overlit whitened face of the young reporter as the hand light picked him up at close range.

He had little to say. A routine foot patrol in the Broadway district of the Falls had been ambushed. A single shot had been fired, fatally wounding a soldier just as darkness was falling. He said that an extensive follow-up operation was still in progress, that the area had been cordoned off and that all cars leaving it were being searched. The camera cut to a harassed-looking officer.

Q. What happened here, Colonel?

A. This is really a most shocking attack, a most cowardly murder. One of my soldiers was shot down in cold blood, quite without warning. A horrible, despicable crime.

Q. Did your men get a sight of the gunman?

A. No, it wasn't till we were engaged in an extensive follow-up operation—which you will have seen for yourself—that we found the place where the gunman was hiding. He was up in the roof of a derelict house, and he aimed at my patrol through the gap left by a missing tile.

Q. Would this have been the work of an expert?

A. An expert in terrorism, yes—in killing, yes. We found sixty-eight cigarette butts in the roof. He'd been there some time. He'd put four chairs on the staircase of the house—it's very narrow anyway. If we'd been chasing him, and had run into the building, those chairs would have lost us several seconds. That's the work of an expert killer. He'd chosen a house which has a communicating passage down the length of the terrace roof. That's the way he got out.

Q. Did anyone see anything on the street?

A. I'm sure half the street knew what was going on. Lots of people, masses of them, must have known a young man was going to be shot down in the gutter outside their homes. But I think your question is, did they identify the gunman to us? The answer there is decisively no, they didn't. But many of them must know who the killer is—I appeal to them to use the police confidential phone and stamp out this type of cruel, cowardly attack.

Q. Thank you, Colonel.

The program changed to an interview in the studio. A Protestant politician and a Catholic politician were arguing over the same ground, with some minute variations, that they'd been debating on the same channel for the last four years. Between them was a host, who had been feeding them their questions and winding them up for just as long. Before the talk was a minute old Mrs. Duncan came forward like a battleship under power and reached for the Off switch.

"There's enough politics on the street without bringing them into my house. Just words. Won't do that young man any good. Mother of Jesus rest with him."

A youngish man, sitting across the table from Harry, said, "If they stayed in their barracks, they wouldn't get shot. If they weren't here, there wouldn't be any shooting. You saw what they did when they came round here a few days ago. Taking the houses apart, lifting men and blocking the streets. Claimed then it was because of that man that got shot in London. But the searches they did were nothing to do with it. Aggro, what they were looking for, nothing more. Harassment."

Nobody in the room responded. The young man looked around for someone to join in argument with. Harry sided with him. "If they were as busy chasing the Prods as us, they'd find things easier for themselves."

The other looked at him, surprised to find support, if not a little disappointed that it was an ally who had put his cap in the ring. Harry went on: "I've been away a long time, but I can see in the few hours that I've been back where all the troops are. I've been abroad, but you still read the papers, you still see the news on the telly bought from the BBC. You get to feel the way things are going. Nothing's done about those Prods, only us."

It was not easy for Harry, that first time. With practice he would gain the facility to sing the praises of the IRA. But the first time around, it was hard going. Never like this in Mansoura. Never went down the souk and shouted the odds about what a fine bloke Quahtan As-Shaabi was, victory to the NLF, out with the imperialists. Just kept quiet there, and scuffed around in the dirt, and watched. But a different scene here. Got to be in the crowd. He excused himself, saying he was tired and had been traveling all day, and went up to his room.

■ 6 ■

It was just after seven when Harry woke. He knew soon enough that this was the day he started working. The euphoria of the farewells, the backslaps and good-luck calls, was over. Now would begin the hard work of moving on to the inside. He checked his watch. Well, twenty minutes more and then it could all begin, then he would get up.

He'd known since his training started that the initial period of infiltration was going to be the difficult part. This was where the expertise and skill entered in his file after Mansoura would count. They had chosen him after going over those files, and those of a dozen other men, because they had thought that he of all of them stood the best chance of being able to adapt in those early critical hours in the new environment.

They'd told him he must take it slowly, not lambast his way in. Not make so much of his presence that he attracted attention, and with that, inevitably, investigation. But they also stressed that time was against him. They pointed to the enormous benefits the opposition was gaining from the failure of the vast military force to catch the assassin.

The dilemma was spelled out to him. How much speed could he generate? How fast could he move into that fringe world which had contact with the gunman? How far into that world must he go to get near the nucleus of the organization where the Man he hunted was operating? These were his decisions. The advice had been given, but now he had to control his own planning.

They had emphasized again and again at Dorking that his own death would be bad news all around. Enormous embarrassment to HMG. No risks should be taken unless absolutely essential. It had amused him, dryly. You send a man to infiltrate the most successful urban terrorist movement in the world over the last twenty-five years, and tell him if he gets shot, it would be awkward. Not much time to mess about with the frills. They'd said if it was going to work out for him, it would be in the first three weeks. By then they expected something to bite on—not necessarily the Man's full name, but a regular haunt, the address of a friend. A hint. Anything to which they could turn the huge and formal military and police machine. The great force was poised and waiting for him to tell it where to hit. That pleased him.

He was starting with little enough to go on. The same available to everyone else in the city—or almost the same. His photokit picture was superior to the one issued in police stations and many posts, but that was all that tipped the scales in his favor. Not much to set against the disadvantages of being a stranger in a community beset by informers and on their guard against them. His first problem would be his infiltration of the Catholic population, let alone the IRA, and becoming known to people already haunted by the fear of army plainclothes units cruising in unmarked cars, laundry vans and ice cream trucks with hidden spy holes, of the Protestant UVF and UFF killer squads. He had to win a degree of confidence among some small segment of these people before he could hope to operate with success.

Davidson had struck a chord when he had said, "They seem to have the ability to smell an outsider. They close ranks well. It's like the instinct of a fox that's learned to react when there's a hostile being close by. God knows how they do it, but they have a feeling for danger. Much of it is how you look, the way you walk, the way you go along the pavement. Whether you look as though you belong. You need confidence. You have to believe that you're not the center of attention the whole time. The first trick is to get yourself a base. Establish yourself there, and then work outwards. Like an upside-down pyramid."

The base was clearly to be the good Mrs. Duncan. She was in the kitchen washing up the first sitting of breakfast when Harry came down the stairs.

"Well, it's good to be back, Mrs. Duncan. I've been away a while too long, I feel. You miss Ireland when you're away, whatever sort of place it is now. You get tired of the traveling and the journeys. You want to be back here. If these bastard British would leave us to lead our own lives, then this would be a great wee country. But it can't be easy for you, Mrs. Duncan, running a business in these times?"

The previous evening he had formally given his name as Harry McEvoy. That was what she called him when she replied.

"Well, Mr. McEvoy, they're not the easiest of times, to be sure. One minute it's all quiet and the place is full. Then you'll have a thing like last night, and who is going to come and sleep a hundred yards or so from where a soldier was shot dead? The travelers from the South find all this a bit near. They like it a bit further away from where it all happens. Having it full like it is now is a luxury. What did you say your business was? I was flustered up a bit when you came, getting the teas and all, yesterday."

"I've been away, ten years or so, just under, in fact, at sea. In the merchant navy. Down in the South Atlantic and Indian Ocean, mainly."

"There's a lot you'll see has changed. The fighting's been hard, hard and cruel these last years."

"Our people have taken a bad time, and all."

"The Catholic people have taken a bad time, and now the Protestants hate us as never before. It'll take a long time to sort it out."

"The English don't understand us, never have, never will."

"Of course they don't, Mr. McEvoy." She flipped his egg over expertly, set it on the plate beside the halved tomatoes, the skinned sausage, the mushrooms and the crisped fried bread. "Look at all the ballyhoo and palava when that man of theirs was shot—Danby. You'd think it was the first man who had died since the troubles. Here they are, close to a thousand dead, and all, and one English politician gets killed . . . You should have seen the searches they did, troops all over. Never found damn all."

"He wasn't mourned much over here." Harry said it as a statement.

"How could he be? He was the man that ran the Maze, Long Kesh. He brought all his English warders over here to run the place for him. There was no faith in him here, and not a tear shed."

"They've not caught a man yet for it?"

"Nor will they. The boys will keep it close. Not many

will know who did it. There's been too much informing. They keep things like that tight these days. But that's enough talk of all that. If you want to talk politics, you can do it outside the door and on the streets all the hours that God gave. There's no shortage of fools here to do the talking. I try and keep it out of the house. If you're back from the sea, what are you going to do now? Have you a job to be away to?"

Before answering, Harry complimented her on the breakfast. He handed her the empty plate. Then he said, "Well, I can drive. I hoped I could pick up a job like that round here. Earn enough so that with a bit of luck I can pay you something regular, and we can agree on a rate. I want to work up this end of town if I can, not in the center of town. Seems safer in our own part. I thought I might try something temporary for a bit while I look round for something permanent."

"There's enough men round here would like a job, permanent or not."

"I think I'll walk about a bit this morning. I'll do the bed first . . . an old habit at sea. Tomorrow I'll try round for a job. Wonderful breakfast, thanks."

Mrs. Duncan had noticed he'd been away. And a long time at that, she was certain. Something grated on her ear, tuned to three decades of welcoming visitors and apportioning their birthplace to within a few miles. She was curious, now, because she couldn't place what had happened to his accent. Like the sea he talked of, she was aware it came in waves—ebbed in its pitch. Pure Belfast for a few words, or a phrase, then falling off into something that was close to Ulster but softer, without the harshness. It was this that nagged as she dusted around the house and cleaned the downstairs hall, while above her Harry moved about in his room. She thought about it a lot during the morning, and decided that what she couldn't understand was the way he seemed to change his accent so slightly in midsentence. If he was away on a boat so long, then of course he would have lost the Belfast in his voice . . . that must have happened. But then, in contradiction, there were the times when he was pure Belfast. She soundlessly muttered the different words that emphasized her puzzlement to herself, uncomprehending.

They don't waste time in Belfast lingering over the previous day. By the time Harry was out on the pavements of the Falls Road and walking toward town, there was nothing to show that a large-scale military operation had followed the killing of a young soldier the previous evening. The traffic was on the move, women with their children in tow were moving down toward the shops at the bottom end of the Springfield Road, and on the corners groups of youths with time on their hands and no work to go to were gathering to watch the day's events. Harry was wearing a pair of jeans that he had brought from Germany, and that he'd used for jobs around his quarters on the base, and a holed pullover that he'd last worn when painting the white walls around the staircase at home. They were some of the clothes the officer had collected when he'd called and told his wife that her husband was on his way to the Middle East.

The clothes were right, and he walked down the road watched but not greatly attracting attention. The time had been noted when he came out of the side road where Mrs. Duncan had her guest house, and into the Falls. Nothing went on paper, but the youth who saw him from behind the neat muslin curtain at the junction would remember him when he came back, and mentally clock him in. There was every reason why he should be noticed: the only new face to come out of the road that morning. Last night, when he had arrived, it had been too late to get a decent look at him. All Mrs. Duncan's other guests were regulars, discreetly examined and cleared by the time they'd slept in her house long enough for a pattern to emerge.

Harry had decided to walk this first morning, partly because he thought it would do him good, but more important, to familiarize himself with his immediate surroundings. Reconnaissance. Time well spent. It might save your life, they'd said. Know your way around. He came down past the old Broadway cinema where no films had been shown for two years since the fire bomb exploded beside the ticket kiosk, and past the open space of the one-time petrol station forecourt where pumps, reception area and garages had long since been flattened. Across the road was the convent school. Children were laughing and shouting in the playground. Harry remembered seeing that same playground, then empty and desolated, on West German television when the newsreader had described the attack by two IRA motorcyclists on William Staunton. The Catholic magistrate had just dropped his two girls at school and was watching them from his car as they moved along the pavement to the gate when he was shot. He had lingered for three months before he'd died, and then one of the papers had published a poem written by the dead man's twelve-year-old daughter. Harry had read it in the mess, and thought it of rare simplicity and beauty, and not forgotten it.

"Don't cry," Mummy said.
"They're not real."
But Daddy was
And he's not here.

"Don't be bitter," Mummy said.
"They've hurt themselves much more."
But they walk and run,
Daddy can't.

"Forgive them and forget," Mummy said.
But can Daddy know I do?
"Smile for Daddy, kiss him well," Mummy said.
But can I ever?

He was still mouthing the words as the Royal Victoria Hospital loomed up, part modern, part the dark crowded red-brick of old Belfast. Staunton and scores of others had been rushed here down the curved hill that swung into the rubber doors of Casualty.

Harry turned left into Grosvenor Road, hurrying his step. Most of the windows on either side of the street showed the scars of the conflict, boarded up, bricked up, sealed to squatters, too dangerous for habitation but remaining available and ideal for the snipers. The pubs on the right a hundred yards or so down from the main gate of the RVH had figured in Davidson's briefings. After a Proddy bomb had gone off, the local Provos had found a young bank clerk on the scene. He came from out of town and said he'd brought a cameraman to witness the devastation. The explanation hadn't satisfied. After four hours of torture and questioning and mutilation they shot him and dumped him in Cullingtree Street a little further down toward the city center.

Davidson had emphasized that story, used it as an example of the wrong bloke just turning up and being unable to explain himself. In the hysteria and suspicion of the Falls that night, it was sufficient to get him killed.

The half-mile of the street Harry was walking down was fixed in his mind. In the log of the history of the troubles since August 1969 that they'd given him to read, that half-mile had taken up fifteen separate entries.

Harry produced a driver's license made out in the name of McEvoy and the post-office counter clerk gave him the brown-paper parcel. Harry recognized Davidson's neat copperplate hand on the outside: "Hold for collection."

Inside was a .38-caliber Smith and Wesson revolver. Accurate and a man-stopper. One of nine hundred thousand run off in the first two years of World War Two. Untraceable. If Harry had shaken the package violently, he would have heard the rattling of the forty-two rounds of ammunition. He didn't open the parcel. His instructions were very plain on that. He was to keep the gun wrapped till he got back to his base, and only when he had found a good hiding place was he to remove it from the wrapping. That made sense, nothing special, just ordinary common sense, but the way they'd gone on about it, you'd have thought the paper would be stripped off and the gun waved all over Royal Avenue. At times Davidson treated everyone around him like children. "Once it's hidden," Davidson had warned, "leave it there unless you think there's a real crisis. For God's sake, don't go carrying it round. And be right bloody certain if you use it. Remember, if you want to fire the damn thing, the yellow card and all that's writ thereon applies as much to you, my boy, as every pimpled squaddie in the Pioneers."

With the parcel under his arm, for all the world like a father bringing home a child's birthday present, Harry walked back from the center of the city to the Broadway. He wanted a drink. Could justify it too, on professional grounds, need to be there, get the tempo of things, and to let a pint wash down the dryness of his throat after what he'd been through the last thirty-six hours. The "local" was down the street from Mrs. Duncan's corner. Over the last few paces to the paint-scraped door his resolve went haywire, weakened so that he would have dearly loved to walk past the door and regain the security of the little back room he had rented. He checked himself. Breathing hard, and feeling the tightness in his stomach and the lack of breath that comes from acute fear, he pushed the door open and went into the pub. God, what a miserable place!

From the brightness outside, his eyes took a few moments to acclimatize to the darkness within. The talk stopped and he saw the faces follow him from the door to the counter. He asked for a bottle of Guinness, anxiously projecting his voice, conscious that fear is most easily noticed from speech. Nobody spoke to him as he sipped his drink. Bloody good to drink, but you need to be an alcoholic to come in here to take it. The glass was two-thirds empty by the time desultory conversation started up again. The voices were muted, as if everything said was confidential. The people, Harry recognized, had come to talk, like an art, from the sides of their mouths. Not much eavesdropping in here. Need to Watergate the bloody place.

Across the room two young men watched Harry drink. Both were volunteers in E Company of the First Battalion of the Provisional IRA. Belfast Brigade. They had heard of the cover story Harry was using earlier in the morning just after he'd gone out for his walk. The source, though unwittingly, was Mrs. Duncan. She had talked over the clothesline, as she did most mornings, with her neighbor. The neighbor's son, who now stood in the bar watching Harry, had asked his mother to find out from Mrs. Duncan who the new lodger was, where he came from and whether he was staying long. Mrs. Duncan enjoyed these morning chatters, and seldom hurried with her sheets and pegs unless rain was threatening. It was cold and bright. She told how the new guest had turned up out of the blue, how he hoped to find a job and stay indefinitely, had already paid three weeks in advance. He was a seaman, the English merchant navy, and had been abroad for many years. But he was from the North, and had come home now. From Portadown he was.

"He's been away, all right," she shouted over the fence to her friend, who was masked by the big green-striped sheet suspended in the center of the line. "You can see that, hear it rather, every time he opens his mouth. You can tell he's been away, a long time and all, lucky beggar. What we should have done, missus. Now he says he's come back because Ireland, so he says, is the place in times of trouble." She laughed again. She and her friend were always pretending they'd like to leave the North for good, but both were so wedded to Belfast that a week together at a boarding house north of Dublin in the third week of August was all they ever managed—then they were full of regrets all the way back to Victoria Street Station.

The son had had this conversation relayed to him painfully, slowly and in verbatim detail by his mother. Now he watched and listened, expressionless, as Harry finished his drink and asked for another bottle. In two days' time he would go to a routine meeting with his company's intelligence officer, by then he would be sure in his mind if there was anything to report about the new lodger next door.

Harry walked quickly back to Delrosa after the second glass of Guinness. He'd never been fond of the stuff. Treacly muck, he told himself. He rang the doorbell, and a tall, willowy girl opened the door.

"Hullo, McEvoy's the name. I'm staying here. The room at the back."

She smiled and made way for him, stepping back into the hall. Black hair down to the shoulders, high cheekbones and dark eyes set deep above them. She stood very straight, back arched and breasts angled into the tight sweater before it molded with her waist and was lost in the wide leather belt threaded through the straps of her jeans.

"I'm Josephine. I help Mrs. Duncan. Give her a hand round the house. She said there was someone new in. I do the general cleaning, most days in the week, and help with the teas."

He looked at her blatantly and unashamed. "Could you make me one now? A cup of tea?" Not very adequate, he thought, not for an opening chat-up to a rather beautiful girl.

She walked through into the kitchen, and he followed a pace or so behind, catching the smell of the cheap scent.

"What else do you do?" Perfunctory, imbecile, but keeps it going.

"Work at the mill, down the Falls, the big one. I do early shift, then come round and do a bit with Mrs. Duncan. She's an old friend of my Mam's. I've been coming a long time now."

"There's not much about for people here now, 'cept work, and not enough of that," Harry waded in, "what with the troubles and that. Do you go out much, do you find much to do?"

"Oh, there's bits and pieces. The world didn't end, and we adapted, I suppose. We don't go into town much— that's just about over. There's not much point, really. Go to a film and there'll be a bomb threat and you're cleared out. The Tartans run the center anyway, so you have to run for dear life to get back into the Falls. The army doesn't protect us, they look the other way when the Tartans come, Proddy scum. There's nothing to go to town for anyway 'cept the clothes, and they're not cheap."

"I've been away a long time," said Harry, "people have been through an awful time. I thought it time to get back home. You cannot be an Irishman and spend your time away right now."

She looked hard at him. The prettiness and youth of her face hardened into something more frightening to Harry. Imperceptibly he saw the age and weariness on the

smooth skin of the girl, spreading like the refocusing of
a lens and then gone as the face lightened. She reached
into the hip pocket of her jeans, straining them taut as
her fingers found a crumpled handkerchief. She shook it
loose and dabbed it against her nose. Harry saw the green
embroidered shamrocks in the corners, and fractionally
caught the motif in the middle of the square. Crossed
black and brown Thompson machine guns. She was
aware he was staring at her.

"There's nothing special about these. Doesn't mean I'm
a rebel and that. They sell them to raise funds for the
men and their families, the men that are held in the Kesh.
'The Men Behind the Wire.' Look. It's very good, isn't it
—a bit delicate? You wouldn't think a cowardly, murdering thug would have the patience to work at a thing
so difficult, be so careful. They think we're all pigs, just
pigs. Fenian pigs, they call us."

She spat the words out, the lines around her face hard
and clear-cut now. Then the tension of the exchange was
gone. She relaxed.

"We make our own entertainment. There's the clubs,
social nights. There's not much midweek, but Saturday
night is okay. Only the bloody army comes belting in
most times. They always say they're looking for the great
commander of the IRA. They take ten boys out, and
they're all back free in twenty-four hours. They stir us
up, try and provoke us. We manage. I suppose all you've
heard since coming back is people talking about their
problems, how grim it is. We manage. Life goes on . . .
bloody well has to, but it does."

"That handkerchief," said Harry, "does that mean you
follow the boyos, have you a man in the prisons?"

"Not bloody likely. It doesn't mean a damn. Just try
and not buy one. You'll find out. If you don't buy one,
there's arguing and haggling. It's easier to pay up. You've
got to have a snot-rag, right? Might as well be one of these

and no argument, right? I'm not one of those heated-up little bitches that runs after the cowboys. When I settle it'll be with the feller with more future than a detention order, I can tell you. And I'm not one of those that runs around with a magazine in my knickers and an Armalite up my trousers, either. There are enough who want to do that."

Harry asked, "What sort of evenings do you have now? What sort of fun do you make for yourselves?"

"We have the caelis," she said, "not the sort they have in the country or in the Free State, not the proper thing. But there's dancing, and a bit of a band, and a singer and a bar. The army come lumping in, the bastards, but they don't stay long. You've been away at sea, right? Well, we've got rid of the old songs now . . . 1916 and 1922 are in the back seat, out of the hit parade. We've got 'Men Behind the Wire,' that's internment. 'Bloody Sunday.' 'Provie Birdie,' when the three boys were lifted out of Mountjoy by helicopter. Did you hear about it? Three big men and a helicopter comes right down into the exercise yard and lifts them out . . . and the screws was shouting 'Shut the gates!' Must have been a laugh, and all. Understand me, I'm not for joining them, the Provos. But I'm not against them. I don't want the bastard British here."

"On the helicopter, I was going through the Middle East. I saw it in the English paper in Beirut."

She was impressed, seemed so, anyway. Not that he'd been to an exotic-sounding place like Beirut, but that the fame of Seamus Twomey, Joe O'Hagen and Kevin Mallon had spread that far.

"Do the army always come and bust in, at the evenings?"

"Just about always, they think they'll find the big boys. They don't know who they're looking for. Put on specs, tint your hair, do the parting the wrong way, don't shave, do shave . . . that's enough, that sorts them out."

Harry had weighed her up as gently committed—not out of conviction but out of habit. A little in love with the glamour of the men with Armalites, and the rawness of the times they lived in, but unwilling to go too close in case the tinsel dulled.

"I think I'd like to come," said Harry. "I think it would do me good. I'm a bit out of date in my politics now, and my voice is a bit off tune. James Connolly was being propped up in his chair in Kilmainham in my time, and they were wearing all their Green. It's time I updated and put myself back in touch. A lot of brave boys have died since I was last here. It's time to stand up and be counted in this place. That's why I came back."

"I'll take you. I'll pick you up here, Saturday, round half-seven. Cheers."

She was away into the kitchen, and Harry to his room.

∎ 7 ∎

The Man moved the last few yards to his home. It was just after two in the morning. Two men had checked the streets near his house and given an all-clear on the presence of army foot patrols.

It was his first visit back into his native Ardoyne since he had left to go to London nearly a month ago. His absence had been noted by the local British army battalion that operated out of the towering, near-derelict Flax Street mill complex on the edge of Ardoyne. It was entered in the comprehensive files the intelligence maintained on the several thousand people that lived in the area, and a week before, two Land-Rovers had pulled up outside the Man's house, made their way to the half-opened front door and confronted his wife. She could have told them little even if she had felt inclined to. She didn't, anyway.

She told them to "Go fuck yourselves, you British pigs." She then added, nervous perhaps of the impact of her initial outburst, that her husband was away in the South working for a living. The army had searched the house without enthusiasm, but this was routine, and nothing was found, nor really expected to be. The intelligence officer noted the report of the sergeant who had led the raid, noted, too, that it would be nice to talk to the occupant of No. 41 Ypres Avenue at some later date. That was as far as it had been taken.

If Harry had been chosen for his role because he was clean, the same criterion had operated with the Man's superiors when they had put the cross against his name midway up the list of those who were capable of killing Danby.

Ypres Avenue was a little different from the mass of streets that made up Ardoyne. The battle it was named after gave a clue to its age; its state of repair was superior to those streets up in the Falls where the Man had been hiding the last three weeks and where the streets took their names from the Crimean and Indian Mutiny battles, as well as from the British generals who had led a liberal stock of Ulstermen into their late-nineteenth-century fighting. But fifty-nine years is still a long time for an artisan cottage to survive without major repairs, and none had been carried out on any considerable scale in the avenue since the day they had been put up to provide dwellings for those working in the mill, where the army now slept. The houses were joined in groups of four. In between, a narrow passage ran through to the high-walled back entrance that came along behind the tiny yards at the rear.

The blast bombs, nail bombs and petrol bombs of four years of fighting had taken their toll, and several of the houses had been walled up. The bottom eight feet of a wall at the end of the avenue had been whitewashed, the work of housewives late at night at internment time, so that at night, in the near-darkness of Ardoyne, a soldier's silhouette would stand out all the more clearly and give the boyos a better chance with a rifle. Most corners in the area had been given the same treatment, and the army had come out in force a week later and painted the whitened walls black. The women had then been out again, then again the army, before both sides called a mutual but unspoken truce. The wall was left filthy and disfigured from the daubings.

The army sat heavily on Ardoyne, and the Provos, as they themselves admitted, had had a hard time of it. This was good for the Man. A main activist would not be expected to live in an area dominated by the military and where IRA operations had virtually ceased. The Man had been careful to link all his work with the Falls, a quite separate Catholic area from the Ardoyne.

Each house was small, unshaped and built to last. Comfort played only a small part in its design. A front hall, with a front room off it, led toward a living area, with kitchen and scullery two later additions under asbestos roofing. The toilet was the most recent arrival, and was in the yard against the far wall in a cinderblock cubicle. Upstairs each house boasted two rooms and a tiny landing. Bathing was in the kitchen. This was Belfast housing, perfect for the ideological launching of the gunman, perfect, too, as the model ground for him to pursue his work.

In the years the Man had lived there he had come to know by the counting of his footsteps, and by touch, when he came to the door of his own yard. The door had been recently greased, and made no sound when it swung on its hinges. He slipped toward the kitchen and unlocked the back door and went upstairs. That back door was never bolted, just locked, so that he could come in through it at any time.

It was the longest he had ever been away. The relief was total. He was back.

He moved catlike up from the base of the stairs, three steps, then waited and listened. The house was completely dark and he had found the banister rail by touch. There were the familiar smells of the house, strong in his nose—the smell of cold tea and cold chips, older fat, of the damp that came into the walls, of the lino and scraps of carpet where that damp had eaten and corroded. On the stairs while he waited he could hear the sound of his family clustered together in the two rooms, the rhythm of their sleep broken by the hacking cough of one of the girls.

There was no question of using the lights. Any illumination through the sparse curtains would alert the army to the fact that someone in the house was on the move unusually late, coming home or going out. A little enough thing, but sufficient to go down into the files and card system that the intelligence men pored over, and which gave them their results. In the blackness the Man inched his way up the stairs, conscious that no one would have told his wife he was coming home this particular night, and anxious not to frighten her.

He moved slowly on the landing, pushed open the door of the back room where he and his wife slept, and came inside. His eyes were now accustomed to the dark. He made out her hair on the pillow, and beside it the two small shapes, huddled close together for warmth and comfort. He watched them a long time, as one of the children wriggled and then subsided with the cough. It had just been coming on when he had left home. He felt no emotion, only the inhibition over how to break in and intrude on their sleep. Gradually his wife became aware of his presence. Her reaction at first was frightened and startled, moving quickly and jerking the head of one of the sleeping children. She was defensive in her movement, the mother hen protecting her nest of twigs. Her aggression went when she saw it was him. With a half-strangled sob she reached out for her man and pulled him down onto the bed.

Beneath him the Man felt the children slide away to continue their sleep uninterrupted.

"Hullo, my love. I'm back. I'm okay. Safe now. I've come back to you."

He mouthed the words pressed hard into the pit of her neck, his voice sandwiched between her shoulder and ear. She held him very tightly, pulling at him as if some force were working to get him away from her again.

"It's all right, love. I'm home. It's over."

He rose to his knees and kicked off his shoes, wrenched at his socks and pulled away the trousers, jacket and shirt. She passed one of the sleeping children over her body and pulled back the clothes of the bed for him to come into the empty space.

Desperately, she clung to him there, squeezing the hardness and bitterness and strength out of him, demolishing the barriers of coldness and callousness with which he surrounded himself, working at the emotions that had been so suppressed in the last month.

"Where've you been?"

"Don't . . . don't . . . I've missed you, I've wanted you."

"No, where've you been?" she persisted. "We thought you were gone . . . were dead. There was no word, not anything. Where? There's always been a word before when you've gone."

He clung to her, holding on to the one person he loved and needed as his life line, particularly over the last weeks of tension and fear. He felt the terror and tautness draining out of him as he pressed down onto her body under him. It was some moments before he realized that she was lying quite still, rigid in shape and yielding nothing. His grip on her slackened and he rose a little from the bedclothes to see her face, but when he was high enough to look down at her eyes, she turned them away from him toward her sleeping children.

"What's the matter? What's this for?"

"It's where you've been. Why you've been away. That's the matter. I know now, don't I?"

"Know what . . . ?" He hesitated. Stupid bitch, what was she blathering for? He was there. Flesh and blood. Bugger this why and where crap. But what did she know? He was uncertain. How much had she realized through the frenzy in which he had held her? Had that crude and desperate weight of worry communicated to her?

"Are you going to tell me about it?" she said.

"About what?" His anger was rising.

"Where you've been . . ."

"I've told you. Once more. Then the end of it. I was in the South. Finish, that's it."

"You won't tell me, then?"

"I've said it's finished. There's no more. Leave it. I'm home—that should be enough. Don't you want me here?"

"It said in the papers that his children were there. And his wife. They saw it all. That the man went on shooting long after he'd gone down. That the children were screaming, so was his wife. It said she covered him from the bullets. Put herself right over him."

She was sitting right up now with her hands splayed behind her, straight, and her breasts, deep from the children she had suckled, bulging forward under the intricate patternwork of her nightdress. The Man's longing for her had gone, sapped from him by her accusation. The moment he had waited for, which had become a goal over the last few days on the run, was destroyed.

She went on, looking not at him straight in front of her into the darkness: "They said that if it took them five years, they'd get the man who did it. They said he must have been an animal to shoot like that across the street. They said they'd hunt for him till they found him, then lock him up for the rest of his natural. You stupid, daft bastard."

Her point of focus was in the middle distance, way beyond the walls and confines of the back bedroom. In his churning mind, the replies and counterattacks flooded through him. But there was no voice. When he spoke, it was without fight. There would be no conflict with her. The little bitch had wrecked it all.

"Someone had to do it. It happened it was me. Danby had it coming. Little bastard he was. There's not a tear shed for him; they haven't a clue to bring them to me. There's no line on me. The picture's no good. The kids wouldn't recognize me on that. They didn't, did they?"

"Don't be so stupid. Do you think I'd hold up two four-year-olds and show them a picture and say 'Do you recognize your Dad? He's a killer, shot a man in front of his kids?' That what you want me to do?"

"Shut your face. Finish it. I told you there'll be no more. You shouldn't have known. You didn't need to know."

"It'll be bloody marvelous. The return of the great and famous hero, with half the sodding army after him. What a future? 'We weren't supposed to know.' What sort of a statement it that? If they shoot you when they get you, there'll be a bloody song about you. Just right for Saturday nights when they're all pissed, so keep the verses short and the words not too long. What a bloody hero. You'll want me to teach the kids the words, and all. Is that the future for us?"

She sank back onto the pillow, and holding the nearest

of the two children, began to weep, in slight convulsive shudders, noiselessly.

The Man rose from the bed and put on his underclothes, shirt and trousers before moving in his bare feet across the room to the door. He went down the stairs and into the front room. Checking an instinctive movement toward the light switch, he groped his way to his armchair by the grate and lowered himself gingerly into it. There were newspapers there, and he pushed them onto the floor. He sat very still, exhausted by the emotion of the last few minutes. She'd clobbered him, kicked him in the crotch, and when the pain had sped all over him, come back and kicked him again. Since Danby, all he had wanted was to get back here, to her, to the kids, the totalness of the family. To be safe with them. The fucking bitch had destroyed it.

In the dark he could relive the moments of the shooting. He found the actual happening hard to be exact about. They had faded, and he was uncertain whether the picture he put together was from his memory or his imagination. The immediate sensations were still clear. The kicking of the Kalashnikov, the force driving into his shoulder—that was as vivid as the day and the time itself. So, too, was the frozen tableau of the woman on her husband. The children. That enormous useless dog. That was all still there. He saw the incident as a series of still frames, not all interrelating. Some of the pictures were in panorama, as when Danby came down the steps and was looking right for the car and waving left at the children. Others were in close-up—the face of the woman he had run past. Fear, disbelief, shock and horror. He could see every wrinkle and line on the silly cow's face, down to the bulging mole above her right cheek. He remembered the blood, but with detachment. Inevitable. Unimportant.

He wanted congratulations for a job well done. He'd

thought that out and decided he was justified in some plaudits. It had been professionally done. The movement would be proud of the effort. He knew that himself, but yearned to be told so out loud. She should have bestowed the accolade. Of course she would guess, no way she wouldn't. Dates were right, the picture. She should have been the one with a nod, and an innuendo. She had guessed. She had to. But she had called him a "stupid, daft bastard."

They had never talked about the Provos. Right from the start, that had been laid down. She didn't want to know. Wasn't interested. No word on the nights he was going out. Went and buried herself in the kitchen, played with the children, got out of his bloody way. She accepted, though, that he needed her strength and support when he came home. That was the concession she gave him. But that was not exceptional in Ardoyne.

The women would hear the shots out in the streets where the battlefield was just beyond the front-room curtains. There would be the high crack of the Armalite, fired once, twice or perhaps three times. Within seconds would come the hard thump of the answering army rifles, a quite different and heavier noise. If the man was not home by dawn, the women would listen to the first news broadcast of the day, and hear what had happened. Sometimes there would be an agony of time between hearing that the army returned fire and claimed hits and the savored moment when the man came in untouched.

Then there would be no words, only warmth and comfort and the attempt to calm the trembling hands.

His wife had once shown him an article in a London women's magazine which had told of the effect on the morale of the army wives stationed in Germany that those same early broadcasts had. He had read how fast word spread around the married quarters that the unit had been in action, and how the women then waited at their windows to see if the officer came around and which house he went to. They would know if one of the men had been killed, because the chaplain or the doctor would be with the officer, and they would go to a neighbor's house first, have a quick word on the doorstep, then move next door and knock, and when the door opened, go inside. The news would be around the houses and maisonettes and flats within minutes.

The Man had been responsible for two of those visits. On the first occasion he had watched the funeral on television, seen the forty-five-second clip that showed the coffin with the flag on it, and a young widow clutching the arm of a relative as she walked surrounded by officers and local dignitaries. Then the staccato crack of rifle fire from the honor party. That was all. The other soldier he'd killed had been buried without a news team there to record the event.

It left him unmoved. He could imagine no soldier weeping if it were he who was shot dead. He had long accepted that it could happen, and apart from the tension of the actual moments of combat and the bowstring excitement afterwards, he had learned a fatalism about the risks he took.

He had started like most others as a teenager throwing rocks and abuse in the early days at those wonderful, heaven-sent targets—the British army, with their yellow cards forbidding them to shoot in almost every situation, their heavy Macron shields, which ruled out effective pursuit, and their lack of knowledge of the geography of the side streets. All the boys in Ypres Avenue threw stones at the soldiers, and it would have been almost impossible to have been uninvolved. The mood had changed when a youth from the other end of the street and the opposite side of the road was shot dead in the act of lighting a petrol bomb. He had been one form above the Man in secondary school. Later that night four men had arrived

at the far end of Ypres Avenue to the rioting, and the
word had spread fast that the kids should get off the
streets. Then the shooting had started. In all, fifteen shots
had been fired, echoing up the deserted street. The Man
was eighteen then, and with other teenagers, lay in an
open doorway and cheered at the urgent shouts of the
soldiers who had taken cover behind the pigs. Abruptly a
hurrying, shadowy figure had crawled to the doorway,
pushed toward him the long shape of a Springfield rifle
and whispered an address and street number.

He had made his way through the back of the houses,
partway down the entry and through another row of
houses, where a family had stared at the television,
ignoring him as he padded across their living space before
closing the door onto the street behind him. When he
reached the address he had handed the rifle to the woman
who answered his knock. She had said nothing and he had
made his way back to Ypres Avenue.

That had been the start.

Many of his contemporaries in the street had thrust
themselves forward into the IRA. They would meet together on Saturday nights at the clubs, standing apart
from other young men to discuss in secretive voices their
experiences over the previous days. Some were now
dead, some in remand homes or prison; a very few had
made it to junior-officer rank in the IRA and after their
capture had been served with the indefinite-detention
orders to Long Kesh. The Man had kept apart from them,
and been noticed by those older, shadowy figures who
ran the movement. He had been marked down as someone
out of the ordinary, who didn't need to run with the
herd. He had been used sparingly and never with the
cannon fodder that carried the bombs into the town
shoeshops and supermarkets, or held up the post offices
for a few hundred pounds. He'd been married on his
twentieth birthday when he was acting as bodyguard to a

member of the Brigade staff, at a time when relations between the divided Provisionals and Officials were at an all-time low. After the wedding he had not been called out for some months, as his superiors let him mature, confident that he would, like a good wine, repay well the time they gave him. They used him first shortly before the twins were born. Then he took part in an escape attempt at Long Kesh, waiting through much of the night in a stolen car on the M1 motorway for a man to come through the wire and across the fields. They had stayed seven minutes after a cacophony of barking dogs on the perimeter fence six hundred yards away had spelled out the failure of the attempt. With two others he had been used for the assassination of a policeman as he left his house in the suburb of Glengormley. It was his first command, and he was allowed to select his own ambush point, collect the firearm from the Brigade quartermaster and lead the getaway on his own route. After that came attacks on police stations, where he was among those who gave covering fire with the Armalites to the blast of the RPG rocket launcher.

On those early occasions he had often missed with the crucial first shot, firing too hurriedly, and then had to run like a mad thing with the noise and shouting of the soldiers behind him. They were heady moments, hearing the voices of the English troops with their strange accents bellowing in pursuit as he weaved and ducked his way clear.

Among a small group, though, his reputation had improved, and his future value was reckoned so great that for nearly a year he had been left to lead what amounted to a normal life in the Ardoyne. Around him, the army removed all but a tight hard core of activists. He was left at home, his name not figuring in the army files, his photograph absent from the wanted lists. In their four years of marriage his wife had borne him twins, both boys, conceived some months before their wedding, and two daughters.

He was still slumped in his chair when his wife came downstairs a little after six. She came into the room on tiptoe and up behind the chair, and leaned over and kissed him on his forehead.

"We'll have to forget it all," she said. "The kids'll be awake soon. They've been upset, you being away so long, and the wee one has the cough. They'll be excited. There's a dance at the club on Saturday. Let's go. Mam'll come down and sit. We'll have some drinks, forget it ever happened."

She kissed him again.

"We need some tea, kettle's up."

The Man followed her into the kitchen.

For Davidson, in his offices up above a paint store in Covent Garden, it was to be a bad morning. He had asked for an appointment with the Permanent Under Secretary at the Ministry of Defence. The Boss, The Gaffer. Appointments with subordinates only when there was a fiasco or a potential fiasco. Davidson had to explain that their operator had gone missing and had never checked into the address that had been suggested to him.

Davidson had been hoping for a phone call, or failing that, at least a letter or postcard to the office, saying, if nothing else, that Harry was installed and working. The complete silence was beginning to unnerve him. The previous day he had authorized the checking of the Antrim Road guest house by telephone for a Mr. McEvoy, but the word had come back that no one of that name had been near the building. There was no way Davidson could find out discreetly and in a hurry whether the package containing the pistol sent for collection had in fact been picked up. He told himself there was no positive foundation for his fears, but the possibility, however faint, that

Harry was already blown or dead, or both, nagged at Davidson. Nagged enough for him to seek a rare audience in the Ministry.

By early afternoon the brandies were on the table in the restaurant of the big hotel on the outskirts of the city. Both the brigadier and the chief superintendent were out of uniform and mildly celebrating the promotion and transfer of the army officer from second in command of the Brigade with responsibilities for Belfast to a new superintendent in Germany. Both knew from their own intelligence-gathering agencies in vague terms of the sending of Harry and the Prime Minister's directive—it had come in a terse, brief message from the GOC's headquarters. There was little more to it than the hunt for Danby's killer, and that all other operations in this direction should continue as before. During the serving of the food, neither had spoken of it as the waiters hovered around them. But with the coffee cups full, and the brandy glasses topped up, the subject was inevitably fielded.

"There's been nothing from that fellow the PM launched," muttered the brigadier. "Long shot at the best of times. No word, I'm told, and Frost in intelligence is still leaping about. Called it a bloody insult. See his point."

"Sunk without trace, probably. They sniff them out, smell them a mile off. Poor devil, I feel for him. How was he supposed to solve it when SB and intelligence don't have a line in? If our trained people can't get in there, how's this chap?"

"Bloody ridiculous."

"He'll end up dead, and it'll be another life thrown away. I hope he doesn't, but if he sticks at it, they'll get him."

"I expect your SB were the same, but intelligence weren't exactly thrilled. What really peeved them was that at first they weren't supposed to know anything, then it leaked. I think the Old Man himself put it out, then came the message, and there wasn't much to show from that. Frost stayed behind after the Old Man's conference last Friday and demanded to know what was going on. Said it was an indication of no confidence in his section. Threatened his commission and everything on it. GOC calmed him down, but took a bit of time."

The Muzak was loud in the dining room, and both men needed to speak firmly to hear each other above the canned violin strings. The policeman spoke. "I think Frost's got a case. So have we for that matter"—in mid-chord and without warning, the tape ran out—"to put a special operator in on the ground without telling . . ." Dramatically conscious of the way his voice had carried in the sudden moment of silence, he cut himself short.

Awkwardly, the two men waited for the half-minute or so that it took the reception staff away in the front hall to loop up the reverse side of the three-hour tape, then the talking began again.

The eighteen-year-old waiter serving the next table their courgettes had clearly heard the second half of the sentence. He repeated the words to himself as he went around the table: "special operator in on the ground without telling." He said it five times to himself as he circled the table, fearful that he would forget the crucial words. Then he hurried with the emptied dish to the kitchen, scribbling the words in large spidery writing on the back of his order pad.

He went off duty at 3:30 and seventy-five minutes later the message of what he had overheard and its context were on their way to the intelligence officer of the Provisionals' Third Battalion.

■ 8 ■

Harry spent a long time getting himself ready to go out that Saturday night. He bathed and put on all clean clothes, even changing his socks from the ones he'd been wearing through the rest of the day, took a clean shirt from the wardrobe, and brushed down the one suit he'd brought with him. In the time that he'd been in Belfast he had tried to stop thinking in the terms of an army officer, even when he was on his own and relaxed. He attempted to make his first impulses those of any ex-merchant seaman or of the lorry driver that he hoped to become. As he straightened his tie, though, he allowed himself the little luxury of thinking that this was a touch different from mess night with the rest of the regiment at base camp in Germany.

He'd spent a difficult and nearly unproductive first week. He'd visited a score of firms looking for driver's work, with no success till Friday, when he had come across a scrap merchant on the side of Andersonstown. There they'd said they might be able to use him but he should come back on Monday morning, when he would get a definite answer. He had been in the pub on the corner several times. Though he was now accepted enough for him to stand and take his drink without the whole bar lapsing into a silent stare, none of the locals initiated any conversation with him, and the opening remarks he made to them from time to time were generally rebutted with noncommittal answers.

It had been hard and frustrating, and he felt that the one bright spot was this Saturday night. Taking Josephine out. Like a kid out of school and going down to the disco, you silly bugger. At your age, off to a peasant hop. As he dressed himself he began to liven. One good night out was what he needed before the tedium of next week. Nearly six days gone, and not a bloody thing to hook onto. Davidson said three weeks and something ought to show. Must have been the pep-talk chat. He came down a little after seven and sat in the chair by the fire in the front room that was available to guests. He was on his own. All the others scurried away on Friday morning, with their bags packed and homes to get to after a half-day's work at the end of the week. Not hanging about up here, not in the front line.

When the doorbell rang he slipped quickly out into the hall and opened the door. Josephine stood there, breathing heavily. "I'm sorry I'm late. Couldn't get a bus. They've cut them down a bit, I think. I'm not very late, am I?"

"I think all the buses are on the scrap yards up the road, stacks of them there, doubles and singles. I'd only just come down. I reckon you're dead on time. Let's go straightaway."

He shouted back toward the kitchen that he was on his way out, that he had his key and not to worry if he was a bit late.

"How do we get there?" he asked. "It's all a bit strange to me moving about the city still, especially at night."

"No problem. We'll walk down to the hospital, get a cab there into town, and in Castle Street we'll get another cab up the Crumlin. It's just a short walk from there. It won't take long, we'll be there in forty-five minutes. It's a bit roundabout, that's all."

In Ypres Avenue the Man and his wife were making their final preparations to go out. There had been an uneasy understanding between them since their talk in the early hours after his homecoming, and no further word on the subject had been spoken. Both seemed to accept that the wounds of that night could only be healed by time and silence. She had lain in bed the first three mornings waiting for the high whine of the Saracens, expecting the troops to come breaking in to tear her man from their bed. But they hadn't come, and now she began to believe what he had told her. Perhaps there was no clue, perhaps the photokit really looked as little like him as he believed. Her mother was busying herself at the back of the house around the stove, where she kept a perpetual pot of freshened tea. All the children were now in bed, the twins complaining that it was too early.

To both of them the evening was something to look forward to, a change from the oppressiveness of the atmosphere as the Man sat about his house, too small for privacy or for him to absent himself from the rest of the family. It had been laid down by his superiors that he was not to try to make contact with his colleagues in the movement, or in any way expose himself to danger or arrest. It meant long hours of waiting, fiddling time uselessly away. Already he felt the restlessness and need for action. But hurrying things was futile. That's how the silly buggers got taken, going off at half-cock when things weren't ready for them. Not like London. All the planning was there. No impatience, just when it suited and not a day earlier. Boredom was his great enemy, and the need was for discipline, discipline as befits the member of an army.

With his wife on his arm, and in her best trouser suit, the Man walked up his street toward the green-painted hut with the corrugated-iron roof that was the social club. He could relax here, among his own. Drain his pints. Talk to people. It was back to the ordinary. To living again.

By the time Harry and Josephine arrived at the club, it was nearly full, with most of the tables taken. The girl said she'd find somewhere to sit, and he pushed his way toward the long trestle tables at the far end from the door where three men were hard at it in their shirt sleeves taking the tops off bottles and pouring drinks. Harry forced his way through the shoulders of the men standing close to the makeshift bar, made it to the front and called for a pint of Guinness and a gin and orange.

As he was struggling back to the table where Josephine was sitting he saw a man come up to her and gesture toward him. After they'd spoken a few words, he nodded his head, smiled at the girl and moved back toward the door.

"Someone you know?" he said when he sat down, shifting her coat onto the back of the seat.

"It's just they like to know who's who around here. Can't blame them. He wanted to know who you were, that's all."

"What did you tell him?"

"Just who you were, that's all."

Everything was subdued at this stage of the evening, but the effects of the drink and the belting of the four-piece band and their amplified instruments began to have a gradual livening effect. By nine some of the younger couples were ignoring the protests of the older people and had begun to pile up the tables and chairs at the far end of the room, exposing a crude, unpolished set of nail-ridden boards. That was the dance floor. The band quickened the tempo, intensified the beat. When he felt that the small talk they were making was next to impossible, Harry asked the girl if she'd like to dance.

She led the way through the jungle of tables and chairs. Near the floor Harry paused as Josephine slowed and squeezed by a girl in a bright-yellow trouser suit, striking enough in its color for Harry to notice it. Then, as his eyes moved to the table she was sitting at, he saw the young man seated there.

There was intuitive, deep-based recognition for a moment, and Harry couldn't place it. His eyes looked, puzzled, at the Man, who stared straight back at him, challenging. Josephine was out on the floor now, waiting for him to come by the girl in yellow. He looked away from the face that was still staring back at him, holding and returning his glance, mouthed an apology and was away to the floor. Once more, from there, he looked at the Man, who still watched him, cold and expressionless —then Harry rejected the suspicion of the likeness. Hair wrong. Face too full. Eyes too close. Mouth was right. That was all. The mouth, and nothing else.

The floor pounded with the motion of a cattle stampede —to Harry, who was used to more ordered dances at the base. At first he was nearly swamped, but survived after throwing off what decorum he had ever learned as he and Josephine were buffeted and shoved from one set of shoulders to another. Sweat and scent were already taking over from the beer and smoke. When the band switched to an Irish ballad he gasped his relief, and around them the frenetic movements slowed in pace. He could concentrate now on the girl close against him, the very pretty girl.

She danced with her head back, looking up at him and talking. Looking the whole time, not burying herself away from him. She was wearng a black skirt, full and flared, so that she had the freedom to swing her hips to the music. Above that, a tight polka-dot blouse. The top four buttons were unfastened. There were no Josephines in Aden, no Josephines taking an interest in married transport captains in Germany.

They talked dance-floor small talk. Harry launched into a series of concocted anecdotes about the ports he'd visited when he was at sea, and she laughed a lot. Twice a nagging uncertainty took his attention away from her to where the man was sitting quietly at the table with the girl in the yellow trouser suit, glasses in front of them, eyes roving, but not talking. The second time he decided the likeness was superficial. It didn't hold up. Face, eyes, hair —all wrong. Before he turned back to Josephine he saw the mouth again. That was right. It amused him. Coincidence. And his attention was diverted to the girl, her prettiness and inevitable promise.

The Man, too, had noticed Harry's attention. It had been pronounced enough to make him fidget a little in his chair, and for him to feel the hot perspiration surge over his legs inside the thick cloth of his best suit. He had seen the door-minder talk to the girl who brought him in, and presumably clear the stranger. But his nerves had calmed when he had seen Harry on the dance floor, no longer interested, now totally involved in the girl he was with. The Man could not dance, had never been taught. He and his wife would sit at the table all evening as a succession of friends and neighbors came to join them to talk for a few minutes and then move on. Along the wall to the right of the door and near the bar was a group of youths, some of them volunteers in the Provisionals, some couriers and some lookouts. These were the expendable of the movement. The teenage girls were gathered around them, attracted by the glamour of the profession of terrorism, hanging on the boys' sneers and cracks and boasts. None of the boys would rise high in the upper echelons but each was necessary as part of the supply chain that kept the planners and marksmen in the field. None knew the Man except by name. None knew of his involvement.

First through the door was the big sergeant, a Stirling submachine gun in his right hand. He'd hit the door with all the impetus of his two hundred pounds, gathered in a six-foot run. Behind him came a lieutenant, clutching his Browning automatic pistol, and then eight soldiers. They came fast and fanned out in a protective screen around the officer. Some of the soldiers carried rifles, other the large-barreled rubber-bullet guns.

The officer shouted in the general direction of the band: "Cut that din. Wrap it up. I want the men against the far wall. Facing the wall. Hands right up. Ladies, where you are, please."

From the middle of the dance floor, a glass curved its way through the crowd and toward the troops. It hit high on the bridge of a nose creeping under the protective rim of a helmet. Blood was forming from the wound by the time the glass hit the floor. A rubber bullet, solid, unbending, six inches long, was fired into the crowd, and amid the screams there was a stampede away from the troops as tables and chairs were thrown aside to make way.

"Come on. No games, please. Let's get it over with. Now, the men line up at that wall—and *now*."

More soldiers had come through the door. There were perhaps twenty of them in the hall by the time the line of men had formed up, legs wide apart and fingers and palms on the wall high above their heads. Harry and the Man were close to each other, separated by three others. At her table, the girl in the yellow trouser suit very still. She was one of the few who wasn't barraging the army with a medley of obscenities and insults. Her fingers were tight around the stem of her glass, her eyes flickering continuously from the troops to her husband.

Josephine's table had been knocked aside in the scramble to get clear from the firing of the rubber bullet, and she stood on the dance floor, interested to see what the army made of her merchant-seaman escort.

Six of the soldiers working in three pairs split up the line of men against the wall and started to quiz each man there on his name, age and address. In the pair, one asked the questions, the other wrote down the answers. The lieutenant moved between the three groups, checking the procedure, while his sergeant marshaled his other men in the room to prevent any sudden break for the exits.

Private David Jones, number 278649, eighteen months of his nine-year signing served, and Lance Corporal Jame Llewellyn, 512387, were working over the group of men nearest the dance floor. The Man and Harry were there. The way the line had formed itself up they would come to the Man first. It was very slow. Conscientious, plodding. The Man's wife was in agony. Charade, that's all. A game of cat and mouse. They had come for him, and these were the preliminaries, the way they dressed it up. But they'd come for him. They had to know.

The lance corporal tapped the Man's shoulder. "Come on, let's have you." Not unkindly. It was quiet in Ardoyne now, and the soldiers acknowledged it.

The Man swung around, bringing his hands down to his side, fists clenched tight, avoiding the pleading face of his wife a few feet away. Llewellyn was asking the question, Jones writing the answers down.

"Name?"

"Billy Downs."

"Age?"

"Twenty-four."

"Address?"

"Forty-one, Ypres Avenue."

Llewellyn paused as Jones struggled in his notebook with the blunt pencil he had brought with him. The lieutenant walked toward them. He looked hard at the Man, then down into Jones's notebook, deciphering the smudged writing.

"Billy Downs?"

"That's it."

"We were calling for you the other morning. Expected to find you home, but you weren't there."

He stared into the young man's face. That was the question he posed. There was no reply.

"Where were you, Mr. Downs? Your good wife, who I see sitting over there, didn't seem too sure."

"I went down to see my mother in the South. It's in your files. You can check that."

"But you've been away a fair few days, Downs boy. Fond of her, are you?"

"She's not been well, and you know that. She's a heart condition. That's in your files, and all. It wasn't made any better when there weren't any of your lot around when the Prods came and burned her out . . . and that's in your files too."

"Steady, boy. What's her address?"

"Forty, Dublin Road, Cork." He said it loud enough for his wife to hear the address given. His voice was raised now, and she listened for the message that was in it. "She'll tell you I've been there for a month. That I was with her till four days ago."

The lientenant still gazed into the Man's face, searching for weakness, evasion, inconsistency. If there was fear there, he betrayed none of it to the soldier a bare year older than himself.

"Put him in the truck," the lieutenant said. Jones and Llwellyn hustled Downs across the room and toward the door. His wife rose up out of her chair and rushed across to him.

"Don't worry, girl, once the Garda have checked with Mam, I'll be home. I'll see you later." And he was out into the night to where the Saracen was parked.

The two soldiers came back to the line, and the lieutenant moved away to the other end where the youths, resigned to a ride back to barracks and an interrogation session at the end of it, snapped back sullen replies to the questions.

Llewellyn touched Harry's shoulder. "Name?"

"Harry McEvoy."

"Age?"

"Thirty-three."

"Address?"

Jones had had his eyes down on his notebook till that moment. He glanced up to hear the answer. Harry saw an expression of astonishment take hold of him, then change to suspicion, then back to bewilderment.

"Bloody hell, what are you doing—?"

Harry's right foot moved the seven inches into Jones's left ankle. As the private ducked forward, caught off balance by the sudden pain, Harry lurched into him.

"Shut your face," he hissed into the soldier's ear.

Jones's face came up and met Harry's stare. Imperceptibly he saw the head move. A quick shake, left to right and twice.

"I'm sorry," said Harry. "Forget it. I hope you'll forget it."

The last words were very quiet and straight into Jones's ear. The men in the line, waiting to be questioned, still faced the wall; the women, sitting at their tables, were out of earshot. The exchange between Harry and Jones seemed to have passed unnoticed. Llewellyn had been diverted by a commotion down at the far end of the hall, where four youths were half carried and half dragged toward the doorway. He was concentrating again now.

"Come on—what's the address?"

"Delrosa guest house, in the Broadway. Just up from Beachmount."

Harry's eyes were fixed, snakelike, on Jones.

"Bit off course, aren't you?" said Llewellyn.

"My girl's local."

"Which one?"

"In the polka-dot, the dark-haired girl." Harry gazed past Llewellyn, his eyes never leaving Jones. Twice the younger soldier's head came up from his notebook, met Harry, and dived back to the writing.

"Lucky bastard," said Llewellyn and moved on.

Apart from the Man, the army had taken nine youths when the officer shouted for his men to leave the club. They went out in single file, the last going out backwards with his rifle covering the crowd. As the door swung to after him, a hail of empty bottles and glasses cannoned into the woodwork.

A tall man at the far end from Harry shouted a protest: "Now come on, folks, we can do better than that. Lob things at the bastards, yes, but not so we cover our floor with our bottles and our glasses and our beer. Now, we're not going to let those swine spoil the evening for us. Let's move it all back and tidy up, and see if we can't get something out of the evening."

It was a good effort on the part of the community leader, but one doomed to failure.

Harry noticed that the girl in yellow was gone before the floor was half cleared. He shifted in his seat.

"We can't go yet. It's the principle of the bloody thing," said Josephine. "You cannot let the bastards wreck everything. What did you say to that soldier?"

"I just tripped against him, that's all."

"You're lucky. You might have got a rifle butt across your face. There's men taken to the barracks for less."

The band had started up again, attempting to capitalize on the angry mood of those left behind.

> *Armoured cars and tanks and guns,*
> *Came to take away our sons . . .*

"Will it wake up again, or is this the lot for the evening?" asked Harry.

> *Through the little streets so narrow . . .*

"I doubt it," she said, "but it's best to give it a few minutes. Let's see, anyway."

Cromwell's men are here again . . .

"It's not that bad, is it?" said Harry. "I heard it in the Baltic when we were working out of a Swedish port. They used to play it about every third disc. Got quite to like it. We had a mate on board who said his son was in the army here. He used to get right steamed up just listening to it."

The men behind the wire . . .

People were edging toward the door. Harry sensed there would be little more of a night out for any of them. "Come on, let's quit. We don't want to stay for the funeral."

"I'm going to powder my nose, then," Josephine said.

"Looks all right to me. Don't hang about."

She smiled, got up from the table and went out through a side door, where a gaggle of girls younger than Josephine had gathered. The band was still trying, but was competing with a wave of talk particularly from a large group that had gathered around a local primary-school teacher who was taking down the names of all those listed by the military. He was promising to go to the barracks to see what had happened to them.

It was a cold clear night as Harry, with Josephine on his arm, walked out of the hall and off toward the all-night taxi rank for the drive down to Castle Street. Then there would be another taxi, and a walk up the last part of the Falls to Mrs. Duncan's.

Harry and Josephine were naked, entwined and asleep, when 275 miles to the south the Garda squad car drew up outside the stone terraced house in the Dublin Road in Cork. There was the sharp mustiness of the docks in the predawn air as the two policemen fumbled their way from the car to the front doorstep.

"It's a sod of a time, God help us, to be getting this poor dear out of her bed."

The sergeant rang the doorbell, twice and firmly, and waited. A light came on upstairs, not fast, then in the hall, and after that the noise of the bolts in the door grating open.

"From the sound of it, you'd think she'd got the Bank of England in there," muttered the sergeant into his gloves.

"Good morning, my love. I'm right sorry to be coming at such a time as this to wake you. But a message has come down over the telephone from Dublin and I'm to ask you some questions. Won't take a moment now. Shall we come on in, out of that wind?"

"We'll do what business you have here. You should be ashamed of yerselves coming at this time . . ."

"That's not our affair, my love. Now, are you ready? We have to ask you when was your boy last here."

"Billy, you mean?"

"That's the lad, love. That's the one they want to know about."

"He was down till the middle of the week. Been here a month, and just gone back. Why do you need to come at this time of night to ask that?"

"You're sure of that now, my dear? No mistakes?"

"Of course I'm sure. Billy was here for a month. And those are bloody silly questions to be asking at this time of night."

She closed the door on them. The two Garda men knocked at the next-door house and again waited for the door to open. They took away the same message. Billy Downs had been there for a month.

The alibi had been passed on to the old lady and her four immediate neighbors some forty-five minutes before the police car had arrived. The wife's phone call to a friend of her man in Belfast had started the chain. Another call had been made to Dublin, another one from there to

Cork, and a young man who had left his car two streets
away from the Dublin Road had completed the process.
The Provisionals' lines of communication were somewhat
faster than the complicated and official process of liaison
between North and South.

Downs had been interrogated twice, maintaining quietly
and without fuss that he had been at his mother's in the
South. He was kept apart from the other prisoners, with
the officers who had questioned him unsure whether they
ought to have pulled him in or not. They heard at 5:30
the results of the checks in Cork, gave him back his coat
and his tie and his shoes and told him to get away home.

■ 9 ■

They'd come into the house on tiptoe and holding their
shoes. Both knew the prim well-scrubbed hallway and
stairs well enough to estimate where the boards creaked,
and where it was safe to put their full weight. Harry held
the girl's hand very tight. At first they had tried to go up
the stairs together, and then, finding that impossible, he
gently led the way. There had been no talk about what
they should do, where they should go when they left the
taxi, no discussion whether she should come back to
Delrosa with him. He had looked into her face at the doorway as he rummaged with his free hand for the latch
key, seen those mocking, querying eyes turned up to his
face, looking as if to challenge or dare him to take her
inside. He'd squeezed her hand, and they'd gone in together. The message of silence was implicit.

Once in his back room, a floorboard had erupted in protest at her foot and he had pulled her away from the place near the basin where she was standing, wriggling out of her coat. That was where it would creak. That was the place where he had prized up the planks two days earlier to find a secure hiding place for his Smith and Wesson revolver.

She slung the coat across his easy chair by the window, and stood waiting for him to move toward her. He felt a tightness streaming through him. Clumsy. Gauche. Inhibited. He reached out toward the tall girl, who gazed back at him, her expression one of interest, curiosity to see what he had to offer.

"You make me feel . . . a bit like someone who's forgotten most of it," he whispered into her ear, one hand holding the nape of her neck, the other flattened into the small of her back.

"You haven't made me feel anything yet."

"Cheeky girl."

"Try a bit of cheek yourself. Might take you a long way."

He pulled his left hand around, drawing back from her to give himself room to unbutton the few remaining buttons on her blouse.

"Not much of an obstacle course here," he murmured as he flicked the buttons, small and transparent, through the tautened and opened holes of the fabric.

"Who said they were supposed to be?"

His hand had moved inside her blouse, and he began to ease the soft cotton over her shoulders and down her arms. "I was never very much one for this. Getting everything off in the right order, like a bloody production line in reverse."

"And it takes so much more time. Let's see to it ourselves. I'll meet you under the sheets in forty-five seconds from now."

In a welter of tights, pants, black skirt, shoes and bra, she stripped herself and was away in the bed and waiting for him. Harry was fighting with his right cuff link. She had started to follow the second hand of her watch with exaggerated interest before he climbed into the narrow bed alongside her. "You took thirty seconds over the limit. Bad marks for that, sailor boy."

"Wasn't for lack of trying."

He had curved his arms around her as she came close up against him. His fingers ran their course across her skin, tight, cool and firm. Beautiful girl. Her eyes closed. She moaned. Calling for him, hurrying him. That first time there were few preliminaries, few subtleties. He found her fast. Deep. Easy. He poured himself into her. Both engaged in a frantic, selfish, uncaring race. He sagged away. Disastrous. Bloody Belfast. Like everything else—crude and rushed. No future for tenderness or patience.

"Got a bus to catch?"

"It'll be better next time," he said, "it happened too quick for me. And I never got around to asking you whether . . . you know, whether you take anything . . . or what?"

"There's Catholics and good Catholics here. I'm one of the first. You don't have to worry about that."

The second time was better. Softer. Calmer. Slower. He took a long time finding the routes and depths and contours of her body. Finding where she moved and squirmed, and when she thrust herself at him. Heat against his chest and his thighs. She called the time she was ready for him to come into her, called quietly in his ear. Her mouth open, almost soundless. He smiled down on her as he felt himself slipping away into the void. It was over and they lay together. Her hair strewn with the sweat out on the pillow, he on her softness waiting for the limpness to come. Still locked together.

"You've no worries, then?" she said.

"What do you mean? I don't think so."

"You can't screw if you're really worried. Did you know that?"

"Old wives. Where did you hear that? Who told you that?"

"Just what one of the girls said to me in the bog to-night."

"Tell me what she said." He lay straddled across her, her mouth an inch or so from his ear.

She whispered to him, "She said she'd tried to do it with one of the big men. But he couldn't manage it. She said he was all so tied up he couldn't make it. She was ever so upset."

Harry raised his eyebrows.

"No, that's what she said. She was there tonight. She told me in the loo. She's a bit frantic at the best of times. Then the army nicked the fellow who'd have had her on the way home. Peeved her a bit. On her own on Saturday night. Not right for her. That's what she said. Big hero. Bid deal. I'm all for cowards in this city."

"I don't believe you," said Harry, very still now, just mechanically moving two fingers in the warm moist cavity of an armpit. "Which girl was it?"

"I'm not telling you the best lay in Ballymurphy."

"I don't believe you. You're making it up."

She pushed him back sideways. In the small bed there was hardly enough room, and he clung to her to save himself from disappearing onto the floor. She rolled over onto him, half her weight supported by his hips and waist and the other half supported by an elbow.

"It was Theresa. In pink. She had the tight skirt. Remember her? Believe me. You'll be up to Ballymurphy sniffing round now. Randy bugger."

"I'd believe anything said by anyone as lovely as you," said Harry.

"Bullshit," she said.

"Who was the big man that didn't slake wee Theresa's thirst?" His hands were on the move again now. Seeking the closeness between her thighs.

She rolled and rose beneath him. "Just like that. Go on. Just like that. The big man . . . the one they're all looking for. The London man. The one that did the politician in London. Don't stop there. Just like that. Faster. There's bugger all time. The old girl's alarm'll be off in half an hour. She's out like a flash then. Makes enough noise to wake half the folks in Milltown Cemetery."

Minutes later she was out of bed, dressed and making her way quietly down the stairs to the front door. She refused to let Harry come and see her off, gave him a sisterly kiss on the forehead and was gone. He stood at his bedroom window and saw her some moments later walking along the main road under the street lights. When she had gone beyond the gap, he lost sight of her.

After she had left, Harry lay in his bed, stretching out his legs, searching out the new-found room, working over in his mind the information she had given him. No problem for the intelligence guys. A girl called Theresa, about eighteen or nineteen, in Ballymurphy. Sleeps around a bit. No problem. Should wrap up the whole thing. Not bad: one good screw in the line of duty, and the big coup. He could scarcely believe his luck—getting so far so quickly, all falling into his lap—and on a night out, at that. And the old woman, Davidson, who didn't rate his chances, who fussed and clucked over him, what would he be thinking when Harry called through? A moment to savor, that would be. I'd like to see his face, thought Harry.

There was still the worry over being recognized by that stupid gawping soldier. But they should have the Man within forty-eight hours, and then what the soldier had seen wouldn't matter. All be academic by then. But where did the soldier come from? He turned over in his mind the military situations he'd been in over the last two years, trying to work out where he had seen the young man who had no doubts about him. Davidson would sort it out. Ring him in the morning. Let him know it's just about wrapped up.

For the first time since he had come to Belfast, he felt the excitement that had been the hallmark of the Sheik Othman operation.

He used to leave little penciled messages in English in an old fruit tin on the Sheik Othman-to-Mansoura road. Nothing as luxurious as a telephone. Sometimes he'd stay around in the afternoon heat the next day when the town was sleepy and out of gear and watch the military come bulldozing into the township in their Saladins and Saracens. He would watch the leather-faced, expressionless men hustled away into the armored cars, resisting the show of force that came to get them only with the contempt of their eyes. That was the reward for the strange job he did—to see the clumsy boots of the army stepping into the exact footprints he had silently prepared for them.

It was a good two and a quarter hours before Davidson would be in the office. He had told Harry that for the first three weeks at least he would be there every day, Sundays included, at eight in the morning and stay till ten at night. Must be playing havoc with his marriage, thought Harry. Can't really see Davidson with a wife, though.

He'd go into town, he decided, and make the call from one of those anonymous call boxes in the city center. Now two hours' sleep. That bloody woman. He was exhausted.

But she was a bit special.

Not like that at home. Couldn't be, really. Nothing in married life vegetating around a barracks square in a line of neat desiccated quarters that matched the drawn bowstring of the city at war. Too many bombs, too many snipers, too many mutilations for people to hang about on the preliminaries. You'd want a few memories as you bumped about in the box up the Falls to Milltown Cemetery. That was the philosophy of life for Belfast.

Across in Germany they'd be asleep now. The wife and the kids, tucked up in their rooms, the familiar bits and pieces around them. The things, semi-junk, that they'd collected from the duty-free lounge and the marketplaces where they went shopping when he was off duty. Knick-knacks that brightened the service furniture they lived off. Josephine didn't fit in there, was outside that world. They'd be up soon. Always had an early breakfast on Sundays. Someone would take the boys out for football. That was regular. And his wife . . . how would she spend a cold Sunday in North Germany? Harry was half asleep. Not quite dreaming, but close. She'd go visiting, walk out along the line of officers' detached houses for a coffee in midmorning, and stay for a drink before lunch, and have to make her excuses, and there'd be laughter when she'd flap about the lunch in the oven. Perhaps someone would ask her to stay and share theirs. That would be par for the course. And they'd say how sorry they were that Harry was away, and how suddenly he'd gone, and fish for an explanation. The questions would confuse her, and embarrass her, because they'd expect her at least to have an idea of why he'd vanished so quickly. And she wouldn't have an answer.

Could she comprehend it even if she did know? Could she assimilate this tatty, rotten job? Could she understand the Man that was hunted, and the need to kill him? Could she accept what might happen to Harry? "I don't know," Harry said to himself. "God knows how many years we've been married, and I don't know. She'd be calm enough, not throw any tantrums, but what it would all mean to her, not the faintest idea."

That would all sort itself. And when the answers had to be given, then Josie would be a fantasy, and over.

The Man was in his bed now, and asleep. He'd come back to find his wife sobbing into her pillow, disbelieving he could be freed, still suffering from the strain of the phone call she had made hours earlier. Many time he told her it was just routine, that there was nothing for them to fear. Relax, relax, they know nothing. It's clean. The trail is old and cold and clean. She held on to him as if uncertain that he was really there after she had mentally prepared herself for not seeing him again as a free man.

The terror of losing him was a long time thawing. He put a brave face on it, but didn't know himself the significance of his arrest. But to run now would be suicide. He would stay put. Act it out normally. And stay very cool.

As soon as he came off duty, in the small hours of Sunday morning, Jones asked to see his commanding officer. His platoon lieutenant asked him why, and about what, but the shuffling private merely replied that it was a security matter and that he must see the colonel as soon as he woke. He was marched up the wide steps of the mill, enclosed by the dripping walls festooned with fire- and parcel-bomb warnings and signs urging the soldiers to be ever vigilant, and was shown into the colonel's office. The colonel was shaving with an electric razor as the soldier put together his report. Jones said that while searching a social club the previous night, he had seen a man he definitely recognized as having been the transport officer at a base in Germany where his unit had refitted after a NATO exercise. He said that the man had given his name as McEvoy, and he explained about his kicked ankle, and the instruction to forget what he had seen. There was a long pause while the officer scraped the razor around his face, doubtful what action to take and how he should react. The minute or so that he thought about the problem seemed to the young private an eternity. Then he gave his orders. Jones was to make no further mention of the incident to any other soldier, and was confined to barracks till further notice.

"Please, sir. What do I tell the sergeant major?"

"Tell him the MO says you've a cold. That's all, and keep your mouth shut. That's important."

When the soldier had about-turned and stamped his way out of the office, the colonel asked for his second in command to come to see him. Sunday was normally the quiet morning, and the chance of a modest stay in bed. The second in command came in still wearing his dressing gown. To the colonel the position was now clear.

"There's all these chaps running round in civvies. I think we've trampled on one. If we say we've done it, there's going to be a hell of a scene all the way round, lot of fluff flying, and problems. I'm going to ship Jones out to Germany this afternoon and have the page of his log destroyed. We can take care of this our own way and with rather less palava than if it goes up to old Frost at HQ."

The second in command agreed. He would ask for the logbook and deal with the offending page personally. Before his breakfast.

Early Sunday morning in Belfast is formidable. To Harry it was like the set of one of those films where there has been a nerve-gas attack and no one is left alive. Nothing but grey, heavy buildings, some crazily angled from the bomb blasts, others held up at the ends by huge timber props. Outside the city hall, vast and enormous and apparently deserted, the pigeons had gathered on the lawns. They, too, were immobile except when they ducked their heads while searching for imaginary worms in the ground. No buses. No taxis. No cars. No people. Harry found himself scurrying to get away from so much silence and emptiness. It was almost with a sense of relief that he saw a joint RUC and Military Police patrol cruising toward him. This typified the difference between Aden and here for him. When he had been on his own in Mansoura, he had shut himself away from the safety of the military and accepted that the run for home would be way too long if his cover was blown or if he gave himself away. Now he had the army and police all round him. He was part of their arm, an extension of their operations.

Yet he felt the very closeness of the security forces was unnerving. The agent operating in hostile territory has to be self-sufficient and self-supporting, but so does the British agent working in Great Britain. Can't be like the little boy with the bloody nose running home to Mum. In Mansoura it had been quite conventional and therefore more acceptable.

Not only was the city center deserted of people, it was battened down for the day. Iron railings, their tops split into sharp tridents, blocked off the shopping streets that fanned off Royal Avenue. The turnstile gates into the security precincts were padlocked. Shops inside and outside the barricades had their windows barricaded and shuttered.

Down near the post office he found a bank of empty phone boxes, with only the work of vandals to prevent him taking his pick from a choice of six. It was cold inside the booth; the wind cut through the gaps where the glass had been kicked out by kids in the days before the army operated in strength in the city center.

He took a pile of ten-pence pieces from his pocket and arrayed them in formation like fish scales on the top of the money box, and dialed the London number he had memorized in Dorking. If he went through an operator, some of his call might be overheard. This was the safe way. The phone rang a long time before it was answered.

Davidson heard the ringing when he was at the bottom of the stairs.

Against its shrill persistence, he fumbled with his key ring to release the three separate locks on the heavy door and stumbled across the darkened room where the blinds were still down. He picked up the receiver.

"Three-seven-zero-four-six-eight-one. Can I help you?"

"It's Harry. How are the family?"

"Very well, they liked the postcards. I'm told."

That was the routine they had agreed on. Two sentences of chatter to show the other that he was a free agent and able to talk.

"How's it going, Harry boy?"

"Middling. I'll get the report over first. Then we'll talk. Going in ten from now."

That was time enough for Davidson to get the drawer in the leg of his desk open, switch on the cassette recorder and plug in the lead to the telephone receiver.

"Going now, okay? The Man is in Belfast still. I'm sure of that. He is apparently under great stress and while on the run shortly after the shooting was with a girl called Theresa. No second name. She's from the Ballymurphy area. He tried to screw her, and she's telling her friends that he couldn't make it because he was so wound up about the shooting. She's late teens or early twenties. She was at a dance last night in a green-painted hut in Ardoyne. She was wearing a pink, tight skirt. The army heifered their way in and picked up about a dozn blokes, some of them in Theresa's group. They should be holding them still, unless they work bloody fast. One of them can identify her. So she's worth a bit of chat and then I think we'll be homeward bound. Seems straight sailing from here. That's the plus side. Now the anti. In the club I was lined up for an ID check. Lance corporal from Wales asking questions, a young boy writing down the answers. The boy recognized me. God knows from when, but he did. I'd like it sorted out. I'm going to lie low for today, but I may have a job of sorts coming up. That's about it, basically."

"Harry, we were worried when we didn't hear anything."

"I didn't want to call in till I had something to say."

"But I won't mess you about. But I know you're not staying where we planned for you."

"Too bloody right. Right little army rest house. Right out of the interesting area, and I take a bloody peep at the place and out comes some squaddie in plains. Bloody shambles that was. You should crucify whoever sold you that pup."

"Thanks, Harry. I'll kill them for it. I'll go high on it."

"I've made it on my own. Quite snug, on the other side of town. Let's leave it that way. I'll call you if anything else shows up."

"We'll do it your way. It's not usual, but okay. Nothing more?"

"Only tell the people who pick the girl up to go a bit quietly. Don't ask me what the source of this is, but I don't want it too obvious. If you can get her in without a razzmatazz, you should have your man before anyone knows she's gone, and can link her to him."

"I'll pass that on. Anything else?"

"Nothing more. Cheers. Good hunting."

Davidson heard the phone click down. The call had lasted one minute and fifty-five seconds."

Harry let the receiver stay a moment in his hands after he'd pressed down the twin buttons with his fingers to end the call. He would have liked to talk with Davidson, unimportant small talk. But that would be unprofessional. Dangerous. Soft. Diverting. Pray God they would get the bastard now. He began the walk back to a lonely day at Delrosa, as the city on half-cylinder sparked to life.

Davidson had been surprised that Harry had rung off so fast. He reached down into his drawer and spun back the spools of his tape a few revolutions to check that the recording had operated correctly. He then wound the tape back to the beginning and played it from start to finish, taking a careful shorthand note of the conversation. He then rewound the tape back again to the start and played it once more, this time against his shorthand. Only when he was satisfied that he had correctly taken down every word spoken by Harry did he disconnect the leads between the tape and the telephone. He searched in his diary, at the back in the address and useful-numbers section, for the home phone of the Permanent Secretary.

"I thought you'd want to know, after our talk the other day. He's surfaced. There's some quite useful stuff. Should give a good lead. He sounded a bit rough. Not having much of a joy ride, I fancy. I'll call you in the office tomorrow. I'm quite hopeful we may be on to something. Yes . . . I'm going to pass it on now."

His next call was to an unlisted extension in the Ministry of Defence.

Minutes later Harry's message was on a coded teletype machine in the red-brick two-story building that housed the intelligence unit at army headquarters, Lisburn. It was of sufficient immediate importance for Colonel George Frost to be called from his breakfast. Cursing about amateurs and lack of consultation, he set up an urgent and high-level conference. He summoned his own men, the 39 Brigade duty operations officer, Police Special Branch and the army officer commanding the unit that controlled Ardoyne. The meeting was called for nine, and the unit officer was given no information as to why he was wanted at HQ, only told that on no account were any of last night's suspects to be released. Davidson had somewhat shortened Harry's message. Believing that an arrest was imminent now, he, too, had decided that the report of the recognition should be suppressed and should go no further. A million-to-one chance. It wouldn't happen again. Could be forgotten. Only cause a flap if it went official.

While he was waiting for the meeting Frost reflected on the punched capitals in front of him, deciphered from the code by one of the duty typists. It was detailed enough to impress him, improbable enough to sound likely, and the sort of material you didn't pick up sitting on your backside in the front lounge. When he had read his riot act to the General about being kept out of the picture, he'd heard of the three weeks' crash-training course and been told the arrival date. The source was now about to start his second week. Five lines of print that might be the breakthrough—and might not.

It was the sort of operation Frost detested. Ill-conceived and, worst of all, with the need for fast results dictated by political masters. If he's working at this pace, involved enough to get his nose stuck into this sort of stuff, then Frost reckoned he had about another week to go. That would be par for the course on a job like this. That was always the way. Crash in hard while the trail is still warm. You might get something when you stir up the bottom. But not discreet. No, and not safe either.

Poor bastard. Frost had seen the body of the armored-corps captain, found shot and hooded, dumped outside Belfast. He had been working with a full team behind him. All the backup he needed. Time on his side. Now this nameless and faceless man was trying to do what the whole bloody army and police couldn't. Stupid. Idiotic. Irresponsible. All of those things, that's how Frost rated it. And there'd be a mess. And he'd have to clear it up.

Harry was nearly at his digs by the time the meeting Frost had called was under way. He had decided this was to be his day off. Tomorrow he would chase the job and try to get a bit of permanence into his life.

But today the pubs were closed. Bugger all to do but eat Mrs. Duncan's mighty roast and sit in his room and read. And listen to the news bulletins.

Theresa and her family were at lunch when the army arrived. The armored troop carriers outside the tiny overgrown front garden, soldiers in fire positions behind the hedge and wall that divided the grass from next door's. Four soldiers went into the house. They called her name, and when she stood up, took her by the arms, the policeman at the back intoning the Special Powers Act. While the rest of the family sat motionless, she was taken out to the back of the armored car. It was moving before her mother, the first to react, had reached the front door.

None of the soldiers who surrounded the girl in the darkened steel-cased Saracen spoke to her, and none would have been able to tell her why she had been singled out for this specific army raid. From the Saracen she was taken into a fortified police station, through the back entrance and down the stairs to the cells. A policewoman was locked in with her to prevent any attempt at communication with other prisoners in the row. An hour or so earlier the nine boys taken from the club the previous night had been freed after sleeping in identical cells on the other side of the city. One of their number, pressed to identify someone who would swear he had been in the club all evening, had unwittingly given Theresa's second name and address.

The decision had already been taken that she would be kept in custody at least until the intelligence operation that had produced the information was completed.

■ 10 ■

Seamus Duffryn, the latest of the intelligence officers of E Company, Third Battalion Provisional IRA, had made Sunday his main working day. It was the fourth weekend he'd been on the job, with a long list of predecessors in Long Kesh and the Crumlin Road prison. Duffryn was working, a rarity in the movement, holding down employment as mate to a lorry driver. It took him out of town several days a week, sometimes right down to the border and occasionally into the Republic. Being out of circulation, he reckoned, would extend his chances of remaining undetected longer than the mean average of nine weeks that most company-level officers lasted. He encouraged those with information for him to sift through to leave it at his house during the week, where his mother would put it in a plastic laundry bag under the grate of the made-up but unlit front-room fire. He kept the meager files he had pieced together out in the coal shed. There was a fair chance if the military came and he was out that they would stop short of scattering the old lady's fuel to the four winds in an off-the-cuff search.

On Sunday afternoons his mother sat at the back of the house with her radio while Duffryn took over the front-room table, and under the fading colored print of the Madonna and Child, laid out the messages that had been sent to him. They were a fair hotchpotch, and it was at this level that the first real sorting of the relevant and irrelevant took place. They concerned the amounts of money held at the end of the week at small post offices, usually a guess and an overestimate, the occasions when a recognized man of some importance drove down the company's section of the Falls, the times that patrols came out of the barracks. Then there was the group that fell into no natural pattern, but had seemed important enough for some volunteer to write down and send in for consideration.

He kept this last group for his final work, preferring to spend the greater part of the afternoon at the detail of the job that he liked best, checking over the information about what was happening at street-corner level. His sifted reports would then go to his company commanding officer, a year younger and three and a half years out of school. The best and most interesting would go up the chain to Battalion.

The afternoon had nearly exhausted itself by the time he came to the final group, and the one report in particular that was to take him time. He read it slowly in the bad light of the room, and then went back and reread it, looking for the innuendo in the ambiguous message. It was a page and a half long, written in pencil and unsigned by name. There was a number underneath which denoted which volunteer had sent it in. He went through the report of probably only one hundred words for the third time till he was satisfied he had caught its full flavor and meaning. Then he began to weigh its importance.

Strangers were the traditional enemies in the village-sized Catholic communities of Belfast. The Short Strand, the Markets, Ardoyne, Divis, Ballymurphy—all were self-sufficient, integral units. Small, difficult to penetrate, because unless you belonged, you had no business or reason to come. They boasted no wandering, shifting groups, no cuckoos to come and feed off them. Those who were admitted after being burned out or intimidated away from their homes came because there were relatives who would put roofs over their heads. There were no strangers. You were either known or not admitted.

What concerned Duffryn now was the report on the stranger in the Beachmount and Broadway area. He was said to be looking for a job and getting long-term rates at Delrosa with Mrs. Duncan. There was a question about his speech. The scribbled writing of the report had the second name of McEvoy. First name of Harry. Merchant seaman, orphaned and brought up in Portadown. No harm in that and checkable, presumably. The interest in the report came later. The flaw in the setup, the bit that didn't ring true. Accent, something wrong with the accent. Something that had been notified as not right. It was put crudely, the reason Duffryn read it so many times to get the flavor of the writer's opinion:

> Seems to talk okay, then loses us for a moment, or a word, or sometimes in the middle of a word, and then comes back . . . his talk's like us mostly but it comes and goes . . . it's not just as if he'd been away as he says. Then all his talk would have gone, but it only happens with odd words.

It was enough to cause him anxiety, and it took him half an hour to make out a painstaking report for his superiors, setting down all the information he had available on the man called McEvoy. The responsibility would rest higher up the chain of command as to whether or not further action was taken. He would keep up surveillance when he had the manpower.

There were difficulties of communication in the city and it would be some days before his message could be passed on.

Private Jones was on board the 1530 Trident One back to Heathrow. He was out of uniform, but conspicuous in his short haircut and neatly pressed flannels.

He had been told he would be met by service transport at Heathrow and taken to Northolt, where he would be put on the first flight to Berlin and his new posting. It had been impressed on him that he was to speak to no one of his encounter the previous night. The incident was erased.

Howard Rennie had made himself a master of the art of interrogation, skilled at drawing out the half-truth and capitalizing on it till the floodgates of information burst. He knew the various techniques: the bully, the friend, the quiet businesslike man across the table—all the approaches that softened the different types of people who sat at the bare table opposite him. The first session with the girl had been a gentle one, polite and paternal. It had taken him nowhere. Before they went into the interview room for the second time Rennie had explained his new tactics to the officer from army intelligence. Rennie would attack, and the Englishman capitalize from it. Two men, each offering a separate tempo and combining together to confuse the suspect.

The detective could recognize his own irritability. A bad sign. One that demonstrated the hours he'd put in that week, the sleep he had forfeited. And the girl was playing him up. They'd given her the easy way. If she wanted to play it like the boyos did, then good luck to her. But she was tired now, dazed by the surroundings and the lights, and hungry, having earlier defiantly refused the sandwiches they brought her.

"We'll start at the beginning again, right? You were at the dance last night?"

"Yes."

"What were you wearing? We'll have that again."

"My pink skirt."

That much was established again by the detective. They'd got that far before. He'd done the talking. The army captain had said nothing as he sat behind the girl. A policewoman was also in the interview room, seated to the side of the desk and taking no part in the questioning. The questions came from the big man, directly opposite Theresa, just across the table.

"Your home in Ballymurphy . . . it's a hideout?"

"No."

"It's used as a hideout. We know that. It's more we want. But it's where the boyos lie up?"

"No."

"We know it is, you stupid bitch. We know they stay there."

"Why ask me, then?" she shouted back.

"It's used as a hideout?"

"You say you know it is."

"How often?"

"Not often."

"How many times in the last month? Ten times?"

"No, nothing like that."

"Five times, would that be about right? In the last month, Theresa?"

"Not as often as that."

"How about just once, Theresa? That's the one we're interested in, just the once." It was the officer behind her who spoke. English. Soft voice, different from those RUC bastards. She sat motionless on the wooden chair, hands clenched together around the soaked and stained handkerchief from the cuff in her blouse.

"I think we know one man came."

"How can I tell you—?"

"We know he came, girl, the one man." The big Branch man took over again. "One man, there was one man, wasn't there? Say, three weeks ago. For a night or so. One man, yes or no?"

She said nothing.

"Look, girl, one man and we know he was there."

Her eyes stayed on her hands. The light was very bright, the tiredness was ebbing over her, swallowing her into itself.

"One man, you stupid cow, there was one man. We know it."

No reply. Still the silence. The policewoman fidgeted in her seat.

"You agreed with us that people came, right? Not as many as five, that we agreed. Not as many as ten, we got that far. Now understand this, we say that one man came about three weeks ago. One man. A big man. He slept in the house, yes or no? Look at me . . . now."

Her head came up slowly to look at the policeman directly in front of her. Rennie kept talking. It was about to happen, he could sense it. The poor girl had damn all left to offer. One more shove and it would all roll out.

"You don't think we sent out all those troops and pigs just for one girl if we don't have it cast-iron why we want to talk to her. Give us a bit of common. Now the man. Take your time. Yes or no?"

"Yes." It was barely audible, her lips framing the word with a fractional fluttering of the chin. The army man behind her could not hear the answer, it was so softly spoken. He read it instead on the face of the detective as he sighed with relief.

"Say it again," Rennie said. Rub it in, make the girl hear herself coughing, squealing. That keeps the tap flowing. Once they start, keep up the momentum.

"Yes."

The detective's face lost some of its hostility. He leaned forward on the table. "What was his name? What did you call the man?"

She laughed. Too loud, hysterically. "What are you trying to do to me? You trying to get me done in? Don't you know I can't . . . I couldn't anyway. I don't know it."

"We want his name." Cut the softness. The crisis of the interrogation. She has to go on from here. But the little bitch was sticking.

"I don't know his name. He was hardly there. He just came and went. It was only about six hours, in the middle of the night."

"He was in your house. Slept . . . Where did he sleep . . . in the back room? Yes, we know that. He's on the run, and you don't know his name? Don't you know anything about him? Come on, Theresa, better than that."

"I don't know. I don't *know*. I tell you I just don't . . . that's honest to God. He came in and went upstairs. He was gone before morning. We didn't see him again. We weren't told anything. There was no need for us to know his name, and when he came we didn't talk to him. That's the truth."

Behind the girl, and out of her sight, the army officer put up his hand for Rennie to hold his questions a moment. His voice was mellow, more reasonable and understanding to the exhausted girl in the chair four feet in front of him.

"But your father, Theresa, he'd know that man's name. We don't want to bring him in. We know what happened that night, up in the man's room. We know all about that. We'd have to mention it. They'd all know at home. How would your Dad stand up to all this, at his age? There's your brother. You must think of him as well. It's a long time he's been in the Maze . . . it would go well for him."

"I don't know. I don't. You have to believe me. He never said his name. It's because he wasn't known that he came, don't you see that? It was safe that way. Dad doesn't know who he was. None of us did."

"You know why we want him?" The detective clipped back in, swinging her attention back into the light of the room, away from the peace she found in the shadows around the soldier.

"I know."

"You're sure. You know what he did?"

"I know."

"Did he tell you what he'd done?"

"No."

"How did you know?"

"It was obvious. I've never seen a man like it. He had a hand like an old man's. It was all tied up. Like a claw. I can't say how he was . . . it was horrible."

"What was his name? We want his name."

"You'll get me killed for what I've said. So help me, Mother of Jesus, he never said his name."

The inspector pulled a photokit picture of the Man from a brown envelope and flipped it across the table to the girl. She looked at it briefly and nodded. Then she pushed it back to him.

"Take her down," he said to the policewoman. The two went out of the interview room and away toward the station's cells. He went out: "Bugger it. I thought we had her. I thought it was all going to flow. I have a horrible feeling the little bitch is telling the truth. We'll have another go at her in two or three hours or so, but I don't think she knows any more than she's said. It makes sense. A strange house, strange people. They're alerted someone is coming. They stick their noses into the box, and he's abed for the night. Come on. Let's get a nap for a bit, and then one last bash at her."

After they had gone Theresa sat a long time in her cell. She was alone now, as the policewoman had left her. In her own eyes the position was very clear. The army had pulled her into the station to question her about the Man who had stayed at the house, the Man she had gone to in the middle of the night. The Man who had killed in London, was on the run, hunted, and in bed couldn't screw. They had pulled her in because they thought something she knew was the key to their finding the Man, arresting him, charging him, sentencing him, and locking him away to become a folk hero in the ghetto, however many years he rotted in a cell like this one. If she was not vital to their case, then, as they said themselves, would they have sent the troops and the pigs to collect her? When he was arrested and charged and all Ballymurphy knew she had spent two days in the station being questioned . . . what would they say? What would the old bags with hate in their slack strops say about Theresa? Who would listen when she denied she had ever known his name? Who would walk away satisfied when she said she had given no information that in any way led to his capture? Who would believe her?

In the legend they'd weave, her name would figure. She went back again over all that she could remember of what she had said to that bastard copper. The one who shouted in the front. Nothing, she'd said nothing that helped them. She'd looked at the photograph, but they knew that he was the Man. All they needed was his name, and they didn't know that, and she hadn't told them. But how had they learned of the night? She told girls, some, a few, not many. Would they betray her? Her friends in a chatter in the bog or over coffee break at the mill, would they tout to the military?

So who was going to believe her now?

She had heard what the IRA did to informers. All Ballymurphy knew. It was part of the folklore, not just there, but all over the city where the Provos operated. The vengeance of the young men against their own people who betrayed them was vicious and complete. There'd been a girl, left at a lamppost. Tarred and feathered, they'd called it. Black paint and the feathers from a stinking old eiderdown. Hair cut off. She'd talked to a soldier. Not loved him—not cuddled or kissed him. Just talked to him, standing with him outside the barracks in the shadows. A boy who lived on the street, they'd shot him through the kneecaps. He hadn't even been an informer. "Thief" was the word on the card they hung around the gatepost where they left him. Provo justice. She hadn't known him, just knew his face. She remembered him on the hospital crutches when he was discharged. Ostracized and frightened. They killed girls, she knew that, and men who they reckoned were informers. They shot them and dumped their bodies, sometimes rigged with wires and batteries. Making a stiff into a bomb hoax. Then they lay a long time in the ditch, waiting for the bomb-disposal man to work his way through his overnight list and come and declare the body harmless. And all the reporters and photographers were there.

It was very easy to imagine. A kangaroo court in a lockup garage. Young men with dark glasses at a table. Hurrican lamp for illumination. Arms tied behind her. Shouting her innocence—and who listens? Pulled from the garage, and the sweet smelliness of the hood going over her head, and bundled into a car for the drive to the dumping ground and the single shot.

She wanted to scream, but there was no sound. She quivered on the bed, silhouetted against the light biscuit-colored regulation blanket with the barred-over light bulb shining down on her. If she had screamed at that moment, she would probably have lived. The policewoman would have come and sat with her till the next interrogation. But in her terror she had no voice.

She knew they would come again and talk to her, perhaps in another hour, perhaps longer. They had taken her watch and she had no sense of time now. When they came again they would ask her if she had ever seen the Man on any other occasion. They would ask that over and over again, however many times she maintained she'd not set eyes on him since the night at her house. They would go on asking that question till they had their answer. They would know when she was lying, especially the quiet one behind her, the Englishman. She was tired, so tired, and slipping away. Could she keep up her denials? They would know and she would say. Before morning they would know about the dance, how the Man had been there with his wife. They had taken him away. So why did they still need the name? Confusion and complicated argument swayed and tossed through the girl. They had taken him but they didn't know him. Perhaps they had not made the connection, and then what she might say in her exhaustion would weave the net around him. Betray him. Play the Judas. If she told the English officer, it would be treachery to her own. The pigs would be out for him, pulling him into another police station, and she would wear the brand. Tout. Informer. Despised.

She looked around the brick and tile walls of the cell till she came to the heavy metal bar attached to the cell window that moved backwards and forwards a distance of two inches to allow ventilation into the cell. As it was winter and the window tight shut, the bar protruded from the fitting. She estimated that if she stood on her bed and stretched up, she could reach the bar. Very deliberately she sat up on the bed. She moved her skirt up over her hips and began to peel down the thick warm tights she was wearing.

When the policewoman came to her cell to wake her for the next round of questioning, Theresa was quite dead. Her mouth was open, and her eyes bulged as if they were trying to escape from the agony of the contortions. The nylon had buried itself deep into her throat, leaving a reddened collar rimming the brown tights. Her feet hung between the side of the bed and the wall, some seven inches above the floor.

Frost was awakened by the duty officer in intelligence headquarters without explanation. The message was simply that he should be in headquarters, and that "all hell is about to break loose." By the time he reached the building, there was a report from the police station waiting for him. It covered only one sheet, was slashed to a minimum and was signed by his own man, who had been present at the interrogation.

> Theresa . . . was interrogated twice while in police custody in the presence of myself. Detective Inspector Howard Rennie, Detective Sergeant Herbert McDonals and policewoman Gwen Myerscough. During questioning she identified the photokit picture of a man wanted in connection with the Danby killing as a man who had stayed in her father's house around three weeks ago. After the second session of questions she was returned to her cell. She was found later hanging in the cell, and was dead by the time medical attention reached her.
> Signed
> Fairclough, Arthur, Capt., Intelligence Corps

No marks for grammar, thought Frost, as he read it through.

"Where's Fairclough?" he snapped at the duty officer.

"On his way back here, sir." It was time for short direct answers when the big man was in this sort of mood.

"How long?"

"Should be here in about ten minutes, sir." Then the sparks will come. Poor old Fairclough, thought the duty officer. Rather him than me.

The colonel went to the filing cabinet behind his desk and unlocked the top drawer, pulling it out on its metal runners and rummaging around for his dog-eared Ministry of Defence extension-numbers book. It was a classified document and also listed the home telephone numbers of senior staff at the Ministry, military and civilian. He found the number of the Permanent Under Secretary whom Davidson worked for, and dialed.

"My name's Frost. Army intelligence in Lisburn. It's a hell of an hour but something has come up which you should be aware of. This is not a secure line, but I'll tell you what I can. We were passed some information from a section of yours about a girl. That was yesterday morning. She was brought in yesterday afternoon and questioned twice. You know what about. She knew the Man we wanted, identified the picture and said he'd stayed in her house within the last month. Found her about three-quarters of an hour ago hanging in her cell. Very dead. That's all I have. But I wouldn't care to be in your man's shoes when the opposition finds out about all this. Thought you ought to know. Sounds a bit of a cock-up to me. Cheers."

The Permanent Under Secretary thanked him for the call and rang off.

Frost locked away his directory and pocketed the keys as Fairclough came in a fraction behind his knock.

"Let's have it, Arthur."

"We got it out of her that the Man stayed at her old man's place. She said they weren't given his name, and that she never knew his name. I think she was leveling with us. We left her for a couple of hours and when they came to get her out to bring her back up, she'd strung herself up with her stockings. One thing should be straight, sir. She was treated quite correctly. She wasn't touched, and there was a policewoman present the whole time."

Right. Put it all down on paper, and soon. I want our version on this out fast. The information from London, on which we pulled her in. It seems to have stood up? It was real stuff?"

"No doubt about that. She'd been with him, all right. No doubt."

Fairclough went out of the colonel's office to type his report. Frost was back on the phone to army public relations, another bedside telephone waking the early-

morning sleeper. He suggested that when the press inquiries started coming, the men on the information desk
should treat this very much as a police matter involving
a girl picked up by the army for routine interrogation. He
then called the head of Special Branch, first at his home,
where he was told he was already at Knock Road headquarters, and then at his office there. His own people had
briefed him. With the slight diplomacy that he could
command, he made the same suggestion about press desk
treatment as he had made to his own people.

"You want our people to take the can for the bloody
thing?" said the policeman.

"Inevitable, isn't it? Your police station, your interrogation. Don't see how we can end up with it."

"**Your** bloody info set the thing up."

"And good stuff it was too. There should be an inquiry
at that damned station as to how it happened."

"The Chief Constable in his wisdom had made that
point. I think we should meet for a talk about the next
move, if there is one, or this trail will be dead in no
time."

"I'll call you back," said Frost, and rang off.

Half-cock bloody operation, and the poor sod, whatever his bloody name is, puts it right under our bloody
noses. And we drop it. Poor devil.

And on top of that we let the little bitch kill herself,
which puts a noose around his neck and a bag over his
head. We've done him well today. Desertion's the least
he's justified in doing.

Harry heard about the girl, with the rest of the province,
on the early-morning radio news bulletin. It was the second story after the European Economic Community all-
night talks. The item was brief and without explanation:

"In Belfast a girl has died after being taken to a police
station in the Falls Road area. She was found early this

morning hanging in her cell and was dead by the time she reached the hospital. Police named her as nineteen-year-old Theresa McCorrigan from Ballymurphy. An investigation is being carried out to find what happened. The Northern Ireland Civil Rights Association has issued a statement calling for a full and independent inquiry into the death. They allege two armored cars and troops were used yesterday afternoon to arrest the dead girl in her home."

Harry switched off the radio. He felt numb. No more playing about. No more kindergarten. These were the powers of the forces at work. A simple, ordinary, decent girl. Wants to get screwed by a bloke who cannot make it. Tells the girls in the loo about it, bit of a giggle, have a laugh together. Thirty hours later she's so terrified—deep-belly fear, balls-shaking fear, arse-pucker fear—that she puts something around her neck and steps off. Throttled. A bit randy, and talks too much . . . and now she's dead. Harry remembered her. Across the far side of the club, in with the toughies and the big kids near the bar. Rolling a little. Too much gin and not enough chips to soak it up.

He was the cause of the fear. He was responsible for the agony of the girl, before she slung whatever it was underneath her chin and swung off into the void. Had she even been questioned by then? he wondered. Had she been able to say anything? Or was it all a lot of boasting?

They all listen to those bulletins, Harry reflected, every last one of them, catching up on the night's disasters, funding themselves with conversation for the day. Josephine would be no different. She would hear it, making her face up, having her breakfast, washing her smalls—the transitor would be on somewhere in her home. She'd hear it, and she'd put it together. Was she that fast, that clever? Had to be, it was there on a plate—and what then?

Harry would have to wait to find out. She wasn't doing teas this week, had a different shift at work. He'd have to wait till the weekend and their next date. Have to sit it out, Harry boy, and sweat it out, and see how bright she is, and if she is bright, what she's going to do about it.

He went down the staircase, across the hall and out onto the street. He heard Mrs. Duncan calling after him about his breakfast, and ignored her as he kept on going up the pavement and turned left toward Andersonstown. As he walked he set out the position, making a chessboard of his job in his mind. Pawns, that's where she rated, and pawns were expendable. Bishops and knights hurt more, but they could also be lost. He and the Man he was hunting were the queens of his game. The superstars, and secondary only to the kings, who were sacred and inviolate. If, as the queens were moved around the board, the pawns toppled over, then that was the nature of the game he and the Man played. There was no time to lament the loss of pawns.

The old theme song. It had been different in Aden. There had been no involvement there. Nothing personal. A clear enemy—all that was on the board was black or white, but definite. Now all the squares were grey, and the figures too. Even the two queens. There would be a problem for an outsider in picking one set of pieces from another.

■ 11 ■

Within four hours of the first broadcast of Theresa's death, a soldier had been killed and heavy rioting had broken out in the Ballymurphy, Whiterock, Turf Lodge and New Barnsley estates.

The soldier had died when he was hit by a burst of shots fired at close range from a Thompson submachine gun. He was last man in a patrol in Ballymurphy, and the gunman was apparently operating from the top floor of an empty council house. Some of the photographers who had gathered outside Theresa's house to get a picture of her parents and collect a holiday snapshot of the girl herself ran in the direction of the shooting. The fleetest managed a hurried few frames as the soldiers lifted the body of their colleague into the back of a Saracen.

In the Falls and Springfield roads, groups of youths had hijacked buses, driven them into the middle of the street and set fire to them. After that the army moved in. Armored cars and Land-Rovers were pelted with milk bottles and rocks by crowds who had gathered on the pavements. The army responded by driving at them, firing volleys of rubber bullets from mountings beside the driver. At one building site a barricade of rocks and oil drums had been assembled by the time the Saracens arrived. They'd crashed into the flimsy wall, fracturing it and scattering the drums crazily across the street, when a lone youth, at the controls of a brilliant-yellow excavator-digger machine, charged back defiantly. The troops, who had been advancing behind the cover of the armored cars, fell back as the mechanical dinosaur accelerated down a slight hill toward the toadlike armored cars. A few feet from the impact, the youth jumped clear, leaving his runaway digger to collide head-on with the Saracens. The armored cars, acting in strange concert for things so large, edged it against a wall, where it spent its force revving in demented futility.

The stoning went on a long time. Unit commanders made it clear in their situation reports to Brigade headquarters at Lisburn that they detected a genuine anger among people. Those who over the last months had shown disinclination to abuse and to pelt the military were back with a vengeance. There were rumors, they said, sweeping the Catholic areas, that the girl who had killed herself in the police station had been tortured to a degree that she could stand no more, and that she had then hanged herself. Provisional sympathizers were on the move off the main roads where the army patrolled, and behind the crowds, giving instructions.

Theresa's parents were on lunchtime television, maintaining that their daughter had never belonged to any Republican organization. They described graphically how she had been taken from the lunch table the previous day. The army press desk received scores of calls, and stalled by saying this was a police matter, that the army was not involved, and pointing out that the girl had died in a police station. At police headquarters the harassed man on the receiving end told reporters that an investigation was still going on, and that the officers who were carrying out that investigation had not called back yet.

Both at army headquarters and within the Secretariat that administered the Secretary of State's office at Stormont Castle there was a realization that something rather better by way of explanation was going to have to come out before the day was over.

Faced with crises, the Prime Minister had called a well-tried formula to fall back on. Identify the problem. Focus all attention to it. Solve it, and then leave it alone. When he finally concentrated on any one subject, his aides found he had enormous capacity to wrestle with whatever political abscess was causing the pain. But they also found that once he thought the situation dealt with, then his interest faded as fast as it had risen. Northern Ireland, comparatively quiet for months, was now on the shelved list. It teetered close to what a politician had once called the "acceptable level of violence." So the transcripts of the lunchtime news bulletins that were brought to him he resented as an intrusion. Violence back again. Streets closed. Casualties. The distasteful death of a young girl in the police cell. It was his habit to be direct.

From the back-room office overlooking the Downing Street gardens, insipid in the November light, too many leaves left around, he called the army commander in Lisburn. Without any interruption he listened to a rundown of the morning's events, and made no comment either when the General launched into the background of the girl's arrest. He was told for the first time of the intelligence reports that had been fed in from London, of her questioning, what little she had admitted to knowing, and then of the finding of the body.

"Is this the first we've had from our chap?"

"First that I've heard of. Certainly we've received nothing else we could act on."

"And it was good stuff, accurate. Something we hadn't had before, right?"

"The information was factual. It didn't take us as far as we'd hoped it might at first. I understand, though, that this is the first positive line we've had on the fellow we're looking for."

"Seems we set a bit of a trap, and it's rather missed its target. We'll have to decide whether our chap's had as much out of the pot as he's going to get. Problem is at what stage to get him out, whether we've compromised him already." He was enjoying this, just like the way it was in the war. SOE and all that.

The General cut across the line. "It's not so easy, Prime Minister. It's faintly ridiculous, but I'm told his controllers don't know where he is, don't even know where to get in touch with him. You appreciate that this chap is not being controlled from here. Your instructions were interpreted very strictly on this point. It's London's re-

sponsibility. He calls in, they don't call him. But my ad-
vice would be that he stays. For the moment, at least.
When you begin this sort of things you stick with it.
There's no out in midstream, because it's a bit too hot.
He'll have to finish it, or dry up completely."

The Prime Minister came back. "We've no reason to
believe yet that he's been compromised? But it would be
difficult, very difficult, if he were to be identified in this
context."

"Those were the sort of questions I assume had been
answered before the instruction was given to launch this
operation, Prime Minister."

The sarcasm bit down the line.

The Prime Minister banged the phone down, then immediately flipped the console button on his deck and
asked abruptly for the Secretary of State in Stormont
Castle. After forty-one years in politics, he could see the
storm clouds gathering long before they were upon him.
He knew the time had come to pull in some sail and close
down the hatches. The combination of an agent working
by the Prime Minister's orders and a teenage girl hanging
herself in a cell would make better ingredients than most
for a political scandal of major proportions. He must start
to plan his defensive lines if the worst should happen
and the chap they'd sent over should be discovered. That
bloody General, not much time to run over there, and his
next appointment already confirmed. Entrenched, which
was why he was so free with the advice. But all the same,
in spite of his eminence it must have hurt him to admit
that this was the best information they'd had so far . . .
and for all that, they'd loused it up.

"He won't have liked it. One bright thing today," and
then he turned his attention to the search for a fail-safe
system. Call the Under Secretary, the man in charge of
this incredible noncommunication setup. In the event
of catastrophe, no statements till the civil servant had

cleared it, and get that away to Lisburn. No acknowledgment for the agent, of course; if all goes wrong . . . deny all knowledge of the mission.

The Secretary of State was on the line. The Prime Minister wasted no time on pleasantries.

"I've been hearing about the troubles today, and the girl. Difficult situation. I thought we were weak at lunchtime, too defensive. We need to be a lot more positive. I've a suggestion to make. It's only a suggestion, mind you, and you should bounce it off your security people and see how they react. But I think you should say something like this—get a note of it and I'll read over what I've drafted. Along these lines, now. That the girl was a known associate of the Man we are hunting in connection with the killing of Danby. That she was brought in quite correctly for questioning, and had been spoken to briefly before being left in the cells for the night. You must emphasize that she was not touched. Leak it that you're prepared to offer an independent post-mortem from one of the hospitals, if you think that'll help. But my thought is to bring it back to Danby. By the by, his memorial service is at St. Paul's this week. You'll be there, I hope. It'll all be in the public gaze again. We'll be all right if we play a bit bold, and attack. Worst thing we can do is to get on the defensive."

The linking of the killing of the British Cabinet Minister with the death of the teenager in the Falls Road police station was splashed across the last edition of the *Belfast Telegraph*, and extensively reported on later television and radio news bulletins. The few men in the city who knew of Harry's existence were uncertain what effect the disclosure would have on the agent's work and safety. They acknowledged an immediate lifting of the pressure on their public relations setup for more information concerning the circumstances of the death.

Harry was not the only man in the city with pawns on the checkerboard.

The scrap merchant would take Harry on his payroll. He'd obviously liked the look of him. He said he had a brother at sea, and asked Harry if he could start then and there. There was not a word about National Insurance cards or stamps, and twenty pounds a week was offered as pay. Harry was told he'd need to spend a month or so in the yard to see the way the place was run. There was to be expansion, more lorries. When they came, if it all worked out, there would be a driving job, and more money.

On his first morning Harry prowled around the mountains of burned and rusted cars. These were the stock in trade of the scrap man, heap upon heap of rough, angled metal.

Harry said to the neat dapper little man who was his new boss. "Is this what the business is? Just cars? You've enough of them."

"No problem with the supplies of that. You must have seen it, though you've been away. Terrible driving here. If you take the number of cars, they say, and work it out against a percentage, of all the people that own them, and the number of accidents . . . then it's worse than anywhere else in the whole of England or Ireland. Maniacs they are here. The boyos down the road do the rest. We'll have a dozen wrecks in tomorrow morning. There'll be a double-decker as well, like as not, but they're bastards to cut up."

He smiled. Small, chirpy, long silk scarf around his neck, choker style, flat hat on his head. They're all the same, thought Harry, likeable rogues.

The scrap merchant went on: "It's an ill wind. Scrap men, builders, glaziers . . . we're all minting it. Shouldn't say so, but that's how it is. The military dumps the cars that are burned out, up there on the open ground. We send a truck up and pull them down here. Not formal, you know. Just an understanding. They want them off the street and know if they put them there, I'll shift them. We'll have a few more today, and all."

He looked up at Harry, the brightness evacuating his eyes. "People are powerful angry about this girl. You'll find that. They get killed in hundreds here. Most of the time it doesn't mean a damn, however big the procession. But this girl has got them steamed again."

Harry said, "It's a terrible thing pulling a girl like that out of her house."

"Poor wee thing. She must have been awful scared of something to want to do that to herself. Mother of Jesus rest her. Still, no politics in this yard, and no troubles. Those are the rules of the yard, Harry boy. No politics, and that way we get some work done."

He walked around with Harry and introduced him to the other men in the yard, six of them, and Harry shook hands formally. They greeted him with reserve but without hostility. When his escort went back to the office to look to the papers, Harry was free to browse. At one stage as he meandered among the cars, he was within eight feet of a Russian-made rocket launcher. It was the RPG 7 variety, complete with two missiles and wrapped in sacking and cellophane, locked in the trunk of a car. There were always people coming into the yard, and the cover was good. Access was easy at night. The launcher, sealed against the wet, had been placed there after the Provisional unit to whom it had been issued had found it inaccurate and unreliable. It had been abandoned until they could come across a more up-to-date manual of operation, preferably not written in Russian or Arabic.

As the little man said, no politics, no troubles. That first day Harry abided faithfully by it, taking his cue from the other men in the yard. Slowly does it here. The high column of black smoke from a blazing Ulster bus was ignored.

The rest of the first week that Harry was there was quite uneventful. He was accepted to a limited degree as far as small talk went, and nothing more. His few attempts to broaden the conversations were gently ignored and not pressed on his part. The death of Theresa and the start of the job probably meant, thought Harry, the start of the next phase. No immediate pointers for him to follow, only the long-term penetration remaining. Three weeks. What idiot had said it could be done in three weeks? Three months if he was lucky. And it relaxed him. Going up the road each day and having the work occupy his mind would ease him. Better than sitting in that bloody guest house. Claustrophobia.

And each day he was watched by Seamus Duffryn's volunteers, from Delrosa to the yard, and back again . . .

Downs was in the kitchen swilling his face in the sink, Monday morning wash, when his wife came in white-faced, shutting the door behind her on the noise of the playing children.

"It's just been on the radio, about you. About a girl. The girl who killed herself."

"What do you mean? What about me?"

"This girl from the Murph, it says she was linked with the man that did the London killing."

"It didn't actually mention me?"

"Said you was linked. Connected."

"What was her name?"

"Theresa something. I didn't catch it."

"Well, I don't know her."

"It said she was being questioned about him because she was a known associate. That was another word they used—'associate.' God rest her, poor kid. She was just a child."

"Well, I don't know her, and that's the truth."

"That's what they're saying on the radio . . . loud and

clear . . . where any bloody ape can hear it."

"Well, it's balls, bullshit."

"When you're shouting, you're always lying. Who was she? What was she to do with it?"

"I don't know her. I tell you, I just don't know her."

"Billy, I'm not daft. You were in town a long time before you came back here. I haven't asked you where you were before you came home. Who is she?"

"What did you say her name was?"

"Don't play the fool with me. You heard the first time."

"If it's Ballymurphy, I stayed there one night. I came in darkness while the family was round the box. There was a girl there. Just a kid who brought me some food in the room. I was away by five-thirty."

"Just brought some food, did she?"

" 'Course she did . . . don't bloody question me . . . like the fucking Branch."

"Just on the strength of that, brought her in and questioned her, just because she brought you some grub? Didn't get her father in—he's giving interviews. Just took her in."

"Leave it," he snapped at her. He wanted out. Escape.

"Just bloody well tell me who the little bitch was and what she meant to you."

"She's just a child a minute ago, now she's a little bitch. She was nothing. Nothing. Must have blabbed her mouth off. Squealed, the little cow."

"How did she know who you were?"

She shouted the last question at him. She would have taken it back once the words were out and had crumpled against him. The noise and aggression slewed out of him. Beseeching. Pleading. Don't make me answer. The found-out child and the hollow victory.

"I'm sorry," she said. "Just forget it."

She turned away, back toward the door into the living

room, where the children were fighting, and one was hungry, and another crying.

"I'll tell you what happened . . ." She shook her head, but he went on: "This is once and for all, never ask again. If I'd wanted her, I couldn't have done anything about it. I was so screwed up. I was sort of cold, frozen, shivering. I couldn't do anything for her. She asked if it was me in London. I hit her. Across the bloody face. She went back to her room. I've only seen her once since then. She was at the dance at the club on Saturday night. I suppose she saw me."

He walked across to his wife and put his arms around her. The children still cried, and the pitch was growing. He pulled her head against his shoulder. There was no response, but she was pliant against him, totally passive.

He continued: "That's when she must have talked. Going home after the dance. Must have said that she knew the man that had been in London. Then some rat, some mother-fucking bastard, squealed. A fucking spy, a tout. Right there at one of our dances, some bastard who'll shop you. That's what must have happened."

"Forget it. We have to forget all these things. There's nothing left otherwise."

He held her for a long time in the darkened kitchen, painfully lit by the inadequate bulb hanging without a shade from the wire. At first she wept silently and without dramatic effect, keeping her grief private, not using it as a weapon to cudgel him with. She controlled herself, and clung to him. Nothing would be different, nothing in his way of life would change.

"You'll go back?"

"When they want me."

"You could end it all now. You've done your share."

"There's no way that could happen."

He needed her now, to recharge him, she knew. When the dose was enough, he would go back into his own vicious, lonely world. Of which she was no part.

She was one of the crowd. The crowd of women who had so little influence over their men that it was pointless, indecent to beg them to stay off the streets. Yet, she was luckier than most. Her man was still with her. The bus that came each Thursday lunchtime to the top end of Ypres Avenue was well enough known. It took the women to Long Kesh to talk to their men for half an hour.

That night the Man opened his door to a treble knock. He was given an envelope by a youth who scurried away into the darkness. His wife stayed in the kitchen, as she, too, had recognized the call sign of the fist against the door. She heard him switch the hall light on, pause a few moments, and then the sound of tearing paper, over and over again.

He went into the front room and threw the half-inch squares of paper into the fire. The message was from Brigade. It was short and to the point. For the moment he was to stay at home. It was believed the girl had hanged herself before identifying him.

Davidson had had a bad week. He admitted it to the young man who was drafted in to share the office with him. The fiasco of the girl had started it off. The Permanent Under Secretary had been on him as well, laying the smoke screen that would be used if the operation went aground. Davidson had tried to counterattack with complaints about the original lodgings and then the foul-up over the girl, but had been rejected out of hand. There had been silence from Harry himself after his first call. Davidson and the aide sat in the office, reading papers, making coffee, devouring take-away fish and chips, take-away Indian, take-away Chinese. The number that had been given to Harry was kept permanently free from all other calls.

When he did call, on Saturday afternoon, the effect was electric. Davidson started up from his easy chair, pitching it sideways, tipping a coffee beaker off his desk as he lunged for the telephone. Papers drifted to the floor.

"Hello, is that three-seven-zero-four-six-eight-one?"

"Harry?"

"How are the family?"

"Very well. They liked the postcards, I'm told."

Davidson was on his knees, his head level with the drawer where the recording apparatus was kept. He pulled up the lead and plugged it into the telephone's body. The cassette was rolling.

"Anything for us?"

"Nothing old chap. No, I'm just digging in a bit. I think it may go all quiet for a few days, so I'm settling into some sort of a routine."

"We're worried about you in the wake of that bloody girl. We're wondering whether we should pull you out."

"No way. Just getting acclimatized."

"I think we all feel at this end that you did very well last weekend. But we want some way to get in touch with you. This may suit you, but it's bloody ridiculous for us. Quite daft. We're sitting here like a row of virgins waiting for you to call us up."

"It's the way I'm happiest. I've been bitten, remember. On the first house. It's going to be a touch trickier getting something further out of this, and this is the way I want it to be. Bit silly, you might say, but that's the way it is."

Davidson backed down and switched the subject. "Are they sniffing round you at all?"

"I don't think so. No particular sign of it yet, but I don't know. More of a problem is that I don't see where the next break is going to come from—what direction. I was very lucky last time, and look where the bloody thing got us. It can't be on a plate like that again."

"You're not following anything particular at the moment, then?"

"No, just entrenching. Getting ready for the siege."

"Perhaps it is time you should come out. Like this weekend. I don't want you hanging about wasting time. Look, Harry, we know it's bloody difficult in there, but you've given the military and security people a lead that they ought to be able to do something about. Come out now. Get yourself up to Aldergrove and get the hell out . . ."

The phone clicked dead in his hand before the dialing tone purred back at him. Despairingly he flicked the receiver buttons. The call was over.

Bugger. Played it wrong. Unsettled him. Just when he needs lifting. Silly, bloody fool. Should have made it an order, not a suggestion, or not mentioned it at all. The military should be following this now. The girl must have left a trail a mile wide.

Davidson could see through his uncurtained window that it was now dark outside. He thought of Harry walking back up the Falls to his digs. Past the shadows and the wreckage and the crowds and the troops, the legacy of the spluttering week-long street fighting he had been the spark to. Keep your head down, Harry boy.

■ **12** ■

It was acknowledged at the higher levels of the IRA's Belfast Brigade command that the campaign was at a crucial stage, the impetus of the struggle consistently harder to maintain. The leadership detected a weariness among the people on whom they relied so greatly for the success of their attacks. Money was harder to collect for the families of those imprisoned, doors generally left unlocked for the gunman or blast bomber to escape through were now bolted, and the confidential phones at police headquarters where the informers left their anonymous messages were kept busy with tip-offs that could only come from the Catholic heartland.

As the pressure grew to near-intolerable degree on the shoulders of the Provisionals' leadership, it was understood that the days of gallantry and chivalry were gone, too. Once a British officer had stood in the turret of his armored car, stiffly upright and with his right arm in the salute position, as the coffin of an IRA man was carried past him, draped in the tricolor. Once British officers, after an evening's celebration and in their slacks and sports jackets, found they had wandered into the Bogside, were captured and returned safely to their embarrassed seniors.

That was all over now. As the IRA fought back against the growing strength and experience of the security forces arrayed against them, the attacks became more vicious and more calculated to shock.

It was the Brigade command that made the reluctant decision to call Billy Downs out from Ardoyne and from inactivity. It was accepted that he was of greatest value when used sparingly, but within seventy-two hours of the earlier instruction, he was given new orders.

The subject of the Brigade's death sentence was an RUC inspector. A priority was put on his death, and it was reckoned important enough to risk the exposure of one of the movement's top cards.

The policeman they wanted shot was Howard Rennie, CID, transferred to Special Branch. Their dossier reported him born in the hills of County Atrim, near the coast. He had been unknown in Belfast till recently, when word had begun to seep into the information system from the holding centers and prisons about a detective with sufficient ability as an interrogator that he was directly responsible for the failure of several suspects to keep their mouths shut.

It had taken a long time, once they'd started, for the Brigade intelligence section to identify Rennie, locate his headquarters at the holding center in Castlereagh barracks and put a plan into operation against him. The final decision to eliminate him was taken after a company intelligence officer reported on the list of police cars' number plates and models that had left the police station after the death of the girl in her cell. One was similar in model and color to that driven by the detective. His association with the events of that night was sufficient to put him several places up the list in priorities, and would win the movement nothing but support when he was killed.

The Man was given a dossier to read, but not to keep. The caller who came to his house late, after the wife and the children had gone upstairs, was to bring it away with him when the Man had done his reading. His wife came down the stairs to see who the visitor was, paled at the sight of the long-haired youth in jeans and heavy quilted anorak coat, who returned her stare and then turned away without speaking to her. She went into the kitchen, aware that the front room was no place for her. When she moved upstairs again, she could hear the voices, talking hurriedly, hushed and with urgency.

The Man was shown a picture of Rennie. Taken five years ago, and one of a group. It had been gained from the copious files of a photographer in the small town where Rennie had then been stationed. It was a fair bet they'd find such a picture when they went into the photographer's shop with guns in their hands, and the competence of the filing system saw them through. The picture was of a group of policemen all celebrating their promotion to sergeant. The picture would not help the Man that much, as it suffered seriously in the enlargement, but it gave him an idea of the build, the hair and the shape of the face of the policeman that he had been ordered to kill. The car the detective would be using was a Triumph 2000 and bottle-green, but the file on Rennie carried a list of a minimum of eight number plates that he might use. He read that Rennie lived in a small detached house in Dunmurray, down a cul-de-sac. The house right at the bottom of the U of the close. Difficult for surveillance and for ambush. The dossier said he used a door direct into the garage. Wife opened the garage doors from the inside and he drove straight out in the morning. They would be open when Rennie came home. The policeman would be armed.

The problems of the ambush were made clear to him.

"It'll not be easy to get the whore. None of them are easy. They often go together—lift each other to work. They'll be using different routes, and all. They've guns, too. One of them would get a shot in if you try it then. They know how to use them. Rennie's a trained shot. And clever—won't be easy to nail the bastard. No chance of sitting down his road: all those women flappin' their curtains from not enough to do, they'd see you and be on the phone straight off. And you don't have time to set it up, next week, next month, when you like. They want it, and fast. Brigade's order. It's a special one, and they want you for it."

His unpolished ankle-length boots were beside the chair. Jeans crumpled and not washed or ironed since he came home. Shirt was off, white and dirty, collar frayed. The fire was small now, needing help to stay alive. He had put the light out when the courier had gone, so that he could concentrate the better on the policeman, Rennie, that they had put him against. He had memorized much of the details of the file and now he savored the problem they had set him, seeking out a plan of action. Like a mathematician attempting the answer to a complex formula, he stayed in the chair, thinking on the method and the manner by which Rennie would be assassinated. He was surprised to have been called out, but the implication was clear. This was a vital and important operation, he was a vital and important operator.

His wife stayed upstairs, aware that this was no time for her to go down to the front and try to break the spell her husband was weaving for himself as his mind took up attack tactics and the weapons he would use.

She drifted into an uneasy sleep that night, tossing through an immediate nightmare. She saw her man cut down by a burst of bullets, caricatures of grotesque soldiers standing over him. Life throbbing away in the gutter. Feet pushing and maneuvering him. When she reached across to see if he had come upstairs yet, she found only the emptiness of the sheets beside her. Back in her half-sleep she witnessed over and over again the firing of those perpetual rifles, and the agony and throes of her man. And then exhaustion and fear took her beyond the stage of the dreams and left her in deep sleep till the morning.

That was how he found her when he came upstairs with a plan maturing well in his mind. He was impressing himself with the cleverness of what he would do. Excited and pleased with his solution to a technical problem.

He lay on his back, elbows outstretched on the pillow, his hands under his neck, going back over his plan, testing each point in it for flaws. He was tired, but elated enough to find none as he checked over each aspect of the killing, each aspect bar the final one—the killing itself. He shut that out of his mind. The actuality of the killing, the pulling and squeezing of the trigger. The Armalite would be in his hands then, aiming the smooth nuggets of steel that killed and maimed.

He seldom tried to work out the values of the killings he performed to the movement that he served. Tasks and projects set for him by his superiors. Others determined the morality. Others had the hatred. Others turned his work into victories. He did as he was told, expertise his trademark. The soldier in his army.

There were some in the movement, men that he had met or, in other cases, heard of, who were said to relish the physical side of the killing. There were stories that they tortured the demented minds of their victims after the sentence of the kangaroo court. Demonstrated the firearm. Went right up to the moment of shooting and then fired with an empty gun. There were beatings, knifings and cigarette burnings. That was no part of the Man. His killing was different. Clever. Organized. Against major targets. His feelings were known and respected by the top men. The ritual was for others. He belonged in the field. His mind reverted to the reconstruction and progress of the murder of Rennie, his plans racing far ahead. It was close to dawn before he slept.

In a room above a chip shop in Monaghan town, just over the border into the Republic, the Army Council met for the first time in a fortnight. Eight men around a table. Businesslike, with their pencils and notebooks in front of them. There was much talk of what they had seen on the earlier television news bulletins, of the film taken on the steps of St. Paul's of the arrival of government Ministers and Cabinet members for the memorial service for Henry Danby.

"Hardly what you'd call security. Sod-all protection."

"They all had 'tecs with them, but by the look of it, only one each. Not the Big Man, though. He had a couple. Little film stars, you get to know them."

"Right open, if we wanted to put a man in again."

"Wide open. What those bloody papermen call a wall of steel. Nothing."

"It would only be a repetition. Took a lot of planning last time. Manpower. What do we achieve? There was good reason for that bastard Danby, but another man, what for?"

"It did a fair bit for us when we got Danby. Keeping our man on the loose, that's not done us bad."

"There was no sympathy for Danby. There's no one else we can get who is in that crowd where we would get the same reaction. The bastard was hated. Even the Prods loathed him."

"In London there's no way they can guard the politicos, no way at all. They have to be out and be seen to be about. They can't lock themselves away. You can do that in the White House, but not in Downing Street."

"Let's have some talk about what we'd get from hitting them again in London." It was the chief of staff who spoke, terminating the knock-about around the table.

He made only rare incursions into the talk, preferring to let it ripple around him while he weighed the ideas before coming down in support of anyone in particular. He was a hard man, with few feelings that did not involve the end product. Like some cost-effectiveness expert or a time-and-motion superman, he demanded value for effort. His training in military tactics had been thorough, and he had risen to corporal in the parachute regiment of the British army. He was in his mid-thirties now and had seen active service in Aden and Borneo. He'd bought himself out at the start of the troubles and set up briefly as a painter and decorator before going underground. When he had been voted into the number-one position in the Provisionals by his colleagues, it was because they knew they could guarantee he would pursue a tough, ruthless campaign. Those who believed in the continua-

tion of the war of attrition on British public opinion had
felt threatened by those they thought might compromise.
The new commander was their safeguard. He was no
strategist, but had learned enough of tactics on the streets
of the Lower Falls where he came from. He had sanc-
tioned the killing of Danby, and was well pleased with the
dividends.

The quartermaster took it up. "It's the trouble with all
spectaculars. You launch them and they succeed, and
where do you go from there? Only upwards."

The older man in the group, a veteran of '56, who
lived now in Cork, said, "It stirs the not well and truly.
How many bombs, how many 'another soldier tonight'
add up to a British Cabinet Minister?"

The quartermaster across the table was not impressed.
"But what's the reaction? If we did it again, they'd tear
the bloody place apart. We'd not survive it. They'd be
all over us. Down here as much as in the North."

"That's what we have to weigh. What would happen
to the whole structure? They'd go mad, knock bloody
shit out of us." The speaker was from Derry. Young, from
the Creggan estate. Interned once and then released in an
amnesty to mark the arrival of a new Secretary of State.
He had been in the Republic's prisons as well, and now
lived on the run as much in County Donegal as in the
maze of streets in the Creggan housing estate. "Our need
at this moment is not to go killing Cabinet Ministers from
Westminster, but winning back what we lost at Motorman
when the army came into Bogside and Creggan. We have
to play on the tiredness of those people across the water.
There's no stomach there for this war. They're soft there,
no guts. They'll get weary of hearing of another soldier,
another policeman, another bomb, another tout. It's the
repetition that hurts them. Not another big killing. All that
does is get them going. It affronts their bloody dignity.
Unites them against us. We have to bore them."

"The bigger man you get, the better." It was a Belfast man. He was of the new school, and had come a long way since Long Kesh opened. He had pitiless eyes, wide apart above his ferret nose, and a thin, bloodless mouth. He chain-smoked, lighting cigarettes one after another from the butt of the one he was discarding. "The Big Man himself wouldn't hurt. They never believe we mean it over there. Somehow the fucking Micks won't actually get around to it, they say. Get the old bugger, himself, that would sort them."

That quickened it. Then the chief of staff chipped in, cutting through the indecision of the meeting as he brought it to heel and away from the abstract.

"We'll think about it. It has attractions. Big attractions. Total war, that's what it would mean. Davie and Shaun, you'll work on it for a bit. Have something for us in a fortnight with something concrete. I don't want it done hasty . . . something in a bit of detail. Right?"

They moved on to other business.

The process of arrests went on with seeming inevitability, with frequent reunions in the Crumlin and Long Kesh. The Provisionals' intelligence officer who should have seen the report of that conversation between the army brigadier and the policeman overheard at their hotel lunch was taken into custody before the message reached him. When there was an arrest, those still in the field shifted around their weapons, explosives, equipment and files, lest their former colleague should crack under interrogation and reveal the hiding places.

That message, closely written on two sheets of notepaper, remained in a safe house in the communication chain while the Third Battalion worked around to an appointment for the vacant position. The clogging in the system lasted more than a week, and when the new man came to sort through the backlog, he had a table covered with reports and documents to wade through. He was into his second day before he got to the paper written by the waiter.

He was sharp enough to sense immediately the importance of what was in front of him. He read it carefully:

> The man with the thin moustache looked like an army man, and from the kitchen I could see the big Ford out in the car park with the uniformed escort sitting there in the front. The other one was talking when the music stopped. He was a policeman, I think. That's when I heard him say "special operator in on the ground without telling." He must have realized I was standing there, and he just stopped and didn't say anything else until I was right away from him. He looked very bothered . . .

That was the guts of the message. The intelligence officer had read it once. Went slightly beyond and then rapidly coursed his eyes back over it. He could imagine the situation. Bloody military and police, not taken in on the act, and feeding their bloody faces, weeping on each other's shoulders, stuffing the food in far away from the "Careless Talk Costs Lives" bit. It was the sort of place you'd expect to hear a major indiscretion uttered, when they couldn't keep their big mouths shut. That was why the waiter had been introduced onto the staff of the hotel.

Undercover men working for the army or D16 were the particular dislike of the Provisionals. They believed there was a much greater secret intelligence and surveillance operation against them than in fact existed. Their traditional hatred was for the plainclothes army squads who cruised at night around the back streets of the ghettos in unmarked cars, looking for the top men in the movement. But this had a more important ring about it than squaddies out in jeans and sweaters and armed. If a brigadier and top copper were not in on the act, and thought they ought to have been, it meant, first, it was top secret, and second, that they considered it important enough for them to have been briefed. Something of critical value to those English swine, so sensitive that top-ranking men had been left out in the cold.

Further down the waiter's report was a paragraph explaining that the tone of the exchange across the lunch table had been critical.

The officer wrote a three-line covering note on a separate piece of paper, clipped it to the original report and sealed it in a plain brown envelope. A courier would take it that night to the next man up the chain, someone on the Brigade staff.

Twenty-two hours later he met Seamus Duffryn for the first time. Duffryn had originally intended that his message should go by hand, but the combination of the new appointment and the nagging worry about this man, Harry McEvoy, had led to the direct meeting, risky as it was.

They met in a pub in the heart of the broken-up and ravaged triangle of the Lower Falls. Taking their pints of beer with them, Duffryn led the other to a corner table. With their heads huddled together, he spoke of the stranger that had come to the guest house further up the Falls. Looking for work. Said he'd been away a long time. Had this strange accent that was noted by those when he first came, but which his latest reports said was not so pronounced. When Duffryn mentioned the accent the battalion officer looked at him, intrigued, and the junior man explained the apparent lapses in speech. Duffryn said that his men who followed McEvoy and heard him talk in the pubs said the oddness about the speech was something very much of the past. Ironed out, muttered Duffryn. He had come to the end of his patience on the matter and wanted a decision. Either the man should be cleared or there would have to be authorization

for more surveillance, with all its problems of manpower. Duffryn himself had personally tried to observe
McEvoy by spending three successive evenings in the
pub on the corner where it was reported that the stranger
came to drink, but he'd stayed alone those evenings, and
the man he wanted to see had not shown himself.

"I'm not that sure what it means," said the man from
Battalion. "You never know with these bloody things. It
could mean he's a man put in by the bastards to infiltrate
us. It could be nothing. It counts against the bugger that
his accent is improving. Would do, wouldn't it? With each
day he spends here, it would improve. There's something
else we have that indicated a few days ago that they could
have put an undercover man in. He'll be a big bloody fish
if it's right. He'll be a bloody whale if what we think
about him is right."

He hesitated as to whether he should bring the young
Duffryn further into the web of reports and information
that was forming in his mind. He dismissed it. The golden
rule of the movement was "Need to Know." Duffryn
needed to know no more than he already knew.

"That's enough. From now on—and this is important—
and I want it bloody well obeyed to the letter—no more
following this McEvoy. Let him ride on his own a bit. I
don't want the bugger flushed before we're ready for him.
We'll just leave him alone for a bit, and if we have to,
we'll move when it's all nice and relaxed. I want it taken
gently, very gently, you see? Just log him in and out of
the guest house, and that's the lot."

Harry had not been aware of the watchers before they
were called off, and therefore had no idea that he had
thrown off a trail when he had gone through the city
center shopping crowds to a telephone kiosk to call
Davidson. On the Friday night when he had been in the
city nearly three weeks, he came down past the cemetery

toward Broadway with his wage packet in his hip pocket and the knowledge that there seemed to be no sign of suspicion from the men he was working with. He had a hired car booked for Saturday for his date with Josephine.

There was a Sinn Fein meeting that Friday night up on the junction of the Falls, and after he'd had his tea Harry wandered up to listen to the speeches. There were some familiar faces on the lorry that was being used as a speaker's platform. The oratory was simple and effective and the message brutally clear. Among the committed there would be no easing in the struggle, the war would go on till the British were gone. The crimes of the British army, the Stormont administration and the Free State government were catalogued, but the crowd of three or four hundred seemed lukewarm to it all. They'd been listening to this stuff for five years or so now, Harry reflected. He'd be a bloody good orator to give them something new at this stage. The army stayed away, and after hearing the first four speeches, Harry left. He'd clapped with the rest, and cheered by consensus, but no one spoke to him. He was just there, ignored. God, how do you get into this bloody mob? How does it all happen, like Davidson said, in that magic three weeks? It'll take months, till the face is known and the background and every other bloody thing.

A long haul. He wouldn't call Davidson this weekend. Nothing to say. Those buggars had sent him here, they could sit and stew for a bit and wonder what was going on. The trail of the man he sought was well chilled now. It would be very slow, and his own survival would take some thinking about. But there'd be no coming out, no trotting up to Aldergrove. One way to Heathrow, please, my nerve's gone and so has that of the bloody controller, thank you very much.

No way. You stay in for the whole way, Harry boy.

▪ 13 ▪

She was waiting at the lights at the junction of Grosvenor and the Falls when he pulled up in the hired Cortina. Tall in the brittle sunlight, her hair blown around her face, and shivering in the mock-sheepskin coat over the sweaters and jeans he'd told her to wear.

"Come on, get that bloody door open. I'm frozen out here." A bit distant, perhaps too offhand, but not the clamoring alarm bells Harry had steeled himself to face.

He was laughing as he reached across the passenger seat and unlocked the near side door and pushed the handle across to open the door. She came inside, a bundle of coat and cold air, stealing the warmth he had built up since he had collected the car.

"All right then, sunshine?" He leaned over to kiss her, but she turned her head away, presenting her cheek for what he hadn't intended to be the brotherly peck they ended up with.

"Enough of that. Where are we going?" she said. She straightened her back in the seat and began to fasten her seat belt.

"You said you wanted some country. Somewhere we can stretch ourselves a bit, walk around. Where do you suggest?"

"Let's off to the Sperrins. About an hour down the Derry and Dungiven road. That's wild country, real Ulster stock. You've seen the slogans on the Proddy walls before the troubles started, 'We will not exchange the blue skies of Ulster for the grey mists of the Republic.' Well, the blue skies are over the Sperrins."

"Well, if it's okay for the Prods, it'll do for us second-class Micks."

"I was brought up down there. My Dad had a bit of land. Not much, but enough for a living. It's a hard living down there. It's yourself and that's all, to do the work. We cut peat down there and had some cows and sheep. Stupid bloody creatures. We were always losing the little buggers. There was no mains, no gas, no electricity, no water when I was born. He's dead, now, the old man, and my Mum came to Belfast."

"Were you involved, at all, with the politics? Was the old man?"

"Not at all. Not a flicker. Most of the farmers round were Prods, but that didn't make much difference. The market was 'nonsectarian,' as they'd say these days. Different schools, different dances. I couldn't walk out with Prod boys when I lived at home. But that's years back now. There was no politics down there, just bloody hard work."

He drove slowly out of town, onto the M2 motorway which within minutes runs into the open countryside, leaving the city with its smoke and its gibbetlike cranes and its grey slate roofs away behind the Black Mountain, which dominates the south of the city. It was the first time Harry had seen the fields and hedgerows, farms and cottages since he came in on the airport bus. The starkness of the contrast staggered him. It was near-impossible to believe that this was a country ravaged by what some called civil war. For a moment the impressions were tarnished by the rock-filled petrol drums outside a pub but that was a flash of the eye, near-subliminal, and then was gone in favor of the hills and the green of well-grassed winter fields.

Josephine slept in her seat, head back against the

column dividing the front and rear doors, her seat belt like some pompous decoration strapped across her breasts. Harry let his eyes stray from the endless, empty road to her.

"Just follow the Derry road, and wake me up when we get to the top of the Glenshane," she'd said.

The road slipped economically through the countryside till Harry reached Toome where the Bann came through, high and flooded from the winter rain, forcing its strength against the medieval eel-trapping cages that were the life-blood of the town. He slowed almost to a halt as he gingerly took the car over the ramps set across the road in front of the small whitewashed police station. Yards of bright corrugated-iron sheeting and mounds of sand-bags surrounded the buildings. It looked deserted. No bulbs showing at the top. After Toome he began to pick up speed. The road was straight again, and there was no other traffic. In front was the long climb up to Glenshane in the heart of the Sperrins. The rain gathered on the windshield, horizontal when it came but light and oc-casional.

As he came to the hills that divided the Protestant farmlands of the Ulster hinterland from Catholic Dun-given and Derry, Harry spotted a damp out-of-season picnic site on his right, and pulled into the car park. There was a sign marking the Pass and its altitude, a thousand feet above sea level. He stopped and shook Josephine's shoulder.

"Not so much of the blue skies and the promised land here. Looks more like it's going to tip down," he said.

"Doesn't matter. Come on, Mr. McEvoy, we're going to do some walking and talking. Walking first. Up there." She pointed far out to the right of the road, where the hill's squat summit merged toward the dark clouds.

"It's a hell of a way," he said, pulling on a heavy anorak.

"Won't do you any harm. Come on."

She led the way across the road and then up the bank and through the gap in the cheap wire fence where a succession of walkers had made a way.

Further on, there was a path of sorts to the top of the hill, made by the peat cutters at first and then carried on by the rabbits and the sheep. The wind picked up from the open ground and surged against them. Josephine had pushed her arm through the crook of his elbow, and walked in step half a pace behind him, using him part as shelter and part as battering ram as they forced their way forward into the near-gale. High above, a buzzard with an awesome dignity allowed itself to be carried on the thrusts and flows of the currents. Its huge wings moved with only a minimum of effort, holding position one hundred and fifty feet or so above the tiny runs fashioned by the creatures the bird lived off. The wind stung across Harry's face, pulling his hair back over his ears and slashing at his nose and eyes.

"I haven't been anywhere in a wind like this in years," he shouted across the few inches that separated them.

No reply. Just the wind hitting and buffeting against him.

"I said I haven't been in a wind like this in years. It's marvelous."

She rose on her toes, so that her mouth was in under his ear. "Wasn't it like this at sea, sometimes? Weren't there any gales and things all those years you were at sea?"

The cutting edge of it chopped into him. Retreat. Back out. "That was different. It's always different, sea wind, not like this."

Poor. Stupid. Not good and not convincing. He felt the tightening deep in his balls as he went on against the wind. Up a cul-de-sac and got cornered. Slackness. The elementary error. He flashed a look down and behind to where her head nestled into his coat. He contorted his head to look into her eyes, and saw what he expected. Quizzical, half confused, half amused: she had spotted it. The inconsistency that he'd known the moment he'd uttered it. Phrase by phrase, he went over it in his mind, seeking to undo the mistake and evaluate its damage. The second time he'd said it, that was when she would have been sure. The first time, not certain. The second time, certain. He'd semaphored it, then.

There were no more words as they went on to the summit. The low jigsaw of clouds scudded above them as they slung together against the power of the gale. In spite of the heaviness of the cloud, there was a clarity to the light of the day. The horizon was huge. Mountains to the north and south of them, the road leading back into the civilization of the hill farms to east and west.

A few yards beyond the cairn of stones that marked the hilltop, the rain running down over the years had sliced out a gully. They slid down into it, pushing against the sandy earth till they were at last sheltered. For a long time she stayed buried in his coat, pressed against his chest with only her black tossed hair for him to see. He felt the warmth from her seeping through the layers of clothes. For Harry it was a moment of beauty and isolation and complete tenderness with the girl. She broke it suddenly, crudely and fast.

"You slipped up a bit there, Harry boy. Didn't you? Not what I'd have expected from you."

Her face was still away from his. He couldn't see into her eyes. It hit home. He said nothing.

"A bit mixed up then, weren't you, Harry? Your story was, anyway. Merchant seaman who was never in a storm like they have in the Sperrins? A bit of a cock-up, Harry."

She'd relaxed in her voice now. Easy. In her stride. Matter-of-fact. "Harry . . ." And she twisted under him to turn into his face and look at him. Big eyes, mocking and piercing at the same time, and staring at him. "I'm saying you made something of a slip-up there. Not the first that you've had. But a good old balls-up, a right big one. Harry, it's a great bloody lie you're living. Right?"

He willed her now to let it go. Don't take it to the brink where explanation or action is necessary. Leave the loophole for the shrug and the open door.

In the town his inclination would have been to kill her, close his fingers on that white, long throat, remove the threat that jeopardized his operation. But on the mountain it was different. On the moorland of the upper hills, still crouched in the gouged-out hollow, and the wind singing its high note above and around them, it seemed time-wasting to deny what she had said. It wasn't in his orders to go strangling girls. That was logical as the solution, but not here.

"It's a bad place, this, for strangers these days, Harry. It will be rather worse if the boyos find your story isn't quite so pat as it should be. If they find you're rather more of a handful than they took you for, then it could be a very bad place. We're not all stupid here, you know. I'm not stupid. It didn't take the world to put eight and eight together after Saturday night, or ten and ten, or whatever you thought too much for an 'eejit' Mick girl who's an easy lay. It wasn't much I said to you. Just a little bit of chat. But there's half the bleeding British army round the wee girl's house for Sunday lunch. What did they find to talk to her about? God knows. Do you know, Harry? It was enough for the poor wee bitch to hang herself, God rest her. I mean, you weren't exactly covering your tracks, were you, Harry?"

The eyes that drove into him were still bright and re-laxed, looking for his reaction. As he listened she grew in strength and boldness. She would close for the kill. She would make the point. Sure of her ground, she began to goad him.

"There had to be something odd about you. Obvious. No family. But you come right back into the center of Belfast. But you've no friends. No one who knows you. People might have gone to a quiet place on the outskirts if they just wanted to come back and work. You've not come to fight, not for the Provos. They don't go to war from a guest house. The voice worried me, till Theresa died. I thought about it and worked it out then. The accent. It's good now. Very polished. You're quite Belfast, but you didn't use to be. So I don't reckon your chances, Harry, not when the Provos get a hold of you. There is some who can talk their way out of it, but I don't reckon you've a chance. Not unless you run."

Harry knew he should kill her. He looked fascinated at the soft skin, and the delicate line that searched down on either side of the little mound in her throat, saw the suspicion of a vein beneath the gentle surface. But there was no fear there, no terror in her face, no expectation of death.

They'd chosen Harry as a hard man, as a professional, able to do what was necessary, to go to the limits for his own survival. He could kill a man either in heat or from cold logic, and if the man's eyes betrayed his fear, that would make it easier, remove the complications.

The endless strands of black hair were playing across her face, taken past her eyes, encircling her mouth . . . and the warmth of her body close to him . . .

There had not been women who had to die in Aden. He was now in an area beyond his experience. Harry had heard it said once that to kill in close combat you had to act instinctively, there were no second chances, the will to cause death evaporates quickly, and does not come again except to the psychopath.

His hands were numbed and useless in the big gloves, and the moment had passed. He looked out onto the moorlands where the spears of sunlight played down from the cloud gaps. He had hesitated, and that would be enough. The buzzard still hovered high above him, and she was still talking.

She was tall, but not strong, he thought. She wouldn't be able to fight him off. He could kill her now. While she yapped on. It would be a long time before they found her. Could be the spring. She'd struggle a bit but she had no chance. But she knew he wouldn't. He could see that. There was no fear in her. The moment had gone earlier when he might have put his hands to her. It was gone now.

"If I went to the bookies more often," she went on, "I'd say you were a real slow horse. I'd say not to put any money on you reaching the finish. I mean it, Harry. I'm not just trying to frighten you, or anything daft. That's the way it is. If I was in your shoes, I'd be carrying spare knickers in my pocket. Well, don't just bloody sit there. Say something, Harry."

"There's not much to say, is there? What would you like to hear me say? If you go off to Portadown and see people there, they'll tell you who I am. Yes. I've been away a long time. That's why the accent was strange. I'm acclimatized. The girl—I can't explain that. How could I? I've no idea about it."

He could not have explained why he had gone back on the resolution he'd made so few minutes earlier not to get involved in a charade of deception. There was no conviction, no belief, and he communicated it to the girl.

"Balls," she said. She smiled at him and turned away to put her head back into the roughness of his coat. "That won't do, Harry. I don't believe you, neither do you. You're not a good enough liar. Whoever recruited you, and for whatever, did a poor job there."

"Let it go, then. Forget it, drop it." Pathetic. Was that all he had to say to the girl?

"Who are you, Harry? What did you come here for? When you touted on young Theresa, it was after I men-

tioned the man that did the killing in London. Is that why
you're here? You're not just run-of-the-mill intelligence.
There's more than that, I hope. I'd want to think my feller
was a wee bit special. What's the handle? The Man Who
Tracked the Most Wanted Man in Britain." She snorted
with amusement. "But seriously, Harry, is that what you
are? A little bit special? The Danby killing?"

She gave him time now. He was not ready. As an afterthought she said, "You don't have to worry, you know.
I won't split on you or anything like that. It's the national characteristic . . . the Ulster Catholics, we don't
inform. But they don't take well to spies here, Harry. If
they find you, God help you. And you'll need Him."

Harry started to move. "There's not very much to say.
What do you expect me to say? Confess . . . dramatic
revelations? Shout you down? Walk away and leave you?
Strangle you? What the hell do you want me to say?"

He got up out of the ditch and moved back toward the
summit of the hill, where the wind took him and fought
him, coming in crude rushes that caused him to hesitate
and sometimes give ground. The rain had intensified while
they had been in the ditch and now it lashed across his
body. He looked only at his feet, head hunched forward,
with his anorak hood up as he stumbled across the gorse
and heather, slipping and falling because he would not give
the attention to the ground in front of him. He'd gone a
hundred and fifty yards from her when she caught him and
thrust her arm into his. They went together down the hill
to the car, hurrying along the worn-out shape of the path.

They ran the last few yards to the car. She stood shaking
by the passenger door as he looked for the keys. It was
raining hard now, and once they were inside he switched
on the heaters. The water ran down the windows in wide
streams, and they were as cocooned and private as they
had been on the hill.

"What are you going to do if you find him?" she said.

"Are we serious now, or sparring still?"

"Serious now. Really serious. What will you do?"

"I'll kill him. Take him out. He's not for capturing. We pretend he is, and they mount the thing on that assumption. But he's dead if we get close enough to him."

"Just like that."

"Not just like that. I've got to find him first. I thought we had him after the dance. It hasn't moved from there. Up a bit of a blind alley now. Perhaps that's just talk about killing him. It should happen that way, but likely it won't. He'll be picked up, and it'll have sod all to do with me."

"Is that what you came for? Because a man kills a politico in England, then they send for you, and you come over here?"

"That's what I came for."

"There's a thousand and more have died here since it all started. And you come because of one of them. He was . . . wait for it, I'm working it out . . . yes, he was a tenth of one percent of all the people that have died here. That's not a bad statistic, is it? A tenth of a percent. He wasn't mourned here, you know. No one gave a damn. Pompous bugger. Always on the box telling us how well he was doing flushing out the gunmen from off our backs. Why was he so bloody special? They didn't send the big team over when they shot the senator in Strabane, or the UDR man who had all the land down the road in Derry. So why have you come?"

"They put the glove down, didn't they? That's what shooting Danby was about. To make us react and see how effectively we could counterattack. They killed him as a test of strength. We have to get the man and the team that did it. Either we do, or they've won. That's the game."

"So it's not just Queen and Country? Forces of Right against Forces of Evil?"

"It's nothing to do with that. They've challenged us. Given us a bait we cannot ignore. That's why we're in there kicking. We have to get the killer before the next time."

"Who are you, then, Harry? Who do you work for? Who pays your check?"

"You won't get that. You've too much already. Christ only knows why, I've——"

"And where does little Theresa fit into this big act? You're here to avenge a death. There's been one more already. How many more people get hurt, getting in the way, to make it still worthwhile for you?"

"Quite a lot."

"So, even in death, some count for more than others."

"Right."

She shifted the ground and softened the attack. "What sort of fellow is he, this man you're looking for?"

"I don't know much about him. I've an idea what he looks like, but not a good description. I don't know his name. He's a cool customer, and he'll be a crack shot. One of the top men, but they'll have kept him out of the main eye of things."

"When Theresa talked about him, do you know what it was made her say it?"

" 'Course I don't bloody know. How could I?"

"I mean, she wouldn't just bring a thing like that out of the blue, now would she? She said to me that the man that did the London killing was at that dance. He was there the whole time with his wife. She was looking such a misery that Theresa said she couldn't have been getting enough. That's how it all started. She said the cow couldn't be having it away, then she went into her own bit. That was to back her story up. She didn't know anything else."

"That's the truth, Josephine?"

"She didn't have to die, alone like that, just with those

bastard coppers round her. All she knew was what I said. I doubt she even knew the man's name."

She had started to shout again, spitting out the unsaid accusation at Harry. The weakness had gone. The heat of her attack burst around the tiny marooned inside of the car.

"You might as well have killed her yourself, Harry. She wasn't involved in any way at all. You came here with your challenges, and the bloody games you play. And a wee girl dies who had nothing to do with it. There's enough innocent people killed here without strangers coming and putting their fingers in and digging out more shit."

She crumpled then. Sobbing rhythmically and noiselessly. Gazing into the steamed-up window beside her. The rain was still falling.

Harry was deciding what he should do during his return to Belfast. His ego was rumpled by the way the girl had broken through him. He ought to have killed her up there on the hill, but she had said she was no threat to him, and he believed it. His ego was of less importance, though, than the news she had just given him. The man whom he searched for had been at the caeli the previous weekend.

She shook herself, trying to shrug away her misery. "Come on, I want a drink. There's a pub just down the road. You can't stop for the dead. Not in Ulster. Like they say, it all goes on. I should have dropped it ages ago. Come on, let's go have a couple of hot tods."

She leaned over and kissed him lightly, again on the cheek. Then she began to adjust her face, working with deftness from her little pouch that came out of her bag, painting over the reddened and flushed valleys under her eyes.

When she had finished she said, "Don't worry, hero boy, I won't tell the big bad Provos about you. But if you've ever taken advice, I'm telling you, don't hang about.

Or whatever medal you're after will have to go in the box with you."

They drove down the hill to where a pub and petrol station were nestled in a redoubt cut out from the big stone. He ordered the drinks she wanted—Irish, with hot water and sugar and lemon.

The faint sunlight that had seen them out of Belfast was long since gone as Harry drove back on the shiny watered road into the city. They spoke hardly a word all the way, and Harry dropped her off where he had met her in the morning, on the corner of Grosvenor and the Falls. Just before he stopped, he asked her where she lived so that he could drop her at the door. She said it would be better at the main road.

"When will I see you again?" he said as she climbed out of the car. The traffic was hustling them.

"Next week, at Mrs. Duncan's. You'll see me there."

"And we'll go out somewhere? Have a drink?"

"Perhaps."

She knew so much more than she had wanted to, or was equipped to handle. What had started as something of a game had become considerable enough to subdue her into a morose silence most of the way home. She darted out of the car, and without a wave disappeared into the Clonard side streets.

Harry dropped the car off at the garage and walked back to Delrosa. He remembered now something Davidson had said to him at Dorking: "Look, Harry. Just as important as getting the background right, and knowing what the hullaboo is about, is how you are going to stand up to this yourself. The thing I cannot gauge is how you'll soak up the punishment of just existing there. You could have an isolation problem—loneliness. No one to confide in, not part of a local team, completely on your own. Unless you're aware of it, and bolt it down, there'll come a time when you'll want to tell someone about yourself, however obliquely, however much at a tangent. You'll say now 'Never, never, in a month of whatevers,' but believe me, it'll happen, and you have to watch it."

It had sounded so astonishing then, Davidson fumbling his way into it because it embarrassed him that his chosen man could possibly fall into so well-signposted a pit, embarrassed even to suggest it. But that's the way it was, because Davidson knew what it was about, was the only one of them who knew what it was about. How many people could transpose themselves into the hostility of this community, live day in, day out with the fear and the strain and the isolation?

Don't go on with it. Harry boy, let it rest there. Don't let it infect you. The cancer of doubt spreads fast enough, Harry. Drop it.

The Man decided he would go for Rennie the next day. Sunday.

The reports that were available from the minders who had been cautiously watching the policeman suggested that he made a habit of going to the interrogation center on Sunday afternoons. He stayed a few hours and reached home around seven in the evening. It fitted with the plan that the Man had made. He discussed none of this with his wife, but as his preoccupation with the killing grew, they moved about their house, two strangers under the same roof. Life was carried on with a series of gestures and monosyllabic phrases.

The Man had been informed of the arrangement by which he would take possession of the Armalite rifle that he would use for the attack, and he had reported up the chain on the timing and the date that he would want the operation set in motion. It had been suggested to him that the Armalite was an unsuitable weapon for a close-quarters killing, but in the face of his wishes the point had not been pressed.

The huge power of the weapon excited him to such a degree that he could think of taking no other. The bullet that he intended should kill Rennie would leave the barrel at a muzzle velocity of 3250 feet per second. He had read the statistic in a sales brochure and it staggered and exhilarated him. It weighed slightly less than seven pounds and would fit comfortably into the poacher-style pocket he had fashioned on the inside of his raincoat. And since he would be far from his safe base area, if he was intercepted by the army or police, the sharp crack of the Armalite would be enough to send his enemy scurrying for cover for the few seconds he might need to get clear. He had asked for two of the weapon's thirty-round magazines, just in case.

A brandy in his hand, Frost sat on his own in a corner of the mess at Lisburn, mulling over the magazines of weekly comment with which he prided himself he kept abreast. He made a point of working his way through the dog-eared *Spectator, Economist* and *Statesman*, and it had become sufficient of a ritual for other officers of equal rank to leave him to himself, when on any other evening they would have joined him.

The mess waiter came over and hesitated beside the chair before plunging in. "Excuse me, sir. Sorry to trouble you. There's a reporter from *The Times* on the phone. Says he needs to speak to you. Says its urgent. He said to say he was sorry to trouble you, but he thought you'd want to hear what he had to say."

Frost nodded, pulled himself up and followed the waiter to the phone cubicle.

"Hello, Frost here. Ah, yes, we've met. A leaving party, in the summer, right? What can I do for you?"

He listened without interruption as the reporter read to him the story that was being prepared for Monday's editions. The Provisional IRA had tipped off one of their favored reporters in Belfast that they believed the British had infiltrated a new secret agent into the city on a mission so sensitive that only the GOC, General Fairbairn, had been told of it. The Provos were claiming that the operation had caused great anger among British army staff officers in HQ. On Monday the story would appear in Dublin papers as well as British ones, and the IRA would be calling for special vigilance from the people to seek out the spy. The Provos, Frost was told, were saying this was a special operation and one quite different from anything mounted before.

"I'm not expecting you to comment or anything, Colonel. This is a private call, just to let you know what's going on. Good night."

The Colonel mouthed his thanks.

He flicked the receiver's buttons up and down till the operator came onto the line.

"Evening. Frost here. GOC at home, please." When he was connected, he told the General he needed to see him immediately. There was no hint of an apology for disturbing the senior soldier in Northern Ireland at that time of night. That would not have been Frost's style. His early-warning antennae were already jangling with the possibility of a major intelligence scandal.

The General and Frost talked for an hour, and agreed to have another meeting at eight on Sunday morning with the benefit of further information. They would then, they thought, get onto the MOD and demand Harry's immediate recall before the awkward business of dragging him out of some hedgerow with an IRA bullet in the back of his head became necessary.

Across the city in Mrs. Duncan's boarding house Harry was asleep, He had been somewhat unnerved by the brutality with which his cover had been stripped aside by the girl. On his return he had lifted the carpet and

floorboards at the place where the revolver was hidden.
The Smith and Wesson, with its six chambers loaded, was
now wrapped in a towel under his pillow, in the corner
over by the wall. As a day, it had been a bloody fiasco.
A shambles. Back in the reality of the city, with the
hardness of the gun near to him, he felt lunatic at what
had passed between him and the girl in the wind and the
rain on the hillside. Out of his tiny mind.

■ 14 ■

Harry was up early again that Sunday morning, and out of
the house well before eight to make his way down to the
city center and the phone that he could use to talk to
Davidson. This time he took the revolver with him, in
his coat pocket, with the roughness of its shape shielded
by the length of the covering anorak. The decision to
take the gun had been an instinctive one, but now that
he had it, and out on the streets and loaded, the situation
that he faced was all the more clear. For the first time
since they had flown him in from Germany he felt uncertain. That was the girl. Up that bloody mountain talking a load of slop when he should have been concentrating,
then letting her go last night, back into the warren that
she shared with his opposition. Madness, and it aggravated
him. Perhaps also there was the knowledge that the trail
which had seemed so warm a week ago had now chilled.

The Smith and Wesson jarred against him as he stepped
out down the Falls to the phone and communication and
Davidson. There were no eyes watching him after he left

Delrosa: the orders of the battalion intelligence officer were being strictly obeyed.

He dialed the number, three-seven-zero-four-six-eight-one. After several desultory clicks he heard it ringing at the other end. It was answered.

"It's Harry here. How are the family?"

Davidson was in early too, and hoping for the call. "Very well, they liked the postcards."

"I've got a bit of a problem." Pause. "I've been blown by this girl, the one that helped me with the business I gave you last week. What a cock-up that was." Pause. "But anyway, putting the finger on that bird has led this girl straight back to me. She knows what I am. Not who I am but what we're here for. I want you to take her out. Get her out of the scene for the duration. You can do that, can't you? She tells me that the Man we want was at the same dance that we were at, a fortnight ago. I half felt I remembered him. But the face wasn't quite right on the photokit. If it's the Man, then the army pulled him in, but that looked routine. He was just one of the ones that were rounded up. He had a woman with him, presumably his wife, in a yellow trouser suit. Have you got all that?"

"I've got it on tape, Harry. Anything else?"

"Hell, what more do you want? No, that's all I have at the moment. But look, I don't want the living daylights bashed out of this girl. I just want her lifted out so she doesn't get involved any more. She's Josephine Laverty, lives with her mother in one of those little streets in Clonard, up off the Springfield on the right. You'll find her, but get to her quick, there's a good lad."

"We'll work something out. Don't worry."

"There's not really much else. It's a bit chill here at the moment, but I think I'm settled in here okay. If you don't wrap it up on what I've just given you, then it'll be a very long time. Do we have time for that?"

"We've plenty, as long as you think it's worth it, Harry.

But we ought, as you say, to kill it this time. It was a hell of a balls-up over the other girl. There was a lot of praise at this end for what you got. Great satisfaction. You're all right yourself, are you? No one following you about, no awkward questioning? Our assessment is that they would be right up to you by now if they were about to blow you, and that you'd probably have been aware of something. That's not just supposed to cheer you up, but if no one is sniffing around you, then it should mean you're okay."

"No, there's nothing like that." Harry said. "I'm working too. Job in a scrap yard in Andersonstown, and paying well. Back to the scene, then."

"Harry, look, you ought to know this. I got well and truly chewed up over your living arrangements, us not knowing. It's not only unusual, it's unprofessional as well. Very unprofessional."

"The whole thing's unprofessional," Harry replied. "Nothing's going to change. You're not going to order me, are you? I don't think it would help, but it's my neck. Thanks very much for caring. Cheers, maestro."

" 'Bye, Harry, I understand. No one else does. Take care, and listen to the news. As soon as you hear we've got him, come whistling out. Give me a call first if you can, but head on up to the airport like you've got a bomb up your backside. Take care."

Harry put the phone down and hurried out into the cold and the long walk back up the Falls. He was concerned that they should get the girl out of the quagmire, and fast, before her involvement became too great for her to extricate herself . . . before she followed the other girl he'd brought into the game.

But things did not move fast that Sunday.

Twenty minutes after Harry had rung off, Davidson called the Permanent Under Secretary. He caught him on the point of going to early-morning service. The bad news first. Always play it that way. Davidson liked to say. Kick them a bit, then produce the magic sponge. They like it better. The agent was still declining to name a contact point. Not refusing, but declining. Don't want to make an order of it. Told him it's damned stupid, but can't do more than that. As he says, it's his neck. Our scandal if he catches it, mind, but his neck for all that. Now the bonus. Good information out of our chap. He'll like that.

"Keep that for a moment," snapped the civil servant. "I've had calls in the night. GOC has been on, and that man of his, Frost of intelligence. Bloody misnomer, that. They want our fellow out, and kicking up a hell of a scene. They think he's blown."

Davidson bit at his tongue. He heard at the other end of the line the Under Secretary call for the rest of the family to go on.

"There's been some sort of leak. Like a bloody sieve, that place. The papers have got a story from the opposition that they know a big man has been put in. There's panic stations over there. Anyway, the order is get the chap out or the General says he'll go to the PM. Consolation is that the men over there say they don't think the IRA have a name. But that'll come soon enough. And you haven't an idea where we could go and just take hold of him?"

"All I have is that he works in a scrap merchant's in Andersonstown. Nothing more."

"That won't do us much good till Monday morning."

"He's done well again, our chap. The man we want was actually at the dance where Harry was the other night. The military had him, and must have let him go, or are holding him on something else . . ."

"Look, for God's sake, Davidson, I'm at home. I'm going to church. There's no point feeding me that sort of material over the phone. Talk to Frost direct. He'll be

in his office, prancing about. He's having a bloody field
day. But if this Harry man should call again, get him out.
That now is an instruction."

Davidson had always had to admit that he enjoyed the
complicated paraphernalia of introducing the agent into
the operations theater. He could reflect on it now, with the
phone quiet and his superior racing down the country
lanes for his communion. Davidson had been on the old
Albania team. There had been the months with the undercover Greeks and Turks in Cyprus. Three years' second-
ment to the Singapore government to train bright-faced
little policemen in the techniques of urban infiltration and
maintaining men in a hostile environment. There was a
gap in his wide experience. He recognized it. The men he
sent into the field, or discussed sending, were all, as Davidson saw them, foreigners. The involvement with the men
who listened to his lectures or acted under his orders was
loose, and in no way binding.

With Harry it had become quite different. The danger
that he now knew his agent to be facing numbed Davidson to a degree that almost ashamed him. He had long
seen himself as a tough, near-ruthless figure, the man in
charge who put his agents onto the ground without sentiment or personal feeling. His defensive walls were being
breached, he realized, as he thought of his man across the
water, with the enemy closing in on him.

Not a bloody idea Harry had of it, and he'd just been
told that all was well and looked good. That made him
vulnerable.

Davidson had a growing feeling of nausea when he
remembered how Harry had been brought to Dorking.
Damn-all chance he'd had of backing out of the operation.
The Prime Minister personally authorized the setting up
of the team, and we've chosen you as the most suitable
man. What chance did he have of side-stepping that little
lot? He'd been belted off on the plane on a wild-goose

chase. If he's not out of there soon, he'll be number a thousand and bloody something pushing up daisies.

He picked up his phone and called Frost direct, in his office, where he'd been told he'd be. At the other end of the line the serving colonel in intelligence left the London-based civilian with no illusions as to what he thought of armchair administrators organizing undercover work without consultation or know-how. Davidson resigned himself to it, letting it blaze over him. Between the interruptions he read over the transcript of Harry's message. He ended on a high note.

"He did pretty well with the first lot of stuff we gave you. We were disappointed in our team that it didn't come to much. You should have it sewn up this time, don't you think, old boy?"

Frost didn't rise. It was a juicy and wriggling bait, but the office was crowded and it was not the day for telephone brawling. That would come after this merry little show was wrapped up and in mothballs—what was left of it. He called the Springfield Road police to request the locating and picking up of the girl Josephine Laverty of Clonard, and then turned his attention to the matter of the Man having been in, and presumably out of, military hands on Saturday night two weeks back. Cool bastard he must be, appraised the colonel. In between the calls he canceled his Sunday-morning nine holes with G2 Ops.

Other operations had gone wrong before, Davidson recalled. There were those endless nights when they parachuted Albanians into the marshlands between the sea and Tirana, and waited in vain with their OSS colleagues for the chatter of radio signals that would let them know all was well. When the Cypriot agents he had controlled had disappeared, there had been days of nagging uncertainty until the bodies showed up—generally tortured and always shot through the back of the head. But they were only aliens, so the recriminations were short-lived, the kickbacks muted. But if they lost Harry, then the ramifications would be huge, and public. The roundup of scapegoats would be spectacular, Davidson had no doubt of that. The Permanent Under Secretary would have faded from the picture by then, would have fetched his sliding carpet out. The old hack would be left holding the baby.

He called his assistant in from the outer office, where, thank God, the man spent most of his time, and told him to watch the phones. He was to tape all calls, regardless, on the cassette recorder, whichever phone they came through on. He slipped out of the building. Sunday morning in Covent Garden. Some sunlight about on the upper reaches of the big buildings. Piles of fruit and vegetable boxes. No people. Davidson walked to the small grocer that he knew would be open and bought bread, and cartons of milk, coffee and biscuits, some butter and lemon curd. The total was about all his cooking facilities would cope with.

There had been no calls when he returned. He phoned his wife, told her he would be in town for a day or so, and not to worry. She didn't sound as if she did. There was an army-issue camp bed in the wardrobe behind his desk, excruciatingly uncomfortable but better than nothing. It would be a long wait, and no one to spend it with but the boring young man they'd sent along to give him a hand. Davidson had realized soon that they had not fully briefed his assistant on what was happening. He had no intention himself of enlightening him. They were on stand-by now, operational twenty-four hours.

That same lunchtime, Seamus Duffryn was summoned to a house in Beachmount and told by the battalion intelligence officer to resume close surveillance on McEvoy. Duffryn was told a squad was going out in the afternoon to find a friend of McEvoy, a girl who had been out with him. Josephine Laverty from Clonard.

A few hundred yards away in Springfield Road, the British army unit that had been asked to find the girl was puzzled that it had no record of her or her mother living in the area. There was no reason why they should have, as the house was in the name of Josephine's uncle, Michael O'Leary. A little after three o'clock the unit reported in that it had been unable to locate the girl. By then a critical amount of the available time had run out.

It took more than two hours from the time Frost called the army headquarters dominating Ardoyne and told them of the tip to the moment when they identified the Man. First the troops who had taken part in the search operation at the caeli had to be located. The lieutenant who had led the raid was in Norfolk on weekend leave, and there was no answer to his telephone. The sergeant, the next senior man out, recalled that he had busied himself near the door on security, but he was able to name the six soldiers who had carried out the split-up question-and-answer work. Private Jones was now in Berlin, but Lance Corporal James Llewellyn was picked up by a Saracen from a foot patrol on the far side of the battalion area. There was no written record, of course. That, along with Jones, were the only two pieces of evidence of the confrontation, and both had now disappeared. Llewellyn stared at the photokit issued in London that had been brought up from the guardroom.

"That's the one it's like, if it's any of them. It's Downs. It's not a great likeness. It's not easy to pick him on that picture. But if he was there, that's the one it was. There was his woman there, in yellow. She ran out across to him."

With the name they attacked the filing system. Billy Downs. Ypres Avenue, No. 41. There'd been a spot check on his story about being down in Cork with his mother.

The guards had been fast for a change, and had cleared him of involvement. They said he'd been there through that period. There'd been a query about him because he was away from home. Otherwise, clean with nothing known. The net inside the headquarters spread wider, to include the policeman who had seen him that night in the small hours.

"He was very cool. Not even a sweat on his palms. I know, as I looked."

It was into the afternoon that they called Frost back.

"We think we've located the man you want. He's Billy Downs, without an 'e' on the end. Ypres Avenue, wife and kids. Very quiet, from what we've seen of him. Unemployed. His story stuck after the guards ran a check on the alibi he gave us to account for his long absence from the area. There was no other reason to hold him. Like to point out that the chaps that have actually seen this fellow say that he's not that like the pics you put out. Much fatter in the face, I'm told. Perhaps you'll let us know what you want done. We've a platoon on immediate. We can see pretty much down the street; I've an OP in the roof of a mill, right up the top."

Frost growled back into the phone, "I'd be interested in knowing if Mr. Downs is currently at home."

"Wait one." As he held on for the answer, Frost could hear the distant sounds of the unit operations room as they called up the OP on a field telephone. "Not quite so hot, I'm afraid. They log comings and goings. We think Downs left his home, that's number forty-one, around twenty-five minutes ago. That's fifteen-o-five hours precisely that he went out. But he goes in and out pretty regularly. No reason to think he won't be back in a bit."

"I'd like it watched," said Frost, "but don't move in yet, please. This number will be manned through the evening and the night. Call me as soon as you see him."

The Man was on his way by car up the Lisburn Road at the time the observation post overlooking Ypres Avenue was warned to look out for him. The two soldiers had noted him as soon as he came from his front door and began the walk up the hill away from them to one of the decreed exits from Ardoyne. When the message came through on the radiotelephone to the troops, the Man was just out of the heartland, standing in no man's land at the top of the Crumlin waiting for his pickup. This was neither Protestant nor Catholic territory. Side streets on either side of the road shut off with great daubed sheets of corrugated iron. Two worlds split by a four-lane road with barricades to keep people from each other's throats. Scrawled on one side was "Up the Provos" and "British Army Out," and beyond the opposite pavement the message of "Fuck the Pope" and "UVF."

He was edgy waiting in daylight beside such a busy road, one used heavily by military traffic, and the relief showed in his face when the Cortina pulled up alongside him and the driver bent sideways to open the passenger door. The car had been hijacked in the Falls thirty-five minutes earlier. A moment later they moved off, weaving their way through the city. By the crossroads in the center of the sprawling middle-class suburb, the car turned left and up one of the lanes that lead to the Down countryside through a small belt of woods. They turned off among the trees.

The driver unlocked the trunk and handed over the Armalite rifle. It was wrapped in a transparent plastic bag. The Man checked the firing mechanism. It was a different weapon from the one that he had used before in his attack on the patrol, and was issued by a quite unconnected quartermaster. But the rifle came from the same original source—Howa Industries, of Nagoya in Japan. It had been designed as a hunting weapon, and that astonished him. What sort of animal did you take a killing

machine of this proven performance to hunt? He released
the catch on the stock to check that the folding hinge was
in working order. He was passed the two magazines,
glanced them over and fitted one deep into the attachment
slot under the belly of the gun. He activated a bullet up in
the breach, and flicked with his thumb at the safety catch
to ensure it was engaged. The volunteer at the wheel
watched the preparation with fascination.

With the stock folded, the Man pushed the rifle down
into the hidden pocket. "I don't know how long I'll be,"
he said. "For God's sake, don't suddenly clear off, or anything smart. Stick here. At least till midnight."

They were the only words the Man spoke before he
disappeared into the growing darkness to walk the half-
mile toward Rennie's house. The only words of the whole
journey. The teenager left behind with the car among the
trees subsided, shivering, into the driver's seat to wait for
his return.

The regular Sunday-afternoon visit to the office to clear
the accumulation of paper work off his desk was no longer
a source of controversy between Rennie and his wife. It
had been at first, with accusations of "putting the family
into second place," but the increasing depression of the
security situation in the province had caused her to relent.

It was now understood that she and the two girls,
Margaret and Fiona, would have their tea, watch some
television and then wait for him to get home before bed-
time.

Over the last four years Janet Rennie had become used
to the problems of being a policeman's wife. A familiar
sight now was the shoulder holster slung over the bedside
chair when he had an extra hour in bed on Saturday
mornings, before the weekly trip to the out-of-town supermarket. So, too, were the registration plates in the garage,
which he alternated on the car, and around the house the

mortice locks on all the doors, inside and out. At night all these were locked with a formal ritual of order and precedence, lest one should be forgotten, and the detective's personal firearm lay in the half-opened drawer of the bedside table, on which rested the telephone, which as often as not would ring deep into the night.

Promotion and transfer to Belfast had been hard at first. The frequency of the police funerals they attended, along with the general level of danger in the city, had intimidated her. But out of the fear had come a fierce-rooted hatred of the IRA enemy.

Janet Rennie had long since accepted that her husband might not last through the troubles, might be assassinated by one of those wild-eyed, cold-faced young men whose photographs she saw attached to the outside of the files he brought home in the evening and at weekends. She didn't shrink from the possibility that she might ride in the black Austin Princess behind the flag and the band to a grey country churchyard. When he was late home she attacked her way through the knitting, her therapy along with the television set. He was often out late, seldom in before eight or nine—and that was a good evening. But she felt pride for the work he did, and shared something of his commitment.

The girls, seven and five, were in the bright, warm living room of the bungalow, kneeling together on the treated sheepskin rug in front of the open fire, watching the television when the the doorbell rang.

"Mama! Mama! Front doorbell," Margaret shouted to her mother at the back, too obsorbed herself to drag away from the set.

Janet Rennie was making sandwiches for tea, her mind taken by fish-paste fillings and the neatness of the arrangement of the little bread triangles. They had become a treat, these Sunday teas, the girls and their mother play-

ing at gentility with enthusiasm. With annoyance, she·
wondered who it could be.

The bell rang again.

"Come on, Mama. It's the front door." Margaret resigned herself. "Do you want me to go?"

"No, I'll do it. You stay inside, and you're not going
out to play on your bikes at this time of night."

She wiped her hands on the cloth hanging beside the
sink, and went to the front door. As her hand came in
toward the Yale lock that was always on, she noticed that
the chain had been left off since the children came back
from playing with their friends of three doors down. It
should have been fastened. She should have fastened it
before she opened the door. But she ignored the rules her
husband had laid down and pulled the door back.

"Excuse me, is it Mrs. Rennie?"

She looked at the shortish man standing there on her
front doorstep, hands in his coat pockets, an open smile
on his face, dark hair nicely parted.

"Yes, that's right."

Very quietly he said, "Put your hands behind your
head, keep them there and don't shout. Don't make any
move. I know the kids are here."

She watched helplessly as through his coat, unbuttoned
and opened, he drew out the ugly squat black shape of the
Armalite. Holding it in one hand, with the stock still
folded, he prodded her with the barrel back into the hallway. She felt strange, detached from what was happening,
as if it were a scenario. She had no control over the situation, she knew that. He came across the carpet past the
stairs toward her, flicking the door closed with his heel.
It clattered as it swung to, the lock engaging behind him.

"Who is it, Mama?" From behind the closed door of
the lounge Fiona called out.

"We'll go in there now. Just remember this. If you try
anything, I'll kill you. You, and the children. Don't forget

it when you want to play the bloody heroine. We're going to sit in there and wait for that bastard husband of yours. Right? Is the message all plain and clear and understood?"

The narrow barrel of the Armalite dug into her flesh just above the hip as he pushed past her to the door and opened it. Their mother was half into the room before Fiona turned, words part out of her mouth but frozen when she saw the Man with the rifle. Even to a child three months short of her fifth birthday, the message was brilliantly obvious. The girl rose up on her knees, her face clouding from astonishment to terror. As if in slow motion, her elder sister registered the new mood. Wide-eyed, and with the brightness fading from her, she saw first her sister's face, then her mother standing hunched, as if bowed down by some great weight, and behind her the Man with the small shiny rifle in his right hand.

Too frightened to scream, the elder girl remained stock-still till her mother reached her, gathered the children to her and took them to the sofa.

The three of them held tightly to each other, as on the other side of the room the Man eased himself down into Rennie's chair. From there he was directly facing the family, who were huddled away in the front corner of the sofa to be as far as possible from him. He also had a clear view of the door into the room, and of the window beyond it at the far edge of the lounge. It was there that he expected the first sign of Rennie's return, the headlights of the policeman's car.

"I'll warn you for the last time, missus. Any moves, anything clever, and you'll be dead, the lot of you. Don't think, Mrs. Rennie, when it comes to it, that you're the only one at risk. That would be getting it very wrong, a bad miscalculation. If I shoot you, I do the kids as well. We'll leave the TV on, and you'll sit there. And just re-

member I'm watching you. Watching you all the time.
So be very careful. Right, missus?"

The Man paused and let the effect of his words sink in
on the small room.

"We're just going to wait," he said.

■ 15 ■

The four men sent to question Josephine Laverty had
none of the problems finding her that the British army
unit in Springfield Road had encountered. Smiling broadly,
the oldest in the group, and the leader, suggested that old
Mrs. Laverty might care to go into the kitchen and take
herself a good long cup of tea.

They took Josephine up to her bedroom far from the
mother's ears. One of the younger men drew the curtains,
cutting out the frail shafts of sunlight, and took up
position by the window. Another stood at the door. The
third of the volunteers stood behind a chair and cursorily
suggested Josephine should sit. The older man they called
Frank, and he was treated with respect and with caution.

The girl was poorly equipped to handle an interrogation.
Frank's opening question was harmless enough, and he was
as astonished as the other three men in the room at the
way she collapsed.

"This fellow McEvoy, that you've been going with. Who
is he?"

There had been no reply, only a dissolve as her head
went down to her lap and she buried her cheeks and her
eyes and ears in the palms of her hands.

"Who is he?" Frank was insistent. "Who is he, where does he come from?"

"You know who he is. Why come to me for it? You know well enough."

Frank paced up and down, short steps, continually twisting around toward the girl when he lost sight of her, moving back and worth between the window and the door, skirting the single bed littered with the girl's clothes.

"I want you to tell me." He emphasized it. Like an owl with a barely whelped mouse, a stoat with a rabbit, he dominated the cringing girl on the wooden chair before him.

"I want it from you. D'ye hear? I've not much time."

Josephine shook her head, partly from the convulsion of her collapse, and reeled away from him as he swung his clenched fist backhanded across her face. Her knuckles took much of the force of the blow, but through the splayed fingers across her eyes she saw the blood welling close and then breaking the skin at the back of her hands.

Frank could see that what had been put to him as somewhat of a routine questioning had become rather more complex. The fear and hesitation of the girl had alerted him. Her inability to answer a simple explicit question. Frank knew McEvoy only as a lodger at the girl's employer's guest house . . . been out with him once or twice. A fair-looking piece, he'd probably knocked her off, but that wouldn't be enough to put her there doubled up and sniffing.

"I'm getting impatient, girl. To him you owe none of the loyalty you should give to us."

He weighed up whether he would need to hit her again.

She nodded her head, very slightly at first, then merging into the positive move of acquiescence and surrender. Frank held back. He would not have to hit her again.

She straightened up, steadying herself as she prepared the words. "He's with the British, isn't he? You know that.

He's British. I don't know what he does, but he's been sent to live among us. He's looking for the man that killed the politico. Over in London. That's his job. To find that man. He said when he found him he'd exterminate him."

She stopped, leaving the shadowy little room quiet. Below she could hear her mother about the kitchen, picking things up and putting them down.

Josephine saw the enormity of what she had said. She'd told him, hadn't she, that his truth was safe with her. One backhander and she spilled it all. She remembered it, outside the pub on the hill at Glenshane. She'd promised it then, when she'd told him to quit.

Frank stared intently at her. "His job was as an agent in here? He's a British agent? Sent to infiltrate us? Holy Jesus!"

"You knew? You knew, didn't you? You wouldn't have come if you hadn't known."

The room was near-dark now. Josephine could barely make out the men in the room—only the one silhouetted at the window by the early street light. Her mother called up for tea for her visitors. No one answered. The old lady lingered at the bottom of the stairs, waiting for the reply, then went back to the kitchen, accepting and perhaps understanding the situation and unable to intervene.

The girl wavered one last time in her loyalties. Upbringing, tradition, community—all came down on the scales and balanced there against the laugh and adulthood and bed of Harry. But there was the wee girl with the tossing feet and the tightening stocking, and the obscenity and the misery of death in the police cell, and that wiped Harry from the slate. She spoke again.

"He was the one that shopped Theresa, the girl that hung herself. She said she'd been with the man that did the London killing, but he couldn't perform. Harry tipped the army about it. He said the killing was a challenge to the British, and they had to get the man who did it, and kill him. Something like that, just to show who ran things. He told me this yesterday."

The volunteers said nothing, their imagination stretched by what the girl said. Frank spoke. "Was he close to the man he was looking for? Did he know his name? Where he lived? What he looked like? Just how much did the bastard know?"

"He said he thought he knew what he looked like." She saw Theresa again in her mind, heard her giggling in the small space around the basin outside the lock-up closet. That was the justification, that was enough . . . to see the girl's face. Hear her choking. "He said he was a good shot and a cool bugger, that's what he called him. And, yes, they were looking, he said, for a man who would be out of the main eye of things. That was the exact phrase he used."

"And you, how did you spot this highly trained British assassin, little girl?"

"I spotted him because of a silly thing. You have to believe me, but we were on the Sperrins yesterday. He said he'd been in the merchant navy and sailed all over, but the gale on the mountain seemed to shake him a bit. I said to him it wasn't very good if he'd been to sea as much as he said. Then he didn't hide it any more. He seemed to want to talk about it."

Clever little bitch, thought Frank.

"Is he in regular touch, communication, with his controller?"

"I don't know,"

"Is he armed?"

"I don't know that either. I never saw a gun. I've told you all I know. That's God's truth."

"There's one little problem for you, Miss Josephine." Frank's voice had a cutting edge to it now, something metallic, cold and smooth. "You haven't explained to me yet how this British agent came to hear about Theresa and what she was saying about the London man. You may need a bit of time for that, you bastard whore. Treacherous little bitch."

He came very close to her now. She could smell the tobacco and beer on his breath and the staleness of sweat on his clothes. He hadn't shaved that day, and his face was a prickled, lumpy mass.

"Just work it out," he said. "Then tell the lads, because they'll be waiting for an answer. To us you're nothing, dirt, scum, shit. You've shopped one of your own . . . a wee girl who hanged herself rather than talk to the fucking British. You betrayed her. You betrayed your lover boy as well. We'll put it about, you know, and we'll let the military know as well. You'll find somewhere to run, but there'll be sod-all people to help you get there, you little cow. But then, when these lads have finished with you, you'll be thinking twice before you go drop your knickers to another Britisher."

Frank turned away and walked to the door. He said to the man who was standing there, "It's just a lesson this time, Jamie. Nothing permanent and nothing that shows. Something just for her to remember, to think about for a long time. Then lose yourselves. If we need you later, we know where you'll be, so split from here. And, little girl, if you've half an inch of sense in your double-dealing painted head, you'll not mention what's happened here tonight, nor what's going to."

He went out the door and down the steep staircase. The old woman saw him in the hall as she turned in her chair by the fire and looked at him. He smiled at her. "Don't worry, lady," he said, "I can find my way out. You just stay where you are."

The three younger men followed him through the door fifteen minutes later. They left Josephine doubled up on the bed, wheezing for air and holding the soft solar plexus of her stomach, fighting the pain and willing it away. Her clothes lay scattered in the corners of the room where the men had ripped them off her.

"Right on your bloody flesh, you little bitch, where it hurts, and where it'll last."

She'd thought they were going to rape her, but instead they simply beat her. She curled herself up, fetal position, her arms protecting her breasts and lower stomach, thighs clamped together. That was how she stayed after they'd gone. Her breath came back to her soon, and after that there was the long, deep aching of the muscles and, mingled with it, the agony of the betrayal. Betrayal of Theresa. Betrayal of Harry.

Perhaps the men had been sensitive about beating up a girl, perhaps it was the sight of her nakedness, but the job was not thoroughly done. The effect soon faded. There was time to think then. Frank would have gone straight to the house to find Harry. He'd be taken, tortured and shot—that would come later, or tomorrow morning. Her reasoning made any thought of warning Harry irrelevant. They would have him already, but did she want to warn him? One good screw, and what had he done? Lifted her bedroom tattle from pillow confidence to military intelligence information. Bugger the bastard. Let him rot with it.

When her mother came up the stairs late in the evening, she was still doubled up, still holding her stomach, and cold now on her skin. The old lady looped the girl's nightdress over her head and twisted her feet under the bedclothes. She spent some minutes picking the clothes up from the floor, showing no more interest in those that were torn than those that formed the general muddle on the floor.

Twice during that Sunday evening Davidson phoned through to Frost. The first-floor office had, with the com-

ing of darkness, taken on the appearance of a bunker.
The telephone that was specified for outgoing calls was
on the floor beside the canvas camp bed, now erected.

Davidson was curtly told there was no information, and
was reminded that he'd already been told that he would
be notified as soon as anything was known. The earlier
elation had left him, and he allowed Frost the last word on
"an operation so inefficient that you cannot even get in
touch with your man when you need to get him out."

But for all his bark Frost was now sufficiently involved
in the operation to call Springfield Road, wait while the
commanding officer was brought to speak to him, and
stress the urgency with which the girl Laverty should be
found.

In their aerie high above Ardoyne two soldiers looked
down on Ypres Avenue. There were no street lights, old
casualties of the conflict, but they watched the front door
of No. 41 from the image intensifier, a sophisticated visual
aid that washed everything with a greenish haze and
which enabled them to see the doorway with great clarity.
On the hour they whispered the same message into their
field telephone. No one had used the front door of the
house.

Frank did not go near Delrosa that night. He had ridden
up to Andersonstown on his bicycle in search of his
battalion commander. It was arranged that at midnight
he would be taken to meet the Belfast Brigade commander.
Frank knew his name but had never met him.

From his home the Permanent Under Secretary had
authorized the sending of a photograph of Harry to Belfast. The next morning, Monday, it was to be issued to
troops who would raid the various Andersonstown scrap
merchants. Less than half a dozen people in the province

would know the reason for the swoops, but each search party would have several three-by-four-inch pictures of Harry. It had originally shown him in uniform, but that had been painted out.

The big television in the corner of the room droned on, its Sunday message of hope and charity, good will and universal kindness expounded by ranks of singers and earnest balding parsons. The family sat quite still on the sofa, watching the man with the Armalite rifle.

The pictures claimed no part of Janet Rennie's attention as she stared, minute after minute, at the man with the rifle across his knee, but for long moments the children's concentration was taken by the images on the screen before being jerked to the nightmare facing them across the carpet. It was a new degree of fear that the children felt, one they were not able to cope with or assimilate. They held fast to their mother, waiting to see what would happen, what she would do. To the two girls the Man opposite represented something quite apart from anything they had experienced before, but they recognized him as their father's enemy. Their eyes seldom left his face, held with fascination by the greyness of his skin, its lack of color, its deadness. This was where they saw the difference between the intruder and their world. There was none of the ruddiness and weight, the life and color that they knew from their friends' fathers and the men that came home with their father.

In the first twenty minutes that the Man had been in the room, Fiona, who traded on her ability to charm, had attempted to win the stranger with a smile. He looked right through her, gap-toothed grin and all. She'd tried just once, then subsided against her mother.

He's never come out into the light, the elder girl, Margaret, told herself. He's been locked up, and like a creature, he's escaped from wherever they've kept him.

This Man was from across the wall, but she knew little of the causes of the separation and the walling-off. She studied the deepness of his eyes, intent and careful, uninvolved as they took in the room, traversing it like the light on a prison camp watchtower, without order or reason, but hovering, moving, perpetually expecting the unpredictable. She saw his clothes too. A coat with a darned tear in the sleeve, and buttons off the cuff, trousers without creases and shiny in the knees, frayed at the turn-ups and with mud inside the lower leg. To the child, suits were for best, for work, not for getting dirty and shabby. His shoes were strange to her, too. Cleaned after a fashion by the rain on the winter pavements, but like his face, without luster, misused.

Margaret understood that the gun on the Man's lap was to kill her father. Her sister, twenty months younger, was unable to finish off the equation and so was left in a limbo of expectancy, aware only of an incomprehensible awfulness. Margaret had enough contact with the boys at school who played their war games in the schoolyard to recognize the weapon as an Armalite rifle.

He'll be a hard bastard, Janet Rennie had decided. One of the big men sent in for a killing like this. Won't be able to distract him with argument or discussion enough to unsettle him. He's hard enough to carry out his threat. She saw the wedding ring on his finger. Would have his own kids, breed like rats the Catholics, have his own at home. But he'd still shoot hers. She felt the fingers of her daughters gripping through the blouse. But she kept her head straight and her gaze fastened on the Man. There was not response to her stare, only the indifference of the professional, the craftsman who has been set a task and time limit and who has arrived early and therefore must wait to begin. Faster than her children she had taken in the Man, searched him for weakness, but the gun across his knees now held her attention. If he were nervous or under great strain, then she would notice the fidgeting of the hands or the reflection of perspiration on the stock or barrel of the gun. But there was no movement, no reflection.

He held the gun lightly, his left hand halfway along the shaft and his fingers loose around the black plastic that cradled the hard rifled steel of the barrel. His hand was just above the magazine, and her eyes wandered to the engineered emplacement where the capsule of ammunition nestled into the base of the gun. Just after he had sat down, the Man had eased the safety catch off with his right index finger, which now lay spanning the half-moon of the trigger guard. Like a man come to give an estimate on the plumbing, or the life insurance, she thought. None of the tension she would have expected on display. Thirty minutes or so before she thought her husband might be arriving home she decided to talk.

"We have no quarrel with you. You've none with us. We've done nothing to you. If you go now, you'll be clean away. You know that. You'll be right out of here and gone before my husband gets back." That was her start. Poor, she told herself, it wouldn't divert a flea.

He looked back with amused detachment.

"If you go through with this, they'll get you. They always get them now. It's a fact. You'll be in the Kesh for the rest of your life. Is that what you want?"

"Save it, Mrs. Rennie. Save it and listen to the hymns."

She persisted. "It'll get you nowhere. It's the Provisionals, isn't it? You're beaten. One more cruel killing, senseless. It won't do any good."

"Shut up." He said it quietly. "Just shut up and sit still."

She came again. "Why do you come here? Why to this house? Who are you?"

"It's a pity your man never told you what he did when he went to work of a morning. That's late in the day now, though. Quiet yourself and stay where you are."

He motioned at her with the rifle, still gently, still in control. The movement was definitive. Stay on the sofa with the children. He sensed that the crisis was coming for her, and that she knew it. With growing desperation she took up the same theme.

"But you're beaten now. It'll soon be all over. All your big men are gone. There'll have to be a cease-fire soon, then talking. More killing won't help anything." Keep it calm, don't grovel to him, talk as an equal with something on your side. There's nothing to counterbalance that Armalite, but you have to make believe he doesn't hold everything.

"We're not beaten. It's not over. We've more men than we can handle. There'll be no talks, and no cease-fire. Got the message. Nothing. Not while there are pigs like your man running round free and live."

The children beside her started up at the way the crouched stranger spoke of their father. Janet Rennie was an intelligent woman and hardened by her country upbringing. That she would fight for her husband's life was obvious; the problem had been in finding the medium. For the first time in nearly two hours, she believed she stood a chance. She still watched the hands and the rifle. The hands were in a new position on the Armalite. From resting against the gun, they were now gripping it. Attack . . . and how can he hit back before Rennie comes home?"

"There's no future for you boys. Your best men are all locked up. The people are sick and tired of you. You know that. Even in your own ratholes they've had enough of you . . ."

"You don't know a bloody thing about what goes on. Not a bloody thing. You know nothing. Nothing. Shut up. Shut your bloody face . . ."

She taunted him, trying to act it with her voice to overcome the fear. "They don't want you any more. You're outnumbered, living off the back of people. Without your guns you're nothing . . ,"

He shouted back across to her, "What do you know of the way we live? What do you know of what support we have? All you see is what's on the bloody television. You don't know what life is like in the Falls, with murdering bastards like your husband to beat the shit out of boys and girls. We're doing people a service when we kill fucking swine like that husband of yours."

"My husband never killed anyone." She said it as a statement of fact. Safe.

"He told you that, did he?" Very precise, low and hissing the words out. "Pity you never asked him what sort of little chat he had with the wee girl what hanged herself in the cells at Springfield."

She had built herself toward the climax. Now he watched with relish the demolition. She remembered reading about the girl, though it had not been mentioned at home. Work rarely was. The rebuttal caught her hard, draining her. The hands. Hold on to the hands, and concentrate on them. The only life line is the hands. The left knuckle was white on the barrel, blood drained out from around the bones. He was holding the rifle with both hands as he brought it up across his face to wipe his forehead with the sleeve on his right arm. He was sweating.

"You're nothing, are you? That's all you're fit for. Sitting in people's homes with bloody guns, guarding women and wee bairns. You're a rat, a creeping, disease-ridden rat. Is that what the great movement is about? Killing people in their homes?"

Her voice was battering it out now, watching the anger rise first in his neck and spreading through the lower jaw, tension, veins hardening and protruding. Safe. What can the gun do now that would not rouse the neighbors who lived through the thin brick-and-cement walls of the estate just a few feet from her own bungalow?

"You've made it all out wrong, Mrs. Rennie. Whatever your bloody man says, you don't kill the Provos just by locking a few up. We are of the people. Don't you know that? The people are with us. You've lost, you are the losers. Your way of life, God-given superiority, is over and finished, not us . . . We're winning. We're winning because the people support us. Go into Andytown, or the Murph or Ardoyne or Turf Lodge. Go in there and ask them about Provo rule. Then ask them what they think of RUC scum."

He was shouting, half rising out of the flower-covered seat of the chair. The rifle was now only in the right hand, but with the finger still close to the trigger. His left arm was waving above his head.

The hate between the two was total. His fury was fanned by the calmness she showed in the face of the rifle, and the way she had made him shout and the speed with which he had lost his control. Her loathing for the Republicans, bred into her from the cradle, gave her strength. With something near detachment she weighed the pluses and minuses of rushing him there and then. He was gripping the gun, but it was pointed away from the family. There was no possibility that she could succeed. She felt the children's grip on her arms. If she surged suddenly across the room, she would carry them like two anchors halfway with her.

He was not so calm now, and she saw the hint in his eyes that he felt the claustrophobia of the room, that the time he had sat in the chair had sapped that sense of initiative and control that were so important to him. She remembered a young Catholic boy who had come around her father's store, idling or loitering or just with nothing to do, and how her father had pulled him up by the front of his collar and shaken him like an animal to find what he was doing there on the corner outside the shop. And there had been then the trapped-rodent fear of the youth, of the second-grade boy who accepted that this would happen, and ran when released, feeling himself lucky not to be thrashed. In the eyes of the Man across from her was the hint that he knew he no longer dominated the situation.

When Rennie turned into the cul-de-sac, he noted immediately that the garage interior light was not switched on. He stopped his car forty yards from the bottom of the road, and turned off his engine and lights. The bungalow seemed quite normal. The curtains were drawn, but there was a slice of light through the gap where they had been pulled not quite together, from the hall light filtering through the patterned and colored glass. Everything as it should be.

But no light in the garage. For months now it had been a set routine that an hour or so before he was expected Janet would go into the kitchen and switch on the light in the garage. They kept the garage empty, without the clutter that their neighbors stored in theirs. That way, there was no hiding place for an assassin.

The detective sat in his car, watching, allowing himself some minutes just to look at the house and search in front of him in detail for any flaw other than the unlit garage. There was no light upstairs. Perhaps there should have been, perhaps not. Usually Fiona would be having her bath by now, but only darkness there. That was another cautionary factor.

Over the years Howard Rennie had been to enough full-dress police funerals to wonder how it could happen to himself. There was only one way. The epitaphs of the dead men were clear enough. Carelessness. Somewhere, for some time, usually minuscule, they had slackened. Not all, but most, grew overconfident and fell into the convenience of routine, began to believe in their own safety. A few were killed in closely planned attacks, but most, as

Rennie knew well, presented themselves as casual targets.

This was why he had a light fitted for the garage that should now be on, and why he noticed it was not lit.

His wife was a meticulous and careful person. Not one to make a silly mistake about the garage. It was the dilemma of the life they led that he wondered constantly how far as a family they should take their personal security. On the one hand, there could be something drastically wrong that had prevented his wife from switching on a light as agreed. On the other, she could be next door for sugar or milk, and stayed to gossip while the children played or watched television.

But it was quite out of character for her to forget.

He eased out of the car, pushing the door to but not engaging the lock, and reached for the PPK Walther in his shoulder holster. He had loaded and checked it before starting his drive home from Castlereagh, but he again looked for the safety-catch mechanism to see if it was in the On position. On the balls of his feet, he went toward the front gate. The gate was wrought iron and had never hung well—it rattled and needed a lifting, forcing movement to open it. Rennie instead went to the far side of the gatepost before the hedge thickened, through a gap, past the roses and onto the grass. The run up to the front door was gravel, and he kept to the grass, fearful of any noise his feet might make. Though the window showed the light from inside, the gap between the curtains was not enough for him to see through.

There were no voices at the moment he reached the window, just the hymn-singing on the television. Rennie came off the grass and stepped onto the tiled step of the doorway. The Walther was in his right hand, as with the left he found his Yale key and inserted it gently into the opening. Steady now, boy. This is the crucial time. If you're noisy now, it's blown—if there's anything to blow. For a fraction he felt sheepish at the stupidity of tip-toeing across his own front lawn. Had the neighbors seen? The door opened, just enough to get him inside. To the lounge door. It was off the latch, and the aperture of an inch or so acted as a funnel to the final crescendo of the program and the choir's lusty singing. As the sound tailed away he heard his wife speak.

"Great hero, aren't you? With your bloody rifle. Need it to make a man of you . . ."

The voice, shrill and aggressive, was enough to deaden the tiny amount of sound Rennie made as he leaned into the door, and the Man in his chair was aware of nothing till the door started moving in on its hinges toward him.

The Man saw the door moving long before the woman and her children.

His body stiffened as he fought to take hold of himself, and to regain his concentration after the debilitating argument across the room. He was still raising his rifle into the fire position when Rennie came in, low and fast, hitting the carpet and rolling in one continuous action toward the heavy armchair between the fireplace and the window.

The movement was too fast for the Man, who fired three times into the space by the door before checking to realize that the policeman was no longer there.

He struggled up from the sitting position in the deep, soft armchair, flooded with the sudden panic that he had fired and missed, and didn't know where his target was.

The metallic click of Rennie's safety catch, and the single shot that howled by his ear and into the French windows behind, located the target.

Rennie was not a marksman. He had been on pistol-shooting courses, most of which simulated a street situation. Once only they'd practiced storming a room. When you go in, they'd said, dive and roll as soon as you hit the floor, and keep rolling till you find cover. You're difficult to hit while you're moving. That first shot came as he balanced momentarily on his left side, his right arm free to fire in the general direction of the dark shape across the carpet. But his momentum carried him on till he cannoned into the solid bulk of the big chair. He was on his right side, the Walther driving into the softness of his thigh when he realized his impetus had wedged him between the wall and the chair. He twisted his head, seeing for the first time with agonizing clarity the Man, his wife and the children, as he struggled helplessly to swivel his body around. His survival depended on that movement.

The rifle was against the Man's shoulder now, eye down the barrel, not bothering with the complicated sight devices, just using the barrel itself to give him a line. He poised himself to fire. Wait for it, you bastard copper, wait for it, now. The triumph of the mission was there now. The bloody slug of the copper on the deck, soft, fat and vulnerable. And dead.

Rennie was screaming, "No, no. Keep away."

For the two children the room had disintegrated in speed and noise. As soon as Fiona saw her father, some four seconds after he had come through the door, she fled across the room toward him.

It was the moment that the Man had chosen to fire.

His vision, misted and unclear, of the man that he had come to kill was blocked fractionally by the checkered dress and the long golden hair.

He hesitated. Staring at the body, feverishly trying to get the child behind it and away. It was the time to shoot, a perfect target. Still he hesitated.

He saw the child with pinpoint clarity, as sharp as the mummified kids back in the street in London. Not part of the bloody war. He couldn't see the face of the girl as she writhed closer to her father, only the brightness of her dress, the freshness of the white socks, the pink health of the moving skin on the small legs. Couldn't destroy it. Rennie was struggling to pull the child under him to protect her. The Man could see that, and when he'd done so, the big policeman would be free to fire himself. The Man knew that. It had no effect. Not shoot a child, no way he could do it. He felt himself drifting away from the reality of the room, concentrating now on his wife. Kids at home, not as clean, scrubbed as these, but the same. If his wife knew he'd slaughtered a small one . . . He saw the slight body fade under the shape of the detective, and the other man's firing arm come up to aim.

Behind the Man were the French windows and the light framework of wood. He spun and dived at the center of one of the glass panels. The wall of wood and glass squares gave way. Rennie, the child spread-eagle under him, emptied the revolver in the direction of the window.

It was the fifth or sixth shot that caught the Man in the muscle of the left arm, just above the elbow. The impact heaved him forward through the obstacle of wood and glass splinters and across the neat patio toward the well-cut back lawn.

The pain was searing hot as the Man ran across the lawn. At the bottom, among the vegetables still in the ground, he crooked the rifle under his injured arm, and with his right, levered himself over the fence and into a cut-through lane.

Struggling for breath, he ran down the lane and then across a field to get to the road where the car was parked. Pushing him forward was the fear of capture, and the knowledge that the failed shooting would bring massive retaliation down on him. Like the fox discovered at work in the chicken coop who flees empty-handed, the sense of survival dominated. The experience in the house and the exhaustion of the running and the pain in his arm combined to create a confusion of images—all returning to the looming blond head of the child thrust into his

line of fire as the detective lay on the ground. It merged
with the memory of the muted stunned children in London
as he fired at their father. Again and again, though, as
with a film loop, came the face of the child across the
room, throwing herself at her prone father. And after
that, as he neared the car, was the knowledge that if he
had fired, he would have killed the policeman. He might
have hit the child, that was the area of doubt; he would
have killed the policeman, that was certainty. He had
hesitated, and through his hesitation, his target was alive.
It was weakness, and he had thought himself above that.

The young driver was asleep when he felt his shoulder
shaken violently and above him the frantic and blood-
etched face of the Man.

"Come on. Get the fucking thing moving. Don't hang
about. Get it out of this bloody place."

"Aren't you going to do something about that . . . ?"
The youth pointed to the still-assembled Armalite, but
cut off when he saw the blood on the arm that was holding the rifle.

"Just get moving. Mind your own bloody business and
drive."

The boy surged the car forward and out onto the road
in the direction of Andersonstown.

"Did it go okay?" he asked.

■ 16 ■

The Belfast Brigade staff met in a semidetached corpora-
tion house in the center of the conglomeration of avenues,

cresents, walks and terraces that makes up the huge housing estate of Andersonstown. It was very different country from the Falls and Ardoyne. Landscaped roads, and flanking them a jigsaw of neat red-brick homes. Ostensibly, the war had not come here with the same force as in the older battlegrounds closer to the city center, but such an impression would be false. This was the Provo redoubt, where the Brigade officers and top bomb-makers had their hideouts, where the master snipers lay in between operations, where five thousand people voted for a Provisional supporter in a Westminster election. Cups of tea were rare for the troops here, and it was the tough and experienced battalions who were asked to hold the ring with the most dedicated and intransigent of the enemy.

The particular house where the Brigade met had been chosen with care. It had been noticed that the combination of a twist in the road and a slight dip shielded both the front and rear doors of the house from the army camp some three hundred yards away. The house could be approached from the rear with virtual impunity.

The Brigade commanders were key figures in Northern Ireland. Some, like Joe Cahill and Seamus Twomey, had become household names around the world, famous as the men who had converted the guerilla wars of Southeast Asia and the Middle East and Latin America into West European terms. Promotion had exposed younger men to the job, none of them any the less hardliners for their youth . . . Adams, Bell, Convery. All had learned assiduously the arts of concealment and disguise. Their capture called for rounds of drinks and celebration toasts in the mess of the army unit concerned, and articles in the national press maintaining that the Provos were about to fold up. But within a week of the one-time commander being carried off to Long Kesh, another young man moved forward into the scene to take over. During their reign in office, however short, they would set the tone of the administration. One would favor car bombs, another would limit attacks only to military and police targets, or direct operations toward spectaculars such as big fires, major shoot-outs and prison escapes.

Each left his imprint on the situation, and all went into the mythology of the movement. The one common factor was their ability to move, almost at will, around the rambling Andersonstown estate. Their names were well known to the troops, but their faces were blurs taken for the most part from out-of-date photographs. One had ordered his wife to destroy all family pictures that included him, and given all his briefings from behind curtains and drapes, so that under the rigors of cross-examinations his lieutenants would not be able to give an accurate description of him. The most famous of all had sufficient mastery of impersonation to be able to win an apology for inconvenience from a young officer who had led a search party through the house where the Brigade commander was giving an interview to a reporter from a London Sunday.

To a portion of the community, their names provoked unchecked admiration, while to those less well disposed, they sowed an atmosphere of fear. There were enough youths with "kneecap jobs" and daubed slogans of "Touts will be shot dead" for the message not to have to be repeated that often.

That there were a few prepared to risk the automatic hooding and assassination was a constant source of surprise to the army intelligence officers. Money was mostly the reason that men would whisper a message into a telephone booth. It was seldom because of the wish to rid the community of the Provisionals . . . Men who felt that way stayed silent, kept their peace and went about their lives. It was because the Brigade commander and his principal lieutenants could never be totally certain of the loyalty of the men and women who lived in Andersonstown that they delayed their meeting till midnight, though their arrivals at the house had been staggered over the previous seventy minutes.

None was armed. All were of sufficient importance to face sentences of up to a dozen years if caught in possession of a firearm. If arrested without a specific criminal offense provable against them, they could only be detained in the Kesh, with the constant likelihood of amnesties.

They took over a back bedroom while below the lady of the house made them a pot of tea. She took it up the stairs on a tray with beakers and milk and sugar. They stopped talking when she came in and said nothing till she had placed the tray on the flat top of a clothes chest, and turned to the door.

"Thanks, ma'am." The Brigade commander spoke, the others nodding and murmuring in agreement. She was away down the stairs to busy herself with her sewing and late-night television. When that was over, she would sleep in her chair, waiting for the last man to leave the house to tell her the talking was done. The woman asked no questions and received no explanations, other than the obvious one that the positioning of the house made it necessary that the men should use it.

There were six men in the room when the meeting started. The Brigade commander sat on the bed with two others, and one more stood. Seamus Duffryn and Frank were on the wooden chairs that, apart from the bed and the chest, represented the only furniture in the room. The present commander had been in office more than six months, and his general features were better known than was common. He scorned the flamboyance of masks. From the pocket of his dark anorak he brought a small transistor radio, the sort that had a corded loop that could be slipped over the wrist, so that he could walk along the pavement with it pressed to his ear. This was how he kept abreast of the activities of the ASUs, the Active Service Units.

The crucial listening times of the day for him were 7:50 A.M., the 12:55 lunchtime summary and then five to midnight. Every day the BBC's Northern Ireland news listed with minute detail the successes and failures of his men. Shootings, hijackings, blast bombs, arms finds, stone-throwing incidents—all were listed and chronicled for him. The lead story that night was of the shooting at a police-man's house in Dunmurry.

The men in the room listened absorbed to the firm English accent of the announcer.

"The gunman had apparently held Mrs. Rennie and her two children a gunpoint in their house for some hours while he waited for her husband to return from duty. A police spokesman said that when Mr. Rennie entered the living room of his home the gunman fired at him. Mr. Rennie dived for shelter behind an armchair just as his younger daughter ran toward him. It seems the child ran into the field of fire of the terrorist, who then stopped shooting and ran from the house. Mr. Rennie told de-tectives that when the girl moved he thought she was going to be killed, as the gunman was on the point of firing at him. The family are said to be suffering from shock and are staying the night with friends.

"In the Shantallow district of Londonderry a blast bomb slightly wounded . . ."

The commander switched off the set. "That's not like bloody Downs from Ardoyne. Not like him to lose his nerve. Why should he do that?"

"Stupid bastard. We needed Rennie killed. Put a lot of planning in and a deal of work to have him rubbed. Then it's screwed. Could be they're just feeding us this crap." It was the Brigade quartermaster who came in.

"Doesn't sound like that. Sounds like Downs just threw it. Hardly going to fool us, are they? The bugger Rennie, he's alive or he's dead. We sent for him to be killed, he's not. So that means it's failure, can't be any other answer. What matters is that our man couldn't finish it."

He pondered on the decision he was about to take as the other men waited for him. He alone knew of the link between Danby in London and the man Downs from Ardoyne. Later perhaps he would include the others in his knowledge, he decided, but not now. At this stage, he felt, the fewer the better. Some of the commanders ran the office by committee, but not the man who now spoke again.

"On from there. What about the man they've put in? What do we have?"

"I think it's watertight." Frank had taken the cue and come in. Frank had been with the Provisionals since the split with the Officials, the "Stickies," as they called them, but this was the first time he had been in such elite company. It slightly unnerved him. "The girl he was laying spills it all. It's bloody incredible, what he told her. She was saying that he says to her that he was sent over to get the man that shot Danby in London. She told him about the girl, the one that was picked up and taken to Springfield, the one that hanged herself. It was because he shopped her that she was taken in. She says she challenged him about it yesterday afternoon. He admitted it."

The Brigade intelligence officer was sitting on the bed beside the commander. Hard face, tight pencil lips and darting, piglike eyes. "What's his name, the Englishman?"

"The name he's using is Harry McEvoy. I doubt if it's real or—"

"Of course it isn't. Doesn't matter, that. They must be a bit touched up then over there, if they send a man over on his own to find us just like that."

Duffryn spoke. "But it all fits with what we had from the hotel. The army man and the RUC. The bit we had about them putting a man in and then not telling the brass. We thought we'd caught the buggers griping about it. It has to be some nonsense drawn up by one of them bastards sat behind a desk in London, in the Ministry."

Duffryn was little more than a name to the commander. He looked at him with interest. "You had a line on the man first, right? Through his accent? Where is he now? What's covering him?"

"He's at the guest house, where he has lodgings. It's called Delrosa, run by Mrs. Duncan, off the Broadway. She's all right. He's there in a back room that he rents. The front and back are watched at the moment, and the lads have been told in the last hour or so that if he goes out, he's to be tailed. But they must stay right back."

"And the girl you've talked to, won't she warn him?"

"We told her not to. I think she understood. She won't do anything," Frank said.

The commander lit his fourth cigarette in less than half an hour, pulled at it, forcing the smoke down into his throat. "I think we want him before we hood him. We would like to talk to him for a bit first. Pick him up and bring him in for a talk. Does he work?"

"In a scrap yard. He leaves to walk there about eight, just a few minutes after, perhaps."

"Take him when he's walking. On the main road, get him into a car and take him up the Whiterock, into the Crescent; it's that or he's away. Remember that, I want him chatted with."

For Frank and Duffryn it seemed the end of their part in the evening. They rose out of the chairs, but were waved down by the commander.

"Where's Downs now?"

The Brigade quartermaster said, "The message came through just before I left to come here. The wound he got, it's a light one, in the arm. Flesh. It's being fixed up now by the quack in the Murph. He's okay, but he hasn't gone home yet. The quack will want to keep an eye on him for the next few hours."

The Brigade commander talked to no one in particular. "What do they say when a driver's been in a crash? A lorry driver, bus, heavy truck? That sort of thing. What do they say? Send him straight back out again. Don't hang about fidgeting and mumbling about it. Get stuck in again. Downs can go on this one. His nerve wasn't too good last night. He'll need this to get him back into scratch again. He'll want to retrieve himself a bit. Get him here in an hour. Downs can finish him after the talking-to."

It amused him: the fox turning back on the hound.

For Frank and Duffryn the briefing was finished. They went out through the back of the house to where a car was parked some three hundred yards away, keys in the dash. Frank would drive on to the doctor and drop Seamus near his home.

Seamus Duffryn was frightened for the first time since he had become involved with the movement. He'd been present three months earlier at an interrogation. A kid from up in Lenadoon. The charge was that he had betrayed colleagues in the movement to the military. The muffled screaming of the youth was still in his ears, bouncing and ricocheting about. They'd burned his naked stomach with cigarette ends while he was strapped in a chair, with a blanket over his head folded several times to deaden the noise. He'd screamed each time the glowing ash met his skin, from a deep animal desperation and not with hope of release. Seamus Duffryn had become involved that night, and would become involved again tomorrow. The paper stuff he did, that was important. But this was when it mattered, and you were either in the movement or you were out of it. There had been an awful, shaming thrill through his entire body when he saw the light-grey material of the boy's trousers turn to heavy charcoal. As the urine ran down the kid's leg, there'd been the steam rising through the trousers, and the hood had gone on, and the gun had been cocked. At the moment they shot him the kid was still screaming.

If McEvoy was British army, how would he take it? Duffryn wondered. That was a nothing from Lenadoon. McEvoy would be different. How would he stand up to their interrogation and the ritual end?

He would find out by tomorrow night. He hurried on his way through the night to his home and his mother.

After he'd made his phone call to London, Harry had spent the rest of the day in his room. Before dark he gazed mindlessly into the abstract of roofs and walls that was the view from his window. He had not gone down to Sunday high tea, and to Mrs. Duncan's inquiries, only replied that he thought he had something of a chill coming on. He was going to have an early night, he shouted through the door. She had wanted to bring him a hot drink in his room, but through the closed door he managed to persuade her that there was no need.

He wanted to be alone, shutting out the perpetual tension of moving in company and living the falsehood that had been planned for him. That girl. It had upset him. Created imbalance in the delicate poise he had taken up. Blown by a silly girl who couldn't stop talking. Up on a mountain, wind and rain, like some cigarette advertisement, and he'd chucked the whole operation. Ridiculous and, worse, so bloody unprofessional. He brooded away the hours. He'd put faith down on the line of a girl whose address he didn't even know. What in Christ's name would they be thinking in London when he put the request in for the special treatment for Harry's bit of tail? Go raving mad, wouldn't they? And reckon he'd twisted. No way they wouldn't. And they'd want to get him out.

He'd heard all the radio broadcasts, searching for the formula announcement that would end it all. Arrest . . . Man wanted for questioning . . . London murder . . . Big operation . . . Tip-off . . . Appear in court. That would be the jargon. There had been nothing.

He had steeled himself to what he would do if he heard of the capture of the Man. He'd be out of the front door, straight out, with no farewells or packing or luggage, onto the Falls, and turn right along the main road, and then right again before the hospital and on down to the Broadway barracks, and in through the front door. But without the news he couldn't end it. He had to stay, finish the bloody job. No arrest, and it was all a failure, abject and complete. Not worth going back for, just to report how it all bobbed. Didn't really matter what Davidson said. No arrest, no return.

But where was the bloody army? Why wasn't it all wrapped up? Big enough, weren't they? Got enough men, and guns, and trucks. He's out there just waiting for you to go and get him. The national bulletins traced their way around the news: there was nothing from Northern Ireland.

The frustration mounted in Harry, welling up against his reason and his training. How much information he had pushed at them in London over the last two, three weeks! How much did they bloody *want*? All sewn up, it should be, cut and dried, taped and parceled—and now more delay. Through Josephine, streak of bloody luck there, about as much information had come out as he was ever likely to get his hands on. The long-term adrenalin was fading . . . he wanted out . . . he wanted it over . . . but when it was finished . . .

As the dusk came he unwrapped the Smith and Wesson. After locking the door he took the weapon to pieces and laid it out on a handkerchief on the bed. With a second dirtied handkerchief from his pocket he cleaned the firing mechanism, then reassembled the gun. He would take it with him next morning to the yard. Put it in the bag where the sandwich box went. It was a sort of therapy, the gun, the instant pick-me-up. It had gone wrong.

Nothing on the radio when there should have been. The girl, that was where it had gone wrong, with that bloody girl. Lovely face, lovely body, lovely girl, but that was where it all loused up. Nothing else, that's the only point where it's gone wrong, but that's enough. Gossip, don't they, and she won't keep her mouth shut any more than the rest of them. Like she talked about Theresa, so she'll talk about me. A lonely man in a back room bed-sitter. The gun was insurance, the disaster was less distinct.

When he went to bed he lay a long time in the dark of the room thinking about Germany, the family, home and the people with whom he worked. The other officers, easy and relaxed, none of them knowing where Harry was, and few caring. He envied them, yet felt his dislike of that easy way of life. His distrust of the others not committed to the front, as he was now, was all-consuming. It was only rarely that he turned his mind to his wife and the children. It took him time, and with difficulty he recreated them and home on the NATO base. The chasm between their environment and Harry's was too difficult for him to bridge. Too tired, too exhausted.

His final thought was salvation and made sleep possible. Of course the man was in custody, but they'd be questioning him. It would take thirty-six hours at least. They wouldn't rush it, they'd want to get it right. Tomorrow evening they would be announcing it, and then home, and out of the hole, another forty-eight hours perhaps, and then out.

In the early hours of that Monday morning, while Harry alternately dozed and dreamed in his bed, and while the Brigade nucleus sat up in Andersonstown waiting for the Man to come, Davidson in the Covent Garden office was scanning the first London editions of the papers. Both *The Times* and the *Guardian* carried reports from Northern Ireland that the Provisional IRA was claiming that British intelligence had launched a special agent into the Catholic areas, and that people in those areas had been warned to be especially vigilant. Both of the writers under whose by-line the stories appeared emphasized that whether true or false, the claim would have the effect of further reducing the minimal trust between the people of the minority areas, the front-line housing estates of the city and the security forces. There was much other news competing for space—on the diplomatic front, the state of the economy, and the general "human-interest claptrap" that Davidson raged about. The Belfast copy was not prominently displayed, but to the man propped up on his camp bed, it presented a shattering blow. He lay deep in newsprint and pondered his telephone, wondering whether there were calls he should make, anything he could usefully do.

Those bungling idiots had still failed to pick up the chap Downs and the girl Josephine. Bloody near a day to get them, and nothing to show for it. He was astonished —too long after the war, too long after the organization had run down, too many civilians who'd never been up the sharp end. Without the arrest, the scheme of which he was an integral part would collapse, and at a rate of knots. In all conscience he could not ring that bloody man Frost again, supercilious bastard, and once more expose himself to that sarcasm. On the wall by the door the clock showed after two. For a moment he comforted himself that Harry might see the report for himself and do a bunk on his own. No, that wouldn't fit, scrap men don't take *The Times* or the *Guardian*, that wouldn't match the cover.

Davidson tried to shut the problem out of his mind, and closed his eyes. He fumbled unseeing above him till his fingers caught at the string that hung down from the light switch. By the time he drifted into sleep he had worked out his immediate future. The early retirement and professional disgrace, and all because that hoof-footed army couldn't pick one man up. The unfairness of it all.

Frost had gone to bed a little after midnight, and lain half awake expecting the phone to ring and unwilling to commit himself to the task of sleeping. It had to come, the message that either the Man or the girl had been found. The bell's shrill insistence eventually woke him. The army in Ardoyne reported no known entries or departures at the house in Ypres Avenue. He authorized the unit to move in and search at 5:30 A.M.

After that he slept, safe in the knowledge that Monday would be a real day, a real bugger.

The doctor had cleaned the wound. He'd found the damage slight, and it lessened further as the cotton wool and spirit cleaned away the caked blood that had smeared itself on the upper part of the Man's left arm. A small portion of flesh had been ripped clear close by the small-pox-vaccination scar. There was an entry and exit wound, almost together and one, and after he had cleaned it thoroughly the doctor put a light lint dressing over the pale numbed skin.

"You can move yourself around a bit. If you need to, that is. But if possible, you should stay still, take it quiet. Go put yourself in the easy chair out the back, and get a rest or something."

"Is it serious? Will I be left with anything?" asked the Man.

"If you look after it, you'll be okay, nothing to worry about, nothing at all. But you must go easy to start with. The only problem is if it gets infected as this early stage. But we'll see that doesn't happen—yes?"

The doctor had been associated with the fringes of the movement since the start of the violence. He asked no questions, and needed few answers. Once every fortnight or so he would hear the square of gravel flick once, twice, against his bedroom window, and in his dressing gown he would open the door to a casualty too sensitive to face ordinary hospital treatment. He had made his attitude clear at least three years earlier, that there was no point their bringing men to him who were already close to death. Take them to the RVH, he'd said. If their wounds were that bad, they'd be out of it for months anyway, so better for them to get top medical treatment or the best hospital than the hand-to-mouth service he could provide. He handled a succession of minor gunshot wounds, was able to remove bullets, clean wounds and prevent sepsis setting in.

He was sympathetic to the Provisionals, but he gave them no material support other than the late-night ex officio surgery. Perhaps if he had been born into the ghetto, he would have been one of them, but he came from off the hill and went to medical school after sixth-form secondary education. Though they had his sympathy, he reflected, he was a very different person from the hard, wild-eyed men who came to him for treatment.

The Man was very white in the chair, his shirt ripped away on the left side and his coat, holed and bloody, draped over the back. He heard the faint knock on the door down the corridor at the front of the house. There was a whispered dispute in the hall. He heard that distinctly and twisted himself around in the chair to see two men push their way past the doctor and into the room.

There was a tall man, in jeans and a roll-neck sweater. "The chief wants you. He's waiting in Andytown now. Said he wants to see you straightaway."

The doctor remonstrated, "Look at the state he's in. You can see that for yourself. He should be here all night, then go and rest. He's in shock."

"No chance. He's wanted at a meeting. There'll be no permanent damage if we take him?"

"You're setting back recovery time, and adding to the risk of infection."

"We'll see you get a look at him tomorrow. Right now we have to go. Come on."

This last was to Downs. Twice he looked backwards and forwards from the messenger to the doctor, willing the doctor to be more insistent. The doctor didn't meet him, avoiding the pleading in the Man's eyes. The tall man and his colleague took hold of Downs under his armpits and gently but decisively lifted him toward the door.

The doctor said, "You may need these to pull him up a bit, if there's something that he has to do. Not more than a couple at a time, after that he has to sleep. If he takes them, they'll help him for a few hours, then it's doubly important that he rests."

From the high wall cabinet in the back room he took down a brown pill bottle, half filled with tablets, half with a wad of cotton wool.

They always said they'd come back, but few did. If they needed further treatment, they headed South, where they could lie up more easily away from the daily tensions of the perpetual hunt by the military for men on the wanted list. The doctor watched them carry the Man to the car and ease him into the back, propped up against the armrest in the center of the seat. He wagered himself the pills would be in use before lunchtime.

The drive between the doctor's house and the meeting place in Andersonstown took twenty minutes. They helped the wounded man out of the car and in through the back entrance, the way the night's other visitors had come. Irritably, he shrugged them off once he was inside the scullery, and independently followed their instructions up the stairs and in through the second door on the left of the landing.

Only the Brigade commander had remained behind to see him.

"How are you, Billy? Have they fixed you up all right?"

"Not so bad. It's only in the flesh. Not much more than a graze, the thing went straight on through. It's bandaged up now and the doc says it's clean."

"I heard a bit about it on the radio. Said you didn't get a shot into the bastard, you didn't hit him. Said his brat got in the way and you didn't fire. Is that right?"

"It's not as simple as that." Oh, Christ, not a bleeding inquest now. Not why, wherefore, how and bloody when at this time of night. "I fired once and missed, then when I had a clear shot at him, the kid came right across. She was right in front of his body and his head. I couldn't see him, so I didn't fire."

The Brigade commander was still smoking, in front of him the clear-glass ashtray mounted with a score of filtered ends steeped in the grey powder he flicked continuously into the bowl. The debris was left in a circle around the ashtray where it balanced on the blanket over the bed.

"If you just fired, child and all . . . then you would have got him, yes? If you'd just gone right on through with it, Rennie would be dead, right?"

"Is that what they said on the radio?" The Man was peeved by the reception, not used to being challenged and questioned. "Is that what Rennie is saying, on the radio? If I had fired through the kid, then I would have killed him?"

Who did this bugger think he was? thought the Man. When was this miserable sod out with an ASU? When did he expose himself? All right for those who give orders and send kids out to carry bombs into tupp'nyhapenny supermarkets. Get out on the streets at night, know the silence of waiting, the terrible noise of action, feel a nine-millimeter slug hit you. Then bloody well come quizzing me. Anger rose in him, but not sufficient for him to shout, to release him from the discipline inculcated in him. Can't shout at the Brigade commander. That's mutiny.

"I don't know what Rennie is saying," said the commander. "The radio said the child was in the way and that you didn't fire. That's all. There's no criticism of you. I know of no cause for criticism."

Cunning sod. "There shouldn't be. Rennie was no soft one. He moved bloody well."

"One or two people, who don't know the facts as we do, might feel, if they only had half the story, that Billy Downs had ballsed it up, gone soft on the job. If they hadn't the big picture, and knew it all, they might say Billy Downs was sent on a job and when one of the copper's brats got in the way that then he held his fire." The Man didn't really know the commander, he was from a different part of the city. They had had no real dealings before, but rank separated them and dictated that he must let him have his say. "These people, they might recall that when we shot Sean Russell, of the UDR, in New Barnsley, that he had his kids draped all over him. Now, two of them were wounded, but Russell was still shot dead. The order had been to shoot him. Now, we all know that it wouldn't be fair to put your escapade tonight in the same category. And we know that your nerve is as good as ever. That you are one of the top soldiers we have. We know that, don't we, Billy?"

"You know it's balls," said the Man. "I'm not soft. My nerve hasn't gone. We're not fighting five-year-olds. Is that what you're saying, that we kill wee girls? Are you saying that I should have fired straight through the girl? Is that what you think I ought to have done?"

"Don't get ratty, Billy. It's just we have to be careful that people who don't know the circumstances might think that. They might point out that getting you that close to Rennie took a deal of time, and that then the front runner botched the whole bloody thing . . . because a kiddie got in the way. That's nonsense, Billy." The voice droned on, repetition of failure dragging itself through the Man. He had to sleep, to rest, to escape from this room with this boring and nagging whore of a man.

"We know it's not true, Billy. We know there was a good reason for you not to shoot. We know you couldn't see the target. We know Rennie wasn't straightforward. I don't know how many other people feel the same way. But that's enough of that. Nobody will have a leg to stand on by tomorrow night. Right, Billy? We have a little job tomorrow, and by the time that's done, they'll be silenced."

The Man looked away, broken by the twisting of the screw. Self-doubt rampant. The commander crushed the ego out of him.

"I'm the only one of Brigade group that knows about London. We've kept it tight for your protection. It's worked pretty well . . . up to now. There's a difficulty come up. The Brits have put a man in to find you. An agent. McEvoy. Harry McEvoy. Lodging down in Broadway. There's a split in their top ranks about him. We think London wanted him but Lisburn didn't."

He let it sink in, watched the color return to the Man's face, watched the fear come back to his eyes and saw the hands begin to clasp and activate.

"His job, the agent's job, is to find you. Perhaps to kill you, perhaps to take you in, or just tell them where to go. We fancy he wants to kill you. He's been near to you already. He tipped the troops that picked up the girl that hanged herself. We think she did that rather than tell about you. Rennie was the one that questioned her. He chatted to that girl till she was ready to hang herself. You couldn't kill him when his brat jumped in the way. You had no cause to be soft with Rennie. You'll have a chance to let people know what you're made of, Billy. Tomorrow we're going to lift this fellow that's come for you, and we'll talk to him, then we'll hood him. That's where you come in. You'll shoot him, like you shot Danby, like you should have shot Rennie."

The Man felt faint now, exhausted by the sarcasm of the top man. He nodded, sweat rising from his crotch across his body.

"When it's over, we'll send you down to Donegal. Sleep it all off, and get fit again. Tonight you'll stay in Andytown. You'll be taken there now, and they'll pick you up at six-fifteen. They'll have the guns when they meet you. This will sort it out, I think. Be just the right answer to those who say that Billy Downs has gone soft."

He wanted out, and this was the chance. They were showing him the way. The way to do it properly, not so as you were looking over your shoulder for half a lifetime, and running. The official way, that was how it was done. One more day, one more job. Then out. Leave it to the cowboys. The heroes who didn't hold their fire, who shot wee kids. Squeeze the trigger right through the scream of a five-year-old. Was that Pearse's revolution, or Connolly's or Plunkett's? Was it, hell. Leave it to the cowboys after one more day.

■ 17 ■

The long night was coming to its close when B Company swarmed into Ypres Avenue. The column of armored cars had split up some hundreds of yards from the street, and guided by coordinated radio messages, had arrived at each end of the row of bleak terraced houses simultaneously. The first troops out sprinted down the back

entrances behind the houses, taking up positions every
fifteen yards or so along the debris-strewn pathways. From
the tops of the Land-Rovers, searchlights played across
the fronts of the houses as the noise and banging in the
street brought the upstairs lights flickering on.

The major who commanded the company had received
only a short briefing. He had been told the man they
were looking for was named Billy Downs, the address of
his house, and that he was expected to search several
houses. He was thirty-three years old, on his fourth tour
to Northern Ireland, and as a company commander in
South Armagh on his last visit, had witnessed four of his
men killed in a culvert bomb explosion. His hatred of the
Provisionals was deep-rooted and lasting. Unlike some of
his brother officers who respected the expertise of the
opposition, he felt only consuming contempt.

What Downs was wanted for he hadn't been told, nor
what his status was in the IRA. He'd only guessed the
reason for the raid when they unpinned the picture from
the guardroom wall and gave it to him. It was the photokit that had gone up five weeks earlier after the London
shooting and remained at top of the soldiers' priority list.
The intelligence officer from Lisburn noticed the flash of
recognition spread across his face as he looked down at
the picture.

Once the street was sealed, there was time to work carefully and slowly along the road. No. 41 was the third
house they came to. The soldiers banged on the door with
their rifle butts. The few who had seen the picture of the
man they wanted were hanging on the moment of anticipation, wondering who would come and open the door.

From upstairs came the noise of crying, which steadily
increased to screaming pitch as the family woke to the
battering at the wooden panels. The Man's wife came to
the door, thin and frail in her nightdress and cotton dress-

ing gown. A tiny figure silhouetted against the light from the top of the stairs when she drew back the bolts, turned the key and stood against the soldiers. The troops in the search party pushed past her, huge in their boots and helmets and flak jackets. They raced up the stairs, equipment catching and bouncing off the banisters. A lieutenant and two sergeants. All had seen the picture, all knew what they were there for. The officer, his Browning pistol cocked and fastened to his body by a lanyard, swung his left shoulder into the front-bedroom door and bullocked his way to the window. The man behind switched on the light, covering the bed with his automatic rifle.

Two faces peered back at the intruders. Saucer-eyed, mouths open, and motionless. The troops patted the bodies of the children and pressed down on the bedclothes around them, isolating the little lumps they made with the blankets. They looked under the bed and in the wardrobe. There were no other hiding places in the room, and that effectively exhausted the search.

They had come in hard and fast, and now they stopped, halted by the anticlimax of the moment.

The lieutenant went to the top of the stairs and shouted down, "Not here, sir."

"Wait there, I'll come up."

The major came in and looked slowly around the room. "Right, not here now. But he has been, or she's a dirty little bitch round the house. There, his pants, vest, socks. I wouldn't imagine they lie around the house too long."

By the window was the crumpled pile of dirty clothes underneath the chair that the Man used to hang his coat and trousers on at night.

"Get her up here," said the major. "And get the floor-board chaps. He's been here pretty recently. May still be in the house. If he's about, I want him found, wherever he is—roof, basement if there is one, wherever."

She came into the room, her two youngest children

hanging like monkeys over her shoulders, thumbs in mouths. Like their mother, they were white-faced, and shivering in the cold away from their bedclothes.

"We were wondering where we might find your husband, Mrs. Downs."

"He's not here. You've poked your bloody noses in, and you can see that. Now get out of here."

"His clothes are here, Mrs. Downs, you and I can both see that. I wouldn't expect a nice girl like you to leave his dirty pants lying on the floor that many days."

"Don't be bloody clever with me," she snarled back at him. "He's not here, and you can see that, now get all your bastard soldiers out of here."

"The problem, Mrs. Downs, is that we think your husband could still be here. That would be the explanation for his clothes being on the floor. I'm afraid we're going to have to search around a bit. We'll cause as little disruption as possible. I assure you of that."

"Big bloody heroes, aren't you, when you have your tanks and guns. Big and bloody brave."

The soldier with the crowbar mouthed an apology as he came past her. He flipped up a corner of the threadworn carpet and with a rending scrape pulled up the boards at the end of the room. In four separate places he took the planks up, before disappearing to his hips down the holes he had made. The major and the soldiers waited above for him to emerge with his torch for the last time and announce with an air of professional disappointment that the floor space was clear. Using ladders, they went up into the loft, shaking the beams above the major and the Man's wife, and swinging the light fitting.

"Nothing up there either, sir."

The ground floor was of stone and tile, so that stayed put, while the expert banged on the walls with his hammer in search of cavities. The coal bunker out in the yard was cleared out, the wooden framework under the sink taken down.

"It's clean, sir."

That was the cue for her to return to the attack. "Are you through now, you bastards? All these men and one little house, and one wee girl alone with her kids, and it takes all of you and your bloody guns and Saracens . . ."

"You know why we want him?" The major lashed out. "You know what he did? We'll go on till we get him. If we have to rip this house to pieces each week till we get him, we'll do that. Doesn't he tell you where he's going at night? Doesn't he tell you what he did last month? Try asking him one day."

He strode out through the house, followed by his search team. It was three minutes after six o'clock. Failure and frustration were how the majority of these raids ended. He knew that, and he'd never lost his temper before, never gone overboard as he'd done with the woman in No. 41. He comforted himself on two points. That it needed saying, and that the intelligence officer who had tagged along hadn't heard it.

Once the army had gone, a clutch of neighbors moved into the house to gather around the woman and commiserate on the damage left behind. None knew of the importance of the Man among the Provisionals and so news of the army outrage at the house would travel fast through the community. Yet those that came to dress the children and help in the clearing-up and the making of tea and breakfast noted how subdued their friend was. Cowed by what had happened. That was not the usual way. The familiar reaction was to greet the going of the soldiers with a hail of insults and obscenities at their backs. But not this woman.

When the friends and neighbors had left her to get their own families ready for work or school or just dressed and fed, the words of the officer returned to ring in her ears.

quietly she paddled about the house, her children in a crocodile procession behind her, checking to see which of her few possessions were damaged or tarnished or moved.

This was the confirmation. God, this was what she had feared. Ever since his first night back home after London, she had been waiting. So much piss and wind, this confidence he had that no one knew him. Like a rat he was, waiting in a barn with the door shut for the farmer to come in the morning with his gun and his dogs. The big, fresh-faced officer, with the smears on his cheeks, with his suspicion of a mustache and posh accent, who hated her, he had laid down the future. He had mirrored her nightmares and hallucinations while she lay sleepless beside her man. They would come, and come again for him, and keep on till they found him.

Last night he had not slept beside her. On the radio in the back room she heard the early news. A policeman shot at . . . an intruder hit . . . in the middle evening. That was the top story. Whoever had been involved should have been home now. Her man was usually home by now, or he would have said something.

Around the passage and stairs and landing of the house, she thought of her man. Wounded, maimed, alone in the dawn of the city. What hurt most was that she was so unable to influence events.

News carried across the city. With the efficiency of tribal tomtoms, word passed over the sprawling urban conglomeration that the terraced house in Ypres Avenue had been raided. Less than an hour after the major had walked through the front door and to his armored Land-Rover, the Man would hear of it. Brigade staff had decided that he should know. They felt it could only enhance his motivation for the job at hand.

Harry's alarm clock dragged him from the comfort of

his dreaming, and woke him to the blackness of his room. His dreams had been of home, wife and children, the makeshift garden behind his quarters, holidays in timber forest chalets, fishing out in the cool before the sun came up, trout barbecued for breakfast. With consciousness came the knowledge of another Monday morning. It was three weeks to the day that he had left the house at Dorking with the view of the hills and vegetable garden. Twenty-one days exactly. "Must have been out of my bloody mind," he muttered to the emptiness of the room.

All day Sunday he had thought of what Josephine had said to him. She'd accused him of interference in something that was basically none of his concern, of causing death when he should have stayed uninvolved. Stupid bitch should have passed the same message to the Man who came to London with the Kalashnikov.

He examined his position and its natural courses. He wanted to finish it. End it properly. End it with a shooting, with the Man in the picture, with his black-and-white-lined face, dead. That was not emotional, there was no wild spirit of revenge, just that such an ending was the only finite one; otherwise, the job was incomplete.

In Aden, good old Aden, it had been so much more simple. British lives at stake, the justification of every-thing, with the enemy clearly defined—Arabs, gollies. But here, who was the enemy? Why was he the enemy? Did you have to know why to take his life? It churned over and over, unanswered, like pebbles in a coffee machine, grating, ill-fitting and indigestible.

In spite of the fact that Harry came originally from the country town an hour or so's drive from Belfast, the army's mold had been the real fashioning influence over-reaching his childhood. Like his brother officers in the mess, he was still perplexed at the staying power of the opposition. But here he parted company. To the others they were the enemy, to Harry they were still the opposition. You could kill them if it was necessary, or if that was demanded for operational reasons, but they remained the opposition. They didn't have to be the enemy to make them worth killing.

But how did they keep it up? What made them prepared to risk their lives on the streets when they took on the power of a British army infantry section? What led them to sacrifice most of the creature comforts of life to go on the run? What made them feel the God-given right to take life, and torture a man in front of his family?

They're not heroes. Bloody lunatics, he said to himself as the pulled his sweater over his head. They rejected all the ordinary things that ordinary people search for, and chose to go on against these massive odds. It didn't involve Harry. The Man he was searching for was quite straightforward. He was a killer. He was a challenge. Simple and clean. Harry could focus on that.

"A cup of tea, Mr. McEvoy?" Mrs. Duncan at the door cut short his thoughts. "What would you be wanting for breakfast? There's the lot if you can manage it. Sausages, bacon, tomatoes, eggs, and I've some soda bread . . . ?"

"Just toast and coffee, thanks. I'll be away down in a moment."

"That won't get you far. It's a raw day, right enough."

"Nothing more, thank you, Mrs. Duncan. Really, that's all I want. I'll be right down."

"Please yourself, then. Bathroom's clear. Coffee's made, and remember to wrap up well. It's a cold one."

After he'd shaved, there was not much to the dressing. Sweater already on and damp from the soap and washcloth, faded jeans, his socks and boots and his anorak. He took the face towel from the rail in the bathroom, brought it back into his room, and when he had finished dressing, laid it out on the bed. About two feet by one and a half, it was bigger than the one the Smith and Wesson was already wrapped in, and he changed them over, putting the revolver in the new towel.

Silly bugger, he thought, clean towels just to wrap a gun in. He needed a towel to disguise the outline of the weapon as it sat in the deep pocket of his anorak on the way to work. But he didn't need a clean towel. That's the army for you: everything clean on a Monday morning. Funny if he got stopped at a roadblock. He thought of that and a whole band of disappointed squaddies, having to hand him over. Wouldn't have cried overmuch, either. Last night, late, he'd decided to put the gun in his coat, easier access than the food bag slung over his shoulder, and the bag with the sandwiches and flash would be lying about in the rest hut through the day, and God knows who could be rummaging around in there. When the revolver was wrapped, it was light and blunt, though still bulky and hard to ignore, bigger than a spectacle case, bigger than twenty cigarettes and the large box of matches that most men carried.

He breezed into the kitchen. "Morning, Mrs. Duncan, all right then?"

"Not so bad, little enough to complain about. You're sure about the toast and coffee?" Disappointment clouded her face when he nodded.

Harry had been in the bathroom during the seven-o'clock news bulletins, and through the closed door he had heard her radio playing faintly downstairs, loud enough to be aware of it but too indistinct to hear the actual words.

"Nothing to note, just the usual. It goes on. A policeman chased a man out of his house and shot him. That's his version anyway, up Dunmurry way, more trouble in the Unionists. Never change their spots, that crowd. They've given nothing to use without it being wrung out . . ."

Harry laughed. "They haven't caught the big man yet, top of the Provos?"

"Well, Mr. McEvoy, if they have, they didn't say so, which means they haven't. They'd be trumpeting it if they had, but that's all the news is, the troubles. Makes you wonder what they used to put in before it all started. I can hardly remember. There must have been something else for them to talk about, but they've forgotten it now, right enough."

"Well then, no big man in the net."

"They don't get the real big men, only the shrimps."

"No, it's just that I read in one of the papers I saw up at the yard that they were mounting an effort to rake in the big fish."

"They say they're doing that each week, and nothing comes of it."

Harry had banked a lot on the Man being in custody. It was twenty-one hours after the call to London, to Davidson. Couldn't be that bloody difficult to pick the bastard up. Shouldn't be taxing the might of the British army. They must have him, but they weren't saying yet, had to be that way. They wouldn't say yet, too early, of course it was. The explanation was facile, but enough to tide him over his breakfast.

It was Monday morning and he was the only guest. Tonight, around teatime, the travelers and the others would be back in the front room. The place then was not quite his own as on Saturdays and Sundays. Lord and master of the household was how he felt over the weekend. Delusions of grandeur.

"Will Josephine be in this afternoon?" He sounded casual, matter-of-fact.

"Should be, Mr. McEvoy. Should be here in time to help me with the teas and a bit of tidying-up that I haven't got round to. She's back on early shift this week. You wanted to see her?"

Shrewd old goat, thought Harry. Beautiful throwaway,

real afterthought. "I'd said I'd lend her a book," he lied
gracefully.

"She'll be here when you get back. I'll need her today,
and all. We're full tonight. It's the way it should be, but
work all the same."

"And money, Mrs. Duncan." It was as much familiarity
as was permitted.

"Your sandwiches are there on the sideboard." She
wasn't drawn. "Some coffee in the flask. I put a boiled egg
in, too, and an apple."

"Very naughty, Mrs. Duncan, you'll make me into an
elephant."

She liked the banter and was still laughing with him as
he walked into the hall and to the front door.

"You've got enough clothes on, then? We don't want
you with a cold and that."

"Don't you fuss, Mrs. Duncan."

The Prime Minister liked to start the day with his
papers, a cup of tea and the first radio news bulletin. He
amused himself by making that first news the commercial
one, maintaining to all those who expressed surprise that
he was not locked onto the BBC, that he was a capitalist,
and as head of a capitalist government he should hear
the capitalist-funded station. The radio acted as window
dressing to his reading, the spoken version of canned
music. He could not do without it, hated silence, but it
took an almighty news story to distract his attention away
from the newspapers. Like all politicians, he had a con-
summate appetite for newsprint, able to take in, extract,
cross-reference or ignore the thousands of words that
made up his daily diet. Included in the pile that rested
on his lap in the middle of the bed were the *Western Mail*
and the *Scotsman*. He would have liked the *Belfast News
Letter*, but the printing times and transportation problems
across the Irish Sea made it impossible, so he compromised

by having the previous afternoon's *Telegraph* sent over. He waded through the politics, diplomatic, economic, pausing fractionally longer on the gossip columns than he would have wanted others to know, and through sport, where he delayed no longer than it took him to turn the pages. The pace was enormous, nothing read twice unless it had major impact.

The frown began deep between the overbearing business of the eyebrows. The degree of concentration extended. The mixture written on his stubbly face was of puzzlement and anger.

The Times had put it on page two, and not given it much. Eight paragraphs. No by-line.

He found the same story in the *Guardian*, a little longer, and above it the resident staff reporter's name. The length of the copy had relatively little importance or significance to the Prime Minister. The content flabbergasted him. He read three, four times that a British agent had been identified by the Provisional IRA, and the population in the ghetto areas alerted so that they might be on their guard against him.

For Christ's sake. Six weeks since Danby was killed. Outcry and outrage over, gone with the memorial service. Whole wretched business faded, and just as well, no leak that Danby himself had asked for his detective to be taken off. And now the prospect of it all back again, supercharged, and with what drifting out? Heaven only knows. With a surge he swept the bedclothes from him and leaned across the bed. He never had been able to make a telephone call lying on his side. He slung the dressing gown over his shoulders and sat on the edge of the single bed he had occupied since his wife died, feet dangling, and picked up the telephone.

"Morning, Jennifer, first of the day." Always something friendly to the girls on the switchboard, worked wonders with them. "Secretary of State for Northern Ireland. Quick as you can, there's a good girl."

He sat for two and a half minutes, reading other papers but unable to turn his full attention to them, till the telephone buzzed angrily in its console.

"The Secretary of State, sir. Seems he's in the air at the moment. Left Northolt about eight minutes ago. He'll be down at Aldergrove in forty-one minutes. He's early this morning because he's going straight down to an industrial estate in Londonderry, opening something. There's a helicopter waiting to lift him down there. That's his immediate program."

"Get him to phone me as soon as he reaches Aldergrove. Let them know I'd like it on a secure line."

He considered calling Ministry of Defence or Fairbairn in Lisburn, and then dismissed it. Protocol up the spout if he did. If they were to be dropped in a monumental balls-up, then the Secretary of State should do some of the lifting and take a bit of the weight. Time to play things straight down the middle, the Prime Minister reflected.

Across London, Davidson was shaving. Wet. With a brush and new blade. He had read his papers again in the daylight. He knew, since he had not been wakened from his sleep by the telephone, that in Belfast Billy Downs and the girl were still at large. He could not be certain at this stage what level of danger Harry was exposed to. When he ditched his logical appraisal, the only conclusion was that the situation must be slightly worse than critical. He said that out loud; the aide was in the other half of the office and would not hear him. The words rolled off his tongue, giving him that almost sexual pleasure that excitement and tension carry in their wake. He stood there in his trousers, socks and vest, with the bowl of tepid water in front of him . . . all so much like the war. The Albania operation, Cyprus. But how to reconcile that when advanced base headquarters, ABHQ they used to call it, was in Covent Garden, West One, Central London?

He patted his face, reddened by the sharpness of the blade and the cool water. Putting on his shirt, he dialed Lisburn military direct. When the WRAC operator came on the line he asked for Frost. The intelligence colonel was already in his office.

"Morning, Colonel. I wanted to ring you to find the up-to-date situation. I fancy there'll be various meetings in the morning. People will want to know, I take it there's been no positive news or you would have called me."

"Right, Mr. Davidson." Had to be the "Mister," didn't it? Doesn't miss them. Not a chance of twisting it. "There is no news. We haven't found the girl. We did Downs's home, and the report an hour ago said he wasn't there, but had been a few hours earlier. There's an off chance he's in trouble. A man of his description attacked a policeman's home late yesterday and botched it up. The policeman thinks he hit him with a single revolver shot as he was escaping. There are one or two blood spots on the escape trail, but we won't get much from them for a bit till the follow-up report is in. It doesn't seem enough to indicate a serious wound. As for your man, well, we're taking out the Andersonstown scrap merchants in about forty minutes. I've nothing else."

"Are you putting it that there's a good chance Downs was out on this shooting last night, or not?"

"There are similarities, but it's not a positive identification. Hair's not the same as the picture, so the policeman's wife says. She was a long time with him. Face is similar. The policeman himself is not able to be very helpful, as he was moving most of the time and getting his gun out and being shot at. He didn't get much of a look. We have the picture you sent us, it's with the unit now that's going to try to round your fellow up."

"Thank you very much, Colonel."

"That's all right, Mr. Davidson. I'm sure we'll never

have the opportunity again of providing a similar service to your organization."

Davidson put the phone down. "Stupid, pompous bugger. Bloody man, does he think we're having a picnic at this end?" He said it with enough ferocity to wake his assistant in the armchair by the door on the other side of the partition.

The younger man shrugged himself out of his sleep. "Any news?"

"Not a bloody dickeybird that matters."

The postcard was lying on the mat, color side down, when Mary Brown responded to the flap of the letterbox in the front door.

"There's a card from Daddy, darlings," she called into the back of the house where the boys were having their breakfast.

"Not a letter, Mum?" her elder boy shouted back.

"No, just a card. You know how awful your father is about letters."

There was a market scene on the card. Men in kaffiyehs and futahs staring blankly from the gold market that stood in the middle distance.

"Hope to see you all soon. Still very hot, and not much to do. Love you all, Harry." That was all there was on the card, written in pen and large in Harry's hand.

Josephine Laverty was late, and hurried in a frantic mixture of run and walk down the Falls to the mill where she worked. She couldn't go fast, as the pain still bit into her ribs. She, too, had heard the early radio news, half expecting in an uninvolved sort of way to hear that Harry McEvoy had been found face down, hooded and dead. It had surprised her that there was no mention of him. This morning she had wondered for a wild moment whether to go see if he was still at Delrosa, but there was no will power and the emotion he had created was now drained from her.

Perhaps she would go to Mrs. Duncan's tonight to help with the teas. Perhaps not. But that could be a later decision. There was now an irrelevance about Harry McEvoy. Forget him. The pillow eavesdropper who had a girl killed. Forget the sod.

With their photographs of Harry, the troops from Fort Monagh raided the five scrap yards in Andersonstown. No one in the operation had been told why they were to pick up the smiling man in the picture who wore his hair shorter than their more general customers. The orders were that if the man was found, he was to be taken straight to battalion headquarters and handed over. Among those NCOs who were the foremen of the military factory floor and who knew most of what mattered, there was surprise that so many men were occupied in looking for a man whose picture was not on the operations-room wall, whose name was completely fresh. They had their regular batch of photographs, top ten for the week, top thirty for the month, four for each day of the week. Made up on little cards and issued to the troops to study before they went out on patrol. But this face had never been among them.

At the scrap yards, the employees who had arrived before the troops stood sullenly against the walls of the huts, hands above their heads, as they were searched and then matched with the photograph. From the five locations the initial report was that a blank had been drawn. But the troops would lie up in the yards till nine at least in the hope that the man they wanted would still come—was just late. At the yard where Harry in fact worked, there was disbelief when they were shown the picture. Never involved, never talking politics, just an ordinary man, too old to be with the cowboys. The little man who ran the yard looked at the armored cars and the soldiers, reckoned Harry must be important and determined to say nothing. He confirmed the picture, that he employed a man called Harry McEvoy, that he had started work recently, that was all. Let them find the rest out for themselves.

"Where does he live?" the lieutenant who led the raid asked him.

"Don't know. He never said. Just down the road somewhere, that's all he said."

"He must have given some impression where he lived?"

"Nothing."

"What about his stamps, his insurance?"

The little man looked embarrassed. The answer was clear enough.

The lieutenant was new to Northern Ireland. The man opposite him seemed of substance, a cut above the yobbos, respectable even. "Look, we need this man rather badly." He said it quietly, out of earshot of the other men.

"Well, you'll have to wait for him, won't you?"

But time was ticking on its way, and as the soldiers crouched behind the wrecked cars and buses and waited, there was no sign of the face in the photograph. Even the little man became worried by Harry's nonarrival. His first reaction had been that it was a case of mistaken identity, but that Harry should be absent at the same time that the military launched this reception led him to suppose that his newest hand was a rather more complex figure than he had believed.

The soldiers radioed in, hung about a few more minutes, then drove back, empty-handed, to Fort Monagh.

■ 18 ■

The Secretary of State spoke to Downing Street from the single-story red-brick building that was the RAF Reception at Aldergrove. They'd offered him a car to take him to the officers' quarters and the use of the group captain's phone, but he'd declined. The message waiting for him was of the sort the Prime Minister rarely burdened him with, must be important and should be returned at speed.

It took several minutes for the connection to come through. The delay came from the need to patch in the speech-distortion apparatus that would safeguard the security of the call and prevent any casual telephone user understanding the conversation. When the instrument rang out in the partitioned office indicating that the call was ready, the service aides discreetly backed out through the door. The Secretary of State's men stayed with him.

"Morning, Prime Minister. I'm returning your call."

"I won't keep you long. I wondered how thoroughly you'd read your papers this morning. *Guardian* and *Times*. Provisionals claiming they've identified an agent of ours, warning the population. All a bit melodramatic but enough to cause anxiety."

"I haven't seen it, I'm afraid."

The Prime Minister replied, "We're a little anxious at this end that it could be the fellow we sent over for Danby. Could be difficult if they nabbed him, and he talked."

"Trifle awkward, no doubt about that. Well, we'll get the people who run him to move him out right away. Get him back to UK and snappy. That's the simple answer."

"The problem lies right there," said the Prime Minister. "It's a bit incredible, but the chaps controlling him in London cannot contact him. Seems he just calls in when he has something to say."

The Secretary of State winced. "Bit unusual that, isn't it? Bit unique. Not standard procedure. What you are saying is that he may not know he's blown, if in fact he is. That we may not be hearing too much from him in the future."

"You're not a million miles away from it."

"And what do we do . . . ? Sorry, I'll rephrase that one. What do you want done about it."

"I'm just letting you know the situation. There's not very much we can do about it beyond the obvious. Stand by to catch the cradle."

"If it comes, it'll be from a fair altitude." The Secretary of State played a slow smile around his lips at the head of government's discomfiture.

"Could be a bit tricky." The Prime Minister was sounding old, tired and a long way away.

"I'm glad it wasn't down to me, this one." He paused to let it sink home. "Still, we'll see what comes out of it. It may be just a kite they're flying. They often do that. I'll keep a weather eye out for the storm clouds. Goodbye, Prime Minister."

There were no confidences with his staff as the group left the building and walked to the big Puma helicopter for the ride to Londonberry. He asked his army liaison officer to keep him informed if there should be any assassination victims during the day.

His remark of "bloody harebrained scheme at the best of times" was heard only by the Scotland Yard detective, his bodyguard, sitting next to him as he adjusted his safety harness while the rotor blades gathered their impetus.

The ambush was in position.

It was a proven, brutally simple piece of organization. A stolen Ford Escort was parked sixty yards up from Delrosa just before the junction with the Falls Road. The car was empty and unlikely to cause suspicion. The number plates had been changed. Harry would walk along on the opposite side of the pavement and turn into the main road. He would be watched by three men who had placed themselves behind the lace curtains of the house in front of which the car was parked. With Harry safely around the corner, the men could come out of the house, start up the car and cruise up from behind him to surprise their target. It was a fast and effective method, and over the years had come to be considered fail-safe. The three men in the room, behind the lace curtains, were Downs, Frank and Duffryn. All were at this stage without their guns, but in the Escort's glove compartment was a Luger, and underneath the driver's seat a folded-down Armalite placed in position, ready loaded and cocked.

To both Frank and Duffryn this was a novel situation. Neither had ever been entrusted with a mission of such importance before, and the tension they felt was reflected in the frequency with which both of them came forward and tugged at the flimsiness of the curtain to view the other side of the road. They talked quietly in staccato style to each other, avoiding the eyes and attention of the Man, who stayed at the back behind them. Neither Frank nor Duffryn knew the third man's name, only vaguely his reputation as a marksman. That was something both had reflected on overnight to comfort themselves as the few hours slipped away before the rendezvous.

Since he had been told of the operation, the Man had had little to say. He burned up his anger and frustration inside himself till he was as taut as a stretched catapult. The pain of his injury told on him, too, and though that was slightly compensated for by the tablets he had taken, he felt weak and, above all, disorganized.

Both Frank and Duffryn looked to the third man for leadership, but he buried himself away from them, not communicating the confidence and expertise they were looking for. He wore a loose overall sweater, with his left arm in a sling underneath it, the sleeve hanging free at his side. He knew he was not fit enough to get into a firefight like that, but for a pickup and at close range he'd see it through. To back him up, he had the strength and fitness of the other two men. He would sit in the front with Duffryn driving, and Frank in the back with the Englishman for the short ride from Broadway to Whiterock.

Frank said, "He's late now. He can't be much longer. He's a big fellow. We'll not miss him. He's the only visitor at the house."

"How long do we leave him after he's away round the corner?" Duffryn asked. He'd been told the answer three times, but kept on asking with the insecurity of a small boy who needs to quiz his teacher in class so that she won't forget his presence.

"Hardly at all," said Frank. "Just a few yards. We want to pick him on the bend near the cemetery, so we need him to move about a hundred yards, not much more."

"Hope the bloody car starts." Duffryn giggled weakly, and looked at the Man. "You done this sort of thing before?"

Duffryn saw the pale, pinched hating face. Sensed the quality of his anger and hostility.

"Yes," said the Man.

"It works like they plan it, does it? I mean, it all seems so straightforward when you put it on paper and work out a timetable and that. But does it really happen as easily as that?"

"Sometimes. Other times it doesn't."

"The thing that worries me"—like a bloody tap, drip, drip, drip, thought the Man as Duffryn chattered on—"is if they have a pig going by as we jump him. Christ knows what we do then."

He said the last to himself as the anxiety built up in him about the caliber of the morose and injured man that he and Frank were depending on for success. Just as Duffryn put it out of his mind, Frank stiffened and edged forward again toward the window.

"He's coming. Here comes the English bastard."

Duffryn pushed his friend to the side to see for himself. The tall figure in the distance, blurred and in soft focus, closing the wicket gate at the front of Delrosa behind him, that was their enemy. He'd thought about him most of the night, about the killing of him—now he came, walking straight, without a sideways glance. Looks as if he bloody owns the place, thought Duffryn.

"Keep back from the window, you stupid buggers," the Man behind them hissed.

Harry was stepping out, aware of his slow start to the morning and conscious that whatever speed he walked to the yard, he would still be late. The combination of Mrs. Duncan's chatter and her insistence on the fresh coffee that percolated interminably had delayed him. He came up the familiar pavement fast, with his sandwiches and flask in the bag bouncing on his shoulder and the weight of the wrapped revolver thudding against his right hip.

He saw the car, one of several parked on the other side of the road. It was small, neat and well kept, but slightly different, something strange . . . the keys left in the ignition. Daft idiot, who leaves keys in his car down the Falls. People didn't leave the keys in the ignition around here unless they'd gone inside for something shorter than a quick crap.

Harry moved on past the car and up to the junction of

the side street and the Falls, where the Catholic community comes into town and where the traffic snarl-ups were beginning. The side of the road that Harry walked on, though, was virtually clear, with just an occasional car speeding past him. He was a punctual man. The army and his aunt's upbringing had disciplined him in this, and his lateness this Monday morning annoyed him. He checked his left wrist to see how far behind the morning schedule he was, and realized with a suppressed oath that he had left his watch behind . . . Where . . . ? Not in his room, not at breakfast. In the bathroom after shaving. He was thirty yards into the Falls, the guest house some seventy-five back around the corner. Damn and blast it. Only a hundred yards back to get it. He wavered. And then, a hundred yards back to where he was now. Two hundred yards. Nothing. It's a naked feeling without a watch. Not as bad as leaving glasses behind or your fly unzipped, but an irritation. Harry swung around on his heel and walked back toward Delrosa.

As he turned the corner, Duffryn was beside the driver's door of the car, at the handle and in the process of opening it. Frank was already in the back seat, and the Man, coming out of the house last, was halfway between the front door and the car.

For a moment all four men froze.

Harry, mind racing like a flywheel, tried to put a situation and background to the familiarity of the face in front of him.

It was fractional, the lapse of doubt before the image slotted. The dance, the woman in yellow, the army crushing in, and as the concentration lasted, so the face confronting him across the street dissolved into the details of the photokit picture. Outline of cheekbone structure, that matched. More so than when the man had been at the club, the contours of the flesh on the face merged with the painstaking impression built up in London. Perhaps it was the strain the Man had been under these last hours, or the pain from the wound, but the features at last resembled those the old lady had seen in the park, that the girl in the Underground station had stared at as she fought to keep her balance.

The first movement. Harry reached into his anorak pocket, thrust deep with both hands to pull out the pistol. He dragged at the sharp white toweling, and ripped it from the blackness of the gun, tearing a ladder of bright cotton on the foresight. Thirty feet away, Duffryn flung himself face down behind the car, his mind clouded by the sight of the gun in his enemy's hand. Frank jack-knifed his body over the front passenger seat to open the glove compartment where the Luger lay, stretching himself over the obstacle of the headrest. The Man bent low, ducking forward toward the back of the car. Out of sight and to the rear right door beyond which his beloved Armalite was resting.

Aimed shots, Harry boy. Don't blaze. Aim and you'll hit the buggers. He shrugged the duffel bag from his shoulder onto the paving stones, and, legs squat and apart, brought the revolver up to the aim position. Knees slightly bent, body weight forward, both arms extended and coming together with the gun at eye level. The classic killing position. Hands and gun as one complete sighting apparatus. Squeeze, don't jerk the trigger. Take it gently. The thumb of the right hand fumbled forward, rested on the safety catch in the On position and eased it forward.

In the big V of the arms, reaching to the barrel of the revolver, was the contorted shape of Frank, still stretching for the Luger. Harry steadied as the man lurched back into the rear seat with the gun in his hand, and fired his first shot. The left side of the rear window disintegrated, and Frank jolted as the bullet hit him in the throat. The effort of getting at the Luger had denied him a clear look

at Harry. Bewilderment was spread over his face as he
subsided onto the back seat with a rivulet of crimson
flooding down onto the collar of his shirt. Not in itself a
fatal shot, but it would become one if Frank did not get
immediate hospital treatment. He was out of Harry's sight
now. The Englishman stood stock-still, looking for the
next target. Come out, you bastards. Show yourselves.
Where's the bloody man we want? Which of you has the
next gun? Who shoots next? Steady, Harry boy. You're
like a big lamppost up there, right in the open. Get some
bloody cover.

Harry knelt on the pavement. Come out with your hands
above your heads. Any attempt to escape and I'll shoot.
Good control, Harry, dominate the buggers.

The Man whispered to Duffryn as they huddled on the
reverse side of the car, "Make a run down the hill. He'll
not hit you with a hand gun. But for God's sake, run and
now!" He pulled Duffryn past him and shoved him out
into the open and away from the sanctuary of the car. The
Man shouted after him, "Run, you little bastard, and
weave . . ."

Duffryn, in deep terror, bolted from the cover. Out of
control and conscious only of the empty space around
him, he sprinted down the street in the direction of
Delrosa. His intention was to shift direction from right to
left and to change his speed at the same time. The effect
was to slow him down and make him the easier target.
Harry fired four times. By the time he pulled the trigger for
the second time, he had sensed that he was after a man
who had never faced this type of situation before. He
heard Duffryn sob out as he ran, pleading, merging with
his shout as the third shot caught him between the
shoulder blades. Duffryn cannoned forward into the
lamppost, spread-eagled against it for a few seconds, and
then slid down to become a shapeless mass at its base.
The fourth bullet, unnecessary, jolted into his sluggish

body. Duffryn would live, since neither of the hitting bullets had found a critical resting place.

Now that he was down and stationary, the confusion ebbed and clarity came to the young intelligence officer. The enemy would kill him, no doubt. Certainty. It seemed not to matter. There was hurt, but not so much as he had expected. He was puzzled that he could barely picture the face of the Englishman who had shot him. The clothes he could see, and the gun resting between the hands and the kick as it rocked back when Frank was shot. But there had been no face. The gun obscured it. He had not even seen his enemy. He never would, now.

The moment that Duffryn had run, the Man eased open the front door of the Escort, forced himself upward into the driving seat and started the engine. The four shots that Harry had fired at the decoy—the hare with the job of distracting him—had given him sufficient time to get the car rolling in the direction of the Falls.

Harry swung the revolver around, tracking his attention away from the fallen boy to the moving car. He saw the head low over the wheel before it swung lower still, below the dashboard. That was the moment he fired, knowing instinctively as he did so that he was going too high. The bullet struck the angle of the roof of the car, exited and thudded into the wall of the house opposite. Count your shots, they always drilled that. He had done so, and he was out, chamber empty, finished, exhausted. Three more cartridges in the picnic bag, down at the bottom below the plastic food box and the coffee flask. Frantically he broke the gun and pushed the used cases out, so that they clattered and shone on the pavement. He slid in the three replacements, copper-plated ends and grey snub-nosed tips.

The Man was out in the traffic of the Falls, desperate to avoid the cars around him but unable to escape from the conformity of the Catholic route into town. As a reflex, Harry ran after him, revolver still in hand. He saw cars shy away from him as he came out into the traffic lanes, heard the grind of acceleration and scraping of brakes as men tried to put space between him and themselves. It was as though he had some plague or disease and could kill by contact. The Man was edging away when Harry worked out the equation. Nine cars back was a Cortina Estate, crawling with the others and unwilling to come past the man waving his revolver. Harry ran to the passenger door. It was unlocked. As he looked into the driver's eyes he shouted at him, "This is loaded. You're to follow that car . . . the white Escort in front . . . and follow it close. For your own safety, don't bugger about. I'm army, but that won't help you if you mess me."

Donal McKeogh, aged twenty-seven, a plastics salesman living outside Dungannon, forty miles down the motorway, gave a mechanical, numbed response, the car trickled forward, its driver's mind still blank.

Harry saw the Escort drawing away. "Don't mess me, you clever bugger." He screamed at the face a few inches away, and to reinforce the effect of his intentions, fired a single shot through the roof of the car. McKeogh surged forward toward the Springfield Road lights. The message was understood now, and would not need repeating. He might have seen me coming out into the traffic, reckoned Harry, but he's unlikely to have seen which car is following him. Little chance of that. McKeogh, swerving through on the inside, crossing the double lines in the center and drawing angry shouts from other drivers, had closed the gap to five cars by the time they reached the lights.

Two bullets remained in the Smith and Wesson.

It had taken the Man little time to work out where he was going. The failure to kill the Englishman dictated the decision. He was going home. Blown, finished, out.

He was tired. Needing a corner to sleep away the

stabbing pains and biting disappointments of the last few hours, needing quiet, and silence. Away from the guns, and the firing, and the blood. Above all, he wanted to get away from the noise of the weapons that blasted out close to his ears, screwing up his guts with tension, then releasing them like an unplugged bladder, flat and winded.

Away from it all, and the only place he could go was home. To his wife. To his children. To his house. To Ypres Avenue. The logic and will power and control that had caused him to be chosen for London were drained from him. No emotion, no sensitivity left. Even the slight bubbling coughs of Frank in the back seat could not disturb him.

Failure. Failure from the Man considered so valuable that only the most important work was earmarked for him. Failure from the elitist. More important, failure against the enemy who was working to kill, eliminate, exterminate, execute *him*. The words kept tempo with the throbbing of the arm wound. Christ, how it hurt. A bad, dangerous pain that dug at him, then went, but came again with renewed force, chewing at his strength and resolve.

The Armalite was still in the car, untouched under his seat, but useless now. It had no further part to play. The Armalite days were over, they didn't settle things. It was over. Concluded, done with, half a lifetime ago.

Driving was hard. He had to stretch his left arm to the gear handle every few seconds, and even the movement from second to third aggravated the injury. He mapped out a route for himself. Down to Divis, then across the top fringe of town to Unity flats, and then on to Carlyle Circus. Could park there, on the roundabout. It was a walk to Ardoyne then, and the car and Frank would be close to the Mater, their own people's hospital. Frank would be found quickly there, and would get the treatment he needed. There were no roadblocks and he moved with the traffic, Frank too low down to be seen and the bullet holes failing to draw people into involvement.

It was nine minutes to the Circus, where the Crumlin and the Antrim roads come together and where cars could be left unattended. He drove on to the space and stopped the car. To get out he had to lever himself up with his right hand, then he looked behind and in the back. Frank was very white, with much of his blood pooled beside his face on the plastic seating. In his eyes was just enough light to signal recognition.

"Don't worry, Frank boy. You're close to the Mater. You'll be there in five minutes. I'm going to call them. I'm going now, and don't worry. God bless. It's all okay, you'll be safe. A few minutes, that's all."

Frank could say nothing.

The Man left the engine running and the driver's door open as he ran away from the car. It was enough to ensure that someone would look inside. The broken window would clinch it. The Armalite was still under the driver's seat, and the Luger lay beneath Frank's body. He ran up the Crumlin, Mater Hospital on his right, huge and red and cleansed, giving way to the prison. High walls, coils of barbed wire, reinforced stone sentry towers and, dominating all, the great gatehouse. The Man went on by them, and past the soldiers on guard duty, and the policemen guarding the courthouse opposite, with their flak jackets and Stirlings. None spared him a glance as he ran.

The sprint gave way to a jog, then to little more than a stumble as he neared the safety of Ardoyne at the top of the long hill. The weight of his legs seemed to pin him back as he forced his feet forward, separating himself from the chaos and disaster behind him. His breath came in great sobs and gulps as he struggled to keep up momentum. The only demand he made of himself now was to get to his home, to his wife, and bury himself in her warmth. The hospital and the prison were far behind down the road when he reached the iron sheeting that divided Shankill from Ardoyne, where he had stood the previous afternoon waiting for the lift that took him to Rennie's home. God-rot that bastard copper and his bloody children. That was where it had all collapsed. The bloody child in the way, smack in the way, never a clear sight at the copper, only the bloody kid's head. Panting and wrenching for air, he slowed up to walk the last few yards.

They were right. He'd lost his fucking nerve. Billy Downs, the one selected by the chief of staff, had slipped it because of a child's head.

And then, this morning . . . Frank with his voice shot out, and the young bugger they'd sent him, down on the pavement, shredded. And you, you clever sod, you told him to run to make room for yourself, and he did, and he bloody bought it.

In the race across the city, McKeogh had several times fallen back in the traffic stream, losing completely the sight of the white Escort before spotting it again far to the front, maneuvering among the lorries and vans and cars. Then Harry screamed and threatened McKeogh, and the salesman would speed up. He doubted his hijacker was a member of the British army, but was undecided whether he was IRA or UVF. That he would be killed if he didn't follow the bellowed instructions, he was certain of. As they came out of the town and reached the Circus, the Escort was gone. Four major routes come together there, including the Crumlin leading up to Ardoyne and the Antrim Road running up to the nearer equally hard-line New Lodge. New Lodge offered the quicker refuge, and Harry aimed his arm that way as McKeogh swung around the Circus and then up the wide road. They drove a mile, and fast up beyond the scorched entrance to the ghetto, before Harry indicated they should turn back.

"Try the Crumlin, it has to be that way."

"He could have got away from us and still be in this road. If he went up the Crumlin, he'll be out of the city by now, up in Ligoniel, halfway to the airport," said McKeogh.

"I know where the bugger can be. Just drive and close your attention on that," Harry snapped back. He would be lucky now to find him again. He knew that, but didn't need any bloody driver to tell him. Neither saw the Escort still parked among the other cars on the Circus, and they turned up the long haul of the Crumlin. Harry was forward in his seat now, peering right and left as McKeogh swept up the road. At the top he shouted. The exultation of a master of hounds throwing off the frustration of a lost quarry. "There he is, at the tin wall!"

McKeogh slowed the car in against the near pavement. "Who is he?" he said.

Harry looked at him, didn't reply and bolted from the car. He ran across the road and disappeared from McKeogh's view through the gap in the silver corrugated fence. The Man had a start of less than a hundred yards.

Talk of the initial shooting straddled the city. The first officer into the road was taken by a lance corporal to meet the tear-swamped Mrs. Duncan. Between gulps and pauses to blow her nose, she told the immediate story that formed the basis of the situation report.

"He'd just left for work, Mr. McEvoy, and I heard the shooting, and I ran to the door. Up the end of the street was Mr. McEvoy with a gun, and one man seemed to run down the street toward this end, and he was shot. Mr. McEvoy just aimed and shot him. Then another man got into the car and started to drive away, and Mr. McEvoy fired at him too, and I don't know whether he was hit or not. It was so fast. Then Mr. McEvoy ran into the road, waving and shouting at people in cars. Then I came indoors."

"Who is this Mr. McEvoy?" the bemused subaltern asked automatically.

"He's my lodger, been here three weeks. Quiet as a mouse, and a gentleman, a real proper man. Never spoke to anyone, and then there he was, crouched behind his gun and shooting it over and over."

The ambulance took Duffryn to the hospital, and bulletins later in the day spoke of his condition as "critical."

Frost, still in the 39 Brigade operations room at Lisburn, saw the reports coming in over the teletype. In rapid succession he spoke to the GOC, the Brigade commander in Londonderry in order that the Secretary of State could be briefed when he arrived there, and finally to Davidson in London.

In each case the message was substantially the same.

"At first sight it looks as though they mounted some sort of ambush for McEvoy this morning. There was a balls-up on the job, and our fellow ended up shooting at least one of theirs. He's in hospital, injured. Another chap escaped in a car, and when last seen, McEvoy was standing out in the Falls trying the old tack of waving down a spot of transport, civilian, for hot pursuit. It gets a bit more droll each stage. He'd holed up in a small guest house just off the Falls in the Broadway section. So he's on the loose again, and it's my wager that by lunchtime the place will be buzzing a bit."

Minutes later the teletype was chattering again. A shot-up car had been discovered in Carlyle Circus, and a man had been taken from the back with serious gunshot wounds.

"This McEvoy, he's one of ours," said Frost to the major from his department who stood beside him.

"Working for us?" said the other man in astonishment. The clerks and corporals and duty officers strained to listen.

"Not as simple. Working for our side, but not working for us, not for this department. It's involved and complicated and a cock-up."

Frost explained the whole situation to the major. "It seems the boyos went for McEvoy this morning to try to get him on the way to a job he'd picked up. He's cool enough, this lad. There's been quite a shoot-out. McEvoy shot at least one of them, maybe more. There's another half-stiff turned up beside the Mater in a car with guns in it. It may be something to do with it. Could well be."

One of the desk sergeants came toward the colonel, pushing a telephone trolly across the floor of the ops room, a light set in the handle flashing brilliantly. "Call for you, sir."

Frost took the phone, identified himself and listened rather more than a minute. Then he thanked the caller, asked him quietly not to move anything and said he would be on his way.

"There's been shooting in Ypres Avenue, that's Billy Downs's street. Looks a bit like *High Noon* apparently, bodies and plenty all over the place." Frost rattled it out, hard and composed. "I think I'll go down there, so hold the fort, please. It'll take me about fifteen minutes to get there. But if there's any word of McEvoy, let me know right away."

And he was gone before the major could stand on any of his dignity and complain about being kept in the dark. That Frost traditionally kept things close to his chest was small consolation. Suddenly the operations room was alive. It was seldom the staff on the first floor of headquarters was able to feel the tension of street-level operations. Frost had brought them into it, though at the expense of his famous discretion.

The sergeant brought the trolley over once more. "It's a call for Colonel Frost, sir. They say it's London and personal and urgent. A Mr. Davidson. The colonel called him a few minutes ago. Will you take it?"

The major took the phone. "It's his deputy here." He waited while the question was framed at the other end, then went on: "We have another wounded man, and a shooting in Downs's street in Ardoyne. Bodies but no names to match them with is the order of the morning so far. You'll have to wait half an hour or so, and then we might have the answer. Sorry, old chap, but that's the way it is."

■ **19** ■

Feverish in the torment of her uncertainty, the Man's wife had sent two of her children to the community infant crèche and dumped the others with her neighbors. In her threadbare green coat, and with her bag and purse, she had taken herself to the shops at the top of Ardoyne. The screw had been well twisted on her exhausted nerves.

The news program less than two hours earlier had carried reports of the shooting at the policeman's house, amplified by eye-witness accounts. The BBC had sent a man to the house, and his story made much of the gun-man who hesitated, the intervention of the child, the wounding of the gunman. There had been a trail of blood, and the policeman was a trained marksman the report said. The *Irish News*, which she had seen when she took the young ones three doors down, had shown a floodlit picture of the neat bungalow and white-faced detectives working with their fingerprint kits by the front door. The paper had also spoken of the wounding of the would-be assassin.

Men from the community association would come in later in the day to help repair the boards pulled up at dawn by the army, but for now the debris and confusion in the house and the noise of the children coupled with the danger to her husband to defeat her.

But the single factor that weighed most with her was the knowledge that the military knew of her husband, had identified him, and that their life together was effectively over. If he had survived last night, then he would be on the run and go underground, otherwise the future held only the prospect of years in the Kesh or the Crumlin.

And for what?

She was not one of the militant women of the streets who blew the whistles and beat the dustbins, and marched down the Falls, and screamed at the soldiers and sent food parcels to the prisons. At the start the cause had not interested her, till, parallel with the growing involvement of her husband, she had become passively hostile to the movement. That a Cabinet Minister should die in London, a soldier in Broadway or a policeman in Dunmurry, was not the fuel that fired her. Her conviction was of far too low a grade to sustain her in her present misery.

Her purse had been full from the social security last Thursday. Now most of it was spent, with only enough for the basics of bread and milk bolstered by sausages and baked beans and tins. At the shops as she queued, many eyes were on her. Word had passed in the streets that the army had raided her house, that they were looking for her man, that he had been out all night. Over the years it had become a familiar enough situation in the little community, but that it was this family that was at the center of the morning's swoop caused the stares, the muttered comments and the pulling aside of the front-window curtains.

She glared back at them, embarrassing the onlookers enough to deflect their eyes. She paid for her food, pecking in her purse for the exact money, and swung out the door and back onto the street. She had forty yards to walk to the top of Ypres Avenue.

When she turned into the narrow long street, the observation post spotted her. The soldiers were concealed in the roof of the mill, disused and now converted into warehouse space. They came and went by the back stairs, and where the boards were too rotten, hauled themselves up by rope ladded. Once in position, they put a heavy padlock on the door behind them, locking themselves in the roughly fashioned cubicle, constructed out of sandbags, blankets and sacking. They had some protection and some warmth: that was all. To see down the avenue, they lay on their stomachs with their heads forward into the angle of the roof, with a missing tile providing the vantage point. The two men in the post did twelve hours there at a stretch, and with three other teams, would rotate in the position, familiarizing themselves enough with the street so that eventually they would know each man and woman and child who lived there. The comings and going were logged, laboriously, in a notebook in pencil, then sifted each evening by their battalion's intelligence officer. A synopsis of life in the street was sent each week to headquarters for evaluation. It was a process repeated in scores of streets in the Catholic areas of Belfast as the security forces built up their enormous and comprehensive dossiers on the minority community.

Lance Corporal David Burns and Private George Smith had been in the mill since six that morning. They arrived in darkness and would leave long after the few street lights had come back on. They had been in Belfast eleven weeks on this tour, five more to go. Thirty-four days to be exact.

To the OP they'd brought sandwiches and a flask of sugared tea plus the powerful German binoculars they used, a folded card that expanded to show a montage of the faces of wanted men, the rifles with daytime telescopic sights and also the bulging image intensifier for night work. They carried everything they needed for the day up the rope ladder to the roof. Only the radiotelephone and the bulk treacle tin for emergency nature calls were permanent fixtures.

Burns, face intent behind the glasses, called out the details on the slight woman walking toward him. "The bird from forty-one. Must have been shopping. Didn't go for long. Can't be ten minutes since she went. Looks a bit rough. Didn't find her husband, did they?" The soldier squirmed closer to the aperture, pressing the glasses against his eyebrows, face contorted with concentration. "Hey, Smithie, behind her. I think he's coming. Right up the top there. Sort of running. That is her old man, isn't it? Looks like him. Have a squint yourself."

"I'm not sure, not at this stage. We'll be definite when he gets down the road a bit." Smith had taken over the hole. "Is he a shoot-on-sight, or what?"

"Don't know. They didn't say nothing about that. I'm sure enough now it's him. Get HQ on the radio. Looks like he's run a bloody marathon. Knackered, he is."

It was the pounding of his feet that first broke through her preoccupations. The urgency of the footsteps dragged the woman away from the images of her wounded husband and the breaking of her home. She turned toward the noise and stopped still at the sight.

The Man was struggling to run now, head rolling from side to side and the rhythm of his arm movements lost. His legs flailed forward over the last few paces to her, uncoordinated and wild. The stitch on his right side bit into the stomach wall. The pallor of his face was sluglike, excavated from under something of permanence. His face was hollow at the cheeks as he pulled the air inside his lungs, eyes fearful and vivid, and around them the skin glistened with a sheen of sweat. He was shapeless, the big sweater worn over the left shoulder and arm giving him a grotesque breadth. But as he came toward her, it was the eyes that held her. Their desperation, loneliness and dependence.

She put down her shopping bag on the paving, careful that it should not topple over, and held out her arms for her man. He fell against her, stumbling, and she reeled with the sudden weight as she took the strain. He convulsed against her as his lungs forced down the air they needed. There were words, but she could not understand them as they buried themselves in the shoulder of her coat. Far distant, on the top street corner, a knot of women had gathered.

"They came for you, you know, this morning."

"I know."

"They searched all over, and they said they'd come again. Again and again, till they got you." He nodded, numbed and shocked by the pain of the running and the throbbing in his arm. "They know, don't they? They know it all. They're not so daft as you said."

"I was told." The voice, the speaking, was a little easier now. The air was there, coming more naturally, and the legs steadied.

As she twisted herself against him, working away from the sharpness of his collarbone against her cheek, she felt him wince and tear away his left arm. "Is that where they hit you? Last night it was you. At the policeman's home. Did he hit you?" The pain came and went, surging and then sagging. "Has it been looked at? Have you seen a doctor?" Again he nodded.

"Where are you going now? What are you going to do?"

"I'm going home. It's over, finished. I just want to go home."

"But they came this morning for you," she screamed, her voice high, hysterical that he could not understand something so simple. "They'll be back as soon as you walk through the door. They'll take you. They were crawling all through, under the floorboards, into the roof, looking for you. They took the bloody place apart trying to find you."

He wasn't listening. "They put a man in, just to find me." He said it with wonder, as if surprised that the enemy would classify him of such importance that they would take a step so great. "We found him first. We went to get him this morning, and it just ballsed up. There's two boys shot by him, by the Englishman. And last night . . . that was another cock-up. That bloody copper, he . . ."

"I heard on the radio."

"Well, there's no point in running now. I'm finished with it. There'd be a reason to run if I was going on, but I'm not."

"You mean all this? It's not just because you're hurt? We can get you away from here, the boys will shift you."

"It's definite," he said. He was very tired now, deeply tired and needing to sit down, to take the great weight from his legs. He picked up her shopping bag with his right hand and draped the injured left arm over the small woman's shoulder. They began to walk by the terraced doors and the chipped and daubed red-brick of the street. It was a grey Belfast morning, rain threatening, wind cold and from the east, coming in over the Lough. The two threaded a path over the fractured paving stones, past the endless heaps of dogs' mess toward the house that had become the Man's goal.

The moment the two had created for each other was broken by the footsteps behind. Instinctively, both knew the noise of pursuit. In Ardoyne the knack of recognizing it was inbred.

The women on the corner were silent as Harry ran by them down the gentle incline toward where the Man and his wife were walking away from him. He held the revolver close to him, reassured by the hardness of the wooden handle, roughened with age and usage. He pulled up twenty feet short of them. The pair swung around to face him.

"Don't move. Don't try to run or get your firearm. If you do, I'll shoot."

Harry barked the instructions. The harshness of his tone and its assurance surprised him. He felt almost detached from the orders he was shouting.

"Put the bag down and begin to walk towards me, and slowly. Your hands on your head. The woman—she stays where she is."

Be strong. Don't mess about with him. You'll be a long time before you shift the bastard. Don't let him dominate you. Keep the gun on him, look at his hands the whole time. Watch the hands, and keep the gun in line. Keep it so it's only got to come straight up to fire, and the catch off. Check with the thumb that the catch is off. It is, certain. Now separate them, don't let them be together so she can shield him. She'll do that, they all will, throw themselves at you to give him a yard. And shoot. If he moves, shoot him. Don't hesitate. Stay still yourself. Don't march about. That disorganizes the shot you may make. Two bullets only. One up the spout, and the other in the next chamber, that's all.

Harry studied him hard. The other man, the opposition. Dirty, cowed and frightened—is that the terrorist? Is that all he is? Is that the killer in all his glory? Not much to look at, not much without his Kalashnikov.

"Start walking now, and remember: keep it very cool, or I shoot. What's your name?"

"Billy Downs. You're the Englishman they sent for me? The one that had the girl killed?" They'd told him the Britisher hadn't come to take him, not to put him in the Kesh, but to kill him. The fight for survival was returning, steadily and surely. "You won't get out of here, you know. Not with me on the end of your pistol, you won't."

He looked past Harry and seemed to nod his head into the middle distance. It was cleverly done. Good try, Billy boy. But you're with the professionals now, lad. A squaddie might have turned and given you the third of a second you needed to jump him. Not Harry. Pivot around. Get your back to the wall. Keep going till you feel the brickwork. But watch the bastard. All the time keep your eyes on his hands.

Faced with troops in uniform, the Man would probably have submitted without a struggle and climbed into the armored car to start whatever segment of his lifetime in captivity they intended for him. But not this way. No surrender to a single hack sent from London to kill him, watched by his wife and in his own road. For a year it would be talked about—the day when a lone Englishman came into Ardoyne and shot down meek little Billy Downs. The day the boy's nerve went.

He was formidable, this Englishman, in his old jeans and dark anorak, with the clear-cut face, softer than those fashioned in the bitterness of Belfast. He had not been reared through the anguish of the troubles, and it showed in the freshness of his features. But he was hard, the Man had no doubt on that. They'd trained him and sent him from London for this moment, and he knew his life rested on his capacity to read the expressionless mouth of his enemy. When he made his break, all would depend on how well the Englishman could shoot, and when he fired, how straight. The Man made his assessment . . . he'll fire, but fire late, and he'll miss. He turned himself now from the waist only, and very slowly, toward his wife.

He was close to her, much closer than Harry, and with his face in profile he mouthed, from the far side of his lips, the one word.

"Scream."

She read it in the shape of his mouth, the way the lips and gums twisted out the message. Harry didn't see the instruction and was still concentrating on the Man's hands when she yelled. It came from deep down. A fierce noise from so small a woman. Harry jerked from his preoccupation with the Man as he searched for the source of the noise, his eyes shifting direction.

The Man made his decision. Now or not at all, either now or the bastard has you in his own time, to shoot like a rat in a cage. He pushed his wife violently toward Harry and started for the freedom of the open street down the hill. His first two strides took him to the edge of the pavement. A flood of adrenalin . . . anticipating the shot, head down, shoulders crouched. This was the moment. Either he fires now or I make it, three, four more paces, then the range and accuracy of the revolver is stretched. His eyes half closed, he saw nothing in front of him as his left foot hit hard on the steep edge of the pavement. For his heel there was support, for his sole there was nothing, only the gap between the flagstones and the gutter eight inches below. His weight was all there, all concentrated on that foot, as he catapulted himself forward, the momentum taking over.

He realized the way he was falling, and tried to twist around onto his back, but there was no time, no room. He hit the rough gravel of the road on his left arm, right on the spot where the flesh had been twice torn open by Rennie's bullet. The frail lint bandages gave no protection. With his right arm he clawed at the road surface, trying to push himself up and away from Harry, who was coming to him, revolver outstretched . . .

Harry saw the pain reach over and cover the Man's

face. He saw the hand scruffing under the body. If the Man had a gun, that was where it would be, down by the waist, where the hand was fumbling now. It wasn't a difficult decision any more. He raised the revolver so that the line went down from his right eye, down his right arm to the V of the back sight and along the black barrel to the sharp foresight, and then on to the Man's upper chest. He held the aim just long enough for his hand to steady, then squeezed the trigger gently into the cup of his forefinger. The noise was not great. The revolver gave only a slight kick, jolting down the rigid arm to Harry's shoulder. Below him the Man's body began to twitch, giving way to spasmodic convulsions. The blood found its own pathway from the side of his mouth out onto the greyness of the road. Like water tracking across dry earth, it kept its course, faster, thicker, wider as the road discolored with its brightness.

There was no need for the second bullet, Harry could see that.

"Why did you shoot him? He had no gun. Why did you kill him?" She was moving toward her husband, looking at Harry as she spoke. "You didn't have to shoot. You could have run after him, and caught him. You know he was shot last night, and hit. He wasn't much opposition to you, you Britisher sod."

She knelt down beside her husband, her stocking dragging on the harsh surface of the road. He lay on his side, and she could not cradle him as she would have wanted. Both her hands touched the face of her man, unmarked in his death, fingering his nose and ears and eyes.

Harry felt no part of the scene; but something was demanded of him, and painstakingly he began to explain. "He knew the rules. He knew the game he was playing. He came to London and murdered the Cabinet Minister. In cold blood. Shot him down in front of his house. Then he went to ground. It was a challenge to us. He must have known we had to get him—you must have known that. It was a test of will. There was no way we could lose—we couldn't afford to."

Harry had wondered how this moment would be. How he would feel if the Man were dead, destroyed. There was no hatred, no loathing for the slight body that lay on the grit of the tarmac. There was no elation, either, that his world and his system had beaten that of the young man who they had told him was the enemy, evil, vermin. All the training, all the fear, all the agony, directed to killing this awkward, shapeless nonentity. And now nothingness. He pushed the revolver down into his anorak pocket, looked again at the wife as she stayed bent over her lifeless man, and began his walk up the hill out of Ardoyne.

She watching him, hands still on the man's body, when the shot came. Simultaneously with the crack she saw Harry stagger, appear to regain his balance, and then sway backward, before thudding against the front wall of a house. His arms were pressed across the middle of his chest. Then he toppled over in slow motion onto the pavement.

In the OP it was Smith who was at the aperture, giving a continuous description to the lance corporal, who relayed the messages back to headquarters over the radio-telephone.

"There's a man running up behind Downs. With a shooter. A revolver, looks like, a little. Tell 'em to shift 'emselves back at HQ. Downs has his hands up, and they're talking. Not much, but saying something."

From the telephone set Burns called, "What about the other bloke, they want to know, what's he look like?"

"Civvies, anorak and jeans. It's a short-barrel revolver he got, not Downs . . . the other man. Scruffy-looking. He's making a run for it, Downs is. Bloody hell, he's down, tripped himself. Fuck me, he's going to shoot him, he's going to shoot him!"

High in the hidden observation post, Burns heard the single shot.

"I can get the bugger, can't I, Dave? He just shot the other bastard. Waving a gun about and all that, it's enough." Smith was maneuvering his rifle into position. The old Lee Enfield with the big telescopic sight, the sniper's weapon, the marksman's choice.

"I've a good line on him from here. No problem." Smith was talking to himself, whispering into the butt of the rifle. Burns was motionless and watched from the back of the OP, nestled among the blankets and sacking as Smith drew back the bolt action and settled himself, shifting his hips from side to side to get comfortable for the shot. He was a long time aiming, wanting to be certain the first time. The firing echoed around under the roof of the mill.

"Did you get him?" urged Burns.

"A real bloody peach."

The soldiers looked over the two bodies, made the decision that they were beyond medical help and left them where they had fallen. En route from headquarters, they had been told over the radio that under no circumstances were the two to be moved unless there was hope of life being saved. Both the Man and Harry were in that awkward, sacklike form that the soldiers recognized as death. Downs lay a few feet from the curb out in the road. The blood had run from him to create a lake, blocked from escaping further by the debris of the gutter. His wife stood now, beside him, with some of the other women of the road who had come to her after Harry was shot.

Harry was propped against the wall, his face still showing the great astonishment and shock that overwhelmed him as his hands and arms entwined across his chest for strength in holding back the scope of the wound in his lungs. It had been an instinctive action, to try and staunch the lifeblood, and his last. Several men had come from the houses and stood in clumps at the doorways, unspeaking, unsmiling, unshocked, leaving the business of comforting and abusing to their women.

In their shawls and head scarfs and short skirts, they shouted at the officer who came with the platoon. "He's one of yours. That bastard lying over there."

"He's a fucking Englishman, English bastards."

"Shot a man without a gun, you gutless bastards."

"SAS killer squads, you murdering bastards."

"Killed an unarmed man in front of his wife, and he never in trouble before."

The crescendo gathered around the young man. In a few moments his company commander and his battalion commander would be there, and he would be spared; till then he would take the brunt of their fury. Braced with the accusation that Harry was one of theirs, the soldiers looked curiously at Harry. They knew a certain amount about the undercover operations of the army—SAS (Special Air Service) and MRF (Mobil Reconnaissance Force) —but to the men in uniform it was a different and basically distasteful world. The soldiers had the rules and regulations to abide by, the book was near to God.

In exasperation, the lieutenant shouted above the babble, "Well, if you say the chap who shot Downs is one of ours, who shot him then?" He phrased it clumsily, expecting no answer. But a chorus of voices had the answer. "The Provos got him. A Provie gunman. One shot and dead. From the bottom of the street."

That end of the street was deserted, dominated by the massive wall of the old mill. The lieutenant looked up at its roof, and winced.

"Bloody hell," he said, and walked over to the colonel's Land-Rover.

"It's just as we found it, as you requested," they told Frost when he arrived. "The chap by the wall shoots Downs, and then is shot himself. I'm not a hundred percent where the second shot came from. Still reports coming in. The indications are that it's the OP, up in the mill roof. But I haven't spoken to the men there yet."

There was no reaction on Frost's face. His eyes traveled around the street, taking in the faces and the scene. He walked from one body to another, skirting Mrs. Downs, his bodyguards hovering at each shoulder. He recognized Harry from the photograph that had been sent the previous night from England. It should never have worked, it had succeeded, and now right at the end was loused up, poor bugger. He paused at Downs's body, looking into the profile of the face and running a mental check on against the photokit they'd issued. Lucky to have spotted him from that, the colonel thought, not really good enough, something to be learned from that.

"It's not for general release," he said to the local unit commander, "but you'll hear it soon enough anyway. The Prime Minister ordered a special chap put in with the sole object of finding Danby's killer, right? The Cabinet Minister shot, what is it, six or so weeks ago. Downs was the gunman. By something of a miracle, and a quite unaccountable amount of good luck, the agent tracked him down. That's not a generous assessment, but that's how I evaluate it. He tracked him and shot him dead about fifteen minutes ago. I think your OP has just killed the Prime Minister's man."

Frost knew how to play his moment. He stopped there, let it sink, then went on: "We'll deflect it as much as we can, but if I were you, I'd leave it to Lisburn to make the statements. It may be some small consolation to you that I was one of the many who didn't know about it either."

The other man considered. They stood alone in the street away from the people of Ypres Avenue, with the bodyguards and other soldiers giving them room for the private talk. He remembered now the social club less than three hundred yards from where they stood. There was nothing to say, nothing that would help the prone figure by the wall, nothing that would do anything except create further unnecessary involvement. Businesslike and brisk as always, outwardly unshaken, he said to Frost, "Is there any reason for us not to clean this lot up now? Our photographer has done his stuff."

"No reason at all, get it out of the way before the bloody press and cameras start showing up."

The press statement from Lisburn was short and took something more than two hours to prepare. It was the result of a series of compromises but owed most of its drafting to the civilian deputy head of the army public relations department who had recently transferred from the Treasury and had experience in the art of communiqué writing.

Billy Downs, a known IRA gunman, was shot dead at 0910 hours in Ypres Avenue, where he lived. He was involved in an exchange of shots with a member of the security forces, an officer engaged in plain-clothes surveillance duties. The officer, who will not be named till his next of kin have been informed, was hit by a single shot in the chest and died before medical treatment reached him. Downs was high on the army's wanted list in Northern Ireland, and was also wanted in London for questioning by detectives investigating the murder of Mr. Henry Danby.

The main thing was to keep it short, pack it with information and deflect the press away from the sensitive bit. There was, he said when he had finished typing it, more than enough for the scribes to bite on without them needing to go digging around any more.

A solitary journalist moved toward the delicate area, but without knowing it, and was easily put off. "Then this man Downs was carrying a gun?" he asked the duty press officer.

"Obviously, old man, it says in our statement that there was an exchange of shots. Have to be armed, wouldn't he?"

There were no other questions to be asked. Among the resident reporters that night, interest was warm but not exceptional, and the treatment of the story was straight and factual.

■ 20 ■

The Prime Minister learned the news at lunchtime. The message had been framed by the Under Secretary, Ministry of Defence, with an eye to the political master's haste, and the order in which he would read of the events in Ypres Avenue had been carefully thought out. First, Billy Downs, identified as the killer of Henry Danby, had been shot dead. Second, he had been identified by the agent specifically sent to Northern Ireland by the Prime Minister. Third, and unfortunately, the agent had been shot in the chest during the incident and had died.

As he read the message that the aide gave him, his attentive smile had switched to a frown of public concern, studied by the bankers around the table with him in the first-floor salon of No. 10. They looked for a clue as to the contents and information that was important enough to intercede in discussions on the progress of the floating pound; albeit the end of the discussions. The Prime Minister noted their anticipation and was anxious to satisfy it.

"Just on a final note, gentlemen." He refolded the typewritten sheet. "You will all be reading it in the papers tomorrow, but you might be interested to hear that we have caught and killed the man that assassinated Henry Danby. He was shot in Belfast this morning after being hunted down as part of a special investigation that was launched from this building a few hours after our colleague was murdered."

There was a murmur of applause around the table and a banging of the palms of hands on the paper-strewn mahogany surface.

"But you will be sorry to hear, as I am, that the man we sent to find this terrorist was himself killed in the shooting exchange. He'd been operating undercover there for some weeks, and obviously carried out a difficult task extremely successfully and with great bravery. The whole concept of this intelligence operation really goes back to the last war. My family was involved in Special Operations—you know, the crowd that put agents into the occupied countries. I had a hell of a job getting the military and police to agree to it. But it just shows, you sometimes need a fresh approach to these things. Perhaps we should get that general over there, who always seems to be wanting more troops, to have a try at banking and running a budget!"

There was general and polite laughter.

"He'll get a medal, won't he? The man you sent over there? They look after the families and all that sort of thing, I suppose?" said the elegantly dressed deputy chairman of the Bank of England.

"Oh, I'm sure he will. Well, I think we can adjourn now. Perhaps you would care to join me for a drink. I have a luncheon, but I'm not off to that till I've had a drop of something."

Later in the day he called the Under Secretary to express his appreciation of the way the operation had been handled.

"It'll get a good show in the papers, I trust," said the Prime Minister. "We ought to blow our own trumpet a bit when we chalk one up."

"I don't think there will be too much of that, sir," the civil servant replied decisively. "MOD has put out a short statement only. I think their feeling is that undercover is bad news in Ulster, and that apart from anything else, it was a damn close thing whether our man got theirs first, or vice versa. They're playing it rather low key I'm afraid, sir."

"As you like. Though I sometimes feel we don't give ourselves the pat on the back we deserve. I'll concede that. One more thing. The man we sent over there, I'd like a medal for him now it's over. What sort of chap was he, by the way?"

"I'll see to that. He already had an MC from Aden. We could make it a bar to that, but perhaps that's a bit on the short side. I personally would favor the OBE. The George Cross is a bit more than we usually go for in these circumstances, and it would obviously provoke a deal of talk. You asked what sort of chap. Pretty straightforward, not too bright. Dedicated, conscientious and a lot of guts. He was the right man."

The Prime Minister thanked him and rang off. He hurried from his study to the Humber waiting outside the front door of the official residence. He was late for the House.

The Army Council of the Provisional IRA, the top planning wing of the military side of the movement, had noted the killing of Downs. The chief of staff had received a letter from the Brigade commander in Belfast relaying the collapse of the Man's morale and his failure in the last two missions assigned to him.

The two members of the Council who had been asked to report on the practicality and desirability of further assassinations in the political arena, particularly the plan involving the British Prime Minister, delivered their assessment at the first meeting of all members after the Ardoyne shoot-out.

They advised against the continuation of attacks on the style of the Danby assassination. It had, they said, been disastrous for fund-raising in the United States: the picture of Mrs. Danby and her children at the funeral had been flashed across the Atlantic and coast-to-coast by the wire syndication services. The Provisionals' supporters in the States reported that November's fund-raising and on into December would show a marked drop. They said that if there were a repeat or a stepping-up of the tactics, the results could prove fatal. And money was always a key factor for the movement: RPG 7s and their rockets did not come cheap, not from Czechoslovakia or Libya or from anywhere else.

The chief of staff summed up that in the forseeable future they would not consider a repetition of the Danby attack, but he finished: "I still defend the attack we carried out against Danby. That bastard deserved to go. He was a straight, legitimate target, and it was well done, well carried out. They acknowledge that on their side, too. There's been no trumpeting on their side even though they've shot our lad. They've been keeping their heads down for more than a week."

There was criticism in the Council, which had not been voiced while Downs was still on the run, of the way the chief of staff had monopolized the planning of the attack. That would stand against him in the future, being one of the factors in his eventual replacement and consequent demotion.

Little of the credit for the killing of Billy Downs landed on Davidson's desk. It jumped with no little agility to the posthumous name of Harry McEvoy via the desk of the Permanent Under Secretary.

Frost put in a long and detailed complaint about the amount of work the independent, and for so many days unidentified, agent had meant for the security services. He logged the man hours involved in the search for Harry at the scrap yards, and for the girl around the Clonard, and described them as wasteful and unprofessional. The control of the agent received scathing criticism, particularly the inability of London to reach their man when they wanted to draw him out. The paper concluded with the demand that such an operation should not be repeated during the following eighteen months that Frost would be on the staff of Northern Ireland headquarters.

The Under Secretary, who had a copy of the document forwarded to him, read it over the phone to Davidson. The response was predictably angry. "He bloody well forgets it was over there on his side of the fence that some big mouth let the cat out of the bag." Davidson already had the transcript of the interrogation of the stricken Duffryn. Still suffering from shock, the young man had given Special Branch all of his limited knowledge of the Provisional IRA and its affairs relating to Harry McEvoy.

"He forgets that our man got the fellow, not all their troops and police and Special Branch and SIB, and whatever they call themselves, SAS and the others," Davidson roared into the receiver.

The Under Secretary soothed, "They have a point, you know. This bit how you couldn't reach him, and he didn't stay where he was supposed to, that was a bit irregular."

"The way they clod about over there, I'm not surprised he didn't go to the house they fixed for him. The fact is we were set a mission, and carried it out, with success. Is that cause for a bloody inquest?"

Davidson had not been told how Harry had died. That was to be kept very close to London. "Need to Know" was being applied with rigor. The Under Secretary decided that if the PM wasn't on the list, then Davidson ranked no greater priority.

"Of course the mission was a success, but it's put a great amount of strain on interservice and interdepartment cooperation. The feeling at MOD is that a similar operation would not be mounted again. That means, I greatly regret to say, that the team we set up to direct our man will have to be dismantled." There was no change in his voice as he delivered the hammer blow. It gave him no pleasure, but Davidson was so excitable that one really did have to spell it out in simple words and get it over with. He went on: "I did have hopes at one stage that if this went off without a hitch, we might have had something a bit more regular going through Dorking. Make a habit out of the place. But that's not to be."

Davidson could recognize the shut-out. The shouting was over. He asked. "And what now? What happens to me?"

"It's recognized here, Davidson, that in fact you did very well on this one, particularly in the preparation of our man. You made him ready for a difficult and dangerous task, which was subsequently carried out with great expertise. You must not take all that Frost says too seriously. You've a great deal of experience to offer, and this showed in the way you got the fellow ready. I want you to think about it carefully, and not come to any hasty decision, but the feeling is that there's a good opening abroad for you."

Here it comes, the old playoff, reckoned Davidson. What would they have for him, sewing blankets in the Aleutians?

"You've built up great experience of counterterrorist operations," the civil servant kept going. Don't lose pace, don't let him interrupt. "I won't beat about the bush. Hong Kong wants a man who can advise them on the posture they should be in. Now, don't say anything hasty, the terms are first class. You'd get more than I'm getting. Good allowances, good accommodation, and pretty much of a free hand. Probably live off expenses and bank the rest, I'd say. Don't give me an answer now, but sleep on it and call me in the morning. Cheers, and we all think you did well."

The conversation was over.

Hong Kong. What kind of bloody joke is that? Who the hell does that bloody man think he is? Up to our bloody eyeballs in all that shit, with a man in the front line and God knows what happening to him, and half a bloody city waiting to chop his balls off if they get their hands on him. I'm sitting here biting my nails, pulling my hair, no proper sleep, no rest, worrying. My man, the one I've trained, and he goes into that murderous great flea pit and kills the top man they have . . . and all they offer is bloody Hong Kong and free gin for as long as I'm bloody fit to drink it.

The buggers didn't even call from Lisburn to say that Harry was dead. That sod Frost and his bloody memos. Had to wait till it was on the newsflash, not Harry's name then, but two dead in Ypres Avenue. Not worth it, Harry boy. Should have bloody stayed at home. Should have bloody stayed with wifey and left it to the goddamn amateurs. What for, Harry? What have you bloody well got out of it? Sod all. And what have I got out of it? Bloody promotion to Hong Kong.

He ranged around the office, fumbling at his papers,

diving into the drawers of the old wooden desk. He aimed a kick at the folded camp bed, away in the corner and not used since the last Sunday night of his vigil. It took around an hour to find the will and inclination to exert some order to the anger of his feelings. The documents and maps of the operation filled two briefcases, the rest was government property, some bloody man could clear that up. Sort it out themselves.

He made a call to his wife. Didn't speak much, just said he'd be home early, that he had some news, they would be going out for a meal. Then he locked up. He'd thought about Harry considerably since the shooting, and by the time he had reached his commuter train, his rage had subsided and he brooded in a corner over the evening paper about the young man who had died in Belfast . . . sent away across the water with all that damn-fool optimism coursing through him.

For days Mrs. Duncan talked of little more than the strange events that preceded the death of her most favorite lodger.

That the man who shared her bathroom, her front room and occasionally her kitchen, who lived in her best back bedroom should have turned out to be an English agent was rather too much for her to serve out in a single session of conversation. Her neighbors came several times to hear the full saga, culminating in the eyewitness description of the final shootout beyond the front garden gate.

She was to remain unaware of her full role in the death of Harry and Billy Downs. She never discovered that it was her chatter over the back fence about the strange accent of the man who lived under her roof that was to start the process that led, near-directly, to the gunfire in the street. She told those who came to listen to her that the thing she found the strangest was the confidence and authority with which Harry was holding the gun as he

shot down Duffryn against the lamppost. The cold me-
thodical power with which the quiet man, a man she had
grown to like but knew little about, executed the youngster
had shaken her more than any of the other horrors of five
years of living on the Falls.

The army had come midmorning and backed a
Saracen right up to the gate. Two men in civilian clothes
had waited till the doors were opened and screened them
from casual view from the pavements, then hurried into the
house. They had searched Harry's room slowly and carefully while soldiers hovered around the house and the
street was sealed to all cars. When the men left, it was
with all of Harry's possessions, slung together into big
transparent plastic bags.

Later that same day Josephine arrived to help with
the teas. It was a wasted visit, as the guests had cried off.
There were no takers for the lodging used by British
intelligence. Some telephoned their apologies and listed
excuses; others simply failed to turn up. Instead Josephine
was told the events of the day. She listened without comment, and sat on a straight chair in the kitchen, sipping
her tea and smoking a cigarette. She was another who
would never learn her full part in the affair. She went
home that night believing her information alone had led
the Provisionals to Harry. In the months ahead she was
to stay distant from any connection with politics and with
violence. Left alone by the IRA, she took to remaining
at home in the evenings with her mother, shutting out the
memories of the few hours she had spent with Harry, of
how he had betrayed her, and of how she had betrayed
him.

Billy Downs's funeral was a bigger day than any in his
young life. A huge and winding crowd of relatives and
friends marched behind his tricolor-draped coffin up the
Falls Road. It had been the army's intention to prevent

the firing of the traditional IRA volley over the body, but the procession diverted into the back streets of the Lower Falls, and before it emerged again, the shots had been fired.

Eight men from Ypres Avenue took the weight of the coffin on their shoulders for the first part of the journey to Milltown Cemetery. Grim, set faces, they slowly marched at the head of a crowd estimated by police to be around three thousand. Behind them came the display of force, youths and girls in semiuniform, the green motif dominating, polished Sam Brownes, shouted commands and the tramping of feet.

At the bleak, overornate Milltown gates, faces in the crowd were recorded by the Asahis of the military from behind the sandbags on the top of the walls of the Andersonstown bus station. Inside the cemetery the chief of staff of the movement, who arrived and departed unseen by those who were hunting him, delivered the graveside oration. They played the Last Post while small children in their best clothes played and skipped among the stones that marked the last resting place of other heroes of the cause.

With the passing of weeks and months, the adulation and estimation in which Billy Downs was held increased. They named a club after him, and wove his picture into a big, wide banner. It was some eight feet across, with slots for two poles, one at each end, so that it could be carried high in procession on the marches the Provisionals organized.

The songs followed, sung with the nasal lament in the bars of Andersonstown and Ardoyne to drinkers who sat silent and rapt. They were heavy with sentiment, helping to cement the legend that in Ulster solidifies so quickly. The brave soldier of the songs had been gunned down by the British killer squads while his wife and bairns were around him. The most tuneful, with a good backing, was recorded by a folk group that specialized in such music. Off-duty soldiers would buy it as a souvenir of their tour in the province in the record shops that had sprung up in the burned-out shell of the old Smithfield market.

His wife lived on in Ypres Avenue, seemingly aloof from the events around her. She was asked several times to take part in anniversary marches organized by various factions of the Republican movement, but always declined. The invitations would eventually dry up, and with them the weekly cash supplied by the Provisionals.

New horrors would overtake the Ardoyne community, new causes requiring sympathy. Soon the Man's wife would no longer be celebrated, pointed out, stared at.

The RAF flew Harry out on a Hercules transporter, along with a load of freight and two private soldiers going home on compassionate leave, for whom there were no seats on the British Airways commercial flight.

The two boys, both still in their teens, huddled in their seats away from the tin box wrapped in sacking and strapped down with webbing to the floor of the aircraft. There was a brown stiffened label attached to the box, filled in with neat handwriting.

"Says he's a captain."

"Yeah, it's the one what did the shooting on Monday morning."

"Says he's got an MC and all."

Across the great tube that was the rattling noisy inside of the transporter, they could read the writing.

"It's the one that tracked that geezer for weeks and all. I heard it said. He lived in amongst them and all."

"I've been over twice, this is the second time. I've never seen a bloody IRA man, or anything like one. All we bloody do is walk up and down."

"Undercover agent they say he was."

"Hasn't done him much bloody good and all, whatever he was."

That terminated it. They spoke no more of Harry as the plane brought them down to Northolt, where it had all started six weeks earlier.

They buried Harry in a village close to where his wife's parents lived. By army standards it was a conventional funeral. An honor party, a volley over the grave, a short address from an army chaplain. In the event, it was not totally different from the funeral accorded to Billy Downs. Smaller, less stylized, less sentimental, but with all the same ingredients. There were few civilians present, mostly soldiers in uniform, stiff and upright as the bugler played the same final, haunting farewell.

There was a wreath from the Prime Minister, and Davidson was there. He was one of the few not in khaki. He didn't introduce himself to Harry's widow, and stayed very much at the back, unknown to the family and to the brother officers who had come over from Germany. When he left the graveside, it was to complete his arrangements for the transfer on loan to Hong Kong authorities.

FAWCETT CREST BESTSELLERS